JUNGLE SALVATION

EVERNIGHT PUBLISHING ®

www.evernightpublishing.com

Copyright© 2019

M.A. Jewell

Editor: Karyn White

Cover Art: Jay Aheer

ISBN: 978-1-77339-985-0

ALL RIGHTS RESERVED

JUNGLE SALVATION

DEDICATION

Jungle Salvation is dedicated to my sister and best friend Robin Owen, the one who is always there when needed and forgives with ease. As a family member, friend, or acquaintance, she advocates for those who need it and empowers those who don't.

ACKNOWLEDGEMENTS

First, foremost, and always, I am forever grateful to my husband Jim, for doing much more than his fair share around the house while I sit at the keyboard. That guy can doctor up a pizza like no one I know, and he runs a mean vacuum cleaner, too. And at the end of the day, he still loves me and encourages me to write the next story. I want to send a huge shout out to the best critique group any author could want, my Friday Night Critique BFFs. These ladies listened to pages for months, and then read the entire manuscript. Their feedback made me look good. Love you all—Deb Hines, Sherri Shackelford, Lizzie Starr, Donna Kaye, and Cheryl StJohn. So many people support an author when a story is brought into the world! I could write a book on the people who helped me create Jungle Salvation. Numerous friends and colleagues beta read this manuscript at varying stages of finish, and I wish there were space here to include everyone. You know who you are. Thank you!

And the cover! Way to go, Jay Aheer of Simply Defined Art. She captured the soul of the story in one image.

A big thank you to my tried and true personal editor Ann Pullum, AKA the WordDetailer. Four years ago, she listened to my fledgling attempts at romance and encouraged me anyway.

I am forever grateful to Evernight Publishing's editor Karyn White, whose keen eye helped take the story to the next level. Thank you!

Finally, thank you the readers. Each of you is a precious gem. I hope you enjoy the story.

JUNGLE SALVATION

Jaguar Queens, 2

M.A. Jewell

Copyright © 2019

Chapter One

Matteo D'Cruz recognized the scent of his old friend Cristiano Salazar in the humid Brazilian Amazon. Even so, territorial invasion raised hackles across his shoulders, and he drove his claws into the bark beneath him. The sensitive lining of his nose told him Cristiano escorted two other jaguar shifters—one an impossibility—*a female.*

A harsh male scent polluted her essence. *Mated.* Adrenaline surged his heart into a gallop. The possessive warning didn't temper her allure, as a mate's mark should. His lack of control triggered alarms in his head, but he ignored them. Base cat instinct overruled his long-lost sense of propriety.

Matteo strained to hear her above the never-ending insect symphony. She was close. A hundred meters, or so. Mated or not, she traveled his territory, and he would have her.

God forgive me.

Driven by ages-old instinct, Matteo barked a series of courting roars into the canopy's understory. He waited a breathless beat. No response. Rocketing from tree to tree, ignoring the branches slapping his muzzle, he raced toward the queen. Flat-out shifter speed wasn't fast enough. Monkeys screeched a warning to the entire jungle and scampered from his path. After an agonizing half-minute, human conversation reached his keen ears, slowing his pace.

"Jaime, keep Kelsi close. Matteo's near."

Odd. Cristiano spoke English rather than Portuguese.

A metered growl came from the unknown male. "*Papai*, your friend flirts with disaster."

Cristiano's son!

"You two act like he's dangerous. Maybe we shouldn't invite him to the wedding." Odder still, the queen's Yankee English was likely her native tongue.

The sound of her voice assured Matteo he hadn't entirely lost his mind. For an instant, he'd suspected his overlong solitude had sparked a hallucination. The soft compost layer of the jungle floor muffled her nearing footsteps.

Compelled to lay eyes on the female, he used a lifetime of hunting experience to glide through the leaf-covered branches. He aimed for a lone rubber tree where his auburn rosettes and tawny hide would fade into the two-tone ochre bark. Careful not to disturb the foliage, he peered down between green leaves.

"He's *Papai*'s oldest friend and—I suspect—very lethal." Jaime added the last with a warning tone, scanning overhead with a predator's eyes.

The younger shifter had Cristiano's features and jet hair. If not for the scar from his ear to his jawline, and

Cristiano's gray streaks, Matteo might have mistaken the two. The graying version of his friend restrained the young doppelganger by the arm.

In a protective motion, Jaime pulled an attractive, fair-skinned girl to him and stepped in front of her. Matteo indulged in a draught of the queen's floral scent and then snorted to clear the male's distasteful mark.

Jaime's her mate! Somehow, an unknown line had produced a female. A tsunami of aggression, a primal drive Matteo had never experienced, overtook the last of his will.

The glands at the base of his whiskers throbbed, demanding release. He had no doubt he could best the younger shifter. After he won the challenge, he'd smother the queen with his scent, eradicating all trace of the cub from her body.

Meu Dios! Furious with his friend for testing him so, Matteo snarled at his murderous jaguar thoughts. He didn't even know this Kelsi, yet he couldn't dredge up the will to turn away from the queen.

Cristiano's attempts to entice Matteo back into society had dwindled over the years. This time, however, he had gambled poorly. Too many seasons in cat form.

Helpless against nature's gale force, Matteo prayed Cristiano could save his son. He stepped from cover, and fixing a predatory glare on Jaime, he roared a challenge. Even the insects fell silent.

The big male charged forward with a dark glower.

Cristiano looked up at Matteo, his mouth a firm line. "Come to us. *Now.*"

Matteo dropped from the three-story-high branch and sailed effortlessly to the jungle floor, landing in a crouch. With eyes locked on his adversary, he stalked low to the ground, set on attack.

Dark light shimmered across Jaime's exposed skin, signaling his impending shift. Scowling at Matteo, he tossed his shirt and pants next to a clump of ferns. "You'll never have her."

Cristiano, face drawn tight with rage, hurtled to block Matteo from his prey. "You'd challenge your own godson for his mate? Kill *my* son? Shift now, or die as feral."

Matteo snarled in anguish, praying Cristiano could make good on his threat.

Kelsi's green gaze darted from him to Jaime. She lunged at Cristiano to tug at his arm. "Just leave him."

He pushed her back, keeping his focus on Matteo. "Not possible. If his humanity's lost, he could mate with a natural jaguar."

"As in sire a litter?" The female grimaced in plain disgust, turning an appalled expression on him. "*This* is who you thought my sister should meet?"

"A selfish misjudgment. I wanted my best friend at my son's wedding." Cristiano's amber eyes shone with tears. "Instead, I'm his executioner."

Sister! Where had the females come from? The last known living queen was Cristiano's mate, Maria. The thought of females in the world overpowered any concern Matteo had for his own life.

"Kelsi, you know genetic diversity is crucial." Though Jaime spoke quietly in her ear, Matteo's sensitive hearing picked up his words, as though he'd spoken aloud.

"No." She turned tear-filled eyes to her mate. "Invite someone else, please."

Pinning his ears back, Matteo snarled in misery and lowered to his belly. He wanted to shift, to stifle his cat, and turn from killing the men before him—*his only family*. Matteo's life meant nothing. If he killed Cristiano and Jaime to steal a mated female, his life would mean even less.

To throttle back his jaguar instincts, Matteo focused on the existence of another queen. The drive to possess diminished by a fraction, allowing him to breathe and sense his humanity. Matteo grappled for the sliver of control.

With more concentration than he'd ever required before, a shift's searing heat journeyed snail-like through his muscles until electric current chased the fever away. Every molecule in his body screamed with the metamorphosis. He couldn't recall another shift so long or painful.

His hoarse bellow of agony rang off the thick foliage above. With his head low, and still on all fours, Matteo took stock of his limbs, ensuring he was indeed human.

Despite the jungle's damp heat, gooseflesh traveled his torso. His skin objected to the loss of his pelt. Or maybe the magnitude of the averted crisis produced the cool shudder.

"Matteo? Are you with us?" Cristiano kept his distance.

Worried he'd lost his ability to speak, Matteo nodded. Ropes of tawny hair moved against dead leaves below him, and curtained his face from the world. Now in human form, his compulsion to claim the jag queen abated. Matteo sent up a heartfelt prayer of thanks.

Shaken by his uncontrollable reaction to the female and his sluggish change, he rose to a wobbly biped stance. He dared a glimpse of the woman. Silent, with wide green eyes, she stared at him with parted lips.

Matteo couldn't imagine his abhorrent appearance—his nakedness being the least offensive. He scrubbed at the irritating beard itch that had replaced his feline muzzle's glandular throb. Years' worth of beard.

A violent urge to return to jaguar form threatened to overtake him. He forced himself to meet Jaime's gaze and remembered the blue-eyed toddler who'd begged piggyback rides. With an iron will born of terror, Matteo smothered the urge to return to cat form.

Jaime retrieved his clothing and then stepped in front of his mate, blocking Matteo's view of the female. Murderous lines carving the younger shifter's face replaced all hint of the adoring child who'd called him Uncle Baddeo.

A gusty breath deflated Cristiano's aggressive posture and a limp smile creased his face. He scrutinized Matteo from head to toe, his uncertain expression dropping to a grimace. "My God, when did you last shift? Are those rosettes?"

Matteo tracked his friend's line of sight to his left shoulder. Rust-colored spots embedded his skin. Worse, sharp, oversized canines filled his mouth. *Dios!* His cat had truly overbalanced his humanity. Part of him was terrified. Another part didn't care.

"He looks like a savage. The hair and beard might even house critters." Kelsi whispered the insults to her mate in her Yankee tongue.

Matteo seethed. The woman must think him uneducated as well as unkempt. Unburying Brit English from his Oxford days, he sneered at her. "Don't worry, Kelsi. I want nothing to do with you—or your sister."

He was grateful he'd formed words; however, his voice sounded gravelly from lack of use—or a partial shift. Along with spots, he may have retained other feline traits. He swallowed, staving off a fearful shudder.

"Sorry." Color crept into her face. At least she had the decency to look embarrassed.

Now dressed, Jaime fired a wad of clothing that

slapped against Matteo's chest. He slid on a pair of cutoffs and threw the t-shirt back at Jaime. "And you, *cub*, never take me on without your father's help. You'll die."

To his credit, the whelp didn't back down. "I'll give you a pass today, old man. Instinct is brutal. But make another move on my mate, I'll kill you."

"Jeesh. Take the testosterone down a notch. No wonder we're nearly extinct." Huffing, Kelsi grabbed Jaime's hand and pulled him toward a path leading to a narrow waterway. The trio could only have come by boat. The male glared over his shoulder at Matteo, until the couple disappeared from sight.

He turned to study his old friend. Cristiano had changed in a way Matteo couldn't identify—subtler than a few added gray hairs. Something was missing.

Cristiano's amber gaze warmed. "I'm glad to see you, *amigo*."

Matteo wanted to enjoy their reunion, but his anger wouldn't allow it. "I won't forgive you."

"I don't care."

"What if I'd killed you? Or worse, Jaime?"

Cristiano snorted. "You think me so weak?"

Matteo followed the young couple's trail, and Cristiano fell in behind him. In tacit agreement, the two males kept an old woman's pace, creating a semblance of privacy.

Cristiano cleared his throat. "How long since your last shift?"

"Not sure—sometime after I left the war. What happened with Hitler?"

Cristiano puffed air through pursed lips. "That was over seventy years ago."

Stunned by the revelation, Matteo was grateful his friend walked behind him. He couldn't have schooled his features. After seventy years, he'd been lucky to shift at all. "Hitler?"

"A few months after you disappeared, he killed himself in his bunker."

"Despicable coward." Matteo spat his disgust.

Cristiano grunted. "Probably sits at Satan's right hand."

When Brazil entered the Mediterranean Theatre with the Allies late in '44, he and Matteo had volunteered together but with different goals. Cristiano, a pilot, fought from the air to rid the world of a tyrant. Matteo battled on the ground in hopes of permanent serenity. When final peace eluded him, he'd returned to the jungle.

Matteo didn't want to talk about the war. "You still like to fly?"

"Yes. I go up almost every day. Manaus is a huge metropolis now, but still no roads to get there. Those with enough money use aircraft. Jaime flies, too." Pride filled Cristiano's voice.

"Bold one. He was ready to take me." Matteo forced a smile. Jaime had been lucky to walk away. "Where did his queen come from? I thought Maria was the last."

Halting, Cristiano sighed before resuming his leisurely pace. "Kelsi's a gift from God. She was a latent when Jaime stumbled upon her in the jungle."

Bewildered, Matteo slowed to pace next to his friend. "You mean latents really exist?"

Cristiano nodded with a chuckle. "Poor boy had thought females were a myth, too."

"Hardly a boy. Must be near eighty by now." Matteo snorted a laugh. Likely, Jaime had had his own instinct crisis and now understood how a queen devastated a male's senses. "That explains the *pass*."

Cristiano's chuckle confirmed his suspicions.

****

A couple hours later, Cristiano led Matteo to a sleek motorboat. Vessels traveled the river every day, but Matteo hadn't been near one in decades. He rapped his knuckles on the white hull. "What's this stuff?"

"Fiberglass. Use it for automobiles, now, too." Cristiano waved him into the padded seats.

Holding hands, and appearing to snuggle while walking, Jaime and Kelsi emerged from a patch of shade on the bank. He lifted her fingers to his lips for a brief touch. Sunlight glinted from his hand. The gold engagement band, circling Jaime's right ring finger, taunted Matteo with what he'd nearly destroyed—and what he'd lost.

The couple's obvious joy in one another poked at a damaged piece of his heart. Kelsi's bruised lips and mussed hair conjured memories that Matteo didn't dare indulge. Seven decades wasn't long enough for some wounds to heal. In self-preservation, he climbed into the boat, focusing on the floor mat.

The ride was quiet aside from the motor and rush of parting water. Conversation became scarce after one tried to steal a man's mate. Jaime and Kelsi spoke in low tones in the rear seat, engine noise keeping their conversation private. Most likely, they discussed Matteo.

Instead of socializing, he passed time reading an unfamiliar current events magazine—*Manaus Now!*. The headlines meant nothing, although he marveled at the photographs—all in color and so crisply focused. And the people in them wore so little, especially the women. At least changes in their culture would hold his interest for a time.

"We taking the river all the way to … where're we going?" asked Matteo.

"The boat's a rental. My chopper's at a dock

about fifteen miles downstream. We'll take it to our home."

"Chopper?"

"Helicopter. You'll see. It flies."

Of course. Matteo recalled the experimental aircraft from years ago. The noisy machines occasionally hovered above the canopy and more appeared each season. *Chopper* seemed an apt term.

Cristiano ferried them north, eyeing an ancient kapok tree with raised, wall-like roots dominating the shore ahead. No doubt, he recognized the ancient marker flagging the edge of Matteo's range. Passing the boundary, he realized he hadn't ventured beyond the tree since 1945.

Dread of the unknown settled in Matteo's chest. He loosened his hold on the boat's trimmed edge lest it crack under his grip. As an added embarrassment, his scent had probably announced his anxiety to the others.

In a barely-veiled attempt to distract him from the milestone, Cristiano pointed to the opposite shore. A cinnamon and black jaguar used the shadows to stalk a caiman. The gator-like reptile glided beneath the surface, its scent reaching Matteo's astute nose.

The male jag was hunting too near Matteo's territory. *Mine.*

Without thought, he lifted to balance himself on one knee. A metered rumble vibrated in his chest, and heat traveled his spine.

With knitted brows, Cristiano cut the engine and gripped Matteo's forearm. "My friend, stay with us. Years from now, caiman will still be in the river."

During the few beats of tense silence, the boat slowed to bob with the current. Cristiano's subtle message came through loud and clear, though Matteo didn't need the warning.

Decades prior, as the shifters' *Enforcer*, Matteo had tracked and executed feral males—always males. *Two.* Killing friends lost in their cats had withered his soul. Anna, his mate, had been his only solace—anchoring him in humanity. He'd nearly condemned Cristiano to the same haunting remorse.

What have I done? Still, part of him didn't care. For now, he would stay human for Cristiano.

Matteo's shift to biped had been a near thing. Going cat within the next three years would almost certainly trap him in jaguar form. Followed by a swift execution as feral. *Or maybe not.*

He studied his aging friend. Cristiano's physical supremacy over the jag males might have slipped over the years. Matteo doubted Cristiano could have executed him alone. Maybe with Jaime's help.

A warm hand on his back startled Matteo. The female's scent announced her mated status, so her touch had nothing to do with attraction. Mated pairs didn't stray—ever.

"Hard to see through the hair, but I think he has a few more rosettes on his back." Kelsi's low voice held concern, not the derision he'd expected. Close behind him, she pushed his waist-length knotted hair to the side. She gave his flesh a soft pat before dropping her hand. "I get it. Caiman rile me to shift, too."

Her olive branch gave him hope. Even more impressive, Jaime had held his possessive instincts in check while his mate touched Matteo. With their support, maybe he could face his biped sentence. Emotion tightened his throat. Avoiding eye contact, he gave a curt nod and reclaimed his seat.

Cristiano started the engine.

Chapter Two

"Mom, I'm sure she's fine." Lying her ass off, Dakota Gorman pressed her cell phone against her ear, cupping a hand over her mouth for privacy in the Brazilian airport.

"You can't be serious."

Her sister, Kelsi, a tediously responsible journalist, intended to marry a near stranger—only weeks after Brazilian smugglers had murdered her photographer and tried to kill her. *She's not close to fine.*

The rapid-fire timeline of events distressed Dakota, too. Still, she needed to reassure her mother. "She *is* thirty-eight years old, remember—and the forever common-sense girl. Maybe she just got lucky and finally found *the one*."

Lavender tendrils escaped Dakota's insufficient hairclip, purchased to match her bling sandals rather than for its functionality. In a nervous habit, she blew the strands out of her eyes.

Seated in an airport cafe next to an expanse of windows, she took in the scenic jungle only a few hundred yards away. The vegetation strained against an unseen boundary, threatening to invade the Eduardo Gomes tarmac.

Supposedly, Manaus, Amazonas, a metropolis of over two million people, was only six miles to the south. Her sister planned to somehow make a life deep in the rainforest, well beyond the reach of any navigation app.

"You call me as soon as you get to the Salazar's place. I can't find a satellite view of their address, only treetops." Celeste Gorman sounded frantic. Known in the business world as the Steel Fox, Dakota's mother never lost her cool composure, even when they'd gotten the news that Kelsi was missing in the jungle.

Dakota's reflection, superimposed over the wilderness, hinted at bloodshot eyes. Opening a backpack-style purse, she pulled out a compact to get a closer look. *Great.* Red streaks clashed with blue-green hazel. Annoyed, she snapped the mirrored case shut and shoved it back into the violet leather bag.

"So why am I the only one here? If you're so concerned, get on a plane." The day prior, Dakota hadn't recovered from the shock of Kelsi's wedding announcement enough to protest. Mom had dished out travel instructions, and Dakota had numbly followed them.

She had departed Omaha, Nebraska, wedged into an economy seat and doomed to sixteen hours of travel, including two layovers. Dakota's assigned mission: Bring Kelsi home.

Now, the Fox sighed in her ear, and Dakota imagined her mother's long-suffering expression.

"I leave right after next Tuesday's board meeting. The reprobates want Gorman Paper to go public before expanding. I can't leave Jasper to deal with those wolves."

"Traveling coach?" Dakota sounded petty to her own ears, but she was too tired to care. A suited woman strode past with a carry-on case rumbling in her wake. Dakota covered one ear.

"Fly first class when you buy your own ticket. Damnation, if she's pregnant I'll kill her." The Fox's tone wavered between worried and furious.

Dakota thought it wise to let the ticket discussion die. "She's not. I asked. She wouldn't get married over a pregnancy anyway."

Unusual concern for her mother needled Dakota. Mom had never been this cranked about anything, not even after retrieving a teenaged Dakota from the Omaha precinct. Just her luck, she and the Omaha police had ended up in the same bar.

"This Jaime Salazar character wants something. I can't find financials on Salazar Holdings—it's a privately owned company. Maybe they're going under." Mom said the last as though thinking aloud. Even for her suspicious nature, this was extreme.

Dakota shifted in the uncomfortable metal bistro chair. "She's way too smart to fall for a con."

"For God's sake, she's vulnerable." A sob punctuated the tremor in her mother's voice. "When she refused to come home after—after … I *knew* something was wrong. What if she's had a mental breakdown?"

Other than a polite tear at a wedding, the Fox didn't cry. In addition, her posttraumatic stress theory made sense. Dakota swallowed her own angst. "He saved her life. Maybe that created a bond."

"She doesn't owe him marriage!"

Dakota didn't know what to do with her mother's escalating anxiety piled atop her own. She didn't dare mention Kelsi's sister-only news. The secret announcement she would only share with Dakota in person. However, Kelsi wouldn't hide a baby from Dakota… *Would she?* "I'll call right away, promise."

"I never thought *she'd* be the one to pull something like this."

A couple beats of silence didn't dull the sting.

"You're wrong, Mom. I wouldn't have bothered you with a wedding." Livid, Dakota thumbed the call to an end. She lifted a quaking cup of coffee to her lips. Thirty-four years old and still, her inner child pouted over her mother's less-than-flattering opinion of her.

Dakota sipped cold coffee until she had her emotions under control. Once calm, she juggled her drained latte along with the backpack and rolling carryon, and headed toward baggage claim. Unfortunately, her empty cup forced a stop at another airport bistro. Inflight coffee sucked. Withdrawal was imminent, and she wanted to be alert the rest of the day.

Her sister needed her.

An incoming text buzzed at her hip.

Mom: **I love you. Forgive me.**

Dakota blinked away the angry sting of tears. At least the tourist sim card worked. She slid the phone back into the pocket of her white cropped pants. Maybe she'd cool off during her limo ride to the Salazars'—if at all.

Her lilac floral luggage floated around the carousel alongside a few other unclaimed pieces. She loaded an airport cart.

Finally approved and stamped by customs, Dakota located the transportation hub. Drivers holding up LED screens and cardboard signs peppered the covered sidewalk. None with her name.

A swarthy, thirtyish man studied her and lifted a screen glowing "Smith". She shook her head. A dark-complexioned teenage boy, with a hopeful expression, waved lavender cardstock at her. "Welcome, Dakota!" crafted in Kelsi's over-sized handwriting graced the heavy paper.

Kelsi's use of her favorite color gave Dakota a warm pang. Shooting her greeter a big smile, she pushed down worry about why her sister hadn't come to greet her in person.

The boy's hooded gaze traveled her form with an appreciative air well beyond his years. *Really?* Her lips twitched with an amused smile. Maybe the adult driver waited in the limo. She strode forward and extended a hand. When the man-child clasped hers, he looked up to her five-foot-nine height, making him appear even younger.

"I'm Tad Mendes. *Senhor* Cristiano send me to drive you." His words were slow and deliberate. If he drove, she'd misjudged his age.

"Hello, I'm Dakota. Nice to meet you. I'm relieved your English is so good. Would you teach me some quick Portuguese on the way to the Salazars?"

Tad's black eyes lit up over a white-toothed grin. "*Sim*! I mean, *sim* is yes!"

He took charge of the luggage cart and led her to a late-model Mercedes sedan idling at the curb. The vehicle stood out among the modest Fiats and Chevrolets rolling past. Tad opened the passenger-side door for her.

"Sit in the front, *Senhorita* Dakota. The water is for you." He pointed at a bottle glistening with condensation in the console's cup holder. "We practice Portuguese."

"Thank you." Butter-soft leather seats and air conditioning welcomed her. She opened the bottle and took a swig to be polite. A nice vehicle didn't mean the Salazars were wealthy, but did cast doubt on Mom's gold-digger theory.

Dakota couldn't imagine her competent, goal-driven sister as traumatized. However, a near execution would break anyone. With the heel of her hand, she rubbed away the prickle of brewing tears. The Fox wasn't the only one losing it.

While Tad returned the cart, Dakota pulled out her phone and tapped the keypad.

Dakota: **Forgiven, of course.**

With the speed of youth, a cart-free Tad rocketed back out through the sliding doors. Her first greeter, Mr. Swarthy, sauntered behind him with his laptop tucked under one arm and no passenger. His fare must have stood him up.

Glancing her way, Mr. Swarthy's narrowed gaze held a hint of animosity, as though she'd offended him. She'd never seen him before he held up his sign at her. Maybe he was a racist or just hated Americans. He turned on his heel and strode in the opposite direction. Tad bounced into the driver's seat and, after checking traffic, pulled the running vehicle into the stream of cars.

Dismissing weird Mr. Swarthy, Dakota focused on Tad. "So, what's the legal driving age here?"

His expression dropped, as though he'd guessed she thought him too young. "Eighteen. I got my license in February."

A whole three months of driving experience. Still, he seemed a sweet kid, and she hadn't intended to hurt his feelings. "Sixteen in the states. Is it a big deal here, too?"

He glanced from the road with a reinstated grin. "*Sim*."

As they worked their way through Manaus, the Amazonas state capital, Tad kept up a running commentary of Portuguese greetings and common phrases, and Dakota bounced back with responses. He finally took a breath. "You pick up words fast."

"I've got a good memory." She wondered why they didn't get on a highway. "How much farther?"

"*Desculpa*—sorry. Three hours."

She settled into her seat to enjoy the scenery and took in the ornate architecture, making a mental list of sites to explore. "How did you learn English?"

"*Senhor* Cristiano has a school for the plantation. English, French, too. Mendes family work for Salazars for many generations. I go to university next year."

Jaime's father sounded like a decent sort.

"Have you met my sister, Kelsi?"

"*Sim*. Very nice lady."

"Why didn't she come with you?" Dakota kept the question casual, despite her concerns.

"Oh, she's with the *senhores*. On wedding business."

Dakota tried to distract herself from her growing worry. Weddings took work, even if a couple hired a professional planner. After she learned how this surprise engagement had materialized, she could plan a course of action to drag her sister home.

A peach-toned Renaissance architectural masterpiece drew her attention. Its domed roof glinted in the sunlight. Dakota craned around to look for a sign. "What was the name of that building?"

"It's the *Teatro*, people sing there. Very beautiful."

A helicopter flew in low over the *Teatro*'s mosaic dome, and fell in behind their vehicle. The bird's presence gave Dakota an uneasy sense of being followed, until another chopper crossed over the skyline at a higher elevation. "Do many fly here?"

"*Sim*. I forget. I'm to apologize for the long car ride. Our helicopter is used for the wedding business."

Helicopter?

Kelsi had never explained how Jaime—in the world's most remote jungle—had materialized out of nowhere to take out the smugglers ready to kill her. With enough money to own a chopper, there could be only one reason to live in the rainforest. *Cocoa plantation, my ass. They're drug runners.*

Irritated she'd missed the obvious, Dakota pulled out her phone. GPS indicated they neared the edge of the city with at least two hundred miles to go. Soon traffic thinned and pavement turned to gravel. Exotic, vine-laden trees crept to the road's very edges, and a tunnel of foliage arched over their route.

She stifled a groan. On her way to vacation with drug lords in a remote wilderness, and her cell would be nothing more than a doorstop.

****

"We are here, *senhorita*." Tad's low voice sounded hollow inside the unmoving, quiet sedan. She'd fallen asleep. Shock that she'd left herself vulnerable jolted her awake, and she peeled her cheek from the window.

Glancing at Tad, she couldn't make herself believe the amiable kid could've drugged her. She straightened and stretched a kink in her neck.

Tad beamed at her. "You don't snore."

She scanned the manicured grounds backed by the jungle's edge. "Ah, thanks, I think."

Somewhere between Manaus and the Salazar drug cartel stronghold, her ever-vigilant guard had slipped, and she'd passed out cold. *Tad's fault.* He was too sweet to be involved with drug lords.

Dakota straightened from her slump and tugged at her rumpled navy silk blouse. At least the creases coordinated with the wrinkles in her linen pants. She tried to ignore her usual concern for her appearance. No need to waste a good impression on drug lords.

After she brought Kelsi to her senses, Dakota would drag her sister's ass back to Omaha. Maybe she'd add a few days in Cancun to break up the long commute. The Fox would be so happy, she might even join them.

Tad's door clicked shut, and he paced to the trunk. He'd parked in a circle drive fronting a sprawling Portuguese-colonial manor house surrounded by carefully placed ferns and orchid-draped trees. A gated, central courtyard, boasting an expansive kidney-shaped pool, welcomed guests to the manse's carved double doors within the enclosure.

Releasing her bling clip, she rewound her hair on top of her head. The layered *Thunderstorm* and *Spring Lilac* color cost good money, so she intended to show it off. Using the visor mirror, she draped her lavender curls over the bed of gray, cringing at a splotchy window print on her cheek.

She slipped on her coordinating rhinestone sandals and stepped out to help Tad with her luggage. Humid heat, blended with hints of rain-drenched earth, swamped her. With any luck, this muggy air would steam the wrinkles from her outfit.

"No, no, *a senhorita*, I do this. You follow me, *por favor*." The wheels of her three stacked bags clunked a staccato cadence along a cobbled path as he led them to an imposing black wrought-iron entry.

One side of the double gates swung open. A plump, middle-aged woman, with a salt and pepper bun and Tad's features, smiled widely at Dakota. "Ah, you're as pretty as your sister. I'm Consuelo, Tad's mother. Welcome."

"I'm Dakota." She extended a business-like hand in greeting, but the woman gently clasped her fingers and pulled her into the covered patio. Dakota's low heels clicked across a blue and orange mosaic floor.

She gawked at the exquisite veranda made for outside entertaining. Realizing her mouth hung open, she snapped her jaw shut and wrenched her attention back to her hostess.

Consuelo's eyes danced, apparently amused with Dakota's reaction. "We're all so excited about the wedding. Now, *Senhorita* Kelsi will have you here to share in her joy. A bride should have her family here for such a time, yes?"

Dakota nodded. Tension she'd tried to ignore since taking off from Omaha eased in her shoulders.

Surprising, considering she was walking into a den of drug lords. She scanned the Hollywood-worthy space for Kelsi. "I've missed her. Is she here?"

"Soon. She and *Senhores* Jaime and Cristiano do something for wedding."

Not at the airport and now, not home to greet her? Worry for her sister bubbled to the surface. Dakota looked left, then right as though Kelsi would materialize. "Did she call? It's not like her to—"

"No concern, all is well. Phones don't work many places. Only three weeks until wedding, and much to do."

Still holding her hand, Consuelo patted it and added a kind smile. The woman was adorable. And the perfect front for a drug kingpin. She pulled Dakota farther into an open-air, columned walkway. They turned a corner, entering a commercial outdoor kitchen.

Idle, utilitarian fans adorned the ceiling, while shiny stainless appliances marked the perimeter of the space. Behind them, latticework panels equipped with hooks held giant spoons, tongs, and forks. Dakota detected a hint of lemon oil, likely used to protect the steel from rust.

"Tad, take her belongings to the parrot room, *por favor*."

"*Sim, Mamãe*." The young man squeezed the stacked luggage between the women and an oven large enough to roast a pig.

After assuring Consuelo she didn't want a meal, snack, or cocktail, Dakota jumped at the chance for a swim to gain some privacy. "Lead the way."

The parrot room, no surprise, housed a parrot. Through the rails of its hanging bamboo cage in the corner, Dakota studied the lifelike indigo macaw. The level of detail made her suspect it was a stuffed animal.

She slid a hand inside and stroked real feathers. However, she'd never seen such a vibrant cobalt bird.

The suite's blue and yellow décor played off the parrot's colors, all in sharp contrast to the conservative Midwest furnishings favored by the Fox. Dakota snapped a few photos with little hope she could send them.

A couple minutes later, in some kind of cell-service miracle, the images of her suite's sitting area—a wicker chair and loveseat, wall-mounted television, and a wet bar—made it to her mother. She hoped the slideshow would convince Mom that Jaime wasn't using Kelsi to build a portfolio. However, the reality could be worse. Adding the international code, Dakota dialed her mother's number.

"Thank God, your phone works." Mom answered in true Fox fashion, short and to the point. "You're there."

Dakota planned to make the conversation as short as possible. "Yeah, finally. Long drive from Manaus, but their helicopter was tied up."

Silence filled the line. "Is she okay?"

"Kelsi's away 'on wedding business'." *Shit.* Dakota had erred calling her mother prior to seeing her sister. She struggled to keep any hint of her own worry from her voice. "She's due any time now."

The Fox sighed. "After you talk to her, call me again."

"From what I see here, you can cross gold-digging off your list. Their household staff is extremely nice, too." Dakota kicked herself. Like nice help made the Salazars good people. Still, she couldn't imagine Consuelo and Tad in with bad guys.

"Maybe. Call me." The Fox gave the order, but followed with a sniff. "I love you. Stay smart while you're there."

"Love you, too."

That chore accomplished, Dakota unpacked her suitcases, planning a dip in the pool while she waited for Kelsi. She hoped she could meet Jaime face to face, too. Maybe in person, she'd get a read on how he'd knocked staid Kelsi off her feet.

From his pictures, he was leading-man hot with sky-blue eyes, bronzed skin, and jet hair. Certainly, he was gorgeous enough to melt most women from the inside out.

However, good looks had never messed with Kelsi's head before. She always held out for the emotional connection, and took her sweet time doing it. Dakota had never suffered such a malady. Drool-worthy guy? She enjoyed him until his jerk shone through, or the wrong thing came out of his mouth.

She grabbed her bathing cap and draped a bionic blue towel over her arm. As an afterthought, she checked her bikini bottom. Wouldn't do to have butt cheeks peeking out. Satisfied, she exited her room's sliding glass door to the veranda and found a lounge chair in the shade.

A blue Fiat, like half the cars in Brazil, idled in the front drive. A man strode to the vehicle, but from this distance, his features were unclear. Something about his gait tugged at her mind, forcing recall that wouldn't cooperate. By his darker complexion he was likely Brazilian, so she couldn't know him. He climbed into his vehicle and studied her while closing his door in slow motion.

Dakota wiggled fingers at him to let him know he'd caught her interest. The man snapped his gaze to the driveway, accelerating to reach the winding lane leading to the road. *Freak.*

Late afternoon sun warmed the air-conditioned

chill from her skin. Stretching out on the shaded chaise, she planned to baste until she overheated, and then shock her body with a headfirst plunge into the pool.

****

Engine noise overhead and a sweltering wind jarred her awake. Blinking, she forced herself to consciousness. A too-close helicopter silhouette flew along the burnished sunset, its trajectory aiming somewhere behind the mansion. Kelsi and the Salazars had finally returned.

Showtime. Her sister would tell all, if Dakota had to strangle her to get it.

As she rose, her head spun from the heat. In the waning light, she could tell that at some point, the shade had moved and left her in the full sun. If she was quick, she had time for a cooling swim before Kelsi got to the house. After carefully tucking her two-tone color job under the rubber cap, she dove in and savored the chill that sluiced over her.

Although it was not yet dark, underwater lighting had come on, illuminating the blue and orange tiled walls. Dakota sprinted a few laps before gripping the pool's mosaic ledge, pausing to catch her breath. During her short swim, the sun dipped behind the treed horizon, and dusk triggered more landscape lighting.

Loud, male conversation erupted from a suite in the wing across the pool from hers. Shamelessly nosy, she crossed her arms on the cool tile ledge, straining to hear their muffled words. She lifted one corner of her swim cap for better reception.

The closed patio door framed two shadows facing each other, one man with hands on hips, and the other with waist-length hair. The low beam meant for ferns reflected off the sliding glass door and made it difficult to see into the room. At one point, Dakota thought she heard her name followed by an animal's snarl, of all things.

"There you are!" Kelsi's familiar voice turned her around. She stood in the threshold of Dakota's suite, illuminated by a light above the door.

Relieved to see Kelsi in one piece, Dakota stroked across the pool and climbed the metal ladder two rungs at a time. Biting her tongue against the scolding she wanted to unleash, she raced to hug her sister.

Dakota held her tight, and a beat too long. "About damn time you showed up."

"Um, you're soaking me." Kelsi laughed.

Ignoring her protest, Dakota pulled back to study her, searching for any sign of stress-induced psychosis. Her overzealous hug left water-drenched cotton clinging to Kelsi. "Where the heck have you been?"

"You look freaked. Relax. We flew out to pick up *Papai*'s friend, and it took way longer than we thought."

Tears welled in Dakota's eyes, and she swiped them away. Kelsi pulled her in for another quick embrace.

"I'm so glad you're here," she whispered.

"Me, too." Dakota glanced over her shoulder at the two dark figures. "So Jaime's father is *Dad* already?"

"Yeah, he's a sweetie."

"That his room?" Dakota cocked her head toward the suite holding the arguing men. One form leaned in toward the other, with arms moving, though their loud conversation had muted.

"His friend's, Matteo. The one we picked up. Can we say *issues*?" Kelsi puffed a breath. "They'll work it out."

"They're not the only ones with drama. The Steel Fox is cranked tight." Dakota motioned for Kelsi to follow her into her room before pulling the door shut behind them. She paused and faced her sister.

"I know. But I couldn't be better. And now that you're here, you can vouch for my happiness—and my sanity." Kelsi cocked one brow and held.

"I'll try. Mom demanded a report tonight." The suite's cool indoor air blasted Dakota with a shiver of goosebumps.

Questions about the Salazar wealth burned her throat, but she didn't want to spoil their reunion in the first five minutes. Kelsi stretched out over the cobalt bed topper and grabbed a parrot decorator pillow for her head. She waited while Dakota carefully selected underwear, shorts, and a girlie t-shirt from a mahogany inlaid highboy.

Kelsi gestured to Dakota's backside. "You've got a new tat! Hummingbird, very cool. When? Where?"

Sliding on a lavender thong and matching lace-trimmed bra, Dakota studied her sister. She seemed herself, not broken or withdrawn. "It's a souvenir from the Bahamas. Mom beat me up over it. She's sure I caught HIV from a dirty needle."

Kelsi pursed her lips. "She may have a point."

Dakota delivered her best *duh* look from under her brows. Between piercings, ink, and a stint at med school, she understood to be careful. "I watched them take the needles out of their autoclave." She twisted in vain to inspect the tat on the small of her back. "Hope I didn't ruin it out in the sun. I used SPF 50, but fell asleep."

"It looks okay, but is the hummer's flower missing a petal?"

"I need another appointment." Dakota huffed, recalling the snap of bone during her final ink session. She switched topics fast. "I made a few boss jumps over Rum Cay. Oh, and I can braid you some rockin' wedding hair. Had a job on the beach for a few weeks."

If all went according to plan, Dakota's new hair-styling skills would not be required.

"You know only adrenaline junkies jump out of perfectly good planes, right? And does Mom know you got another degree—in French braids?" Kelsi sounded too much like the Fox.

Ignoring the oft-heard jab at her skydiving hobby, Dakota pointed a warning finger. "No, and she doesn't need to, either. And lucky for you, I progressed way beyond French."

With a hint of apology, Kelsi curved her lips into a tight grin. "Okay, you do the hair."

Dakota, now dressed and marginally warmer, turned to Kelsi. "Enough small talk. How did this wedding pop up out of thin air?"

"Jaime's a wonderful man." She patted the bed for Dakota to join her, bringing back memories of late-night girl talks after lights out.

Dakota lay on her side next to her sister, snatching a pillow for her head. "And if you've lied to me about being pregnant, I'll kill you. After the Fox is done with you."

Kelsi snorted and smothered a laugh with her hand. "Not yet, that I know of, but we're trying."

"You're *what*?" Dakota groaned. Her sister had been possessed. A pregnancy would make it almost impossible to bring her home.

"I'm not getting younger. And we want a baby." Kelsi's brows furrowed, her narrowed gaze daring Dakota to argue. Lately, most of their friends who got married jumped right into motherhood, too. The risk of infertility skyrocketed after age thirty-five. She shouldn't have been surprised.

She choked back a million comments. Maybe she

could slip some birth control pills into Kelsi's food.

Chapter Three

"If you lacked the courage to execute me, you should've left me in the jungle." Matteo cringed at his unfair charge. Cristiano's judgmental scrutiny and his own embarrassment had made him surly.

From the lavatory's etched mirror, a gutter rat's image, complete with meat-tearing canines, taunted Matteo. The refined bamboo mosaic in the background of his reflection drove home his deteriorated state. He'd shifted too late to ease back into polite society.

Scowling, Cristiano stood in the tiled threshold as though overseeing a child's first attempts at hygiene. He seemed to guess Matteo's thoughts and waved newfangled electric clippers at him.

"Be silent and cut the damn hair." Cristiano flicked the motor on and off and shoved the device at Matteo. "Simple. You'll look human enough."

With a feline snarl, Matteo snatched the clippers. Years ago, he'd seen ads for the novel powered shears, however he'd never used them. Apparently, now, everything was electrified, not just light bulbs. At least the comb and scissors Cristiano laid on the stone vanity looked familiar.

"You'll catch up with technology."

Matteo snorted. The boat had impressed him, but flying inside the remarkable *chopper* had told him just how far he'd fallen behind the civilized world. He turned the buzzing razor on and off. Not only did he burn endless energy in a never-ending battle to stay human, the most menial tasks required interminable questions.

He grunted at his reflection. "If I were ready to move on, I'd have scheduled a visit."

"Jaime's godfather should be at his wedding."

Cristiano used his *Patron*'s tone, the one that brooked no argument from anyone save Matteo. "Times are dangerous. The new digital technology threatens to expose us every day. We need our *Enforcer* back—and I need my friend."

Interest in his appearance gone, Matteo laid the razor on the washroom counter. "Liar. You want a breeding bull. Pick another male for your save-the-species campaign."

"Now who lies? You ignored my visits for decades—until a queen's lure drew you out."

"A foolish stunt." Matteo shrugged. However, the fact he'd responded to a taken female disturbed him to his marrow. "You have no idea what you gambled."

As a mated male, a female's trace wouldn't affect Cristiano. He had no concept of just how close Matteo had come to killing his only child.

"A calculated risk worth taking to bring you back to us, whether or not you choose to court Kelsi's sister." Damn him, Cristiano's kind eyes showed nothing but sincerity.

Matteo refocused on his wildman reflection, unable to ignore Cristiano, but unwilling to respond.

"Is it so offensive I want my best friend to meet her first?" Cristiano hesitated, the way he'd always done when withholding information. "She might not even be a jag queen. However, if she is, you're the most genetically diverse from my line."

"Bloodlines. Pedigree papers will be next." Matteo huffed and lifted the clippers to his face.

"How many more years, Matteo? Anna, God rest her soul, is gone. You have a chance to rebuild a life."

The clippers clattered against the green stone counter. With a knife-like pain gouging his heart, Matteo glared at his friend. "What the hell would you know about it?"

Cristiano's face blanched, and several seconds of silence stretched. His color returned, and fury filled his eyes. "If you'd thought of any but yourself in the last seventy-three years... You've got spots for Christ's sake."

"And you! You're gray at the temples. How long since *your* last shift?" The something missing slammed into Matteo. Maria's scent no longer entwined with Cristiano's trace. *Oh God, please no.* Matteo hung his head. Dread stole his voice, and he barely forced a whisper. "What happened?"

Cristiano's eyes shone, and he blinked the tears away. "A car wreck. Jaime was eight. Nearly killed him, too."

Regret pummeled Matteo, and he laid both hands on the cool stone, his body laden with heavy grief. "I should've been here."

"Yes, you should have." Anger, likely years' worth, hardened Cristiano's features.

Matteo blew out a gust of air. He deserved the unforgiving tone. A knock sounded at the suite's door.

"Enter," Cristiano commanded, his voice rough. He turned on his heel, and strode into the bedroom.

Matteo paced after him with an apology on his lips. However, Consuelo and Tad trundled into the chamber, toting laundry baskets of clothing and shoes. With privacy gone, Matteo straightened and lifted his chin. The woman looked from one man to the other before dropping her cargo on the bed. "Tad, come. We'll stop back later."

"Stay—I was just leaving." Cristiano pushed by the pair to exit.

Consuelo raised a halting hand. "Before you go, *Senhor*, a man stopped by earlier. Said he is from

Manaus Now! magazine. He wishes an interview about the wedding."

Cristiano's scowl deepened.

"I understand." She smiled with a hint of indulgence. "His card is on your desk."

He gave a curt nod and then pulled the bedroom door shut behind him.

Matteo, though uncomfortable, strode forward to greet Consuelo and her son. The three made their introductions.

"I remember your father-in-law. A good foreman for Cristiano. Knew the cacao business like no one else," said Matteo.

"Thank you. He and his wife have passed on. My husband, Alejandro, is supervisor now. We're so glad to have you with us, *Senhor* Matteo. You'll be good for our *patrono. Senhor* Cristiano..." Consuelo paused with a quick glance at Tad, and busied herself organizing Matteo's hand-me-down wardrobe.

He returned to the bathroom to tackle his Moses-worthy beard, closing the door for privacy. Immediately, he regretted the isolation. Maria was gone. And so long ago. *Poor Cristiano.* As few could, Matteo understood his pain.

His sweet, delicate Anna's death had wrecked him. Sobbing like a child, he'd begged her to shift to cat and stop the bleeding. Allowing crimson to blossom through the bedding, she'd ignored him, cuddling their stillborn daughter's body. Even now, Matteo snorted against the unforgettable pungent copper tang of the birthing room. *She'd left without a backward glance.*

Cristiano and Maria, with Jaime on her hip, had stayed with him through the funeral and long afterwards. Old sorrow combined with new. When his friend suffered through his loss, Matteo should have been here, in this home. His throat constricted with his own sorrow for Maria—and his guilt. He'd been a self-centered asshole.

A tap at the bathroom door shook him from his regrets. "Come."

The door cracked open. At Matteo's nod, a smiling Tad delivered towels to stow in the linen closet. Before leaving, he halted, shifting his weight from one foot to the other as though ready to burst. "How did you live in the jungle so long?"

Matteo was grateful for the distraction. His own thoughts were killing him. "A lot easier than here."

With a fleeting look of open envy, the boy gestured to Matteo's knotted ropes of hair. "Your dreads are cool. Mamãe won't let me have them. Says if I look like a street soccer player, I won't get into a good university." A chagrined look crossed the boy's expression. "Sorry."

"Dreads?"

"Your hairstyle. They're cool, though."

Matteo eyed the mirror. "Your *mamãe* is right."

"I'll be back in a second." Tad jetted out of the room on a mystery errand.

"Walk!" Consuelo scolded him from the suite's sitting area. Scooping a stack of folded shirts from one of the two leather loveseats, she stowed the clothing into a tall chest of drawers. She ambled toward the hallway and looked over her shoulder. "I'll make sure he doesn't bother you, *Senhor*."

"Just Matteo, please. And Tad's helping me," he called as she disappeared.

Relieved to be alone, he pushed the bathroom door closed and groaned at the image in the mirror. Grabbing his beard in one hand, and scissors in the other, he snipped. He stuffed the wad of tan and gold into the wastebasket. Mimicking Cristiano's demo, he put a plastic guard on the clipper's tiny blades.

After he buzzed the shears over his cheeks and chin, his stubble-covered face finally looked familiar—until he opened his mouth. Newly prominent canines still dominated his bared-tooth grimace. The door swung open behind him, banging against the wall.

"Oops." Thumping his knuckles once on the door in a belated knock, a breathless Tad held out a bead-decorated leather strip. "I got this hair tie at the market when I hoped to grow mine out."

Gathering his *dreads* at his nape, Matteo decided to tackle his hair in the morning. He snugged them into a fat ponytail, exposing the animal print on his shoulder. "Thanks."

His reflection mocked him. Discouraged, and unable to look at himself another minute, he turned from the mirror. No wonder the queen had called him a savage. He couldn't change the past, but somehow, he'd make it through the wedding. Cristiano deserved that much.

Tad looked up from Matteo's back with widened eyes. "Is that your jaguar pattern?"

Having hit his tolerance for human contact, Matteo feigned a search in the top lavatory drawer. "Thanks for the hair tie."

Tad's reflection frowned from the mirror, obviously wounded by the dismissal. "Uh, sure."

He trudged out of the room, minus his youthful energy. With brief remorse over hurting the nice kid, Matteo waited for the suite door's latch to snick shut before leaving the confines of the washroom. If he planned to stay in the human world, explaining his retained feline traits would be a challenge.

For tonight, solitude suited him. He eyed the

over-sized bed littered with foliage-print pillows. Atop the bookcase-style headboard, an oblong planter hosted leaf-covered bamboo stalks. The bamboo room, they'd called it.

He sought Maria's scent and found nothing. Regrets poked at him, again. It was a wonder Cristiano hadn't gone mad. Maybe he had, in a way.

Shifters didn't age, yet he had gray hair, and tiny wrinkles bracketed his eyes. He and Maria had loved running their jungle. Maybe Cristiano couldn't return without her, just as Matteo had loathed his empty human home. Maybe, while he had hidden in the jungle, Cristiano had escaped into the human-world and his Salazar Holdings empire.

Mouthwatering aromas of barbecued beef and fresh-baked cheese bread preceded a knock from the hall. Cristiano had remembered Matteo's favorites. Suddenly, privacy wasn't essential. He swung open the door to a beaming Consuelo.

Glancing at her delivery, Matteo's first smile in ages was a foreign sensation. "Yes."

She lifted a two-handled platter by way of greeting.

Matteo opened the door wide.

"You arrived too late for a sit-down dinner." Marching in, she didn't wait for a formal invitation and, with a wink, deposited her bounty on the coffee table. "I suspect you're getting hungry."

A plate of perfectly pink, sliced, barbequed peccary accented with grilled pineapple dominated the meal. Despite the delectable entrée, a side of *pão de queijo,* cheese-stuffed biscuits, captivated his interest. "Thank you *very* much."

He tore his attention from the food, and Consuelo chuckled. "*Senhor* Jaime always enjoys starchy meals when he returns from the jungle."

Later, with a full belly, and expecting to wallow in the bed's cushioned luxury, Matteo flopped onto the mattress. Instead of enjoying the softness, sinking into the pillow-like padding made him feel trapped, and the absent insect song rang loud in his mind. With an irritated groan, he rose and pulled the bedding with him.

****

The next morning, dawn's earliest light filtered through the sheer green curtain. Across the veranda from Matteo's suite, clinking utensils mingled with the familiar cadence of Consuelo's footsteps. Along with spots and fangs, keen jaguar hearing had followed him into human form.

He rose from a pallet of bamboo-patterned linen on the floor and peered out the patio door. The housekeeper bustled toward a metal table toting a pitcher of juice and a plate stacked with pastries.

Despite devouring the mountain of cheesy biscuits the night before, his mouth watered, and his stomach rumbled. After so many decades in cat form, Matteo's human body screamed for carbohydrates.

He blasted to the chest-of-drawers, pulled out a pair of shiny-blue elastic waist shorts and slid them on, hoping they weren't actually underwear. If he hurried, he could bring his breakfast back to his suite before anyone else arrived.

As he stepped from his chilled room, damp heat welcomed him. Air-conditioning required one more adjustment to this new world. Schooling his stride to a casual stroll, he skirted the pool to the serving table.

Consuelo paused at the home's kitchen entrance, turning to him. "*Senhor*, good morning. Did you sleep well?"

"Yes, thank you." He'd frozen his ass off. On top

of that, he'd slept naked, since the pajamas abraded his furless skin.

"I'm just setting up. I'll be back with more in a few minutes. Make yourself at home."

Matteo paced to the nearly empty buffet and poured a tall tumbler of juice. After draining the acai-banana blend in gulps, he refilled his glass, and scanned for a small plate. Finding none, he zeroed in on the mountain of round, cinnamon-sugared balls and just picked up the platter.

The fresh pastries' warmth heated his hand through the glass plate, and the blossoming cinnamon triggered a rumble from his gut. A furtive glance over his shoulder confirmed he could escape to privacy.

Lavender, with a low note of vanilla, filled his nose. Confused, he looked down at the fried confections. *Oh God...*

Chapter Four

Dakota smelled *coffee*. Consuelo's shadow had passed by earlier, followed by sounds of utensils and dishes. The housekeeper must have planned an alfresco breakfast. Inklings of the brew seeped into her room. Dakota threw on cutoffs and her Bahama Mama t-shirt. When she opened the patio door, heaven-sent coffee fragrance magnetically pulled her outside.

Giant ferns and a small blossoming tree framed the back of a shirtless man who stood at the buffet. She paused to enjoy the view. As he served himself, an auburn animal print tat rippled in harmony with his muscular torso.

Lion-colored dreadlocks fell from a ponytail, complementing the superb ink job gracing broad shoulders to narrow hips. In an added bonus, the pattern extended over his left deltoid. He had to be the shadow man from last night. Too bad, he was hooked up with dealers. Brazil could've been a great time.

Lifting his nose to a sniffing position, the man froze. His tense stance—and big-cat pattern—gave the impression of a predator scenting prey. As Dakota approached, he looked over his shoulder in a hesitant movement. The dreadlocks ponytail swung to the side, exposing more of the exquisite skin art.

"*Boma dia*," Dakota offered, trying out her new Portuguese.

He stood unnaturally still for an instant, and then turned, holding a platter of donut holes. Maybe he hadn't heard her.

When his molten-copper gaze met hers, her lips parted in stunned surprise. Bronzed lashes and a few days' worth of beard almost matched his golden skin tone, adding punch to his already exotic eyes.

After recovering her wits, she tried her Portuguese again. "My name is Dakota. Nice to meet you."

His steely regard gave the impression he saw her every flaw and found her lacking. She shook off the ridiculous idea, recalling the most important phrase she'd learned from Tad. "Where's the coffee, *por favor*?"

As she padded barefoot toward him, his eyes widened and his nostrils flared. She wondered if the Brazilian heat had overpowered her deodorant. Or maybe, he was just a freak. Still silent, he studied her for an unnerving moment with knitted brows. "Your hair is *blue*."

Even in Portuguese, she got that he didn't like her hair. Suddenly, coffee became even more important. Pursing her lips against the insult, she strode toward the buffet. He jumped aside as though frightened of her.

The coffee scent grew more enticing with every step, but no carafe or pot was on the buffet. No food either. Dreadlocks still held the single platter of pastry. With a sigh, she poured herself a glass of some kind of purple juice that smelled like bananas.

The dog hadn't even said hello before cracking on her hair. Not bothering with eye contact, she switched to irritated English. "It's *Spring Lilac* and *Thunderstorm*."

"I'm sorry. I've not seen hair that color before." His clipped Oxford English didn't gain her forgiveness.

She returned her best droll stare. "Whatever."

Seeming frozen in place, he gaped at her with parted lips. He tilted his head a fraction, but still said nothing.

Despite her annoyance, she tracked the cobblestoned muscle paving his abs up to his stacked chest and finally his face. She gestured to the pile of sugar-crusted donut holes he held at groin level. "Were you setting those out? Or are you eating them?"

Enjoy the view and that's it. His jerk had already shone through—and he dealt drugs. She waited for an answer, quirking a brow.

The man blushed as much as his golden skin would allow. For an instant, she suspected her less-than-discreet appraisal had embarrassed him. He looked over the pastry for a long moment, as though making a grand decision, and finally offered up the tray in slow motion. "Oh, have some, please."

The dirt bag had intended to take the whole platter.

"No thanks, I'll come back." Turning on her heel, she marched past him toward her room.

Coffee scent burgeoned, halting her. Another search told her she hadn't overlooked a pot. *Him!* Maybe he filled his pockets with coffee beans. After all, the weirdo planned to take a whole plate of cinnamon balls.

Faking a sniff of the donut holes, she took in a delectable espresso. "On second thought, I will grab a couple."

She paced to the buffet for a napkin. When she returned, coffee overwhelmed her again, but this time the trace did strange things low in her pelvis. Or, maybe the hot-bod view affected her in spite of her jerk-o-meter. *I've lost it.*

****

Unmated. Matteo gripped the edge of the steel buffet table for support. Out of nowhere, a fresh lavender *Ardor* fragrance had conquered his body and stolen his mind. With her so near, he'd almost dropped the glass platter shielding his awakening male parts.

He'd thanked God when she finally strutted

away. Until the exaggerated sway of her hips hardened his unused cock to the point of misery.

Having been a eunuch since he'd lost Anna, he'd marveled at his first very painful arousal in nearly eighty years—seventy-seven to be exact. *Your hair is blue.* No wonder Dakota had tortured him with a take-that sashay.

Apparently, his pecker was ready to move on. Using Kelsi's sister to scratch that itch would complicate his life beyond measure. *Disastrous.*

To gain relief from Dakota's dissipating *Ardor*, Matteo circled the pool to a table near his patio door and claimed a cushioned seat. The mated female, Kelsi, had prompted an urge to possess her, but not arousal. Matteo hadn't responded to any female since his mate had passed.

He popped a pastry ball into his mouth and savored the sugary warmth. Another shifter would find a human. Hell, many had married them. Not an option for Matteo. He brushed crumbs from his chest. Human females had never drawn him—he'd tried. Dakota was off limits. He would just have to suffer the torturous three weeks until the wedding.

Vertical strips of fabric—a type of blinds he supposed—moved to the side behind Dakota's sliding glass door, and he met her sea-green gaze. An arched brow and high cheekbones offered certain contempt. Dark silver hair draped around her oval face, blending to *Spring Lilac* over her shoulders. Holding a fistful of blue hair to his nose and entangling their bodies would surely be heaven.

Schooling his trigger-happy dick, he acknowledged her bold study with a nod. He hoped his coffee scent had made her equally uncomfortable. While he held her gaze, he popped another fried sweet into his mouth and deliberately licked sugar crystals from his lips. Two could play her game.

The long blinds swung as though shoved. Rather than smug satisfaction, Matteo had the hollow sense that, yet again, he'd been an asshole.

As she carried out more food, Consuelo's sharp gaze shifted to the still swaying window covering. She dropped two steaming trays on the metal buffet with a clatter and paced around the pool to Matteo's table. As he reached for a pastry, she pulled his unfinished breakfast out from under his hand. The lift of her chin told him he'd lose an arm if he tried for the leftover sweets.

She glanced to the breakfast spread just outside of Dakota's suite. "Help yourself. To the food. Even though he's too young for her, I fear the *Senhorita* Dakota will break Tad's heart. He's quite taken with her. Sweet girl, don't you agree?"

Great, Consuelo had witnessed Matteo's base behavior. Worse, an urge to pummel Tad accosted him. *Jealous of a boy—over a female I don't want.*

"Good luck to him," Matteo croaked out.

Too irritated, and possibly too feral, to socialize, Matteo nearly jumped to his feet, the metal chair legs squawking against the concrete. He ignored Consuelo and returned to the solace of his room.

****

Mid-morning sun shone over the garden's decorative trees and dodged the table's umbrella, threatening to bake Dakota and the two women who'd thought to enjoy the dancing hummingbirds. Beads of condensation coated their tea-filled glasses.

"I've been in eight weddings, but now that it's my turn, I can't make a single decision." Kelsi groaned. She sent a furtive glance after Jaime and his father, who strode along a cobbled garden path toward the helipad.

Again, the wedding planner sent Dakota a desperate, pleading look before turning a weak smile on Kelsi. "The bride's bouquet of the wild white orchids will be exquisite."

In her transparent distraction, Kelsi's gaze lingered on her betrothed. A few minutes prior, he'd stopped to say goodbye before leaving for the Salazar headquarters in Manaus. The two seemed to touch each other about once per minute. Kelsi's obvious joy relieved Dakota's worry and warmed her heart.

She nudged Kelsi's arm. "Go. Walk him to the chopper. Go to work with him, if you like."

"Really?"

"I got this. All orchids, right? How tough can it be?"

Her sister's green eyes sparkled before she engulfed Dakota in a fierce hug. "I love you!"

As though they hadn't seen each other in weeks, Kelsi blasted off to join her man, who swung her around into an embrace. Giving them a wide berth, Cristiano beamed at the pair, likely counting the months until he had grandchildren. He probably measured Kelsi's hips in his mind to confirm her childbearing potential. *Male granny-lust.*

"Those two are so smitten," said *Senhora* Vargas. "Poor thing, she couldn't even think while he was near."

Wistful longing pushed a sigh from Dakota. No man had ever filled her heart to bursting. Only a lucky few found their true soul mate. And no one deserved the fairytale more than Kelsi.

When relating her near-death experience, Kelsi's eyes had appeared vacant, and she'd clipped out a sketchy tale. A poacher had held a rifle to her head. An instant before he'd pulled the trigger, Jamie had wasted the dirt bag. Dakota shuddered. Given that history, he'd earned a lot of leeway. Maybe the trauma *had* made Kelsi vulnerable.

Dakota prayed she was wrong about the drug connection. Tonight, she would find the courage to ask where the Salazar money really came from. *Like they would tell Kelsi.*

She screwed on a smile before turning to *Senhora* Vargas. "Okay, now let's plan a wedding."

The woman practically wilted with relief. "We'd accomplished nothing. *Obrigada!* Apologies, I forget myself. Thank you, very much!"

"The sun's on the way up, so let's move things along." Dakota rose to adjust the umbrella to shade her guest, earning another look of gratitude. "If it gets too hot, we'll go inside."

In the distance, Dreadlocks, clad in shorts and a sleeveless tee, walked the tree line. His stride and long V-shaped torso gave him the balanced look of a world-class athlete. Chiseled biceps and quads made her think martial arts, or maybe an Olympic swimmer. Jerk or not, the guy was hot.

As though she'd called out to him, he turned, pinning her with his copper gaze.

Reminding herself to breathe, she snapped her attention back to Mrs. Vargas. "First things, first. What's our budget?"

The fifty-something, dark-haired woman raised penciled-in brows over a new kind of smile. "The best. *Senhor* Jaime said, 'give *meu anjo* anything she desires'."

"Well, well." Spending money topped Dakota's skill set. "Let's get busy!"

The liberal funding hadn't surprised Dakota. During last night's mandatory call to the Fox, her mother announced the Gorman clan would arrive in Manaus via chartered plane, courtesy of Cristiano Salazar.

Little impressed her self-made CEO mother. However, five-star accommodations, including amenity allowances for the wedding guests, had taken her aback. Word was, despite the short notice, relatives were scrambling to get tourist visas and arrange time off work.

With Dakota's firm report of true love, and a reassuring show of wealth, her mother had apparently resigned herself to a Salazar marriage. Dakota hadn't shared her drug cartel suspicions.

Two and a half hours later, with ceremonial and reception battle plans in place, Dakota escorted an elated Mrs. Vargas to her Chevy sedan in the circle drive.

"I'll send a venue diagram and pictures of the selections to share with the bride." The matron dabbed her glistening cheeks with a tissue and tapped a command on her phone. "There. Our team will arrive very early. All will be perfect, I promise."

Dakota used the rest of the day to organize the wedding planner's catalog screenshots and knocked out a draft of the agenda. Late in the afternoon, when Kelsi walked in with the Salazar men, Dakota was ready with her packed folder.

****

Matteo's need for starchy food beat at him. The low-hanging afternoon sun now peeked over the distant canopy. It had been hours since he'd last eaten. With Consuelo annoyed at him, he doubted room service would arrive.

As he trudged across the courtyard to the kitchen entry, the thought of encountering people darkened his mood. However, the savory aroma of black beans mixed with peccary leftovers overcame his reluctance to socialize, increasing his pace toward the kitchen.

When he opened the door, Dakota's scent rushed

over him. Determined to keep his wits, he focused on the food. A casual buffet graced the eating bar with the expected fair of beans, steamed rice, and barbeque. He spotted some kind of pastry weeping chocolate pudding.

Dakota and Tad sat at one end of a trestle-style table, conversing amiably over their meals in Portuguese. The boy's adoration for Dakota gleamed in his eyes. Her aquamarine gaze sparkled back at the young man, and she giggled at his teasing quip.

A rush of aggression pulsed through Matteo, and he rolled a shoulder in irritation over the unbidden jaguar urge. *It's only instinct.*

The pair looked up at his arrival, and Dakota's scent blossomed to a new level. Despite how quickly she returned her attention to Tad, at the least, she was attracted to Matteo. The realization quickened his pulse.

Turning his back to them to fill a plate, he reminded himself that she had no real interest in a clod who had insulted her appearance. She simply couldn't control her physical response any more than he could.

Like this morning. He'd thought a jungle hike would relieve his edginess, but aborted the plan after her siren scent had carried to him, whipping him around to the sight of her curvy frame.

Instead, he'd read a stack of newspapers Cristiano had left in his room. Overwhelming information emphasized his lost years. He'd forced himself to finish and jotted a lengthy list of terms to research.

"*Senhor* Matteo, welcome. The food's great." Tad rose and delivered his stacked dishes to the kitchen sink.

"I'm counting on it." Matteo sculpted a food mountain on his plate and shot a smile at the boy. He'd come back for the pudding puff creations.

Tad halted at the threshold, turning his attention to Dakota. "I'll talk to Papai. We'll fly to Manaus, tomorrow. Tonight, you search shops and have addresses ready."

"Awesome." Dakota responded to Tad. "Have a seat." Still speaking Portuguese, she met Matteo's gaze with a half-smile. Not particularly polite or inviting, her sea-green eyes held more of a dare, and maybe mischief.

Matteo could never ignore a challenge. He forgot his escape plan and claimed Tad's vacated wooden chair adjacent to her, placing his *to-go* plate on the oak surface. "So, what sends you into Manaus?"

"I need a dress for the wedding." Dakota responded with crisp pronunciation and only a hint of accent. Matteo was impressed. She topped off her coconut water and lifted the pitcher in silent offer to pour. "Kelsi said to get whatever I want—she has no idea how dangerous that is."

"*Real* spends as quickly as dollars." Matteo smiled and held up a tumbler. The small courtesy eased the tension in his shoulders. Maybe she'd forgiven his blue-hair blunder.

"Even faster, when it's not mine." She chuckled.

Her smooth command of the language piqued his interest. "Your Portuguese is excellent. You've been in Brazil before?"

She shook her head. "Thanks. It's similar to Spanish—and I have a knack for diction and word patterns."

Matteo raised his brows. From his recall, few in the United States bothered to learn a second language. "You speak Spanish, too?"

"It's the only language that I'm truly fluent in— besides English." She smiled. "But Spanish makes Portuguese easier to grasp."

"So this morning, the wedding planner didn't need to waste her English skills on you?"

"I needed it then. Too many new words flying around." Dakota smiled. An instant later, she pursed her lips to a straight line and lowered her forkful of pastry. "You were a football field away."

"I've got excellent hearing." He'd done it again. She likely thought he'd snuck back to the garden patio to eavesdrop. "Your voices carried."

"Whatever."

He translated *whatever* to mean *bullshit*. She'd given the same response to his blue-hair-comment apology. Pride wouldn't allow him to offer more explanation.

Cristiano's warning came to mind. *She might not even be latent.* Well she was. Certainly, he had detected her queen's scent.

Matteo wondered how they planned to inform Dakota of her hidden self. "So, has your sister talked to you about the family traditions—heritage?"

"A few things. We're not Catholic, so an indoor wedding surprised me. Ouch on that. When I saw the gardens, I thought for sure…"

"They're beautiful." *She doesn't know she's a cat.* Leaping three-quarters of a century into the future had capsized Matteo. Every action involved learning how a new invention worked. However, Dakota faced an even larger challenge—a fundamental shift in her reality. As though she were under his care, protective instincts welled in his chest. Shifters safeguarded all females.

She means nothing to me. However, he would help her all he could. "Dakota, earlier we began poorly. You're Cristiano's guest and Jaime's future sister-in-law. Can we begin again?"

Her smile lit her eyes to a brighter teal, adding an impish glint. She rose from her seat. "Yes, of course."

The genuine smile and quick forgiveness melted

Matteo. He tracked her trip to the sink and then followed her exit, relishing the sashay that had earlier taunted him.

Chapter Five

The sisters sat cross-legged on Dakota's bed, wedding-related printouts littering the indigo coverlet. The intimate wedding didn't come close to Dakota's definition of small.

With a tired smile, Kelsi closed her laptop. "It's only midnight and nearly everyone has already RSVP'd."

"About that…" Dakota extracted the bride's three-page Gorman family invitation spreadsheet from a folder. "What gives with the lopsided guest lists?"

Kelsi had plucked every second and third cousin from their mother's side of the family. The majority, who hailed from Arizona, would think Kelsi was flaunting the Salazar wealth. But she wasn't built that way.

She gave a wry smile. "You noticed."

"Hard not to. Aren't you afraid the Gorman clan will overwhelm Jaime's fifty or so guests?"

"Doubt it." Kelsi laughed at a joke Dakota didn't get.

She tried again. "We haven't even spoken to the Thornburg girls since grade school. What happened to *an intimate service*?"

Kelsi shrugged, stacking the laptop and folders on the nightstand. "It's still small."

Dakota snorted. She stretched out on her stomach, propping herself up with a squished a pillow, and gave her sister a droll look. "Not an answer."

"I know. I just can't decide the best way to tell you." Kelsi retook her spot on the mattress. "The weird list is connected to the secret I warned you about."

Dakota perked right up. Earlier, all Kelsi had said about her big announcement was that she wasn't pregnant. "Okay, out with it. Don't make me strangle you."

"You remember Mom's *Jaguar Princess* stories?"

"Your epic reveal has to do with a Honduran *legend*?" Irritation put snark into Dakota's voice.

Unfazed by her sarcasm, Kelsi scooched off the bed and undid the top button of her blouse, disrobing. "The stories are part of my news."

Totally confused—and even more annoyed—Dakota arched an eyebrow. "You get some jaguar ink?"

Kelsi's eyes danced. "*Way* better. Mom's stories are *true*."

Dakota's mouth dropped open, and she struggled for words. "*What?*"

"Go stand by the wall." Kelsi stepped out of her panties.

Swinging off the mattress, Dakota joined her at the foot of the bed. Unexplained anxiety and a sudden need to protect her sister, made her stay near Kelsi. Dakota glanced through the open blinds to the lit pool and accent-lighted courtyard, wondering where Kelsi's schoolgirl modesty had gone. She wore a one piece to the nude beach.

"You're creeping me out, Kels. The Jaguar Princess is a myth, not family history. You're smarter than that."

Smiling as though she'd eaten a canary, Kelsi piled her clothes on the corner of the bed and stretched out naked on her stomach. "So you won't be afraid, I'll lie real still. It's okay to touch me if you want to. And remember, no matter what, I won't hurt you."

"What the hell are you talking about? This cloak and dagger act's getting old." Even more concerning, with each bizarre statement, Dakota's sister seemed more like a stranger.

"I'm going to change into a jaguar like the Princess did."

"Oh my God!" Dropping onto the bed, she hauled Kelsi to a sitting position.

Kelsi struggled against her. "Stop. It's okay."

"No. Just—*no*." Holding her sister's arm with one hand, Dakota grabbed Kelsi's blouse with the other. Draping it around her shoulders, she tugged her sister close, holding on for dear life. "We'll get you home. Tomorrow. Mom will hire the best therapist in Omaha. Promise."

Tears blurred Dakota's vision. The Fox's famous intuition had called it. Kelsi had truly broken from reality, and her condition appeared critical. Heavy-duty drugs had to be involved.

Breaking from Dakota's embrace with unexpected strength, Kelsi laughed. "See, this—this *weirdness* right here," she waved a hand in vague reference to Dakota, "is why I've got to *show* you."

Dakota grabbed Kelsi by the shoulders and desperate, she tried to shake her back into her normal, boring, reliable sister. "Stop this, right now."

"Last chance to move back." Kelsi's expression lost its crazed enthusiasm, and she quit fighting, leveling a glower at Dakota. "Fair warning, *you'll* want the shrink, not me."

A dark glow engulfed her sister's slender frame, hiding Dakota's hands. She yelped, scrambling in reverse until her back slammed against the wall—the same spot she'd refused minutes prior.

The radiant halo around Kelsi expanded to a massive cat shape, and then melted into … an enormous white panther with chestnut spots. Their hue matched her sister's hair color—exactly. Familiar emerald eyes stared up at Dakota, and round, tufted ears flicked as the oversized, great cat nestled its muzzle atop its paws. The mattress sagged under what must have been several hundred pounds.

Dakota's heart knocked against her breastbone, and she let loose a full-throated scream. Way too experienced with panic attacks, she squelched the burgeoning fight or flight compulsion. *This can't be real.* Her sister couldn't have hidden that fast, but somehow Kelsi had swapped places with this beast.

The white cat didn't move a muscle, but kept its gaze trained on Dakota. Certain she'd been punked, she scanned for any trace of Kelsi. Even if she bought into a bizarre transformation, the change in mass defied the laws of physics. Had she really even considered her sister had morphed into a—what? She skirted the huge cat by several feet and dropped to peer under the bed from a not-so-safe distance. Not even dust bunnies.

Heavy footsteps pounded inside the main mansion, vibrating the wood floor under her hands. Her hysterical shrieks over an apparently domesticated panther had rallied the troops. Keeping her motions methodical, she rose and edged toward the sliding door. The stunning feline's unnatural stillness spoke to its training. Only its eyes moved, following Dakota.

"Okay, kitty, I'll figure this out later." Intelligence in the eerily familiar green gaze gave Dakota the sense the jaguar understood her.

Now, last night's snarl made sense. Her sister would have a pet panther. Recalling a tour of Kelsi's beloved Omaha zoo cat complex, Dakota realized the sable spots were actually rosettes. *A white jaguar.* She braved a few steps toward the beast, unsure if she had the courage to touch the lush fur.

The cat's gaze snapped to the sliding-glass door behind Dakota, and she wheeled around. Outside on the dimly lit veranda, a wide-eyed, dark-skinned man smashed his face to the pane, peering into the suite. From his distorted, rapt expression, the smoke and mirrors trick had stunned him, too.

A deafening roar vibrated the dresser mirror, and the jaguar leapt the breadth of the room, crashing into the sliding glass door. The cat's massive weight shattered the panel, leaving a crackle-patterned, bowed shell of security glass hanging from the frame. An eighteen-inch hole flagged the point of impact.

In the next instant, the intruder's scream harmonized with a wailing siren. Exterior security lights popped on, and Dakota met his terrified gaze before he wheeled and sprinted away. *Mr. Swarthy!*

He'd followed her. The realization made her legs weak, and she dropped back against the wall. Maybe he thought she delivered drugs, or he was scoping her out for the skin trade. Slavers had tried for Kelsi. Dissecting scenarios only made her brain useless.

Taking a deep breath, Dakota shut down all thought, and focused on the oddly predictable pattern of cracked safety glass.

Matteo, barefoot and shirtless, dreadlocks streaming behind him, rocketed past the damaged window. Her sister's shattered reflection peered back from the damaged pane. The image snapped her to life.

Kelsi! Dakota whipped around. Unharmed, but trembling, Kelsi slid her arms into her blouse.

Dakota scanned the room. "Where did the white—"

Jaime burst through the interior door and rushed to Kelsi, spilling Portuguese. "What happened? Are you okay?"

"A man, in the courtyard." Her voice quaked, and she raised frightened eyes to Jaime. "He saw me shift."

"*Cristo!*" Jaime's dark bronze skin paled.

Dakota settled next to Kelsi, putting an arm around her shoulders. Worry over the intruder trumped her million questions about the big cat. She'd get the goods later. "Matteo's on his tail."

"I can't leave either of you unguarded to give chase." Jaime absently rubbed the back of Kelsi's neck.

She finished dressing as Jaime paced to the demolished door. Grim-faced, he appeared a bundle of barely leashed fury. Apparently unaware he was barefoot, he strode over the glass shards to scan outside then returned to her. Crimson footprints stained a trail along the hardwood.

Keeping a hand on her back, Jaime seemed to need Kelsi as a touchstone to pull in his next breath. Equally drawn, she leaned back into him.

This drama hadn't followed Dakota from Omaha. Mr. Swarthy was Brazilian. In addition, before coming to the Amazon, Kelsi had never used drugs or showed any sign of delusional behavior. Everything traced back to the Salazars.

In a moment of difficult decision, the fierce devotion Dakota detected between the couple saddened her. Drug dealers fell in love, too, she supposed. However, when it came to Kelsi's safety, Dakota wouldn't allow emotion to shake her resolve.

Matteo entered from the hall breathing hard, perspiration highlighting his muscular torso. He looked right at her. "Are you okay?"

He's in the Salazar clan. She nodded with pursed lips, anger nudging her shock aside. Cristiano and Tad followed him in.

"Did you see him?" Matteo focused on Dakota as though she was the only person in the room.

Lifting her chin, Dakota cleared her throat. "I did.

You don't know him?"

Cristiano's eyes widened. His surprise appeared genuine. "Why would we?"

"He was at Eduardo Gomes when I landed." Determination to get Kelsi home gave Dakota courage, and she straightened her spine. "Do any of you know why he'd follow me?"

"What was he doing at the airport?" Matteo snapped, ignoring her question and taking a step toward her. He wasn't so dense that he'd missed her accusation. He was just unfazed—or investigating. Maybe the Salazars really didn't know Mr. Swarthy.

"Yes. *Mr. Swarthy* stood with the limo drivers, holding a sign. It's him, only with a two-inch gash in his forehead. He might've been in the driveway earlier, too. Drove a Fiat." Dakota's gut told her he was the same man, but without actually seeing his face, she withheld that opinion.

"You're observant. Good job." Matteo looked at her as though seeing her for the first time, and she detected genuine admiration in his regard.

"Good memory is all."

He'd noticed something positive about her. A drug dealer's praise should have meant nothing, yet she couldn't deny the hint of pride nosing its way into her heart.

"I don't like it." Matteo stiffened and surveyed the room with piercing eyes, resting his gaze on Jaime. "Patrol a close perimeter until dawn. I'll stand sentry in the courtyard for the night. Have Alejandro put trusted men on the gates, too."

Interesting. Cristiano owned this estate, yet no one questioned Matteo's authority to dish out orders. Jaime sent a subtle glance to his father and nodded. At least he seemed to notice Matteo's odd assumption of leadership.

Cristiano glanced at Dakota with an expression she couldn't interpret. "Matteo, work with Alejandro to coordinate security. I trust him, as I trust you. Our females must be protected."

"I'll find him." Matteo glanced her way, too, making her think they referred to her, personally. *Females?* As though this night couldn't get any weirder.

Consuelo bustled into the suite, wiping her brow and sending an anxious look around the room. "What's happened?"

"An unauthorized visitor. Where's Alejandro?" asked Cristiano.

"Tad, find your father, now. Tell him to hurry," ordered Consuelo.

The teen nodded and raced out into the hall. His staccato footsteps trailed off in the tense silence.

No one had mentioned the cat. A nervous grin tugged at Dakota's lips. "Just turn that white jaguar loose in the courtyard. That cat made him squeal. The goon's tighty whities are brown, for sure."

Jaime furrowed his brows. "Kelsi, you didn't tell her?"

"Tell me what?" Dark portent washed through Dakota, making her lightheaded. What had Kelsi said? *Saw me shift.*

"I showed her, but the peeping Tom freaked me out. I almost got him, too." Kelsi gestured to the misshapen sliding door. "The security glass saved him."

"What?" Dakota rose unsteadily from the bed, and the creepy sensation grew. They talked over her, saying impossible things—carrying this cat stunt too far.

Matteo closed the few steps to her, his coffee scent caressing her, soothing her ire. Swelter had already invaded the room, but with his nearness, the temp jumped another few degrees.

Gently cupping her face, his lids lowered over his warm copper gaze. "You're one of us. Welcome to the jungle, *gatinha*."

Kitty? Before she could stop herself, she turned her cheek into his palm. The rest of his statement was slow to register. "What—"

"You're sure?" interrupted Kelsi.

"Without doubt." Matteo stepped back, and his luscious mocha faded. Dakota shook off an urge to follow him.

Suddenly, the spacious suite walls closed in, and the small crowd sucked the air from the room. In a reaction usually reserved for rodents, an invisible band squeezed Dakota's chest, and her breaths came in shallow puffs.

"Sure of what?" Her voice came out in a squeak.

Backpedaling into the dresser, she rocked the bureau, rattling the handles. Her agitated scan of the floor didn't stem the panic attack. Gripping the dresser's edge at her rump, two fingernails snapped off as she lifted onto it.

"It's okay, really." Kelsi rose from the bed and pulled Dakota back to her feet. She folded her in her arms. "There're no mice. Our phobias are part of our nature."

Kelsi's whispered assurances didn't slow the surge of adrenaline in Dakota's veins. Turning to the household ogling them, Kelsi kept an arm around Dakota's shoulders. "Everyone, out, please."

Cristiano pushed the audience into the hall. Passing near her, Matteo slowed. Glass crunched overloud under his tennis shoes. Dakota stared at the floor, humiliated and desperate to regain control of her mind. A pair of untied Nikes entered her view. *Matteo.* In a moment's clarity, Dakota was grateful he'd donned shoes.

"I'm sorry I frightened you. No one here would ever harm you." He left the room, pulling the door closed behind him. The clicking latch echoed in the sudden quiet.

Tears distorted Dakota's view of the suite. With significant effort, she had choked back a sob until alone with Kelsi. Dakota hated her rodent phobia, always embarrassed over disgusting mice. All three women in her family had a different trigger.

Fear turning to anger, she glared at Kelsi. "Are you going to explain this shit?"

Her sister puffed air through tight lips, a sure sign Dakota wouldn't like what she had to say. "The white jaguar wasn't a pet. It was *me*."

Dakota wanted to scream her denial, but Matteo's words held her back. *You're one of us.*

"Our phobias *are* genetic, like we suspected. When you see mice, part of you—the cat part—sees lunch and wants to snatch it," said Kelsi.

"I don't even like cats. I'm a dog person," whispered Dakota.

"I denied being a shifter, too. Look, it's really cool—and fun. Best ever, we hardly age after we start shifting." Kelsi turned pity-eyes on her. "Please. Just give yourself a chance to understand."

"I'm afraid." Maybe they had already given Dakota drugs, and she was too far gone to fight them. Her heart kicked under her sternum, and she wondered if only adrenaline caused the flutter. "For both of us."

Kelsi hugged her, and held her tightly for several seconds. "I love you. Matteo told you the truth. Any one of them would die to keep us safe."

Dakota's shakes subsided, and after a couple

minutes, her chest loosened and breaths came free and easy. Mice had never really frightened her. However, her *reaction* to them was terrifying. *The cat part of you sees lunch.*

"Okay," Dakota challenged, even as her mind waffled in uncertainty. "Do it again."

Chapter Six

Dakota's stricken sea-green eyes still had Matteo's heart in a knot. He'd only returned to his suite to find a safe distance from her pain. Voices carried through his wide-open patio door, and he strained to hear hers. Her sister soothed her.

When terror had frozen Dakota, her wild jaguar scent had shot through the room, and an unbearable urge to wrap her in his arms had accosted him. A hint of stubborn pride in her eyes, proof of her inner strength, had held him back. That, and the fact they were barely on speaking terms.

Matteo had seen the reaction before, many times from men facing one too many battles—or imminent death. Later, in those same men, the strange lockdown occurred for no discernable reason. However, Dakota showed subtle differences. She appeared aware of her surroundings, and her will had seemed intact.

Carrying a canvas bag by its handles, Alejandro arrived at Matteo's veranda threshold and entered with assumed authority. "*Enforcer*, you need to be armed. You served army time, right?"

Matteo nodded. The old moniker seemed foreign. "Thank you, I do need a sidearm. But my *Enforcer* years were long ago."

Alejandro eyed the makeshift pallet of linens on the floor without comment and dropped the duffle on the bare mattress. "Cristiano never selected a replacement. All understood he held the position for you."

Nodding, Matteo had no words for Cristiano's faith.

If not for the females, he'd ask Cristiano to find another for the policing role. Now, with Dakota in danger, delegating the task didn't warrant consideration. And, he admitted, instinct had nothing to do with it.

Alejandro offered him a pair of brown and green foliage print pants. "Put these on while I talk."

Matteo appreciated the man's crisp approach. He changed into the utility camo, and soaked up the handgun demonstration. "How many rounds?"

"Depends on the magazine. This one, ten." Alejandro popped a black cartridge into the weapon's grip and racked the slide. He leveled a grave expression at Matteo. "Just don't forget about the slug in the chamber."

While Alejandro schooled him, Matteo loaded his pockets with extra ammo, listening to every word. He'd used a semi-auto Colt in the war. However, knowledge of today's weaponry was imperative. He'd have to rely on Alejandro's counsel to regain competence.

The foreman claimed a seat on the sofa and spread a Salazar plantation map across the coffee table. Before Matteo could join him, Consuelo arrived. Without any preamble, she paraded through the open patio door to her husband. "Sorry to interrupt, but *Senhor* Cristiano would like a report within the hour."

"He couldn't text?" Alejandro didn't hide his irritation. "*You* couldn't text this?"

Text? Sounded like a type of communication. Though they bickered around him, Matteo politely ignored the byplay, focusing on loading and unloading the Browning nine-millimeter semi-automatic handgun.

"They all hurry to replace the door." Exasperation evident in her tone, she waved to the veranda as proof. "And my phone turned on by itself twice, today. It's dead. So no texting."

Alejandro narrowed his eyes, suddenly focused on his wife. "You charged it this afternoon. I'll look at it.

Sweetheart, stay inside on your way back. I don't want you exposed. Please."

Seeming unfazed by his mild rebuke, Consuelo nodded before marching out the suite's hall door.

Alejandro provided a synopsis of their armory, and they laid out patrol routes and sentry stations. The man's competence relieved Matteo.

He gestured to their battle plan. "Do we need mercenaries for extended coverage?"

An out-of-place smile curved Alejandro's lips. "All the cacao workers are cross-trained for security— though we've never needed them. We'll pull our manpower from the plantation."

He explained drug cartels and his long-standing defense plan for a possible conflict. Over the last twenty years, he'd conducted monthly training exercises for his troops. No doubt, a significant expense.

"Good thinking." Matteo couldn't help but be impressed by his foresight. "And I appreciate the weapon. Can I impose on you for the full course? Tomorrow?"

"No problem. Tomorrow afternoon." Alejandro folded the map, while Matteo belted a holster at his waist. The familiar motion reminded him of his army days, just over seventy years ago. They exited onto the veranda and parted ways. Matteo strode to Dakota's suite.

Under bright security lighting, Tad dumped broken glass into a wastebasket, and two workers adjusted the new patio door. With the lengthy transport time for building supplies, it wasn't surprising Cristiano kept construction materials on hand.

"Thanks for your help, Tad." Matteo approached the youth, glancing at the new entry. "Will Dakota sleep here tonight?"

"I will." Dakota closed the kitchen door behind her and strode toward him. "But first, Kelsi has, like, a million things to tell me."

With a smile for both of them, Tad hefted the trashcan and left.

"I suppose she does. Feeling better?" Matteo made a discreet scan of their surroundings, disturbed that she'd left the safer confines of the mansion.

She glanced down as though in deep thought. Spiked lashes graced her cheeks. "Kelsi said some crazy things." With an almost pleading look, she found his gaze. "Are they true?"

It seemed even saying the word *shifter* frightened her. The vulnerability in her eyes nearly made him weep. Matteo touched her cheek. "You're a very special part of an extraordinary world. We'll help you adjust—and keep you safe."

"You're really staying outside my door? All night?" She sounded less than happy about the idea. Not being in charge of her life was, no doubt, a rare event for her.

Matteo didn't know if the irritation he sensed in her tone was for him or herself. Neither concerned him. She would have a guard. "Yes, unless you prefer another."

"You'll do." She glanced at the door to her suite and nodded, leaving him to wonder if she found his skills lacking. He refused to justify his suitability.

****

The knowledge Matteo babysat her disgruntled Dakota. Even worse, the fact that she found his presence comforting filled her with self-loathing. Like she was some damsel in distress. She took care of herself—always.

Portable halogens shone through the verticals of

her room, casting surreal shadows on Kelsi's features. Facing each other, they lay under the covers in the wee hours, the scene reminiscent of slumber party ghost-story challenges, years ago. Tonight, they had plenty of paranormal activity. The only thing missing was the flashlight.

Earlier, Kelsi had floored Dakota with two more shifts into the same ginormous white jaguar—once while Dakota had held her in her arms. Like a damned sci-fi film. Her sister's eyes had never changed. Unbelievably, she had sensed Kelsi's essence within the cat.

"Paradigms have shifted, and I need to catch up." Jumping into a world that included jaguar shifters had stressed Dakota's belief systems. "Microbiology and med school didn't prep me to accept the existence of werewolves, or werecats."

"My break-it-to-you-easy plan failed." Kelsi took her hand. "Mr. Swarthy's visit made everything awful and screwed with your head. It wasn't supposed to be like that."

"Tell me straight, who is he?"

"Cristiano thinks he's a reporter chasing the local urban changer legend."

"If so, why was he waiting for me at the airport? I'm not really a shifter, and how could he know about me anyway?"

"No one knows yet, but we will. Promise." Kelsi glanced toward the veranda where Matteo stood sentry. "Supposedly, your self-proclaimed bodyguard's the toughest jag on the planet. They say the *Enforcer* is back."

Dakota looked his way in irritation. *They* hadn't seen his immature sugar-lips taunt, as if he was a damn teenager. "Can he hear us?"

Kelsi wrinkled her nose. "In all honesty,

probably. He's different."

"Remember, this is a tell-all night." Dakota whispered so quietly, she almost didn't hear herself. She scooched closer, hinting for Kelsi to keep her voice low.

"Okay, here goes."

Dakota listened to Matteo's bio with rapt attention. A lost love so devastating tested her comprehension. "He sounds like damaged goods. All that time, he never got over Anna?"

"It's way harder to lose a mate than a spouse. Surprisingly, he's more normal than I first thought. So, give him a shot, okay?"

Dakota's lips parted, speechless for a beat. "You know that's not a resounding recommendation, right?"

Kelsi chuckled. "How about this? Shifter sex is the *best* in the world."

Stunned that her prim sister could even say "sex" without blushing, Dakota giggled. "For real?"

"Oh yeah." Kelsi gave a vigorous nod, and the pair burst out laughing. Sobering, she tugged a lock of Dakota's hair in an old big-sister move. "Seriously, no pressure. Take your time, and see who's at the wedding. Nearly all of the Salazar guests are shifter males."

Kelsi acted like Dakota would commit to some random guy. Not happening. "Shopping around is my specialty. I'll keep it that way, thank you very much."

"You might." Doubt clouded Kelsi's raised-brow expression, and her thinned lips said Dakota wouldn't like what came next. "Just don't mark a male, or you're stuck forever."

"What?" Apprehension put her on guard, and she lifted to an elbow.

Kelsi pulled the sheet up over her shoulder. "Jaguar shifters mate for life. I'll only want Jaime, ever. And he's bound to me—forever. Until death do us part—

the real deal."

Dakota panicked. *One guy for life.* "WTF? How do I dodge that?"

"We've got to be in cat form to scent-mark a mate. The glands are under our whiskers." Absently, Kelsi rubbed her cheek. "Once the deed is done, the marking shifter is bound."

"Okay, noted." More stuff that sounded nuts, but Dakota wouldn't take any chances. She held on to the *cat form* part of the scenario. At some point, she'd stepped into the *shifter's-are-real* camp. "Do you think *I* can be a jaguar, someday?"

"We're from the same gene pool, and you're for sure latent, so why not? It can't happen until you're around shifters for a while though." Kelsi's eyes danced with excitement. "The first few changes start out like a panic attack."

"Does it hurt to shift?"

"Not really. Heat and static shocks travel through your body. Then it feels kind of like being pushed and pulled inside. And you'll like this. While you're in cat form, you have Wonder Woman strength and speed."

Dakota's pulse quickened with her smile.

****

At the poolside table, where he and Cristiano ate breakfast, Matteo stifled a yawn. The uppermost curve of morning sun peeked over the distant canopy, casting a wall of shadow across the grounds fronting the estate.

Matteo's body protested last night's sentry duty on the concrete, and he rolled his shoulders to relieve the payback aches. Before his long-term jungle vacation, a few minutes in jag form would've cured the minor ailments. Now he had to grit it out.

A guard in camo fatigues passed the manse's front gate at a methodical pace, carrying an automatic rifle. He surveyed the courtyard and the surrounding parklands. A quarter-mile beyond the wrought-iron fence, a similar pair traveled the perimeter where lawn met jungle.

As they'd planned, Alejandro had increased security. He'd launched patrols within an hour of their late-night meeting. "I'm impressed by your foreman's preparedness. Deployment was efficient."

"When he proposed his cartel defense plan years ago, I thought him a young gun trying to prove himself. He kept at me, though." Cristiano gave a half smile. "I'm waiting for the 'I told you so'."

Matteo laughed. Ability to admit an error was one of Cristiano's best leadership qualities.

Humor left Cristiano's eyes, and he knitted his brows together. "We have a new security breech. This morning, Alejandro's checking everyone's electronics."

"What do you mean?" Asking numerous who-what-where-why questions wore on Matteo's nerves.

Cristiano's patient expression showed no hint of annoyance. "Any computers. He found a tracking program in Consuelo's phone."

"A what?" Matteo came to attention. He didn't understand the program reference, but he recalled the couple's odd conversation about Consuelo's phone the night before.

Pulling a blue rectangular device from his pocket, Cristiano turned it over in his hand between them. "It's a surveillance bug for cell phones."

Since Matteo's arrival, nearly everyone had used a portable phone in his presence. He needed immediate education. "An enemy can learn your location?"

"Within a few feet and in real time—instantly. Plus, listen to every conversation, read every text and then transmit the data hundreds or even thousands of kilometers. They're called smart phones."

"Why do you even use something so easily turned against you?"

"You'll see." Cristiano smiled. "This is the information age. And you, my friend, need information."

Matteo snorted. He couldn't argue the point. Again, he wondered what a text was.

Before he could ask, Cristiano set the demon-spawned portable receiver on the metal table and slid it toward him. "This one's yours. Alejandro's cleared it."

"The hell you say!" Were it a snake, Matteo would've cut off its head. Clinking buffet utensils reminded him of their surroundings, and he lowered his voice. "How did he discover this scheme?"

"The program needs power and used the phone's battery up too fast." Cristiano leaned back in his metal patio chair, hints of fury deepening the lines around his mouth. "When Consuelo greeted the supposed reporter, her phone was charging on the dining room table. Our spy must've planted the tracking program while she searched for me. Dakota suspected last night's intruder was the same man—Alejandro strung the events and his wife's phone trouble together. He is ever vigilant."

"I like him even more." Wiretapping and radio transmitters were familiar to Matteo, but this type of surveillance seemed like science fiction.

"He's methodically searching the house and checking all cell phones."

Matteo turned the gleaming blue square over in his hand, realizing it framed a dark screen. "Looks like a paperweight. I'm not sure I want it."

"You do." Cristiano showed him how to use programed phone numbers to call and text. "Communication is essential for security."

Glancing at the females a few meters away,

Matteo agreed. He'd carry a rotting peccary with him to keep them safe. Later, he'd explore the search engine icon, a place to ask any question about anything. That, Matteo could use.

Dakota, with coffee mug in hand, slid open the new door to her suite for Kelsi, who carried a tray of pastries and juice. Dakota's discreet sniffs at her steaming cup, then again in his direction, amused him.

He wondered if Kelsi had explained the meaning of his scent. Or that Dakota's *Ardor* had absolute power over him. He wanted to chafe at her control, but his attraction to her squashed his motivation. She was so worldly, and still, so innocent.

Cristiano tracked the women's exit. "Do you know Kelsi shot a man, and then risked her life to save Jaime? All while she believed he was nothing more than a cat. Those girls are exceptional—tough. That strength could save us."

Matteo had already glimpsed Dakota's backbone. Inner battles were the hardest to win. Yet, he couldn't see how two females would save the shifters from extinction. "You're ever the optimist, Cristiano."

"Someone must be. I have something to show you. Over here." Rising, Cristiano motioned to a notebook and picked up a cardboard cylinder on an adjacent table.

Curious, Matteo joined him. Cristiano extracted a furled blueprint-sized sheet from the mailing tube and spread the heavy paper out on the table.

An involved family tree with multiple lineages inked the page. Gender designations and other cryptic notes dotted several entries. Matteo raised a questioning look.

Returning a warrior's mien, Cristiano stabbed the bottom row of names with an index finger. "Mendel's work has grown to a specialized field—genetics. We can save the species!"

"You think human science will help us? They're more likely to cut us open." Matteo wondered what new threats endangered shifters in this age of advanced technology. Along with a phone's spying ability, last night's intruder came to mind.

"We've always had trusted humans in our lives. That didn't change while you were in the jungle."

Many human familiars, like Alejandro's family, traced their origins to the Amazon's indigenous tribes, or more recently, to the dark days of slavery.

Under the shifter umbrella, education and resources elevated the oath-bound humans above their peers. In return, they kept the shifters' existence a secret from the world. Betrayal had only one penalty—death. Fortunately, none had defected during Matteo's tenure as *Enforcer*.

"True enough, but kinship binds those people to us. You've recruited scientists?" he asked.

"Not yet. Until we found the females, there'd been no need." Cristiano jabbed his chart again. "Now we have real hope. My research says more latents are in the United States, and they will attend my son's wedding."

Becoming infected with his friend's enthusiasm, Matteo perused the scribbled family tree. "Where's Dakota in this mess?"

"Here, in the purest line." Cristiano trailed his fingertip from her name at the bottom straight to the top of the bracket, to a central bold entry: **Comizahual, Jaguar Princess**. "See?"

Matteo looked up to Cristiano. "She's a direct descendant? You're certain?"

"As certain as can be. I've scoured our written

records, and combined the data with what I can glean from the online human ancestry sites. The Gorman girls go back to the Lenca tribe on their mother's side."

"They're fair-skinned, too."

"Yes, the *white* Jaguar Princess." Cristiano nodded at his paper.

"Why so far from us? In the United States?"

"Only a theory, but I suspect full shifters stayed near the jungle. With no need for the rainforest, latents traveled north instead."

Matteo nodded. So, the shifters hadn't migrated north of Central America during his jaguar sabbatical.

"Interesting holes appear in their histories, too." Cristiano pointed out a couple of asterisked names. "The stars indicate an individual with an unrecorded date of death, either in a cemetery or by death certificate."

"Your records go back nearly a thousand years. Undocumented deaths mean nothing."

"The earlier ones, of course. But some are as recent as fifty years ago. Look here. A few family names occur in our lines, too." Cristiano's eyes shone with his fervor. "More latents exist in the United States."

"Perhaps." Matteo looked towards Dakota's patio door. Only one latent interested him.

Cristiano rolled up the paper and returned it to its protective cylinder. They retook their seats, and he buttered a croissant. "Do you believe the intruder is a reporter?"

"No. Our uninvited guest's scent held traces of gunpowder residue. And the bastard was extremely fit— he outran me." With every stride during the chase, Matteo had fought the urge to shift, to rip the human to shreds for threatening his—a female.

Cristiano held the butter knife still as he looked up. "He's human?"

"Yes." Admitting a human had outrun him dented Matteo's pride. "We'll find out who he is—and learn his motives."

Delegating the job to someone else didn't warrant thought. None could ignore the instinct to protect an unmated female. It was a natural drive, the same as the need to eat and drink.

Matteo would sleep on Dakota's doorstep until they'd caught the mangy cur.

Chapter Seven

The fawn-colored Chihuahua trembled so much with his high-pitched growl, even his ears shivered. Colonel Brad Shelton returned the sentiment. He half-hoped the yappy mutt would attack his ankle, so he could kick him through imaginary uprights. The skinned rat parked on a green and maroon plaid couch. Dr. Mason Valentine, alias Captain Einstein, sat behind a wooden desk cluttered with stacks of paper and yellow sticky notes.

His pointed nose and sparse comb-over gave the doctor an eerie resemblance to his annoying dog. He'd arrived at 9:18 for their 0900 meeting. Obviously, this civi-nerd PhD got away with murder at the hidden Army Research Lab. The ARL had embedded their lab within Fort Hood, disguised as a specialty health clinic.

"Dr. Valentine, what's wrong with Lieutenant Liu?" asked Shelton.

Last week, his most promising jungle-trained commando had disappeared off his roster without explanation. The mandatory ARL detail came on the heels of a two-man loss from Shelton's personal team—on what was supposed to have been a simple package delivery.

In addition to his men, Shelton had lost significant income, since the trafficker, Erico Guterre, died alongside Nuno and Andre. Dead men don't pay bills.

Now, this dweeb doctor only half attended to their conversation. "Nothing's *wrong* with him, Colonel—"

"Then I need him back with his squad."

"Soon. David—Lieutenant Liu—has interesting

genetics. We'll take some samples, do some assessments, and send him back to you in good shape as soon as we're done."

"Done. When?" Shelton's face heated. Not many stood up to his full bird insignia. However, this man appeared more oblivious than brazen.

Valentine rose to scoop up the shaking mutt. Seeming to ignore Shelton, he pulled a bacon-shaped treat from his pocket. The dog scarfed it down.

"Taco, be a good boy while Daddy talks to the nice man." Reclaiming his computer chair, Valentine snugged the dog into a tender football hold and glanced at Shelton. "Couple weeks, maybe more, depending. Can't always tell what we'll find, can we, Taco?"

The ridiculous soprano baby talk grated on Shelton's last nerve. He put three Middle-East tours worth of threat into his voice. "An office dog's against regulation."

"Taco's a service animal. The vest chafes his little sides." Valentine rubbed noses with the Chihuahua. "Doesn't it?"

Taco responded with a disgusting display of canine French kissing.

Service animal, my left nut. Shelton pinched the bridge of his nose to block the images of what service this fleabag performed. "I need my man back with his team."

"Do you have high blood pressure? There's a distended vein in your temple. I don't think that's healthy."

The man was an imbecile. Shelton launched to his feet. "Liu. I want to see him. Now."

The dog growled, squirming in Valentine's arms.

"Oh, my." With widened eyes, the doctor jumped from his seat and scurried around the desk to open the office door. In a small show of intelligence, he gave Shelton a wide berth. "Sergeant Davis?"

"Yes, sir?" Sitting at a reception desk, a mature brunette in uniform raised her head.

Shelton closed the distance to stand behind Valentine, fighting an urge to wrap both hands around his neck. Some people were too stupid to live.

"Could you locate Lieutenant Liu and escort Colonel Shelton to meet him? Oh, and stop down by intake and check his blood pressure, too, please."

Sergeant Davis glanced at Shelton, and amusement lit her eyes. She seemed to stifle a smile. "Follow me, Colonel. We'll get you fixed up."

Without a word, Valentine turned back into his office, soothing his upset dog.

Davis seemed normal enough, if exceptionally plain. Shelton followed the plump, forty-something woman into the hallway before a homicide could occur. The no-nonsense bun at the nape of her neck reassured him she attended to details.

"This way, sir." After passing a door marked Intake, they exited the front entry into humid, eighty-degree air. Shelton pulled shades from his pocket to temper the bright morning sun. After a short distance along the compound sidewalk, Davis turned a neutral expression on him. "So you met our famous Dr. Valentine."

"Surprised no one's strangled him yet," Shelton grunted. "Or his dog."

"What dog?" Davis posed the question so innocently; however, lines around her mouth hinted at tension.

Shelton could have her stripes for ignoring the mutt's presence, but decided ARL could handle their own civilian problems. "I see."

Her features relaxed, and she added a smile. "Don't be too hard on him. I think his brilliance pushed social skills right out of his brain. Make no mistake, he's totally committed to his work. And he's the *kindest* man I know."

The last, she said with bold censure. Shelton took note of her surprising loyalty.

****

Sitting across from Shelton in the Killeen, Texas, steakhouse lounge, Lieutenant David Liu wore fatigues and nursed his cola. Shelton studied him with a new perspective, trying to identify what Valentine found so intriguing.

Mixed Asian of some kind with odd-colored eyes. Without access to his performance stats, Shelton wouldn't think him anything special. At just over six foot with close-cropped dark hair, Liu looked like any other well-conditioned soldier. Not that it mattered, but Shelton supposed women found him attractive. Certainly, no outward sign of a genetic anomaly.

The late lunch crowd had thinned, leaving them in relative privacy. Unable to have a beer in uniform, Shelton sipped iced tea, wishing for dark ale, while the lieutenant plucked buffalo wings from their appetizer tray.

"So, son, why's Valentine so interested in you?"

"Got me, sir. Something about genetics. They drew blood, and I've done a ton of fitness assessments." Liu eyed his plate of chicken bones. "Oh, and tomorrow, I start a no-meat diet."

From the wistful look the kid gave the drumette he held up between them, Shelton could guess what he thought of going veggie. "What the hell for?"

"No idea, sir. After a week of vegan, they'll draw more blood."

Shelton couldn't fathom what vegetarianism had to do with Liu's genetics. Maybe Valentine was trying to find a decent diet for all the new-age sensitives who refused to eat meat. More in the ranks every day. However, studying a soldier's physical abilities made sense, especially those trained for the jungle.

"They got wind of your CIGS performance. Lousy timing." With his team down two men, Shelton needed Liu in Brazil and eventually, Manaus. "You missed your evaluation."

"Yes, sir. Had to catch the plane here. I did well enough, though." One corner of Liu's mouth rose.

Cocky bastard. Obviously, he knew he'd smoked Brazil's elite jungle warfare course. Only a few American candidates qualified for the Chief of the Imperial General Staff's Amazon training program. This U.S. Army Ranger had raised their bar.

"Your C.O.'s report said, 'picked up Portuguese within a few weeks' and 'performance is well above that of our indigenous tribal recruits'. You got someone's attention."

"Yes, sir." Liu smiled in a show of bold confidence.

Shelton lifted his mug in salute. "You got my attention, too."

"Thank you, sir." The lieutenant squared his shoulders.

"I'll get to the point. I run a private team. Money's good. You interested?" Recruiting an active-duty Ranger could end in a court martial, but Shelton had done his homework.

Until a recent diagnosis of breast cancer, Liu's single mother had scrubbed floors to provide for his sister. Since then, chemo treatments had kept her unemployed. Liu sent her every dime.

"Maybe." Doubt, or possibly suspicion, shrouded Liu's narrowed gaze. "Doing what?"

"Military support. Escorting civilians, mostly. Bodyguard work with a show of force." Shelton smiled. "An occasional kidnap extraction pays the best."

The lieutenant lifted his chin. "How much?"

"You could help your mama and baby sister in L.A., plus set aside a nest egg for yourself. My word on it."

Liu frowned and set his jaw, but to his credit, held his tongue.

"Don't look so insulted. I investigate everyone before offering a spot on my team."

And Shelton intended to be more selective. Nuno and Andre had lacked high-level military skills. However, he'd needed Portuguese- and Spanish-speaking men, so he'd hired them.

The live package pickup had been an easy assignment. None could have anticipated a mutant jaguar attack. Still, like any good officer, Shelton blamed himself and mourned the loss of his men.

"How much?" Liu's repeat question brought him back to the present.

"Ten thousand US for an operation, two hundred hourly for escort work."

After a beat with widened eyes, the kid sobered. "I'll think about it."

"I understand. We'll talk more when you return to Manaus." Shelton would've preferred a firm commitment, but pushing would gain nothing. "I'll have my driver drop you at your barracks."

Shelton tossed cash on the table and led the way out into the Texas afternoon heat. Liu's few cryptic follow-up questions during their return trip assured Shelton the kid was interested and wouldn't report him to the brass. Relief lightened his mood. Liu would be a valuable asset.

"I look forward to your return to the Amazon, Lieutenant." Outside the guest officers' quarters, Shelton stepped from the olive-green jeep. He returned salutes before his driver sped off with Liu and then strode inside.

Before Shelton could wave off the formalities, the desk clerk rose, snapping to attention. "Good news, Colonel. You get the place to yourself, tonight. Luggage is in the room."

"Nice job, Private. Thanks." He took the offered key card.

At one time, an aide would've ensured a private suite and scheduled drivers to be at the ready. Oh, for the days before Madeline and her fabricated charges to save her own ass.

Sexual harassment was more than a buzzword in the military. And it didn't matter if the supposedly harassed was willing—or a lying, conniving bitch. None of the General Sheltons peppering his family tree had had to worry about that bullshit. After significant maneuvering, his attorney had negotiated a court martial into an Article 15. Still, brigadier stars were not in Shelton's future.

His fall from grace had some benefits, like his private security team. With minimal responsibility for overseeing jungle trainees in Brazil, he had time and resources to pursue other interests. Walking down the hall to his efficiency apartment, he retrieved his vibrating phone.

Pantoja: **I have a personal matter to discuss.**

Code for *find a secure line*. Since the jaguar killings, vengeance had driven ex-Brazilian Lieutenant Jose Pantoja to find his *special friend's* executioner. He believed a human handler had directed the big cats.

Pantoja's message piqued Shelton's interest.

Entering the studio, he placed his camo cap on the coat-closet shelf, facing the front. As promised, his suitcase waited on a luggage rack against the wall. He opened the secured latch and rifled through his belongings to find an unused burn phone.

Pantoja answered on the first ring. "Evening, sir."

Shelton never wasted time on pleasantries. "Report." Dead air reigned, trying his patience. "Pantoja?"

"Hard to say words, sir. But, to start, I no drink in a long time."

Shelton barely stifled a groan. He put up with Pantoja's drunken days because when sober, no other helicopter pilot touched his skill. "You've done well, I give you that."

"Thank you, sir. Tail number say chopper belong to Salazar Holdings. The big boss, Cristiano Salazar, is big man in Manaus."

"The bird had the SZH logo on it. Get to the point." Shelton hated repetition.

"Yes, sir. When Nuno die, Salazar leave airport alone. Same day, he bring son and woman—writer back with him. I watch them close."

The package. "Go on."

Pantoja shuddered a sigh. "Last night, the woman, Kelsi Gorman, changed to a white jaguar. While I watching."

Frustration deflated Shelton's optimism. Sensing that temple vein bulging, he pinched the bridge of his nose to staunch a flood of profanity. "No booze?"

"No."

"None of that *ayahuasca* your granddaddy likes?" More than one of Shelton's men had experimented with the local tribes' favored hallucinogen.

"No waking dream drugs. I tell you, woman glowed, then she—the jaguar—nearly killed me."

Losing his boyfriend had escalated Pantoja from raging alcoholic to deluded nut-job. Remorse over his lost men put compassion into Shelton's voice. "Look, I miss Nuno and Andre, too. Take a couple days off, no argument. And, no goddamn booze, or wacky vine stew either."

"The cat was giant—like giant who killed smuggler." Challenge sounded in Pantoja's measured words. "I don't have a reason to lie."

After Shelton disconnected, he let out a gust of air. Pantoja followed orders well, knew a chopper inside and out, and usually made good field decisions, but finding his lover shredded may have sent him over the edge. Shelton hadn't escaped the site of the gruesome massacre unscathed, either.

A massive feline *had* killed Guterre. Forensic bite analysis dwarfed the lab's known jaguar stats. A different, normal-sized, set of jaws had killed Nuno and Andre. Unheard of, at least two cats had attacked simultaneously to bring down a team of three fully armed men. Then a single human hid the bodies. Shelton needed solid intel.

Someone had bred trainable, oversized jaguars— and he would find them and solve the murders of his men. At the same time, he needed to stay abreast of all potential jungle assets. The answers were behind the Salazar logo. Shelton picked up the hardline receiver and dialed the desk. "Private, my schedule's changed."

Chapter Eight

Matteo and Alejandro had prepped the plantation for a siege, and anyone not wearing fatigues stayed inside. The day prior, Dakota had corralled Kelsi into finalizing most of the wedding, with the exception of last-minute tasks. Now, she needed a run, dammit.

Plantation workers turned armed security flooded the estate, complete with combat gear and assault rifles. A pair of guards patrolled the lawn side of the jungle. Looking at her, one held a mic to his mouth. *Busted.* Dakota waved at them.

She jogged at what should have been an effortless pace over hibiscus-lined stone paths in the Salazar garden. Instead, she sucked in thick humidity with each labored breath. Millions of insects chirped in the nearby jungle, jeering at her poor fitness level. Perspiration stung Dakota's eyes and trickled between her breasts with no hope of cooling her body. It wasn't even noon.

Taunting her misery, fearless jewel-toned hummingbirds rocketed across her path. At the garden's edge, she slowed to a walk, watching a bold, emerald hummer floating nearly inside a cupped purple bloom. If the tiny bird noticed her approach, it paid her no mind.

Still absorbing her new non-human status, she wished some of the little bird's courage would rub off on her. According to Kelsi, there was no downside to being a jaguar shifter. Dakota wasn't so sure. They mated for life. The same man forever. She shuddered. In contrast, the idea of changing into a beautiful jaguar stoked her imagination, and she cast a longing look at the jungle.

An arched, claustrophobic tunnel delved into the green morass of tree trunks and straining saplings. She supposed some would call it a path. According to Kelsi, the undergrowth died away deeper into the canopy.

A two-foot long tailless rat meandered from the opening, snuffling through leaves on the ground. The animal had walked right out of her worst nightmares.

Anticipation of impending out-of-control tremors ripped a strangled gasp from Dakota, and a raging urge to violence rose in her chest. The insolent rodent lifted his nose at her and twitched its evil whiskers.

Fury over her reaction to the nasty thing didn't stem the rising panic attack. Her wheezing breaths came faster until they locked down altogether. Years of this crap were enough.

She glared at the vermin through welling tears. In that instant, she longed to be a great cat and wreak havoc on one over-sized, helpless mouse.

****

Matteo fingered the semi-auto nine-millimeter side arm holstered at his hip, courtesy of Alejandro. Yesterday's review of twenty-first century small arms had impressed him. Another area in which Matteo had fallen behind. He'd spent the morning huddled over his phone, devouring information on Alejandro's arms inventory.

Instinct drove Matteo to find their intruder. Aside from the spy's surprising fitness, he'd displayed an unusual level of confidence during the chase. As though he'd scouted the terrain and had a plan to evade capture. Matteo needed answers only the spy could provide.

With Dakota's tendency for sharp observation, maybe she could recall more about him. Matteo strode across the courtyard to her patio entrance and rapped on the glass.

No one answered. Giving up, he turned to enter the house. Tad, in cutoffs and a t-shirt, exited the kitchen onto the veranda.

Glancing at Dakota's door, then back at Matteo, a slow smile curved Tad's lips. "She jogs in the gardens. I'll take you to her."

He appeared too eager to help, triggering Matteo's possessive instincts. The compulsion to claim the queen irritated him. With an iron will, he crushed his inner cat, allowing Tad's words to sink in.

"She's unattended?" Sudden fear for Dakota sharpened his tone.

Tad frowned. "I didn't think."

"I've been sleeping on cement to keep her safe, and she runs alone in the gardens?" With a growl, Matteo shouldered past Tad into the home and through the kitchen. Pulse pounding in his ears, he jogged past the stainless-steel appliances, his reflection streaming alongside him.

Recalling a rear entrance, he rushed through a utility room, swiping hanging laundry from his path and burst outside into the rear grounds. Damp heat chased the air-conditioning chill from his skin, though he barely noticed.

With her back to him, Dakota stood near one of the garden's many stone benches, her posture showing off her aquiline profile. Tall and curvy, she appeared unharmed. He drew a relieved breath. Gray and lilac hair fell from a clip, and tendrils curved into the shadow of her high cheekbone. With her skimpy top and shorts up to her squeezable ass, sudden desire replaced his alarm. He adjusted his gait to a casual walk.

Striding toward her, he passed a detached garage that likely held more of Cristiano's toys. Atop the roof, a large dish pointed skyward, but Matteo hadn't seen any radios in the house. Several meters behind the building, a tall metal pole topped with finned panels further marred the view.

The unsightly giants must perform critical functions for Cristiano to tolerate their presence. At the far side of the garden, the impressive metallic blue helicopter rested on its cement square.

As he neared Dakota, he realized she hadn't moved. Like a predator in stalking mode, she stood stock-still and stared at the edge of the jungle. Fear-tainted lavender hit his nostrils, and he broke to a run. "Dakota?"

The sound of her name seemed to break a spell, and she turned toward his approach. Her lustrous alabaster complexion had bleached to a pasty white. Tear-filled sea-green eyes met his gaze, before she jerked her attention back to the jungle wall.

"Is all well with you, *senhorita*?" Though he'd caught no one's scent but hers, he scanned the perimeter for any hint of an enemy.

"I'm fine." Her dilated pupils and quaking voice said otherwise. She darted glances toward a jungle path where a mama agouti searched for seeds.

Recall of Kelsi's soothing words, *No mice here*, made him give the rodent tidbit another look. The agouti had disappeared into cover. Matteo studied Dakota more closely. With the acrid scent of fear abating, her natural perfume became more alluring by the second.

Matteo disciplined his features to disguise his amusement. However, her distress reignited his need to protect her. Had he been in jaguar form, he'd have charged after the rodent as if it were a giant peccary boar. "The agouti frightens you?"

Dakota blew a gust of air into the charcoal wisps outlining her eyes, anger replacing the terror in her scent. Her jaguar essence rose, and a wave of color pinked up her fear-blanched cheeks. "It's none of your business."

First, he'd offended her by insulting her hair, and

now he'd embarrassed her. He gentled his tone. "I'm sorry to intrude, but you're alone. I'll stay with you if you like, or you may return to the house."

"I want to kill it." She kept her attention riveted on the path and stepped toward the jungle. Lavender and vanilla, laced with her fury, mingled with a white orchid's fragrance. The wild flowers clung to a dwarf tree behind her. Color filled her cheeks once more, and for an instant, she brought to mind a warrior maiden.

"The agouti?"

"Yes, the fucking rat, if that's what you call them."

A foul-mouthed maiden—with luscious, pouting lips. He wondered if all twenty-first-century women swore so readily. "Why?"

"I've got no idea, but I want him dead. I want all the wicked, sneaky little bastards gone for good."

Maybe her family's panic disorder caused her profanity. He looked into her stormy eyes. "You're a jaguar. Kill it."

Chapter Nine

Incredulous over Matteo's nonchalance, Dakota stared at him in astonished silence. He'd made his recommendation so casually, as though anyone would rip a helpless mammal to shreds. Or, even more bizarre, knew how to turn into a big cat on command.

Apparently, he thought his tattoo counted as a shirt. He had yet to wear more than shorts around her. He folded well-defined forearms across his ripped chest. "You've not shifted yet?"

With Kelsi's theories whirling in her mind, Dakota shook her head. "I don't know if I can."

He jutted his unshaven chin toward the jungle, and his tawny dreads shifted to the front of one muscular shoulder. Glancing at her, he lifted his brows as though in challenge. "If your cat erupts, don't run. I can't shift to keep up."

His coffee scent curled heat low in her abdomen and made her heart pound harder than at first sight of the rat. That he wouldn't join her if she turned into a jaguar caused a strange disappointment. "Why not?"

"It's not safe." He pursed his lips to a firm line, before he turned and led the way to the jungle path.

She let the touchy subject drop and followed in silence for a few yards.

You panic because you see prey. If Kelsi's theory held true, the jungle rat gave her the best chance at shifting. A rush of energy pulsed through her, and the jaguar spots on Matteo's back sparked her imagination.

Her fingers itched to touch the lifelike rosette pattern peeking through his dreads. They were too perfect. Almost three-dimensional. "You really think I'm a shifter?"

"Definitely." Slowing to walk at her side, he took an exaggerated sniff, and one corner of his mouth lifted. "No mistaking a queen's lure."

With his mocha scent filling the air, his shoulder brushed hers, and heat slammed into her core. If only she could taste the hollow of his neck.

The subtle grimace replacing his smirk gave Dakota small satisfaction, imagining that she might affect him, too. "Being part animal is so far-fetched."

"We don't consider ourselves to be part jaguar or part human. We're simply—*more*."

"Sorry." For some unknown reason, she apologized for his elitist attitude. Needing to learn all she could about her new world, she tucked her human affront away.

"No offense taken." He smiled at her for the first time, evaporating her irritation. The copper in his eyes warmed against his golden complexion, and his full lips revealed dazzling white teeth. Prominent canines made him appear dangerous, which she supposed he was.

Bad boys always appealed. Her return smile came unbidden.

"Your desire to catch prey is part of you, of all of us. The only question is when—or if— your cat will make an appearance."

"If?" A stab of disappointment came from nowhere. Now that she had discounted her smoke-and-mirrors theory, the idea of shifting appealed—*a lot*.

"Latents are mostly legend. Lore says you must be around full shifters for a while, though your sister shifted after only three days in Jaime's company."

Excitement sped her heart into a staccato rhythm, like that extra second of freefall before pulling the cord. The adventure seeker inside her took over. "Let's do it!"

Matteo chuckled and stepped into the darkened

tunnel. "Follow closely. Nothing here can harm you in jaguar form, but you're vulnerable while human."

As she stepped under the arched foliage, the sunny morning turned to evening dusk. Damp, loamy-scented air barely parted for them to pass, making Dakota wonder what molds might invade her lungs.

After several yards, Matteo halted and lifted his head in the subtlest of sniffs. He pointed between trees toward nothing, and bent his head near her ear. "She's this way."

The undergrowth thinned, allowing Dakota to walk alongside him and, sneaking glances, she studied the rosettes on his deltoid. If he had enhanced feline smell and hearing, along with oversized canines, maybe the tat wasn't ink afterall.

Red-capped mushrooms and stalk-shaped yellow fungi dotted the rotting leaves on the rainforest floor. The agouti was nowhere in sight. She mimicked his whisper. "You know it's female?"

He nodded and pressed a finger to his lips.

Approaching a plant hosting two-foot-wide, heart-shaped leaves, Matteo motioned her into hiding. They squatted thigh-to-thigh close behind the tropical shield. Lifting one of the parasol-sized leaves, he pointed. Dakota peered through the opening at the rat-agouti. The rodent sat up on its hind legs and sniffed in their direction.

Violent tremors shook Dakota's frame with the onset of an all too familiar panic attack. The thick air wouldn't fit into her lungs. Despite the fight-or-flight reaction, enough of herself remained to wish for privacy. Having a witness to her weakness always made the humiliation harder to bear.

Matteo placed a warm hand on her shoulder and pressed his lips against her ear. "Your cat scent is wild—

and strong, very near. Whatever grips you, don't resist."

After years of disciplining herself against the adrenaline surge, she doubted she could release that control. Dakota opened her mouth, but words wouldn't form. She tipped her head in a fraction of a nod.

The she-rat bolted into the trees. With shaking hands, Dakota crouched, ready to spring, and parted the curtain of leaves. A human growl sounded. Stunned, she realized the snarl had come from her.

Matteo rose and grabbed her arm. "Your skin glows! You'll shift soon." His words tumbled out. "You must disrobe or go back to the house naked. I'll step to the side."

Though not focused on his exit, she sensed his absence. Dimly, she recalled Kelsi had undressed before each shift. With the echo of Matteo's touch still warming her ear, she toed off her running shoes then ripped off her shorts and workout tank top. She didn't bother with the thong.

While a dark shimmer covered her skin, heat surged over her torso, spreading to her arms and legs. Focused on the rodent's trail, the agouti's scent grew stronger, with a wealth of added information. The rat was terrified.

"Chase the agouti, now!" Matteo was only a few feet away, though she couldn't tell exactly where.

Sprinting from cover, she raced after the tailless squirrel, following her suddenly keen nose. Footfalls at her rear told her Matteo ran several feet behind her. The agouti's scent grew stronger, triggering fiery waves over every inch of her skin, and she yelped before falling to her knees.

Sizzling current traveled her spine and found pathways down her arms and legs. Bones shifted, with a pain similar to an over-aggressive arm bar hold. Her terrified shriek didn't drown out the crunch of bone in her head. If only she could tap the mat. *Doesn't hurt much, my ass.*

Her cry melted into the high-pitched yowl of a tortured animal. Alarmed because the noise came from her own throat, she snapped her jaws shut in a loud crack of teeth. Insects seemed to crawl over her skin, hidden under an ultraviolet glow. The dark glimmer dissipated, revealing her arms—that were now legs. *White fur!* She blinked in surprise.

However, the vermin's enticing scent along the ground assaulted Dakota's sinuses, laying out a blazing trail. Squeaks and chirps, now loud to her ears, announced the agouti's location yards away.

An overwhelming urge to give chase accosted Dakota, and she maneuvered her four legs in a failed attempt to stand. With a jubilant expression, Matteo slid to his knees in front of her. He threaded his fingers into the fur on either side of her jowls, and forced her gaze to his. "You're magnificent! Your blue-green eyes look like crystal lakes in the snow."

She wondered when he'd seen snow in the Amazon.

He released her, and she glanced to her *paws.* Very broad cream-colored paws with café-au-lait rosettes trailing up her legs. To think only days ago, she would've called them spots. *I'm really a jaguar! S*he should be terrified, but euphoria overtook her common sense.

Matteo ruffled her ears. In reflex, she licked his arm and instantly wanted to taste the rest of him. He leaned his forehead against hers. "You are a stunning queen."

He'd finally complimented her, and it was because she looked great—as a cat. Apparently, jaguars couldn't roll their eyes. Dakota pushed to her paws and wobbled to a four-point stance. She snarled at her clumsiness.

"In moments, you'll be agile. Don't forget—stay near me." He rose, and Dakota realized how large she must be. Her back almost reached his waist.

The rat. Recall of sweet vengeance pulled her attention. After a few attempts, she commanded her legs into a walk. In minutes, jungle floor scents overloaded her brain with information, chasing the rodent from her mind. She sorted through a genetic memory of plants, animals, myriad insects, and even an image of tribesmen flashed at a particular scent.

A few feet away, Matteo leaned against a wide tree trunk, with arms crossed, watching her with a widening smile. He pointed behind her into the never-ending acres of tree trunks reaching up to an unseen sky. "The agouti is that way."

With less interest than she had anticipated, she padded over the spongy ground after the giant squirrel. Muffled mewling and clicks came from a vine-covered log, pulling her off course. Sniffing along its base, her nose told her more of the agouti rats hid within the wooden hull.

Dakota pushed the fifty-foot rotting trunk with a single paw, surprised by her strength. Rocking it from its earthen cradle, a cacophony burst from within. She peered through a jagged opening into a hollow filled with the female agouti's hair.

Three pairs of beady black eyes glistened at Dakota, and the babies' squeaky cries grew louder. Round ears, no more than membranes, lay flat on their heads, their whiskers twitching at the speed of light. They were … cute. Releasing the log to roll back into place, she realized her hateful need for vengeance had disappeared with her shift.

Matteo watched her with an expression she couldn't read, before glancing to a cluster of ferns a few feet away. The female agouti emerged from cover, dancing to-and-fro, and then rose to her haunches, squeaking at Dakota. The mama rat's scent permeated the nest.

Dakota snorted and returned to Matteo.

He gave her a lopsided grin, settling a hand on the back of her neck. "Suddenly, not so vicious? I understand your sister hasn't warmed to hunting either." He almost sounded pleased. "Your scent will keep the innocent young safe for weeks."

The mama agouti skirted the nest, peeking at Dakota, as though gauging the risk. Finally, the mother rat dashed inside. Dakota's relief over the babies' fate surprised her. With the absence of full-blown panic, killing the entire rodent genus had lost its appeal.

Matteo ruffled her fur. His coffee fragrance curled around her, so much more tantalizing with her new, sensitive nose, drawing her to sniff at his thigh. A throbbing pain, like steroid-fed acne, materialized at the base of her sensitive whiskers. Twitching them only aggravated the discomfort.

Matteo's rough beard would give her the best relief. With the thought came an overwhelming desire to pin him to the ground for a thorough rubdown.

Do not scent-mark a male. Kelsi's warning rang in her head. The thought sent raging goosebumps along her back, spiking her fur. Dakota backed away from Matteo and snorted again in a vain attempt to expel his alluring scent.

Dropping to her belly, she scratched her muzzle with a dangerous claw. When that failed, she buried her nose in the composting jungle floor. Even the rotting vegetation's odor gave no relief from his magnetic coffee attraction.

Matteo seemed to guess her problem, and an annoying smile creased his face. "I suspect you've had enough of the jungle. Relax. Close your eyes and breathe in and out, slow. Think of human arms and legs—and lilac hair."

The man had no sense, taunting her that way. Did he not notice her very large teeth and coordinating claws? However, fear of being stuck in furry mode overrode her reaction to his lame sense of humor. She nestled her chin between her paws.

This time, when the fever wave started, she opened her eyes to watch her forelegs. A white glow obscured her view for a moment before melting into human arms—her arms. With the fur's disappearance, a chill traveled her bare skin. She heaved a sigh of relief. Not only was she human, but this change hadn't been as painful as the last.

Matteo strode to her and took a knee. He reached for a lock of her hair and, oddly interested, rubbed a wisp between his fingers. "Are you okay?"

"More like exhilarated." Dakota looked up at him, and a huge grin came unbidden. She scrubbed at her chilled, goosebump-covered arms. "That's a rush, for sure."

"We all remember our primary shift with the same awe." Offering a hand, he helped her rise, and she recalled her nakedness. Consumed with excitement, she'd forgotten.

"Where're my clothes?"

His darkened gaze scanned her head to toe, pausing at the apex of her thighs with widened eyes. Expression breaking to a wide smile, he finally looked her in the eye. "Nearby, unfortunately."

"A Brazilian who's never seen a Brazilian wax?" Her amusement helped her ignore the heated flutter his letch-look had caused.

He snorted through his smile. "Apparently."

She scanned for her running outfit, her loose locks brushing her shoulders. "And my hairclip?"

"Your tresses are lovely down, by the way."

Irritated by his scrutiny, and her reaction to it, she fisted her hands on her hips. "Like you're looking at my hair."

With mischief in his eyes, he reached into his denim pocket. "The clasp fell away when you shifted." He opened his hand, cupping a wad of lavender lace. "Along with ... is this underwear?"

In stunned mortification, she snatched the shredded thong from his hand. "Do you mind?"

His dancing eyes and half smile said he didn't mind at all. Ignoring her ire, he turned and strode off, waving her to follow. "The best privacy I can afford is to lead you to your clothing. Most shifters are as comfortable naked as dressed."

She sneered at his back. "I might be, too, if you didn't look at me like I was lunch."

All the rainforest looked the same here, but if needed, Dakota could find her own way out. Unfortunately, her change into a saber-toothed whatever had been too distracting for her to note where she'd dropped her clothes.

The bastard chuckled. "My apologies. It's been many years since I've been near a queen. Not all my manners survived."

After changing into a giant cat and then returning to human, Dakota walked in the jungle—naked—behind a man with suspiciously real-looking rosettes down his back. More than once, her panic disorder had made her doubt her sanity. But this? *Unbelievable.* However, she was over it.

I'm a jaguar shifter.

Kelsi was right. The perks were outstanding. And, as Matteo had said, she was—*more.*

Chapter Ten

With dreads swinging, Matteo jogged to the patch of moss-covered ground where Dakota had shifted. He strode back and returned the clasp to her. "Your hair thing."

She wrenched her gaze from his eight-pack abs. "Thanks."

His fingertips lingered for a delicious instant over the tender inside of her wrist, chasing shivers up her arm. Coffee scent surrounded her, and sent a thrill through her core. In mutiny, her body announced her reaction, tightening her nipples to pebbles in the open air. Mortified over her lack of control, she avoided his gaze in hopes he hadn't noticed.

Swirling her sweat-dampened hair onto her head, she clamped it in place and followed him, enjoying the athletic grace of his movements. Even at a walk, she perceived his harnessed power. "Are you really over a hundred years old?"

"One hundred thirty-three." At his clipped response, she held her zillion follow-up questions.

True to his word, after a short distance, Matteo picked up her folded clothes and handed them to her with a smirk. Snatching the spandex pile, she stepped behind a tree and dressed. As though modesty mattered now.

Returning to their hike, she found Matteo fixated on a branch several feet above with a confused expression. Tracking his gaze, she couldn't see anything unusual. "What is it?"

"A new species of dragonfly. New to me, anyway." He pointed at an atmosphere saturated with bugs. "It makes a high-pitched sound."

Dakota singled out the prehistoric-sized insect

amid the swarm of flying creepies. Aside from size, nothing made the creature stand out. It swooped out of sight. "How can you isolate one chirp in the zillions creating this racket?"

"My jaguar senses followed me into human form." He studied the dragonfly's last location, a spindly low-hanging branch.

Sniffing, she checked for an enhanced sense of smell. During her few minutes as a cat, the nearly bare jungle floor told a multitude of stories. Now, all she detected was Matteo. "Why do you keep your abilities, and I lost mine?"

"With more shifts, your cat senses will linger." He grimaced. "But too many decades as a jaguar…"

Curling his lip back in a silent snarl, he tapped a canine. When fully exposed, the long, curved tooth screamed great cat. Teeth might not be the only jaguar feature he'd kept. His markings had a realistic quality that begged for her touch. Unable to resist, she ran her hand over his rosette-covered shoulder. In contrast to his smooth golden skin, the raised pattern had a rough texture, like stubble. No ink slinger did that.

Coffee scent curled around her, teasing her body with invisible caresses. She fought a wave of dizziness and struggled to keep her expression casual. A low-metered growl came from his chest and his lids lowered over copper heat. Years' worth of sexual tension smoldered there. She wondered when he'd last indulged.

Everything about him spoke directly to her core, making the flesh between her legs clench. After nearly pinning him down in a mating frenzy, Dakota slammed the brakes on her body's heated response. Trying for cool composure, she lowered her hand and quirked an eyebrow. "Really?"

One corner of his mouth kicked up. "It's been

even longer since a queen has touched me."

Dakota snorted. "Keep waiting. That didn't count."

He laughed, and the passion left his gaze, giving no hint her rebuff had offended. He turned to hike a pathless route between the trees, and she fell in behind him. With new interest, she studied the animal print covering his torso. He belonged here, stalking amid the shrub-sized plants and vine covered trees.

"So, those rockin' auburn rosettes are part of your jaguar pattern?"

"Yes. Rockin' is good?"

"*Sim, boa*—good. Damn, I wanted to get the artist's name. I need someone to finish a tat."

****

"The half-drawn flower?" Even as Matteo tossed the words over his shoulder, he regretted his admission to looking. A knowing smile told him she'd caught his confession. He'd broken every shifter protocol by lusting after her flexing ass while she chased the agouti. Remorse eluded him.

"How perceptive of you." Her smug tone was irritating.

She enjoyed his misery. The teasing view and her burgeoning lavender scent had thickened his cock. Jaime's new sister involved with a potential feral. Playing out the consequences in his head cooled some of his arousal.

"You led the hunt. It was hard not to notice." His feigned nonchalance miscarried, sounding forced. "Why didn't the artist finish?"

"He, um, couldn't." Though relieved that Dakota didn't sound frightened, from her hesitancy, Matteo suspected something about the event had stressed her. He doubted the bastard tattooist had run out of ink.

Lack of detail fueled his imagination, and the mental image of another male's hands on her curves made his chest rumble. He glanced over his shoulder. "Do I need to find this man and kill him?"

Half-jesting, he could hardly blame another. Nipping along the trumpet vine's curving trail down the small of her back had an irresistible appeal. When she had dropped to her hands and knees, another battle to stay human had nearly bested him.

"Don't bother. A broken arm is punishment enough." She laughed as if releasing buried tension.

In stunned surprise, he halted, turning to her, and she nearly ran into him. "You broke his arm?"

She planted her hands on her hips. "I didn't mean to." Defiance withering, her shoulders sagged. "It was an accident. Too much juice in my submission hold."

"I'm impressed. The pond scum deserved it. You have no reason for remorse." Matteo wanted to cause the cretin pain.

"What?" Her confused expression broke into a self-possessed smile. "Oh yeah, he had it coming. I only regret my timing. He's the best in the Bahamas. I wanted him to finish the tat."

"And just how did you come by this bone-breaking skill?"

She shrugged. "I dated a jujitsu instructor for a while."

This female's bold confidence astounded him. In addition, she backed it up with real ability. "You have hidden depths, *senhorita*."

Feathery, dark lashes fanned her cheeks, making her appear almost sweet. Matteo smiled. She would most certainly find the thought insulting.

"Few men appreciate a woman who can kick their ass." She batted her lashes one more time.

Fighting an urge to plunder her lush lips with his mouth, he smiled. "A strong woman can be very attractive. But then again, I have no worries you're able to kick my ass."

Desire flared in her eyes, and Matteo leaned in, his lips hovering over hers. The temptation nearly bested him. Instead of closing the distance, he caressed her cheek. "We need to get back, *senhorita*. Alejandro will send out a search party."

"Sure." Affront chased the subtle heat from her gaze, and she jerked from his touch.

He'd hurt her feelings. "I'm sorry. It's—"

"It's fine, is what it is. Leave it." She stomped off, seeming to know the way.

Unable to find better words to apologize for an aborted kiss, he resumed his stride. If only lust drove him, he was no better than the maggot tattooist. Until he knew his heart, he'd keep his distance.

Catching up to her, he pushed a saber-leafed frond from their narrowing path. They neared the Salazar garden where the increased sunlight from the manicured lawns thickened the jungle's edge.

After a minute, she glanced at him and cleared her throat. "I'm sorry, I overreacted."

Her sincerity, or at least her effort at it, relieved Matteo. He tried to lift the mood with a new subject. "You did well during your primary shift. Did it frighten you?"

"Sort of, but in a good way. Like the best rollercoaster ever, with no seatbelts." Her eyes danced. Fortunately, it seemed her exhilaration over her first shift overrode her affront.

He'd overlooked a deep mettle within this woman who fractured arms. He found that inner strength intriguing. "Most shifters are terrified when the primary comes upon them."

"I'm sick to death of feeling terrified. While I was a jaguar, the rat was—just a rat." She smiled wide. "I think Kelsi's right, and our panic disorder goes away after our jaguars come out."

"We're learning about latents along with you. It makes sense you'd suffer if you need to shift, yet are unable to do so. And to manage that for years?" He shook his head. "I don't know how you've borne it."

Dakota gave him a double take, seeming surprised by his perception of her panic attacks. "It's not easy."

Maybe if Anna had had a similar core of strength, his life would've been different. Matteo had loved her, no question. Sweet and devoted, he'd thought her the perfect mate and mother for their planned children. Until she'd held their lifeless baby girl. Even seventy-seven years later, Matteo missed them both, loved them both.

Stillborn infants, combined with a lethal form of melancholy, had taken many of the queens—too many. In Anna's case, none could stop her from following their child to the afterlife. Cristiano may be on to something.

If Dakota's display of backbone was any indication, the latent females might bring a much-needed fortitude to the species.

"Your dragonfly followed you," Dakota whispered from behind him.

Her prompt, and the high-pitched whine, pulled him back to the present. Without noticing, he'd led them back through the jungle archway into the gardens. "I hear it."

When he scanned above, Dakota stepped close and placed a hand on his cheek, as if a lover demanding a kiss. His body took flight with the contact, and he discarded his altruistic ideals. Dragonfly forgotten, he slanted his lips over hers.

Her caress turned into a grip of hair at his temple, halting him. Kissing along his jawline, she stopped near his ear. "Don't look now. Wait 'til we leave. On the fuchsia plant. I think it's a camera drone."

What the hell?

Chapter Eleven

"A high-tech surveillance device. Video. I don't know if it picks up sound." Fury made Dakota's voice quake.

Matteo framed her face in his hands and met her gaze with hardened eyes. He dropped a dry, mechanical kiss to her lips. "They have the pictures already?"

"Likely." She whispered as quietly as he did. "If you can catch it, maybe we'll learn something about the handler."

"Let's sit for a while." Matteo's acting ability would never pay the bills. Touching the small of her back, he gestured to the stone bench.

With a single step, he lunged in a blur at the dragonfly, crashing into the tiny decorative tree beyond the fuchsia. As though anticipating Matteo's move, the robotic insect took to the air, its motor whirring like a quiet dentist's drill. The bug disappeared into an impassable tangle of vines edging the rainforest.

Incredulous over his turbo acceleration, Dakota's mouth dropped open. Matteo righted himself and glared at the spot of jungle that had swallowed the dragonfly, his livid expression cutting off her twenty questions. Restrained rage vibrated from him, and his control made the threat even more foreboding. He looked every bit the *Enforcer* she'd heard about.

"Come." He touched her elbow, and they sprinted to the house.

Grateful for her regular cardio workouts, Dakota held her own as she and Matteo raced to the house. Or maybe her shift had made her a stronger runner and able to keep up with him.

They catapulted into the kitchen, and Consuelo

turned from the counter, gripping a serrated hunting knife. "What's happened?"

"Another spy. Where's Alejandro?" In spite of his dreadlocks and beard scruff, Matteo telegraphed military authority.

Consuelo turned on her heel and muttered. "First my phone, now what?"

"Phone? What does that mean?" Dakota halted Matteo with a touch to his arm. Before he could follow the housekeeper, she arched a brow, demanding full information.

"Hers was tapped."

Dakota's stomach dropped, and she steadied herself with a hand on the counter. Mr. Swarthy was a very aggressive journalist—or something worse. "Why?"

"We're trying to find out." Footsteps sounded, and Matteo glanced past her. "Alejandro, we have a problem."

Petite Consuelo nearly jogged alongside her husband to keep pace. Alejandro had a sidearm strapped at his hip, and creases around his dark eyes gave him a grim, resolute appearance. He nodded in lieu of greeting. "Sounds like more than one. Portuguese?"

Matteo glanced at Dakota, and she put all kinds of threat into her return gaze.

"English, please." Matteo described their small intruder. "They might have pictures of a shift."

Alejandro's widened eyes held unasked questions. "Unfortunate you didn't catch it. This reporter is more ingenious than most."

"And way better funded," added Dakota.

"I find listening device in the parlor." Alejandro's speech slowed while he searched for words. After Matteo's conversational English, Alejandro's heavy accent surprised her. "All phones are cleaned."

Dakota gasped. "Who is doing this?"

"Nosy reporter," Alejandro answered too quickly.

They couldn't rule out someone inside the home, but Dakota didn't know these people well, so left the thought unspoken. Whoever had set up the surveillance had access to serious resources.

The tiny spy drone had appeared cutting-edge tech, possibly even military grade. The fact that the surrounding jungle hadn't blocked its incoming command signals spoke to the device's elite construction. In annoying irony, the handler must've used the Salazar cell tower to transmit.

"My phone's been with me or in my room the whole time. Is it okay to use?"

"Yes, I checked it while you were out." Alejandro frowned. "I fixed."

"You found spyware on *my* phone?" Dakota nearly shrieked.

Alejandro nodded. "I'm sorry."

"You're certain no one was near your phone? Not even for a few minutes?" Matteo took her hand.

Alejandro met her gaze, his expectant expression practically begging for her answer.

These people had been together forever. She couldn't imagine suspecting a family member or lifelong friend of betrayal. "If the reporter is Mr. Swarthy, he was at the airport. Maybe before I got here? I'll think about it."

His solemn eyes brightened. "Still, be careful what you say or—" He air typed with his fingers. "Write on your phone. We will catch them, *senhorita*, I promise."

As though she had to do something, Consuelo bustled among the stainless appliances, preparing beverages for the group. With frequent glances their way, she certainly listened to every word.

"I'm sure you will." Dakota hid her doubt as best she could, turning her attention to Matteo. She gulped a half glass of water, suddenly thirsty. "We'll talk later? If you've got the time, I have a million questions."

His smile reassured her. "And I for you. Smart phones make me feel quite stupid."

"Sure thing. I'll find you." She grabbed a couple shortbread cookies from the tray Consuelo held under her nose. "Thanks."

Unexpectedly ravenous, she bit into one. Smiling, Matteo took the plate from the housekeeper and offered it to Dakota. "Take the platter. You'll want all of them. Trust me."

"Okay … thanks." She *was* starving, and had no idea why. Toting her cookie fix, she paced to her suite's hallway. The two men followed her and paused in a small sitting room, probably seeking privacy for discussion not meant for her or Consuelo.

At the hall's arched entrance, she placed a hand on the wall and turned back to look at Matteo. She'd never met a man like him. When she'd panicked over the agouti, he had empowered her. *Kill it.* Not the usual placating, *just relax, a mouse can't hurt you.* Accepting her need to destroy the enemy, he had taken her hunting, paving the way for her miraculous shift to jaguar. "Thank you—for everything."

His smile warmed his eyes, and he lifted his chin. "You're welcome."

Towering over the foreman in the domestic parlor, Matteo's jaguar pattern and mane of tawny dreads looked uncivilized. The wildness called to her feminine flesh, dropping heat to her core. His eyes widened with his broadening smile. Clearing his throat, he returned to his security discussion with Alejandro.

Shower, now!

****

As Shelton strode through his Manaus office building's tiny parking lot, a late-morning text buzzed at his hip. He glanced at the screen.

Jose: **New findings need immediate attention.**

Shelton had intentionally kept his return trip a surprise. Now, he wondered what he'd find in the office.

Dressed in khakis and a polo shirt to avoid attention, he lengthened his stride. Maybe Pantoja's discovery was worth an overnight flight from Austin. His Fiat sat parked by the front door, so he had disobeyed orders to take leave. In a couple minutes, Shelton would decide if he cared or not.

Embedded in a retail area of southern Manaus, the non-descript AAA Security's entrance wasn't designed to instill client confidence. On the sidewalk, Shelton jiggled open the rickety screen panel fronting the dilapidated entry door.

However, an artistic paint job camouflaged a steel core and numerous locking bolts. He waved his chipped card in front of the hidden reader. At the heavy click, Shelton stepped inside.

Loud whoops from within halted him in the threshold. Pantoja, his dark features jubilant, pirouetted on the linoleum, adding a fist pump, as though he'd scored a Super Bowl touchdown. The center monitor on the desk in front of him showed only a tropical garden. Still consumed with his war dance, Pantoja hadn't noticed he had company. Shelton cleared his throat.

After a double take at his C.O., the surprised man came to attention. "Good you're here, sir. You've got to see this!"

"You sober?" Shelton scanned the four-desk office for empty liquor bottles. All the other computer screens were dark.

"I'm clean. Now you'll know I'm not nuts. First, I need to bring my bug out." A mass of vibrating energy, Pantoja had slipped into Portuguese.

"And what the hell happened to your face?" Fluent himself, Shelton ignored Pantoja's breach of his English-only mandate, and responded with his own Portuguese.

"Five hundred pounds of cat is what." Pantoja dropped onto his computer chair, picking up what looked like an elaborate video game controller. "Damn, they spotted me."

Shelton studied the image of a shirtless man, who whirled in a special-effects lunge at the camera. A jaguar-patterned tattoo covered his back, and along with ropes of ratted hair, he looked like a jungle savage.

Pantoja whooped again and tilted toward the screen with a broad smile. "Too slow, catman."

Given the brute's impossible speed, and Pantoja's crazy story, he must have meant the term literally. Shelton leaned in and squinted. "What the fuck is that?"

"Can't prove it yet, but that is a mythical changer—half-man, half-jaguar."

"He sure looks like someone who might train jaguars, I'll give you that much." Shelton mumbled, wondering if Pantoja had just edited the video with a few frames of fast-forward.

However, his reaction appeared legit, just as he had sounded truthful the night before, recounting the impossible metamorphosis of the Gorman woman. The glimpse of potential on the monitor stirred Shelton's analytical mind and higher hopes for a groundbreaking jungle asset. If Pantoja's werejaguar story theory panned out.

A minute later, Pantoja jutted his chin at a larger screen on his right. "I'll boot up the replay—you'd better sit down."

Shelton pulled a rolling computer chair next to Pantoja. Expecting a replay of the savage's moves, dizzying shots of streaming foliage, seen from the perspective of a bumblebee surprised him. Motion sickness threatened. "Can you move this along?"

Pantoja nodded and fast-forwarded to a steadier part of the video. "Here, we're in front of them now. Watch—and hold on to your ass—sir."

An athletic, nearly naked woman burst from cover, seemingly focused on a chase. Yelling, she fell to her hands and knees. She needed help. However, the wild man running behind her stopped, hovering a few yards away, agape, as though waiting for the rapture.

Dark light rose from her body, and the glowing shape of a large animal obscured her human form. Glare briefly obliterated the image before receding. In the woman's place, lay an over-sized great white panther. The jungle man smiled from his vantage point.

"What the hell kind of cat is that?"

"A *new kind*, sir." Pantoja slanted an amused glance at Shelton. "In jumbo size, anyway. It's a jaguar. See the markings?"

After padding through a short distance of forest, the girl-beast paused to search the ground. Then she rolled a log with one paw that would've taken several men to move. That monster could rip off a man's head. Heart racing with the implications, Shelton leaned in, gripping the edge of the desk. "Show it again."

After several viewings, not daring to believe his eyes, he rose to pace the gray linoleum. He'd all but given up his suspicions that Pantoja had doctored the clip. The cat in the video could have killed the smuggler

Erico. He had to be certain the mammoth-sized jaguar truly existed. "We retrieve your toy together."

"Absolutely, sir." Pantoja's wry smile said the man guessed Shelton's suspicions and hadn't pulled a digital fast one. Military applications raced through his mind, and he recalled Lieutenant Liu's interesting genetics. Though far-fetched, he wondered if Valentine searched for werejaguars.

****

Admiring the blue and yellow parrot mosaic on the wall, Dakota dried off and wrapped her wet hair in a lush towel. After the tepid shower, the indoor air chilled her skin. She grabbed her blow dryer from the granite counter and pulled the towel from her head.

Staring into the mirror, and transfixed by her reflection, she shrieked in fury. *Blah brown!* It had been years since she'd seen her natural color.

Your hair is beautiful. Probably preferring the plain brown over *blue*, he hadn't even mentioned her color change. He could've warned her. On the other hand, given his clunky start with her, a smart man might consider the whole hair-color topic off limits.

In momentary panic that her ink had disappeared, too, she looked at her inner arm. The dainty, rose-colored feather with three tiny birds in flight appeared intact. Turning her back to the mirror, the vibrant hues of the hummingbird masterpiece earned a sigh of relief.

Dakota wanted to rail at Kelsi for not warning her she'd lose her two-tone dye job, but likely, she hadn't known. Her sister never colored over her perfectly highlighted chestnut mane. While Dakota dried her drab hair, she brought her temper under control. The truth was, if Kelsi had told Dakota she would go bald with her first shift, she would have done it anyway. No jump from a plane had ever given her such a juiced high.

Fluffed and puffed, she threw on shorts and a girlie t-shirt, and a moment later, she strode out onto the veranda.

Just outside the kitchen, Tad and Matteo sat side by side at a table, huddled over a phone. She paused to enjoy the coffee scent and didn't bother searching for the pot. The teenager pointed to the keypad and Matteo nodded. Both looked up to greet her.

Tad stopped midsentence. "*Olá, senhorita!* You changed your hair. Very nice."

Matteo scowled at the teen, but turned a smile on Dakota. "Yes, your hair's lovely."

He seemed sincere, and after all, Matteo hadn't turned her hair blah brown. Although it was clear he preferred to avoid the subject. "Thanks. I'm still adjusting to the look. Is Tad getting you up to speed on your phone?"

"*Sim*, I *texted* our new insect discovery to Cristiano, and he actually answered me." Matteo raised his phone between them. "He's on his way home."

Dakota laughed at his archaic take on the common-place technology.

"I'll be inside if you need more help, *Senhor* Matteo. New electronics are always challenging." Tad smiled, glancing from one to the other, before he rose and paced to the kitchen entrance.

She beamed at Matteo and claimed Tad's empty seat, enjoying the flare of mocha. "I promised to help, too. What're you working on?"

****

Matteo indulged in Dakota's shower-fresh scent, lavender caressing the lining of his nose. Mild now, compared to her excited mix earlier in the jungle. Leaning toward her, he placed his cell between them. "Show me how to ride the internet, so I can learn."

Her eyes lit with mirth, and she chuckled. "It's *surf* the internet. But no one says that anymore, just 'hop on the net'."

Matteo nodded and then followed her instructions to connect. In mere seconds, a search of automobiles yielded hundreds of articles and photographs of marvelous machines. With the wondrous search engines, Matteo could catch up on technology and culture. No wonder Cristiano had insisted he learn how to use this device. Implications of the information age took shape in Matteo's mind.

"So, we could learn about an individual with this device? Sitting here?" He tapped the screen, turning it into a list of words. "Damn, how did I do that?"

"Happens all the time. It's a selection menu. This takes you home." Dakota pressed the round button below the screen. "And here, we can search."

Matteo released the miniature television box into her capable hands. While she typed in Matteo D'Cruz, he studied her actions. One result, *Deserters of World War II*, glared back at him. She glanced his way, and he hoped she couldn't read Portuguese.

Dakota opened a new picture and scanned the text. He gritted his teeth. As though the phone had heated in her hand, she set it down with a metal clunk. Meeting his gaze, a tiny V formed between her brows. "Is this really you?"

"*Sim.*"

"You're no coward. Why?"

Matteo fisted his hands with the onslaught of unburied emotion, not understanding why it should accost him now. But he knew. This queen's opinion of him mattered more than it should.

She placed a light hand on his forearm. "I'm sorry. I—"

Unable to face her inspection of a past he longed to forget, he rose from his seat. "There are many kinds of cowardice."

"Don't go. I was rude to pry."

Pulling from her touch, he rounded the pool to reach his own room and yanked the door open. He couldn't help a glance back. Dakota sat with her head in her hands, her light chestnut waves hiding her face from view. Cristiano had almost convinced him he could return to the world.

Chapter Twelve

Shelton observed Pantoja place his drone on the Fiat's back seat, making an effort to be discreet. His suspicions had steadily lost their steam. Pulling a stack of folders from the Fiat's door pocket, Pantoja handed him several dossiers, before he settled behind the wheel. "Read these on the way back."

Apparently, Portuguese was the language of the day. Shelton wanted to keep him engaged in their mission, so made no objection.

He flipped open the top manila file, finding an ancient black-and-white military portrait of a Brazilian soldier. From underneath, he slid out a freeze-framed color shot of the jungle savage. Confused, Shelton raised his brows. "This is?"

"The catman in the video's a mystery. My facial recognition search found only a deserter from World War II. If it is him, his name's Matteo D'Cruz. And he's over a hundred years old."

Incredulous, he glanced at Pantoja, ready to call him nuts.

Pantoja's narrowed eyes stopped him. He lifted his chin. "Compare the photos and see for yourself."

Shelton held the images side by side and frowned, noting stark similarities in the eyes and cheekbones. By today's appearance, the man had deteriorated into a homeless drug addict. Shelton had to admit, the men in the photographs could be identical twins.

Cloistered in the Fiat sedan, bouncing over rut-lined roads, Shelton replayed the woman's metamorphosis in his mind. Pantoja had serious computer skills, but if he'd used special effects, he could make a lot more money in Hollywood. Nor had he ever

M.A. JEWELL

shown this much acting talent. At some point, Shelton's disbelief had transformed to anticipation, which quickly became goals and an action-plan to achieve them.

The silent drive and boat ride into the wilderness had eaten up most of the day, and now the afternoon heat competed with the Fiat's air-conditioning.

Shelton glanced again at the drone's leather case on the back seat. As Pantoja had predicted, they'd retrieved the robotic dragonfly from a shoreline river fern just outside the Salazar property.

Bristling with new energy behind the wheel, he tracked Shelton's gaze. "They're the jaguar changers, I know it. My great-grandfather claimed one traveled our lands."

Shelton snorted, unwilling to admit his optimism. "A *legend*?"

"I used to think so. He said they live between the human and jaguar worlds, taking either form, as they will. Some people believe the ancient city unearthed in Honduras was the Jaguar Princess—Comizahual's capital. A temple held her stone talismans. She was a sorceress."

"You don't believe in magic anymore than me." Shelton snorted.

Pantoja slanted a glance at him. "How does a woman change to a giant jaguar, if not with the black arts?"

"There's a scientific explanation. And we'll find it." Closing the folder on a Dakota Gorman *Omaha World Herald* file photo, Shelton tapped the cover. "This girl's whiter than me. She's no Honduran native."

"Yes, very white—as was the Jaguar Princess. So the legend says, anyway."

Shelton snorted. He wouldn't allow himself to be suckered in to a fable. "Her sister morphed the same

123

way?"

"Both girls are changers. D'Cruz has to be one, too. He moved too fast, and he was happy to see the jaguar. The Salazars must be neck deep in this."

"The sister killed Erico. She was there."

Grave lines carved Pantoja's expression. "Maybe not. Both Salazars were close enough. They could've been at the kill site."

No doubt, Pantoja was still mourning. Shelton regretted bringing up the massacre. "Men always discount the female threat. A beautiful woman is the most vicious animal on the planet."

Pantoja chuckled, the desired result. "Very true."

Shelton only half-joked. *Bitches.* "Surveillance in place?"

"Not sure what's working. After they spotted me, the place turned into a military camp. Living room mic went offline this morning. With luck, the phones might still be hot. I'll check when we get back."

Waving Pantoja to silence, Shelton opened Cristiano Salazar's dossier without reading it. A team that could live in the rainforest as jaguars and change to human when necessary would be unstoppable. Shelton needed indisputable intel.

Pantoja was the obvious choice to research werejaguars, but Shelton needed him to man surveillance. Genetics was way outside of his own wheelhouse. Normally, he'd assign an aide to prepare a brief, but thanks to General Butler's plan to move along Shelton's retirement, staffers were nonexistent. *The asshole.*

Despite what Butler might think, Shelton was a damn patriot. The U.S. military wouldn't miss this opportunity—not on his watch. He would deliver a super soldier to the brass, and at the same time, keep the South and Central American governments on the sidelines.

Liu's interesting genetics kept coming to mind—and his odd eyes. Maybe they weren't an Amerasian trait, like Shelton had thought. With the kid's jungle abilities, and the fact that Valentine studied his DNA, there had to be a connection. And if the doctor actually searched for werejaguars, the Pentagon suspected the changers' existence. However, Shelton didn't dare tip his hand by nosing around.

If indeed, the brass had known about the shifters, they had put him in Brazil for just this purpose. They had stationed him in country to pick up the ball when the action broke.

The revelation eased his bruised professional pride. An unmatched, jungle-born operative could reverse Shelton's circumstances. With the right plan, he could still add one more two-star General Shelton to his family tree.

Slapping the top manila folder closed, he jabbed the stack with an index finger. "Intel on these subjects is your new priority. Use all available resources."

"Way ahead of you, sir."

****

The next morning, Dakota knocked on Matteo's sliding door. While she waited, she wondered if he had even missed his phone, he'd been so insulted by her insolent question. Her left eye would've twitched all night knowing her electronic lifeline was out of reach. She hoped he'd mellowed with some sleep.

He pulled the green sheer to the side and raised an index finger. She translated, *just a minute.* If he was dressing, she hoped he stayed with the shirtless look.

One minute stretched to forever, before rollers sounded with the opening door. Bare-chested and newly clean-shaven, his copper eyes appeared neutral. A healthy step up from yesterday's affront. *"Bom dia, senhorita."*

Enjoying the view, Dakota waved his cell between them. "Missing this?"

His eyes widened, chasing the reserve from his expression. "You've had it? The whole time?"

The rapid change in his demeanor made her grin. She handed over the phone. *"Sim.* And I didn't plant spyware on it, promise."

A smile split his face, as he slid the device into the pocket of his jean cutoffs. He stepped out onto the veranda, and his shoulder brushed hers, giving her a welcome sense of intimacy. He pulled the door closed. "Thank you."

"I thought I'd run this morning. Want to come along? I wouldn't want to make the security czar chase after me." Imagining him hunting her down in the jungle sent an internal shudder though her body. She leaned in near his ear, sneaking a whiff of coffee. "I want to go cat again, too."

"Good you came to me. I'll check for small visitors before you shift." Matteo's smile spread ear to ear. "And I'll try to be a gentleman."

With his scent beating at her, Dakota wasn't so sure she wanted a gentleman escort. She motioned to his face. "You clean up pretty good."

He rubbed his chin. "I'll cut my hair for the wedding. Just haven't made time."

"No!" Dakota reached for a waist-length dread resting on his chest, lifting it to his line of sight. "We'll cut a few and bead some—give you rockin' dreads to match that crazy-hot inkless tat."

"Beads? If I show up like a wildman, I'll scandalize Cristiano."

"He can eat dirt. You look great as you are. And

I've got serious hair skills. Give me a shot. If you don't like the look, we can cut your dreads." Releasing his hair, she turned to lead them to the kitchen door.

He laughed. "As you will, *senhorita*."

They strode through the house, and his sideways glance lingered on her with a hint of a smile. "You're an interesting woman, Dakota."

Her name on his lips, tinged with his faint accent, made her wonder what language he would whisper in her ear if they... She shook off the thought. "Um, about yesterday. When I typed in your name, I overstepped—pried. I didn't think anything would come up. Still, searching your name on the net was tacky. I'm sorry. One of my many personality flaws."

Ushering her into the gardens, he gave her a weak smile. "And I overreacted. Leaving the war was nothing private. All know. Again, my manners are out of use."

Dakota sighed in relief. They stepped onto the cobbled pathway, and hummingbirds greeted them. Their wings barely sounded above the insect chorus. Matteo strode alongside her with no sign of yesterday's tension. At least he didn't seem to hold grudges.

As excited as she was to try another shift, she wanted to know more about him, and if he could move on from his wife's passing so many years ago. His WWII service had followed Anna's death too closely. Anna, the war, and his desertion had to be connected. "Do you want to talk about it? If not, I understand."

"It's a short story." Matteo snorted, glancing away from her towards the distant jungle. "I hid from life. Too long."

Dakota wished she could gauge his reaction. If he was too absorbed in the past to live in the present, she needed to know. "Kelsi said—said you lost your wife and baby girl. I can't imagine coming back from something like that. I'm sorry."

Striations of muscle lined Matteo's clenched jaw, and the path held his rapt attention. "A grieving mate is rarely sane. I was no exception. I left the war because it didn't give me what I needed."

Be it shifter or human, grief was grief. In med school, an attending had made an offhand comment about a new widow—that she had seemed determined to follow her husband right into the grave. *Matteo had wanted to join Anna and his daughter.* Dakota's eyes stung, and she blinked. Another worthless *I'm sorry* hovered on her lips.

"And now? What do you need, now, Matteo?" She held her breath, uncertain if she feared his answer or craved it.

He halted and met her gaze head on. "I don't know."

At least he'd been honest. He resumed their stroll at a faster clip, and she decided he'd hit his sharing limit. She searched for a lighter subject. "I've never truly known what I needed. And now that I'm not human, I really have no clue what I want from life."

Not *homo sapiens*, but something else. She couldn't wrap her mind around her new place in the food chain.

"We'll help you adjust to the shifters' world. We've faced extinction for so long, finding females has energized all of us. Given us hope."

"I bet. I've got a whole new take on the endangered species list." She laughed uneasily. "Never thought I'd be on it."

He smiled with a nod. "Much of shifter life is very human, with human values. Did you have ambitions as a child?"

She cringed at the thought of her resume. Flighty,

according to the Fox. "For a while, I planned to be a doctor. But in America—the U.S.—parts of medicine are a racket."

"Corrupt?"

She shook her head. "Not like you might think. It's complicated. I started medical school because I wanted to help people."

"But you didn't finish?"

"No, I dropped out. Money was way more important in the industry than I could tolerate. I tried computer programming, too—fun for a while, but meh. What do you do?"

With a frown, he turned from her to snatch a lily from its stem and handed it to her. "Not sure, anymore."

"Sorry. I should've asked what you used to do." She'd traveled into weird territory and kicked herself. He'd been in the jungle since World War II, so he'd been chasing deer—or whatever jaguars ate. Self-conscious, she twirled the four-inch lavender bloom.

"Cristiano says I still have a business." Pulling out his phone, he unlocked the screen and tapped an icon labeled "D'Cruz". "Salazar Holdings has managed my plantation."

"Cool. What kind?"

After studying the screen for a minute, he looked up at her with a smile. "Apparently, I still grow coffee."

Dakota grinned. "I should've guessed."

"Can we stop for a minute? I need to see if I can afford a wedding gift."

"Sure." They claimed the same stone bench near the jungle entrance, and the iridescent hummers danced around them. Matteo scrolled through what appeared to be a financial report. Not wanting to pry again, she refocused on the hummingbirds.

"Jaime already has all he could want. What does

your sister need?"

Dakota surveyed the exquisite garden surrounding the Salazar mansion. "Since she's marrying the guy, likely nothing. But for Christmas, last year, she asked family to donate to a jaguar rescue preserve—I forgot where."

"Excellent. Shifters support the natural jag—" Matteo's eyes widened, and he angled his cell at her. "What's this?"

The camera had activated for an incoming video call, reflecting a moving selfie image.

"Tad's playing with you. Press here." Laughing, she tapped to open the connection.

Matteo positioned the screen between them, and as though the camera flew, an image of moving foliage came to life. Dakota's heart pounded with dread. "Oh, hell no."

Matteo narrowed his eyes at the screen, and his features hardened.

When the dizzying motion halted, the camera angled down, showing Dakota's spectacular shift. Threats to her and her family, all shifters, she corrected, scrolled through her mind. CNN features. Tabloids. Science experts seeking study subjects. *A cadaver lab.*

On the screen, Dakota's naked backside disappeared into the darkened forest, ending the clip. Shock sent her reeling, and she dropped her head in her hands.

Next to her, a rumble came from Matteo's chest. "The man who followed you did this. After we recover the film, I'll kill him."

"Not if I get to him first." Her mumbled words frightened her. She meant it. Dakota pressed an index finger to her lips.

He narrowed his eyes, but complied.

Gripping his wrist to steady the phone, she tapped the mute button.

"I shut off their sound."

"Good thinking. But it's as well the caller knows their fate." He glowered at the cell, holding it at arm's length.

"You don't understand. There isn't a single copy to find. Whoever did this backed that video up on more than one server—I would have. Even the U.S. government couldn't track it—"

Mechanical, broken English interrupted her.

Dakota snatched the cell from Matteo and activated the speaker. "Jaguar changer girl, I see you at night. We keep your secret, yes? Give us changer blood and hair for quiet. If you do not, we show pictures on Internet."

Her worst fears were now realized.

****

Livid that he was so helpless to protect Dakota, Matteo pried the phone from her death grip. The screen had returned to rows of tiny pictures. He hated his confusion. Alarm over the unknown had his pulse pounding in his ears. "He is gone?"

She wiped a hand down the side of her face. "Yes, the call's disconnected."

"Why do they ask for blood rather than money?"

Raising a steely gaze, she frowned. "Because they can use our DNA to give humans our traits—well, they'll try real hard to, anyway. Until yesterday, I thought my life was half over. Now, I might see another century or two."

Comprehension dawned on Matteo. Cristiano's excitement over scientific advances began to make more sense. "Mendel's work has gone so far?"

She nodded and blew loose strands of hair from

her eyes. "Compared to a human's lifespan, a shifter's existence is like being immortal. We're the fountain of youth,"

"And humans will do anything to possess the golden chalice." Foreboding placed a physical weight on his body.

Deep in her own thoughts, she didn't look at him. "Exactly."

Guarding Dakota was his biggest priority, though he couldn't recall when she'd gained such importance in his world. Likely, at first sight of her. He'd been a fool to pretend otherwise.

Only a true shifter could protect her, one who lived in the human world. Not a male forever trapped as a jaguar. Dakota was a formidable female—and deserved an equal partner for a mate. The thought finalized his decision. No matter what it took, he would stay human for the three years.

Wanting to curl her into his chest, he put a supportive arm around her trembling shoulders. "Our history is filled with humans' stories about us. Even if he exposes the video, no one will believe it."

"A digital forensic expert can tell if the video is faked."

Her distracted, matter-of-fact pronouncement sank his hopes that a leaked recording would drown in skepticiscm. Years ago, people ridiculed tall tales about the changers.

Next to him, she straightened. "He said, *we*. Mr. Swarthy's not working alone, not with all these resources." She waved above them at nothing. "I doubt a drone with that kind of image resolution is sold retail— I'll check it out."

"Image resolution?"

"The quality of the picture and sound, too. It

might even be military." The steel in her voice told him that rage shook her frame rather than fear.

"We'll hire a specialist to dispute anyone's claims. For enough money, our expert will be a fervent opponent." The technology of the twenty-first century might be beyond him. However, human greed hadn't changed. Matteo hoped his projected confidence hid his uncertainty.

"We don't dare let it get that far." She launched to her feet, pulling him by the hand and led them toward the house at a brisk walk. "Genetics are big business. Governments and corporations worldwide will want to study our DNA. Whoever's behind this won't stop until they get samples, or worse, a subject—one of us—to work on. We need to find the snake and cut off the head."

The truth of Dakota's lineage swirled in the tempest of her ocean eyes. Even without armor, she appeared every bit the Jaguar Princess of legend.

Chapter Thirteen

Ever since the blackmailer's demand had arrived that morning, plans for finding the extortionist and his handlers had consumed Matteo. The whole shifter nation was at risk. When he'd left for the jungle after the war, only one mated female was left on the planet, all but assuring their demise. Now, with the discovery of the latents, they had a fighting chance. And Matteo, their *Enforcer*, would rise to the challenge.

Cristiano and Dakota sat side by side at his office desk, while Matteo hovered behind them, peering over their shoulders at the amazing laptop. They'd grabbed a quick lunch and had stayed huddled around these screens for the last two hours. She focused on the text more intently, and Matteo sensed she'd made progress.

Her fingers flew over the attached horizontal typewriter—a keyboard. The tapping sounded muffled, compared to the metal keystrokes he recalled. The flat display resembled the television in Matteo's suite.

Text flashed into boxes only to disappear, and then more of the same followed. Dakota paused, glancing at a larger screen to the right. A Manaus street map appeared. "There we go."

Ignorance created dependence. Both disturbed Matteo. "Do you know what she's doing?"

"Not a clue, my friend." Cristiano's admission gave him small comfort. Maybe Matteo should spend his biped sentence at Oxford.

After he'd ensured Dakota's safety. The maggot had threatened her specifically. Now, having her near wasn't enough. He placed a hand on her shoulder. "You learned this with your computer school?"

She glanced over her shoulder, eyes determined.

"Not school exactly." She refocused on the monitor. "But I *did* date a hacker for a while."

Possessiveness came from nowhere, sinking jealous claws into Matteo's chest. "Is there *anyone* you haven't dated?"

Either she ignored his growled comment, or didn't hear him. However, from his seat beside her, Cristiano stifled a chuckle.

Matteo tried to regain his dignity, focusing on facts. "What's a hacker?"

Still fighting a grin, Cristiano glanced at him with dancing eyes. "A criminal who breaks into computer programs."

Though he didn't understand, Matteo nodded. The all-knowing Internet would educate him later.

"The phone that sent the vid belongs to Jose Pantoja." Dakota pointed to a blinking, upside down teardrop on a Manaus street grid. "And it's right here."

At least Matteo understood the map.

She turned to Cristiano. "And somehow, they used your cell tower to transmit—both ways."

Grim-faced, Cristiano nodded. "Good job, *senhorita*. Find all you can on him."

"You got it." She appeared so confident—and driven. While she tapped away, words rushed to the smaller laptop's display. Matteo studied her actions for patterns and found none. A return to university was imperative to catch up with the world.

Thirty minutes later, she straightened. "Well-well, looky here." A military headshot popped up on the screen. "Mr. Swarthy, in person, sort of."

"That's him?" asked Matteo, leaning in near her shoulder, unable to ignore her scent.

"Yep. Your army booted our friend here—something about tequila, a naked girl, and another soldier named Nuno Sanchez. Nothing on record after their discharge. They could've gone off-grid."

Cristiano snapped his attention to her. "Nuno? You're certain?"

Focused on the whirring printer in the corner, Dakota hadn't looked at Cristiano and appeared oblivious to his surprise. However, his subtle reaction piqued Matteo's interest.

"Yes." She snatched some papers off the top of the machine, and turned with a grin. "Here you go."

"Could be a coincidence." Murmuring almost to himself, Cristiano read the report. Matteo caught his concern, but Cristiano lifted a neutral expression to Dakota. "Impressive. You got into the military database."

"Oh yeah. I'm sizzlin'." Touching her arm with a finger, she yanked her hand back as though burned. "Don't ask—I won't tell."

The mirth in her eyes infectious, Matteo laughed, and Cristiano joined in with a chuckle.

"While I'm up, more coffee?" She didn't wait for an answer. "Never mind, I'll bring the pot."

Relieved Dakota had missed Cristiano's unease, Matteo quietly closed the door behind her. Leather creaked, as he claimed the office chair across from Cristiano. "So, who's Nuno?"

"Not sure. But I don't believe in coincidence." Cristiano had never looked so grave. "During Kelsi's abduction, Jaime overheard radio transmissions. The traffickers called their helicopter pilot Jose. And one of the mercs on the ground answered to Nuno. Both are common names, but together?"

Interesting. "So, if our Jose flew their helicopter, he's connected to skin traders?"

"Hired by them, at the very least."

"How did mercenaries jump from slaving to

blackmailing for DNA?"

Cristiano snorted. "No damn clue—except money's involved."

The doorknob turned, and the men fell silent. Dakota entered with carafe in hand, halting just inside the threshold. Her smile dropped into a firm line. "If you want my help, no secrets. Got it?"

Matteo didn't know if her boldness came from being an American, or if all women had become brazen. Anna would never have spoken so. A glance at Cristiano gave him no help. The ancient shifter looked to the side, as though telling Matteo he was on his own.

After she refilled their mugs, Dakota clunked the glass pot on the leather blotter, sloshing the brew precariously close to the rim. She dropped onto the seat next to Matteo, and cocked her head with an arched brow. "You've got something to share?"

He recalled her hesitation to kill the agouti's young, wondering now if she could stomach a shifters' war. "We were discussing your sister's brush with slavers."

"And?"

"We think Pantoja was involved, just not how, exactly." Matteo explained the possible connection between Jose Pantoja and Kelsi's abduction. Dakota listened with a steely expression and an occasional nod.

Pulling a pad of notepaper from Cristiano's desk organizer, she jotted notes. "Forensic evidence could've confirmed the presence of a giant jaguar. Then if they got the bright idea to check DNA—and lab analysis would've taken significant resources." She shook her head, talking almost to herself. "But they had enough money to buy a kickass drone. Our bad guys are well connected."

If emotion intruded on Dakota's logic, she held it

at bay. Additionally, her theory that the enemy already had genetic material had merit. Yet again, her analytical mind impressed him.

Cristiano gave an authoritative nod. "It's the most likely scenario."

Dakota leaned in, resting crossed arms on the mahogany desktop. "So what's our plan?"

Without a choice, Matteo forged ahead, including both in his gaze. "We are agreed to eliminate this enemy?"

Cristiano leaned back in his chair. "Yes. I've no reason to believe intimidation would be effective."

"Eliminate?" Dakota sat up in her seat, darting a glance from one man to the other. "As in assassinate?"

Matteo cringed at the shock on her face. Dreading her reaction, he put a gentle hand to her cheek.

"We've no choice but to cut off the head." It was unfair to use her own words against her, but he would honor her wish to know all. "If, as you said, our genetic material could possibly extend human life, or give humans our abilities, they'll stop at nothing. I'll die before I let them dissect you—or any shifter—on a laboratory slab."

****

Dakota pulled from Matteo's touch and stared at the two men who proposed murder. Her own disgust was disturbingly absent, and she couldn't help but admire Matteo's protective nature. No wonder Cristiano had put him in charge of defense.

Still, she hesitated. "Cutting off the head won't keep the shifters hidden from the world. We're too late. If they retrieved even a few strands of Jaime's hair from Kelsi's rescue site, we're outed."

With graven lines bracketing his mouth and hardened copper eyes, Matteo couldn't look more dangerous. "And already they want more. Knowledge of our DNA won't be enough. They'll come for us."

And he was right. *I'll never be a victim.*

Like when she'd snapped the ink artist's arm, she controlled her life. Their murder plot would appall Kelsi. She'd demand police involvement. However, her safety and their new family's existence hung on the decisions made in this office. All creatures were empowered to protect themselves.

Dakota's gaze fell to Cristiano's mailing tube, propped in the corner behind him—the one he carried nonstop, the one labeled "FAMILY". *An entire species. My people.*

Confident in her decision, she squared her shoulders. "I'm in."

Cristiano nodded with a furrowed brow. "Then we are committed."

Dakota glanced from one man to the other. "Promise me you won't tell Kelsi our plan."

After exchanging a look, they both nodded.

"So in your little huddle while I got coffee, did you think of a way to find the head?"

"Yes." Matteo laid out a three-tiered plan to work their way up to the enemy's puppet master. Dakota picked it apart in earnest. After two hours of debate, Matteo announced they were prepared. "Now, let's set up a meet with our blackmailer."

Dakota returned to the keyboard, her fingers moving rapid fire, cracking into the carrier's database to identify the caller's blocked number. After several minutes, she glanced at Matteo. "I need your phone."

He placed his cell next to the keyboard and pointed at the Manaus street grid. "We need to meet him there."

As she dialed, keypad tones played from the

speaker, and all three stared at the tiny screen.

"*Olá*," said a male voice.

Another glance at the white cardboard cylinder steeled her against her human-hearted doubts. "I'm the woman in your video..."

"Changer-girl Dakota, you smart to find a private number." As she had hoped, he switched to heavily accented English. No surprise he knew her name. Still, she shook off a creepy sense of invasion.

"It took a while." Pointing to the blinking cursor on the Manaus map, she mouthed to the men, "he's here". Matteo nodded. Behind her, Cristiano gripped the back of his executive computer chair, and the base creaked.

"Is the catman with you?"

"We want the video and a guarantee all copies of the file have been destroyed or no deal. I found you. I'll know if you saved a back-up." Let him think her an imbecile.

"That can be arranged." This guy shoveled horseshit faster than she did. A secure server housed the video, and they both knew it.

With promises of blood, hair, and saliva samples, the blackmailer agreed to their terms in mere seconds.

Matteo leaned into the speaker. "You'll not survive a betrayal, tapeworm. Come alone."

She pressed the end button, and the disconnection clicked. Falling back against the padded leather chair, she heaved a sigh of relief. Only for the moment. The shit would get several feet deeper before any chance of success.

Cristiano patted her hand. "You did well."

"He'll have a team in place," said Matteo, grim-faced.

****

Thunder erupted from Dakota's phone resting on the wicker end table's glass top. Ten PM. Staring at Mom's contact photo on the screen, she wished she could skip the conversation. Not an option. "Hi, Mom."

"You didn't call last night." The Fox demanded an explanation, but as usual not in question form. Her tone held that hint of reprimand.

"I got swamped with wedding stuff." *A stalker. And I turned into a jaguar.* Dakota set aside her laptop and note book. The search for the video's server trail was going nowhere.

"I've been inundated with calls from excited family. A chauffeured jet to a jungle wedding has them all in a tizzy."

"It's gonna rock, for sure. Mom, the Salazars aren't what we thought."

"Something's happened." Again, implied demand. Sometimes, like now, the Fox's intuition seemed downright clairvoyant. Dakota couldn't imagine what in her tone had slipped.

"Sort of. Nothing bad." Yet. In a couple of days, Dakota might be real famous. *Oh, and by the way, I plotted a murder.* Dakota panicked. She'd said too much and couldn't fill in the blanks. "It'll have to wait. I'm sorry I mentioned anything."

"Oh, I think now is fine. I have time." Expected compliance underscored each polite word.

Dakota kicked herself again. She'd have to give her mother something. "I didn't want to upset you. We had a peeping Tom in the pool area the other night, so when you come, don't be surprised by the armed guards."

The bloated pause told Dakota that her effort to reassure had crashed and burned. Glancing at the security-lit veranda and knowing Matteo would be outside the door most of the night made it easier to recall Pantoja's intrusion.

"Just how armed?" The Fox didn't miss a thing.

Dakota's sigh didn't buy nearly enough time to conjure a plausible response. "Military-grade weapons, camo, everything. But the Salazars aren't part of a drug cartel, I swear." Dakota scolded herself for volunteering her crime-lord suspicions. "It's just different here."

"The plantation simply happens to have an army? They didn't call the police?"

"I don't think there *are* cops. It's very remote. I bet everyone who lives in the jungle has their own security."

"A prowler hardly requires a military response. There's more."

"Yeah, you're right, but it's actually kinda good. Just not something to discuss on the phone." Dakota didn't dare reveal her cell might be bugged. The Fox would freak.

Dead air reigned for several seconds. "All right. Even though I think I should grab the next plane, I'm trusting you. I'll expect good news when I arrive next Tuesday."

"Definitely. Mom, the wedding planner has me booked all day tomorrow. I've got to get some Z's."

"I understand. Kelsi's thrilled you've taken over, by the way."

Dakota chuckled. "Yeah, she just doesn't want to give up one minute with Jaime."

They said their goodbyes and, with a sigh of relief, Dakota disconnected. At least she'd put off dealing with her mother a few more days. Glancing at the patio door, she wished Matteo would return. Worried. She was worried about him.

Chapter Fourteen

About an hour ago, the few working streetlights of the thriving Manaus market had turned on, and the blackmailer's team had vacated the area. Not once had Matteo caught Pantoja's scent. However, several armed men had surveilled the meet site. Their extortionist was one cagy son of a bitch.

After a last scan of the poorly lit, canopy-lined street, Matteo nodded at Jaime, and the two rose from behind a dumpster. For the last several hours, they had endured the narrow alley's rancid fishmonger garbage stench mixed with assorted bodily fluids. More than once, Matteo had cursed his sensitive nose.

His jaguar night vision hadn't deteriorated, either, and now that the sun had dropped away, the dark hid nothing. Fortunately, jaguar pupils were round, or he'd have another feline trait to hide.

A light rain pattered the cement walkway bordering the tattered market booths. Wavering along the dropped-canvas storefronts, a happy couple helped each other navigate the straight sidewalk.

In reflex, Matteo reached for the semi-automatic at his hip, courtesy of Alejandro. The foreman's twenty-first century weapons refresher class had taken a good chunk of the afternoon.

The couple's laughter grew faint, and Matteo relaxed until he sensed raindrops on his face. He looked up at the concerning murky night sky, while beads of water covered his open palm. "If rain washes away the blackmailer's scent, our hunt is over."

"A little shower won't hide a trail from me in jag form. I'll go cat if needed."

"You black like your *papai*?"

"Yes. I'll be nothing but shadow to human eyes." Pausing in obvious thought, Jaime's dark brows knit together. "Since we didn't show, you don't worry they'll publish the video?"

At least he'd had brains enough to think the scenario through. One more time, Matteo played it out to reassure himself as much as Jaime. "If they do, they lose their leverage and any advantage over other contenders."

Jaime nodded, apparently satisfied.

Matteo led him along the alley paralleling the business stalls. Zigzagging back and forth between the booth tents, he checked for their blackmailer's scent.

After interrupting a drug sale, and more than one carnal transaction, he glanced at Jaime. "I'm sure the tapeworm was here, but I can't find his trail."

"We've got all night, my friend. Keep looking."

His words bolstered Matteo. Though he had no need of the younger shifter's acceptance, he truly regretted his base mating challenge.

"I never apologized for my feral greeting when we met. I was … not myself." He couldn't meet Jaime's eyes. Had a male tried to take Anna, only one would have walked away—Matteo.

Jaime snorted. "When I first caught Kelsi's scent, I was no better. Men died."

"Cristiano told me. Justified, every one. Protecting a mate is non-negotiable." Matteo gave an apologetic half grin. "And I was too quick to judge you an unseasoned whelp. You've grown into a good man. That's why I assigned you to this mission."

As they paced through yet another narrow lane between tents, Jaime seemed to walk taller. Matteo thought him young, but at seventy-eight, Jaime was well into maturity. While Matteo had run to ground in the jungle, life had gone on.

"I should've spotted this from the beginning. Best view of our meet, right here." The wide-leafed shrubbery edging a corner barbershop carried Pantoja's scent. The higher vantage point and cover explained why the merc had never showed himself. No need to. They'd found other scents, but this was the man they sought. "You detect the hints of gun residue?"

Jaime turned in a small circle. "Yes, faint to my human nose, but I caught the same outside Dakota's door."

"We've got what we came for. It appears he has a well-trained team for back up. In a few hours, we'll return, track him, and with luck, find him alone."

****

Buzzing atop the wooden nightstand jolted Dakota from a comatose sleep. The day before, hours of wasted effort tracking the blackmailers' server trail had nearly made her head explode. Then, last night, worry while Jaime and Matteo chased bad guys until after midnight had put her in the near dead category.

Conscious, if not fully oriented, she grabbed the offending cell phone and stared at the Fox's contact picture. *Three o'clock in the morning?* Dakota groaned.

In small comfort, Matteo's shadow still showed through the verticals. He sat outside her veranda threshold. After returning way late from his scouting mission, he'd parked there, as though sleep were optional. The reassuring thought of him near made her smile.

Somewhat bolstered, she opened the Fox's text.

Mom: **I'm too worried. I'm on the next plane.**

Great. Dealing with her mother in this mess would be brutal. One thing Dakota had learned over the years: it wasn't worth arguing with the Fox. *I'm nothing like her—Kelsi's so wrong.*

145

Dakota: **Let me know arrival time ASAP. I'll arrange for their helicopter.**

Mom: **No seats on today's flight, so I'll be in tomorrow evening.**

Dakota: **Great. I'll shop in the city. I can meet you at the airport whenever.**

Today's flight. Like all days started at three AM. Another text gave a flight number and arrival time. Dakota dropped the back of her hand on her forehead, shielding her eyes from nothing. *Epic disaster.* First thing in the morning, after coffee, she'd tactfully prepare Kelsi for Mom's imminent arrival.

****

Alejandro took over sentry duty outside Dakota's room at around four AM.

"Thanks. If all goes well, we'll be back around eleven." Before leaving, Matteo opened her patio door and found her soundly asleep. Innocent, curled on her side, she hugged a pillow to her chest. Indulging in her scent, he lingered longer than needed to ensure her safety.

Matteo met Jaime and Paulo at the helipad. Neither shifter male had wanted to stay in Manaus, so far from the queens.

Jaime tossed a light backpack into the cabin. "Paulo, just a drop off at the airport. We'll use other transportation for our return."

"*Sim, senhor.*" Paulo climbed into the right-hand pilot's seat.

Hauling their prisoner out in broad daylight would be too risky. Someone would spot them and notify the police. Matteo and Jaime leaped into the passenger cabin.

Yawning, Matteo clicked his four-point harness into the shiny round buckle. "You wish we'd stayed the night in Manaus?"

Jaime gave a half smile. "No. Not at all."

Mates didn't tolerate separation well. Matteo imagined Dakota snuggled in the sheets again. "Me neither."

Both males napped for the short trip through the star-filled night. When the wheels touched down, Matteo woke fully alert. "Your driver reliable?"

"Absolutely. He'll be waiting." Jaime tapped Paulo's shoulder and handed him several bills. "Tell Bento this arrival is discreet. He'll understand."

Paulo nodded. "I'll make certain."

Matteo and Jaime met Jaime's chauffer at the helipad's private parking lot. *Samuel's Limousine* stamped the bleary-eyed man's navy polo shirt. He dropped them a kilometer from Pantoja's apartment.

Late the night before, when they'd returned to the plantation, Dakota had provided an impressive portfolio on their blackmailer, including his address and his Fiat's license plate number.

She'd casually explained that she couldn't sleep. However, after Matteo took up his station outside her door, she'd drifted off within minutes. He tried not to read too much into it.

Jaime handed Samuel some cash.

The driver's eyes brightened at sight of the folded bills of *real*. "A full day, *senhor*?"

"Yes. However, we were never here." Jaime stared at Samuel until the driver's smile fell away.

"*Sim*." He nodded and slid the cash into the pocket of his khaki-colored slacks. "Never here."

Matteo scanned the sky. The moon still hung well above the trees. They'd made good time. He and Jaime jogged to the nearby apartment building. Pantoja's blue sedan sat in the rear parking lot. The plates matched up.

Thank you, Dakota.

The two males crouched behind yet another stinking dumpster, awaiting their prey. Matteo fingered the plastic zip-ties in the pocket of his lightweight utility pants. In the quiet night, a solitary plover chirped a melody. The little bird seemed to urge the sunrise. In apparent response, a lamp came to life behind their target's first-floor window, silhouetting the moving figure inside.

Minutes later, tall, dressed in jeans and an untucked yellow knit shirt, Pantoja emerged from the building's back entrance. A bulge at his trim waist hinted at a weapon.

Pausing at the threshold, he surveyed the dimly lit parking lot. With his rounded tribal features, the dark-skinned mercenary made Matteo think of the savvy jungle men who searched a shoreline before drawing water. *Patience.*

As Pantoja approached his Fiat, Jaime tensed, but Matteo gripped his forearm in a soundless command to wait. Jaime froze, and the plover fell silent.

Pantoja circled his car, inspecting the exterior and undercarriage, as though he expected a hidden explosive device. After Dakota found him, and the shifters stood him up, he had to know he was at risk. Apparently satisfied, he returned to the driver's side door and reached into his pocket.

With a lift of his chin, Matteo launched their attack. The pair rocketed around either side of the car. Pantoja looked up too late, not that it would have mattered. Matteo gripped his throat, simultaneously trapping the merc's right arm under his own. Slamming the scum's head into the car's roof, he left a dent.

Pantoja roared with the impact. Jaime stayed close, but didn't interfere.

"I give." Air hissed through Pantoja's closed larynx. No doubt, the trained soldier knew death loomed.

"You live at my pleasure. Do not forget." Snarling next to his ear, Matteo spat his quiet words. He glanced at Jaime. "Disarm him."

Already holding Pantoja's semi-auto handgun, Jaime stowed the man's car keys in his jeans pocket. He looked into the merc's terror-filled eyes. "My friend here has a short fuse. Don't light it."

Pantoja nodded, lowering a fisted hand to his side.

Jaime patted him down, and extracted a twenty-centimeter knife from a calf sheath. Gripping the blade's spine in his teeth, he continued his search.

Even though Jaime had vowed to stay on task, Matteo had worried he'd take revenge over his mate's near murder. Jaime's control amazed Matteo. He doubted he could do the same.

Waving a cell phone between them like a prized find, Jaime pulled his lips back in a sinister smile around the blade. With quick movements, he dismantled the device and slid the parts into his pocket.

He released his toothy grip on the knife and held it loose at his side. "His owners might be able to track his phone without a battery. However, it's worth the risk. Alejandro, or maybe your Dakota, can make use of it."

Matteo nodded. *My Dakota.* The phrase sounded natural, right. Others had already detected his sense of possession. Somehow, he'd been the last to notice. "Good work. Search the vehicle—under seats and all compartments."

Jaime rifled through the car and shook his head at Matteo. His quick rummaging hunt had appeared thorough. After he scanned the parking lot, he snapped the slide back on the confiscated nine-millimeter.

Returning to Matteo, who still restrained their prisoner, Jaime leveled the gun at Pantoja. "I've got him."

Matteo nodded. Loosening his grip, he allowed Pantoja a deep breath. "When I let go, you're going to get behind the wheel for a Sunday drive. Got it?"

With a wordless, hateful glare, the black-eyed man nodded.

Still keen to rip out Pantoja's throat, Matteo released him. Pantoja had stolen a joyous experience from Dakota. Instead of reveling in her primary shift, this man's threats of exposure had terrorized her.

The worm complied, sliding into the car without a fight, leaving Matteo deeply disappointed.

****

While Dakota searched for her sister in the huge home, she sipped coffee with an urgency unusual even for her. She'd slept late, and a headache threatened. "There you are."

"Good morning, Sleeping Beauty." Kelsi sat at a table in the breakfast nook. She pushed out a wooden chair with her foot. Behind her, an expansive bow window framed a panoramic view of the Salazar hibiscus garden.

"I've got a good excuse." Dakota plopped onto the upholstered seat. "Mom texted me around three AM."

Kelsi knitted her brows. "Everything okay?"

"For me or her?" Dakota didn't allow an answer. "No. I screwed up big time."

Kelsi propped her elbows on the table, cradling her chin on her hands. "How so?"

Dakota replayed her conversation with the Fox. "She seemed okay—then bam—she's on the way."

Kelsi looked down at the table in obvious thought. "It might be better she's early, anyway. We have lots of explaining to do. Maybe she'll have time to adjust before the wedding day."

Relieved by Kelsi's logic, Dakota sighed. "I suppose."

Glancing at her phone, her sister grimaced. "The dressmaker's coming for my final fitting tomorrow afternoon—can you meet Mom at the airport?"

"Sure." Dakota puffed a breath. The Fox annoyed the hell out of her, but she couldn't imagine life without her mother. "It's weird. You always think your parents will die first. Now, knowing I'll live a couple hundred years, the thought of outliving Mom sucks. You think the Fox is a latent, too?"

"I want her to be—so bad." Kelsi's gaze misted over.

Her own eyes stinging, Dakota clasped her sister's hand. "But we'll have each other, no matter what."

"You have no idea how relieved I am. I was afraid I'd outlive everyone." Kelsi squeezed back and dabbed her eyes with a napkin. "You liking it? Being a shifter?"

"Oh yeah." Dakota laughed. "*Meow.*"

Kelsi joined in with a mood-lifting chuckle. "When are you going back out?"

"Soon. There's just too much to do for the wedding. And I still need to buy a dress." *And kidnap a guy, maybe kill another.* Guilt over keeping Kelsi in the dark beat at Dakota. Her lips parted before she squelched the urge to tell all. Some secrets were necessary. A bride should focus on her wedding, not blackmailers.

"Speaking of ... *Senhora* Vargas sent a confirmation email. She'll be here in twenty." Kelsi gave a half-smile. "I'm glad you got up on your own. I didn't want to wake you."

Dakota raised her mug. "All good. I just need

more liquid motivation."

"Oh, and Alejandro says he needs to talk to her, too. Security stuff. He'll look you up."

"Okay. Thanks." Dakota rose with her empty cup in hand and headed toward the buffet, pleased she didn't have to find him to arrange the chopper.

Sipping another jolt of caffeine at a poolside table, Dakota checked her neglected social networks while waiting for the wedding planner. Possible posts scrolled through her mind.

Life event: **Hi all, big news. I turned into a ginormous white jaguar and it was awesome!**

"Good morning, *Senhorita* Dakota." Alejandro perused Consuelo's breakfast fare, loading a plate of eggs and sausage. He poured a glass of juice. "The wedding lady meets you here?"

"Any minute. Glad you're early, though. I need a favor."

He pulled out a chair, the metal legs scraping the concrete, and sat across from her. Cutting his eggs and coating his entire breakfast in the creamy yolks, he seemed more intent on the food than her favor. "Anything, *senhorita*."

"My mother's changed her schedule and arrives at Eduardo Gomes tomorrow evening. I need to meet her. Could I get a helicopter limo ride?"

"We send the chopper—easy." Pausing mid-bite, Alejandro lowered his forkful of yolked-drenched sausage. His lips thinned to a line, and he glanced at the camo-clad sentry passing by the wrought iron façade. "But *Enforcer* want you to stay on plantation. Bad security."

The thought of needing Matteo's approval for anything scorched her hide. She tried to keep her tone civil. "If you send guards for her, she'll freak. So, I need to meet her. How can we make that happen?"

"I ask Cristiano."

"Thank you." Needing Cristiano's permission didn't set any better with her.

Alejandro tapped his phone's keypad and then drained his glass. Dakota sipped her coffee, trying to stay casual. After a couple donut holes disappeared, his phone chirped. "Cristiano say schedule chopper and Matteo decide the rest."

****

Matteo guarded a cuffed and shackled Pantoja in the back of their rented boat. The convenient toothed-plastic ties had impressed Matteo. Midmorning sun beat down on all three men. Jaime manned the helm, navigating the backwaters he knew so well. Twisting in the rear-facing bench, Matteo handed him a wide-brimmed hat and plopped another on his own head.

As planned, they'd ditched Pantoja's car in the jungle before hiking to an unmarked river. Considering they had traveled at a human pace, they'd made good time. The merc still refused to confirm his name. They would learn all soon enough.

Little appeared familiar to Matteo. The waterways had shifted since his last travels here. The current sluiced against the dilapidated craft, rocking the small motor boat. Matteo glanced at the mat-covered floor again to make sure they hadn't taken on water from an unseen leak.

Small wonder, the sight of Jaime's wad of *real* had evaporated the boat owner's curiosity. Suddenly blind, the river man had obligingly disappeared.

In the back seat, sweat beaded on Pantoja's forehead, and streamed down his cheek to a wet ring circling his collar. A drop of perspiration slid into his eye, and he showed no reaction to the certain sting.

Glancing at a baseball cap resting on the bench's cracked padding, Pantoja clung to his stoic silence.

"It probably has lice." Matteo snatched the bill of the hat and reached to place it on Pantoja's head. "Parasites avoid us, but it's all yours."

Pulling back, the blackmailer narrowed his eyes. "Fuck you."

Matteo dropped the cap beside him. "You should take what comfort you can. It's *very* early."

"Time to blindfold him," Jaime tossed over his shoulder.

Nodding, Matteo lifted his pantlet and unsheathed the confiscated knife at his calf. "Your holster and blade are top quality."

Matteo rose and reached for Pantoja's midsection with the knife, and the man startled. It didn't hurt to keep him on edge. Grabbing the hem of his yellow shirt, Matteo cut a wide strip off the bottom.

"Sit up." He made quick work of the blindfold, wrapping it twice to fashion a sweatband. Odd, he concerned himself with this small comfort, when he intended to torture the man. Years in the jungle had made him soft.

An hour later, the cross on the Salazar chapel came into view.

Jaime throttled back, and the straining motor slowed. He steered the craft to the shore and lined up with the dock.

****

Seated in a cream-colored armchair with papers strewn on the matching ottoman, Dakota checked her phone again. Eleven-thirty. Matteo and Jaime should arrive with their captured blackmailer any minute, but she'd heard nothing from Alejandro or Cristiano. She needed to wrap things up with *Senhora* Vargas, sitting across from her.

The experienced event manager had taken Alejandro's security protocols in stride. The venue now included a metal detector, cell phone check station, and discreetly armed guards. Before he'd taken his leave, Alejandro asked Consuelo to set the women up in the air-conditioned comfort of the parlor. *It hadn't been that hot.*

"So only the closest family in the sweet little chapel?" *Senhora* Vargas's question brought Dakota back to their conversation.

Half attending, she nodded.

"While here, I should see the space. I need more measurements." The *senhora*'s comment jolted Dakota. The dock sat right next to the chapel.

"Today isn't good. We have—have—" Panicking, her lack of an excuse short-circuited her brain.

Senhora Vargas lifted a penciled-in brow. "The wedding is only days away. I need the measurements now."

Oh, shit! Dakota had to get rid of her. It was steaming outside. The scenic route without a courtesy four-wheeler should scare her off. "Um, okay. It's quite a walk, but follow me."

Taking the rear exit onto the Salazar grounds at an impolite speed, Dakota led the planner toward the cobbled path. Perspiration dotted *Senhora* Vargas's round face, and, breathing hard, she hustled to keep up.

Dakota flinched inside. *Necessary cruelty.* She pointed into the distance. "It's near the river, over the rise. See the steeple and…"

At the far edge of the garden, Cristiano and Alejandro strode purposefully toward the chapel—and the boat dock. Those dogs were leaving without her. Stopping dead, Dakota glared at the pair, and the rushing plump woman collided with her backside.

Grabbing the matron's arm to steady her, Dakota was out of time for diplomacy. "I'm so sorry, but I just remembered something I've got to do. It can't wait."

The stunned woman widened dark eyes. "But-but—"

"Absolutely *cannot wait.*" Dakota wheeled toward the house, practically dragging the sputtering wedding planner with her. "We'll get whatever you need—*tomorrow.* Promise."

She handed the flummoxed *Senhora* Vargas off to an equally dumbfounded Consuelo and bolted out the back door, breaking into a ground-eating jog. Fortunately, she'd been anticipating a hike and had donned running clothes first thing. Cresting a rise, Dakota spotted the two men.

Cristiano must've heard her closing in on them. Halting, he turned, and at sight of her, heaved a sigh. His disappointment was visible from yards away. The men waited for her.

Dakota stopped with her hands on her hips. "Not cool, Cristiano. Why?"

The two men shared a look, and Alejandro shrugged his shoulders. Cristiano frowned. "This is ugly business, *senhorita.* We only wish to protect you."

Alejandro gave a sage nod, making Dakota want to smack him.

They'd grounded her to the plantation, and now they'd tried to leave her behind. Stepping into Cristiano's personal space, she used every bit of her five-foot-nine height to get nose-to-chin. "Too late. I'm in this. You can't bench me now that it's game time."

****

Alejandro and Cristiano stood look out from the stone sanctuary's higher ground. Matteo waved an arm at the pair, as they strode down the hill to the wood-decked landing. Dakota emerged from the steepled building and broke to a jog to join them.

As she trod over the boardwalk to a gazebo over the water, Matteo couldn't take his eyes from her. Her favored fake-diamond clip secured her hair atop her head, and the graceful lines of her neck made him want to nip her flesh. Stretchy pink fabric shaped her firm breasts, and snug matching shorts barely covered the top inch of her taut thighs.

Turning back to the rear of the boat, looking at the bound prisoner, Matteo's heart sank. Dakota had been too softhearted to kill her hated agouti prey. A shifter interrogating a human might scare her from Brazil—and Matteo.

Jaime groaned. "*Papai* failed us."

He tossed a line to Alejandro, who tied the aged-nylon strap to a post. Jaime leaped onto the dock, and together, they secured the boat.

The Enforcer cell was a good hour's hike into the jungle. While Jaime greeted their welcome party, Matteo cut the merc's ankle ties.

"Stand." Closing in nose-to-nose with the prisoner, he allowed a feline snarl into his voice. "Even as human, we're faster, stronger. Any trouble—you'll meet my other half. Understand?"

The blindfold blocked a good read of Pantoja's response, but his clenched jaw hinted at defiance. Matteo gripped his upper arm. "Step up. Two feet to the dock."

Cristiano nodded a greeting, and Dakota smiled. Alejandro waved their group toward the shore, allowing Matteo to lead with the prisoner. The foreman must have schooled all to silence, and once again, earned Matteo's approval.

He loathed that Dakota walked so near this

miscreant, his shifter instincts demanding he remove the female from risk. Sharing a look with Cristiano, Matteo jutted his chin at her, hoping his friend got the hint. She should go style her hair or select wedding flowers.

Instead, Cristiano shook him off.

Matteo seethed. Females had always been fewer in number, so protecting them was a priority. Never had their women participated in military action. Aside from his concern for Dakota, it was ludicrous to risk injury to either of the two queens they'd found.

****

Following behind Alejandro en route to the Enforcer cell—whatever that was—Dakota batted a fan-shaped leaf from her path. Matteo led their silent party over the moss-covered jungle floor. At least the bugs weren't biting as bad as usual, and her body seemed to be adapting to the swelter.

Still fuming over Cristiano's attempt to exclude her, she embraced Alejandro's order to silence. She tried to read the men, not surprised to detect tension between Cristiano and Matteo. Likely, they'd plotted together to keep her from the interrogation, and her very presence caused the strain.

Or, like her, maybe they weren't as comfortable abducting a man as they'd first thought. With an uncertain prayer for help, she'd failed to leave her worries over kidnapping in the chapel.

Matteo slowed at the base of an unusual, rock-faced hill. Even though bits of rare sunlight dappled the rise, only weak saplings had taken root, as though something unseen prevented their ascension to glory. High above the stunted trees, the far-reaching canopy still obscured any aircraft's line of sight.

Handing his automatic rifle to Cristiano, Alejandro used a machete to hack away a woody vine, exposing a ground level crevice. Surprisingly cool, dry air came from the cave's entrance.

Her gasp of wonder earned a quelling look from Alejandro.

Since an adult needed to stoop to enter, the scene brought Hobbits to mind. In other circumstances, the unusual hollow would have intrigued her sense of adventure.

Jaime led them into the oppressive passageway with a flashlight, followed by Pantoja and Matteo. Cristiano gestured for her to enter and brought up the rear.

After a few yards, the cavity widened and allowed them to walk upright to negotiate the steady descent. Dakota couldn't tell how far they traveled, but several minutes passed before they hit level ground.

Eerie light, akin to dusk, shone in the distance, illuminating foliage claiming the far tunnel's floor. The startling sight prompted a sense of anticipation within Dakota. Matteo, too, it seemed, since he took the lead and quickened their pace toward the patch of green.

The passageway opened to a prehistoric cathedral, housing acres of primeval jungle. Wide irregular-shaped pillars dotted the expanse, seeming to support a domed ceiling a few stories above.

Dakota sucked in an awed breath. No one shushed her this time.

Immense vine-covered rock walls, terraced with plateaus of tropical greenery, climbed to meet the natural vaults above. In crowning glory, a narrow thirty-foot waterfall filled a tiny stream, lifting a miniature cloud of mist. The bubbling water laced through the center of the underground jungle. Expecting a T-rex sighting, Dakota had the sense she had teleported back to primordial Earth.

As they marched for several minutes over rocky terrain, Dakota realized the enormity of the cave. Matteo raised his fist, and they halted at a rugged cliff face covered with tropical greenery. On closer inspection, creeping foliage obscured a wall of bars set in stone.

Adding to the mystery, in the rock above the opening, the eyes of a primitive jaguar relief peered through the woody vines. The hewn cat's gaze followed her, giving her the sense that the inanimate beast watched with sentient awareness.

Again, Alejandro put his machete to work, the sound of metal on metal pulling her attention. The vines dropped away and revealed a rusty barred gate securing a bedroom-sized niche. A prison cell. The Enforcer cell.

The rounded space held the foul stench of a poisoned mouse found too late. Inside, at precise intervals, smaller feline carvings adorned the rounded cave wall. A tattered mattress on the floor and a sturdy ladder-back chair furnished the chamber. Varying shades of reddish-brown stains on the pallet brought bile to Dakota's throat, and she shot a sympathetic glance at Pantoja.

Alejandro keyed open an ancient padlock, and the heavy rusted links clunked free of the bars. Jaime forced the gate open and its hinges objected, their screech boosted by the natural stone amphitheater. Dakota covered her ears, wondering how Matteo could stand it.

Seeming unaffected, he escorted Pantoja inside and pushed him onto the wooden chair. He removed the shredded yellow blindfold.

Pantoja blinked and looked around. His gaze darted to the small cat carving behind Matteo. For an instant, the prisoner's eyes widened with what could only be fear. Something about the relief frightened him. Dakota studied the cat's face. Like the one outside, the eyes seemed to look sideways at her.

"This cell's made for our kind. There's no escape. For now, we'll leave your dainty fetters in place."

Fetters? Matteo likely used English for her benefit, but his take on the plastic-tie handcuffs gave her pause. Seventy-plus years of catch-up must be overwhelming.

Looking at him with new eyes, she sensed a determined, charged fury—and no sign of the impetuous bum who'd taunted her with sugary lips. She wondered what had changed him.

"Yes, Pantoja, look around." Matteo waved at the stone walls and gestured to the bars separating them from Dakota and the others. "Or should I call you swine?"

Mr. Swarthy—Pantoja—lifted his chin with a sneer.

A blur of motion shot from Matteo's side. In the same instant, blood gushed from Pantoja's nose, and a spray of crimson marred Matteo's sleeveless white t-shirt. The lightning-fast strike had been invisible.

"Just, *wow*." Dakota mouthed the words to no one.

"I give you nothing." The prisoner spat blood and Portuguese. He sent a hateful glare to the group, settling on Jaime. "You murdered my friends and—and…"

Chapter Fifteen

One to pick up languages easily, Dakota wasn't surprised she understood Pantoja. However, both his emotional charge of murder, and the ease with which Matteo inflicted damage, disturbed her. As far as she knew, Jaime had only killed the traffickers who had kidnapped Kelsi.

At Dakota's side, Jaime's exposed skin glowed an ominous ultraviolet, the halo adding size to his already formidable bulk. Narrowing ice-blue threat at their *guest*, he bolted into the cell with whirlwind speed and shouldered in front of Matteo. Jaime leaned his radiant mass over Pantoja, dwarfing the human male.

Heart racing, Dakota clutched the cell's metal bars, bracing for a nuclear detonation.

"You claim *murder*?" A rumbled growl stole any human quality from Jaime's voice. "I'd already given up, but your friend Erico slit my mate's throat. He left her to bleed out for fun."

Dakota's mouth fell open, and her own flesh took on an iridescent sheen, reflecting against the bars she held in a death grip. Kelsi had edited her harrowing abduction story.

Blinding rage, well beyond anything she'd held for the rodent world, threatened to take her wits. Silently urging Jaime to rip out Pantoja's throat, her conscience ignored her unspeakable thoughts.

"Not my friend, I swear." His defiant bravado disappeared, and breathing hard, white edged Pantoja's rounded eyes. "I transport large jaguar. I didn't know about the girl until after."

In his terror, Pantoja bounced between Portuguese and English. He shot a tear-filled glance to

Dakota. Knowledge of imminent death carved his expression, and filled with wrath, she had no sympathy. She glared at the rat bastard who'd tried to murder her sister.

Grabbing his hair, Jaime cranked the prisoner's head back, leaning in nose-to-nose. His jaguar roar vibrated the bars under Dakota's sweaty hands, and she flinched. Grim-faced, Cristiano and Alejandro looked on with no sign they'd intervene.

Unintimidated by Jaime's meltdown, Matteo stuck close to his side, giving the impression he might halt the unfolding insanity. However, Jaime appeared unstoppable. And Dakota couldn't make herself eke out a protest—part of her still rooted for Jaime to end the slimeball.

Pantoja twisted in the chair, screaming, and turned terrified, pleading eyes to her—*human* eyes. Bright crimson pulsed from his nostrils, and fluid streamed from under his seat, a dark puddle blooming beneath him. Urine odor joined blood's copper tang in the stone cell. *Oh Jesus!*

Unable to control her shocked reaction, Dakota gaped at the real-life nightmare. Jaime gripped Pantoja's throat, forcing the prisoner to look at him. "Your voice is familiar—*Jose*—you called on *Nuno's* radio. *Nuno* couldn't hear your hails, but *I* did."

For an instant, Pantoja sidelined his terror, and rage flashed in his eyes. "Worthless scum, don't you dare say his name." Then, his expression contorted to grief. "You—you slaughtered him."

Dakota's gasp underscored their prisoner's sob. Seeing Jaime on the cusp of violent homicide, she *knew* he'd killed Nuno. Making it worse, Jose Pantoja hadn't taken an active role in Kelsi's capture—he'd been in the air. With a shuddering breath, she leaned her cheek against the cool steel bars. Dakota believed Pantoja. And clearly, Nuno had been more than a teammate.

Kelsi's life had been on the line, making Nuno's death necessary. Dakota would never fault Jaime for saving her sister. Still, her gut said Pantoja hadn't been involved. Guilt weighed heavy in her chest, made worse by dreading Jaime's next move. She sent Matteo a pleading look. Meeting her gaze, he sighed.

Instantly, he wrapped an arm around Jaime's torso and, with deceptive ease, Matteo manhandled the much larger, furious male to the wall. Swinging ham-sized fists, Jaime gave no quarter. Cristiano said nothing, but his jaw clenched so tight, Dakota wondered if he'd crack a tooth.

Wedging a forearm at Jaime's throat, Matteo held him against the stone wall. "I'm with you, but use your head. We need him alive."

Jaime snarled in Matteo's face, and after a tense few seconds, the menacing blue-black halo receded. He seemed to regain control, lowering clenched fists to his sides. Dakota dropped her forehead against her arm in relief.

Matteo straightened, releasing him. "Good man. Take everyone out. I work alone. Lock us down and leave the key within reach."

Jaime complied, steadfastly ignoring the prisoner as he exited the cell.

The grieving Pantoja, whom Dakota had wished dead, hadn't kidnapped Kelsi or even harmed her. *I would've let them kill him.* She trembled with the realization. Dakota had committed to eliminate—*assassinate*—their enemy. Now, with Pantoja's blood and piss pooled on the stone, her appetite for vengeance waned.

Worse, like Jaime, Dakota had allowed her

emotions to blind her. Pantoja was their only source of information. However weak her stomach, they still had to deal with Pantoja—and his handlers. Even if he hadn't tried to kill Kelsi, he wasn't innocent. If they exposed Dakota and Kelsi to the world, she and her sister would end up in a lab somewhere. Or, more likely, as Matteo suspected, Pantoja's powerful owners would find a way to study the shifters on the down-low. A dreadful shiver ran through her.

Cristiano met Jaime with a man hug, and Alejandro set the key on the ground just outside the cell. Ready to leave, the three men looked expectantly at Dakota.

With a glance at Pantoja, she retreated a step. "I'm staying."

"*No.* You're not." From inside the cell, Matteo slammed the barred gate shut, and the metallic bang reverberated like a gunshot.

They needed the information in Pantoja's head to protect themselves. And Matteo seemed to know how to get it. A disgusting, cowardly part of Dakota wanted to let him. However, leaving wasn't an option.

Shaking her head so hard her hair fell from her clip, she glared at him. "I led you to Pantoja, so I'm responsible for what happens here. I'm not leaving."

Scanning the small group, Matteo returned his attention to her. "Suit yourself, but I still work alone."

"Sure, no problem."

After sharing a hesitant look with Jaime, Alejandro gestured to a backpack leaning against the rails. "*Senhorita,* water and supplies are inside."

"Dakota, this is no place for a lady. You need to come with us." Cristiano's paternal tone reminded her of her late father's troubled warnings after little-girl schoolyard scuffles.

Daddy had been gone for years, and she missed him most during big events, like graduations and big decisions—like *should she allow torture*. Finally, she'd pointed her stubborn nature in the right direction. Daddy would be proud. The Fox, too, if she knew—but she'd never hear a word about today.

"I can't." She lifted her chin in defiance. "I won't."

****

Jaime had let the swamp scum Pantoja have two seconds of eye contact with Dakota, and now Matteo had an audience. He riveted his gaze on her, daring rebellion. "No entrance into the cell for any reason, understood?"

"Yes," she whispered.

In the decades before Hitler's war, Matteo had hidden his *Enforcer* role from Anna. As any good mate, he'd protected his queen from the darker parts of their world. Now, he allowed a female to witness an interrogation.

Disgust already lined Dakota's elegant features, though the swine suffered nothing more than a broken nose. *I repulse her.* Shifters' lives depended on this intel. He couldn't allow her presence to shake his resolve. They needed Pantoja's master.

Matteo's expression must have shown his unexpected reticence, because hers softened. "I understand what's at stake."

It was the best he'd get. Matteo nodded before stepping to his prisoner, still seated and cuffed. "Do *you* know what's at stake? For you?"

Pantoja darted fearful eyes at Dakota. Matteo slapped him, holding back on a closed fist. Irritated with himself, he snarled. "Every time you look to her for mercy, I'll answer. Are we clear?"

"When I'm dead, she'll hate you." Glaring at him,

Pantoja honed in on his Achilles' heel. Matteo had failed to hide his vulnerability for the queen.

Somehow, he had to regain control of this interrogation. No prisoner had dared to speak to him this way, nor had Matteo ever withheld punishment, barring a strategic objective. Worse, his exposed weakness had given the merc hope.

Focusing on Pantoja, Dakota pushed wisps of hair from her face, her expression a mix of sympathy and fear. Tears hovered on her lower lashes. After today, she would always see Matteo as the thug who had tortured a defenseless human. *Hope's keen edge cuts shifters, too.*

Resigned to his loss, he gripped Pantoja's trachea, squeezing until a dusky blue tinged his lips. The man writhed on the chair, sliding his tethered feet in the dirt in a vain attempt to escape.

Leaning in, Matteo switched to Portuguese. "You're wiser than you look, Jose. Forget about me. Let's focus on you—and the fragile human larynx. Who owns you? Each time you breathe out, a name better come with it."

Matteo loosened his hold, and low-pitched wheezes accompanied Pantoja's two labored gasps. "Fuck. You."

Squeezing his throat again, Matteo silenced Pantoja's harmonic breaths. Red spider veins burst into the whites of his swollen, watering eyes. Again, he bucked against Matteo's grip.

The gate hinges shrieked. *Goddammit.* Matteo kept his gaze riveted on Pantoja, and the man slanted his eyes toward the approaching Dakota. Matteo slapped him, but still allowed him another wheezing breath.

Pantoja looked past Matteo, and his pupils dilated.

Unable to resist, Matteo looked over his shoulder.

Dakota faced the wall, tracing a lazy finger over one of the jaguar carvings. Pantoja's gaze never left her. She turned toward Matteo and his prisoner, her fingers absently stroking the stone muzzle. "Please. Let me talk to him. Just for a minute. Then I'll leave, I promise."

She paced to Matteo and rested a damp hand on his shoulder. The cool cave temperature hadn't caused her clammy skin.

Uncertain of what he'd just witnessed, he released Pantoja's throat and waited for his seal-bark coughs to still. The merc gaped at Dakota as though she had three heads. For some reason, Pantoja feared her. Matteo grabbed the man's face, furtively digging into submandibular pressure points.

As he intended, the maneuver forced the prisoner's gaze to his. "If I even think you might harm her, you're a dead man."

"Did you just threaten to kill him?" Dakota understood more Portuguese than Matteo realized. The censure in her voice stung him anew.

With a warning glare at Pantoja, Matteo released him and straightened. "I instructed him to be respectful."

Pantoja tried unsuccessfully to rub his jaw with his shoulder. "*Sonofabitch.*"

Matteo looked away. No matter how necessary, inflicting pain always stole something from him; however, his squeamish audience made it impossible to keep his remorse buried.

Dakota lowered to her haunches, putting her eye level with the seated man. Placing both hands on his face in a near caress, she lightly massaged Pantoja's jawline—in the nerve's exact location. Flinching at her initial touch, he relaxed within an instant. Dakota had detected the small punishment. Since she had broken a man's arm, Matteo should've guessed she had formal martial arts training. Women *had* changed.

Even without eye contact, her tender care of the prisoner telegraphed her disapproval. "Did you know that your friends planned to kidnap my sister, Kelsi?"

Breathing freely, now, Pantoja shook his head. He lifted a hesitant glance at Matteo.

"Did you know Erico planned to sell her to a slaver in Russia?"

"No."

"Is that the kind of man you are, Jose? One who thinks women should be slaves?"

"No."

"And your friends? Did they know Erico's plot?"

"They hunt big jaguar."

"But they abducted Kelsi. Your friends followed Erico's orders and tied her up. Nuno didn't tell you about her, did he? He said, 'get the chopper ready for a big cat,' didn't he?" Dakota had switched to very good Portuguese, likely attempting to make Pantoja more comfortable.

His eyes brightened, and he squared his shoulders. In that instant, Matteo sensed genuine hope take root in the dog's heart. The lying swine nodded with enthusiasm. "Yes, *sim*."

It would take hours to undo the damage Dakota caused his interrogation. At least he would have privacy—that is, if she kept her word to leave. *Like her promise to not enter the cell.*

"Your friends didn't want to kill anyone. Did they?"

"No." Pantoja appeared more encouraged with every answer.

"However, Erico slit her throat." Dakota's voice broke. "I want to kill him, but he's already dead. That same evil man lured your friends into something wicked."

Pantoja's eyes shone with unshed tears. She used psychological warfare, putting the two of them on the same team. Watching transfixed, Matteo fell under her spell. Either Dakota's compassion was genuine, or she was the best actress he'd ever seen.

"You loved Nuno, didn't you?"

"*Sim.*" A sob hitched Pantoja's voice, and a tear slid down his cheek.

Dakota's eyes shone with sympathy, and she laid a hand on his forearm. "Jose, I'm so very sorry for your loss."

Pantoja appeared as surprised as Matteo. After a beat, the mercenary seemed to believe her. "Thank you, *senhorita.*"

The soldiers had followed Erico's orders without hesitation. Since Pantoja flew the helicopter above the jungle, he might not have known of his lover's complicity. However, Matteo didn't buy his innocence. Mercs had few morals. Plus, Pantoja worked for someone bigger and badder. There's no way Dakota had overlooked that detail. What was she doing?

Using partial truths, she had sounded so heartfelt—and absolutely frightening. Matteo cleared his throat, signaling her to get to the point.

"Jose, your friends helped a bad man. They stumbled onto the shifters. Will you help us protect ourselves?"

He shook his head. "They will kill me—with ease."

"We can protect you. Tell us who's after us, and you can walk away." She made promises for the shifters. However, if Matteo had thought of it, he'd have done the same. He let the offer stand.

Silence stretched while Pantoja looked from her

to Matteo, and then at the floor, plainly distressed, while weighing his options. The worm appeared truly forsaken. "Your enemy is too strong."

Even without the facts, Matteo recognized Pantoja's desolate honesty, and his heart sank.

By her troubled frown, Dakota must've sensed the same. Leaning in with a pleading expression, she turned those sea green pools on Pantoja. "Tell us who ... please."

The merc glanced at the jaguar relic again and groaned. "The United States."

"You spy for the U.S.?" Dakota's voice sounded almost strangled.

"No. I look for Nuno's murderer. My boss a U.S. colonel—Army. After he see video, he order assets come to Brazil in hiding." As though it made it easier to answer, Pantoja switched to whispered English.

"Assets?" Dakota didn't seem to understand the term.

Floored by the admission, Matteo stepped toward them. "Military assets?"

At Pantoja's nod, Dakota dropped her head in her hands. Matteo fought the urge to do the same. The Yanks always stuck their fingers into everything. In addition, according to Cristiano, their power and influence had grown exponentially since World War II.

****

An unexpected sense of betrayal assaulted Dakota. "My own country's attacking us."

Seeming unsure how to help, Matteo placed a hand on her shoulder. "I'm sorry."

U.S. military involvement meant serious treachery loomed, trumping any concerns over a leaked video. Scientists solved mysteries, and the military always exploited their discoveries first. "They can only want one thing with our DNA."

Matteo cocked his head a degree, the question in his eyes boring into her. He had no idea of the potential genetic applications.

But Pantoja did. He sucked in a breath. "They make *super* jungle soldier."

"This is true?" Matteo's slack jaw and widened eyes flashed incredulous, before his *Enforcer* mien returned.

She nodded, still processing the implications of U.S. involvement. With America's vast resources, they could run the shifters to ground in no time. Especially any living in Omaha, Nebraska. Having just discovered her true nature, she hadn't had time to do any life planning.

Kelsi would stay in Brazil with Jaime. Dakota admitted that with her own new jaguar persona, she would live here, too. A jaguar needed a jungle, after all. With the decision, she straightened and glanced at Matteo.

"My family's first." To drive home her decision, she switched back to Portuguese. This was about more than protecting Kelsi and herself. Her *species* was under siege. "And my people."

Matteo squeezed her shoulder, bolstering her resolve.

Pantoja just became more important, and Dakota didn't have a clue what she was doing. The prisoner's help was essential. For both their sakes. And when this night was over, she needed to live with herself. To do that, Pantoja needed to cooperate—and to stay in one piece. She would give him every chance, but to keep their people safe, in the end, if she had to, she would leave him to Matteo.

Rising, she paced to the bars and retrieved two

bottles of water from the backpack, along with a hand towel. The clothes and sheets crammed inside told her Alejandro had expected a live prisoner after the interrogation. Relieved they hadn't planned to kill Pantoja, she soaked a healthy corner of the terrycloth.

"Matteo, could you please cut him free? He's been cuffed for hours, and I'm sure he's thirsty."

His *Enforcer* scowl made her smile. After he'd hit the defenseless man, she'd seen the self-disgust in his eyes. He was like a prickly pear, with a harsh exterior and squishy soft middle.

"Jose can't harm me any more than he can hurt you. Plus, you're right here to save me." She batted her lashes twice. If she had to guess, he fought an eyeroll.

However, as Matteo pulled a knife from under his pant leg, all traces of humor disappeared. For a moment, he truly looked like he might use it on Pantoja's throat. In quick, precise moves, Matteo cut the plastic strips at their prisoner's wrists and ankles, and Dakota released a held breath. He leaned in close to Pantoja's ear. "Remember our conversation about respect."

Pantoja worked his shoulders and groaned, rubbing his wrists. Dakota sat quietly, giving him a minute to tend his aches. He stilled and, grimacing, took a deep breath, before he gingerly pulled his nose straight. His eyes teared. "Goddamnit."

"We're sorry about that," Dakota murmured, not quite sure of her own sincerity.

Eyeing them, Matteo pulled a finger across his blade's edge, likely for Pantoja's benefit. He glared at the merc, while he sheathed the weapon at his calf. Dakota was relieved that Matteo kept his thoughts to himself.

Putting concern into her gaze, she knelt next to Pantoja and offered him the open water bottle. He guzzled, collapsing the plastic container, with overflow streaming from the corners of his mouth. She handed him the towel and a fresh bottle of water. "Jose, did you know the shifters are a Brazilian treasure?"

Pantoja didn't respond, but he darted a furtive glance at the jaguar relief. His returned gaze grew more intense.

"You know the Jaguar Princess legend? From the Lenca in Honduras?" Dakota asked.

"A children's tale. Until I saw your sister change, I'd thought my grandfather's stories came from the *ayahuasca* cup." He lifted his chin.

Supposing he meant some kind of jungle moonshine, she smiled. "No, Grandpa wasn't drunk. The princess came from Brazil."

His skittish peek at the jaguar carving confirmed her suspicions. She kept any hint of a threat from her expression, as she rose and paced to the icon. Holding his gaze, she ran a finger down the cat's face. "She's my great-great-great grandmother."

Pantoja mouth formed an O, before he dropped his head in his hands.

She had him.

Matteo stood stock still, as though a move would break her spell on their prisoner.

Returning to kneel next to Pantoja, Dakota placed a gentle hand on his forearm. "The U.S. government wants to steal Brazil's birthright. Help us, and your slate is clean with the shifters."

"What kind of help?" Pantoja's tone was wary. He wasn't that enthralled.

"Matteo, what do we need from *Senhor* Pantoja?"

"Names. Locations of the hidden assets. We need him to hide surveillance devices." Matteo sent Pantoja a derisive look. "He's good at that."

Ignoring the jibe, their prisoner turned dark eyes to her. "I'll fight the Yanks for *you*. But I need money, three million *real*—and I protect myself."

****

Dakota raised her brows, appearing as surprised as Matteo. Obviously, she'd done the math—nearly a million U.S. dollars.

More than once, Matteo had compared Dakota to the warrior princess of legend. Now, it appeared Pantoja might believe her to be Comizahual incarnate. Dakota had played him—for the moment. However, the merc wasn't a fool. Later, he'd realize his mistake. Maybe money could reinforce that gap.

Matteo jerked a nod. "Payments after results."

Returning her attention to the awestruck Pantoja, Dakota widened flirtatious sea-green eyes. "We can do that. Maybe one day, you'll be family, too. People who know about us seem to be employed for life."

A very short life, Pantoja!

Dakota's creamy breasts practically rested on the maggot's arm. Clenching and unclenching his fists, Matteo took a step toward them. Dakota darted a narrowed gaze at him. The warning evaporated, and she quirked another smile at Pantoja.

While the woman worked their prisoner, awe replaced Matteo's fury. They had a mole. He'd never considered recruiting Pantoja as an asset, and the move was nothing short of brilliant. That she had seemed to pull it off stunned him.

Pantoja gave up U.S. Army Colonel Brad Shelton and some useful addresses, as well as user IDs, passwords, and server names. Though the computer talk only confused Matteo, Dakota seemed excited by the information, following up with questions about the *dark web,* whatever that was.

With the intel, Matteo agreed to the first blood-money payment, pending validation. Trusting a mercenary never ended well. However, he had confidence the three-million-*real* gleam in Pantoja's eyes would keep him in the right camp.

"We have a good start, Jose. Thank you." Placing a hand on his cheek, she traced a ruby-red fingernail along the shell of his ear. Dakota beamed at Pantoja, and Matteo seethed.

"Just remember, *Jose*, a woman scorned is a dangerous animal. Betray us…" A feline claw appeared at her fingertip, and a seam of blood welled under its path. Her luscious mouth thinned to a line. "I'll rip you to shreds."

Chapter Sixteen

Pantoja wrenched from her sharp caress as though burned.

Matteo's jaw dropped. Not only had Dakota played Pantoja like a violin, at the last instant, she'd shifted her fingernail to a talon. Only a handful of ancients could perform a partial transition. He wrestled his features back to neutral. And he'd wanted this formidable queen to go shop for a dress.

Smart, fearless, and strong, Dakota was one contradiction after another. He wanted her. Lust slammed into his body, and she jerked her gaze to his. No doubt, his coffee *Ardor* had filled the room.

The air sizzled between them, and the cell faded away. Shaking her head as though dispelling a thought, she seemed to recover. She stood and looked down at the prisoner. "We'll be back. Try to rest."

Still not convinced their efforts would bear fruit, Matteo followed her lead to gain Pantoja's allegiance. At Dakota's insistence, they equipped him with a change of clothes, sheets, and a towel soaked with stream water.

She placed a battery-operated light near the mattress. "I'm not sure how much life this has. Use it sparingly."

Pantoja nodded with a cautious gaze.

After clanging the barred gate closed, Matteo secured the lock, screwing some kind of concern onto his face. "When you've proved your loyalty, we'll find better accommodations."

Pantoja returned a level look, openly skeptical of Matteo—with good reason.

Outside the cell, Matteo shouldered the light pack containing a couple remaining bottles of water and a flashlight. Escorting Dakota through the subterranean wonder world of ferns and stunted trees, he marveled anew at the cave's majesty. The underground jungle should be a haven, free of the evils that found their way into the Enforcer cell.

Dakota's phone glowed in the dim light. "Do we have time to look around? It's a little after six."

"Certainly. Consuelo will hold dinner for us," Matteo said.

The jungle cathedral high above so completely captured her attention he feared she might trip. Twenty minutes later, they crossed the brook at a narrow stretch and climbed the short rise on the far side.

"This is about halfway to the entrance. There's a spot I'd like to show you." Matteo turned from the direct route, loosely following the stream's shoreline.

He halted several meters from the misty falls, recalling the restful sanctuary from years past. Dewy ferns glistened along the rocky perimeter, providing a shining welcome. After the evils of the Enforcer cell, he'd often sought the water's healing rhythm to soothe his mind. Thanks to Dakota's intervention today, he didn't feel the need.

"Just wow." She drew up beside him in the clearing, scanning the cavernous ceiling above the cascade. "It's like forever evening in here. I've never heard of a cave ecosystem that includes plants."

"Years ago, Cristiano and I explored and found openings beyond the plateaus." Matteo pointed to upper terraces where small trees strained toward the unseen wall behind them. "Sinkholes from above allow airflow, and some light filters in during the day."

"Fascinating." Taking in the falls, she strode on for a few more meters and halted. Matteo stayed at her side, allowing her to browse the wonders. Furrowing her delicate brow, she glanced over her shoulder in the direction of the cell. "Shouldn't we post a guard? We can't afford to lose Pantoja."

"No one has ever escaped."

The shallow V in her forehead deepened. "But a venomous something could sting him. Escaped or dead, he can't help us."

Matteo had believed her soft heart fueled her concern; however, her analytical mind was still in charge. "All insects avoid a shifter's scent, and he's covered with it."

She glanced at her arms. "Bugs do stay clear, don't they? Now that I think about it, since my first shift, I haven't swatted at anything."

He gave her a broad smile. "I'll have Alejandro assign a bug lookout, just in case."

She laughed a natural laugh, and the glimpse of her unguarded self showed her inner zeal for life.

"Snakes aren't as intimidated, so posting a sentry is actually a good idea. And, by the way, your instincts about Pantoja were incredible. He's in love with you and terrified at the same time. You did very well."

She beamed. "I did, didn't I?"

"And so modest, too." Matteo's chuckle sounded foreign to his own ears. And when her mirth joined his, his upgraded belly laugh seemed altogether alien.

Dakota's lavender *Ardor* assaulted him, but she appeared oblivious, innocent. As her fragrance caressed his body, he hoped she suffered the same.

"Actually, I just got lucky and spotted him eyeing the jag carving. Do we have time to look around? This is seriously cool."

"We'll lose all light soon. But we have some time." Matteo glanced at the waning twilight, disappointed Alejandro had left him a flashlight. A night with Dakota trapped in the dark appealed.

Slowing to inspect one of several stalagmites at the edge of the clearing, she circled the column, pausing at a cluster of pink teardrop-shaped flowers. "Pantoja might be playing me. Since I opened the door for him, he'd be stupid not to. But my gut says he's solid. You were smart to propose the tiered payment plan. That'll hold his interest, if not true loyalty."

"I suspect a beautiful woman with razor sharp claws will have more influence." Recalling the merc's wild-eyed reaction to Dakota's curved talon, Matteo chuckled. "I can't believe you cut him."

Releasing the purple fern that had drawn her attention, she cocked a brow. "I couldn't let him believe I'm entirely soft, now, could I?"

Still shocked at her ability, he wondered what other surprises she had hidden away. "I think he got the message. And that partial shift?" He. smiled. "I might even dream of you."

"Me? Star in your dreams?" Her laugh sounded light and sophisticated. In the next instant, however, her blossoming *Ardor* said that she liked the idea.

She reached an open palm toward the gleaming stone column, and Matteo pulled her back against his body, careful to angle his hips, and his thickening cock, to the side. "Skin oils will ruin the majesty of the cave formation."

He'd wanted to touch her for days. Reluctantly, he released her, and she turned to face him, her mouth dropping into a pouty frown. "Are you playing me, Matteo? Putting out your coffee scent for a good laugh?"

Only days ago, he'd suspected she'd teased him, swinging her round ass in cutoff shorts that tortured a man. "It's not something we control. I'm sorry if you thought so."

"At first, I didn't know it was you. I thought I'd missed the coffee pot."

"If you'd grown up a shifter, you'd have known instantly what you did to me. And I've really never seen lilac hair."

Her lips twitched, apparently fighting a smile.

An errant lock escaped from her hairclip, and he reached for it, rubbing it between his fingers. "Chestnut is beautiful, too."

Leaning in, he pressed his cheek to hers, and her lavender scent stole his reason. Over seventy years of pent-up lust beat at him.

Sliding her hand along his face, not sharing his hesitation, she kissed him with surprising confidence, and he was lost. The fleeting thought that Dakota deserved tenderness passed through his mind. Unfortunately, he had none to give. Devouring her plump lips, he nipped them first and then plundered her mouth.

Breaking the kiss, he tasted the skin at the hollow of her jaw, relishing the intimacy of her *Ardor* and the subtle notes of just her—clean, fresh woman. She rewarded him with a moan and roamed caressing hands over his chest. Her touch reached deep inside, soothing an anguish so old, so much a part of him, he couldn't remember being without the lonely ache. How fast he could lose himself in her loving embrace. But he didn't dare.

Common decency demanded gentlemanly behavior with his godson's new sister. It took all his resolve to pull back from her soft lavender-scented skin. "I can't declare myself—I'm sorry, but not yet."

She pushed from his chest, wrinkling her nose. "Declare what?"

Kicking himself for his ineptitude, he realized she had no such expectation. Still, he needed to do the right thing. "Matings happen easily, and I'm not ready."

With a dainty snort, she glanced down. "You look ready." Something in his expression took the humor from her eyes. "Is there any way to mate for life in human form?"

Matteo shook his head. "But it's not so—"

"Easy-peasy. We keep our jaguars and their pesky scent glands caged—no mating anyone, agreed?"

Simple, he finished. So easy for her, but in this minute, he feared his cat more than anything. "If I shift, I'll live out my days in the jungle."

His concern surprised him. Until this moment, had he gone forever cat, he wouldn't have cared—that much. Stormy teal eyes and lavender scent had left him wanting—needing—life, people, *her.*

"Kelsi told me. Dude, I'm not looking for a wedding proposal, so forget about long-term anything. Let's just have a good time." She tilted her head and arched a brow, trailing a finger along his lower jaw. "No strings, okay?"

Helpless against her pouty-lipped invitation and his burgeoning lust, he pulled her curves against him, burying his face into her hair with a groan.

She massaged his length through the gray cotton pants before lowering the zipper, nipping his ear. "Oh yeah, I want you."

Matteo had never known a woman so brazen. Dakota's blatant desire fired his own, and his dick hardened into agony. Retaking her mouth, his last sensible thought left him. Her scent and knowing hands roamed his body. He needed relief. Gripping her ass with a splayed hand, he trapped his painful length against her pelvis.

"You're dying here." Stroking his shaft, she chuckled and then dropped to her knees. She worked his zipper until his phallus sprang free. Poising her sumptuous mouth over his straining member, she sent him a playful smile. "Commando. Nice. Now, tell me you want it."

Matteo moaned, and he dropped back against the ancient column, the cool limestone the only thing keeping him vertical. He'd imagined her plump lips circling him so many times. She suckled the turgid head of his cock, and he groaned. Swirled nut-brown curls begged for freedom. He fumbled her hair clip loose and tossed it aside, and fisted her silky locks in both hands.

Wisps of chestnut teased his manhood, while she ran the tip of her tongue around his sensitive crown. The reality of Dakota surpassed his wildest dreams. He thrust, half-crazed against her slick lips, nothing short of begging.

Laving his taut skin, she gave him all he desired, taking him deep into her throat while her expert hand played his sac. Without any hope of control, his balls tightened against her palm and, all too fast, he erupted with a guttural cry. A long-overdue release shuddered through him, sapping his strength. He fell boneless against the stalagmite and gasped while aftershocks wracked his frame. Finally, he stilled.

Her amused chuckle dragged him into the present. "In hundreds of years, your back print will tell all our secrets."

"They'll know a man was held captive against the stone." Smiling down at her, remorse over the precious cave formation eluded him. Lowering to his knees, he slanted his lips over her salty mouth in a kiss. The musky reminder of her claiming surged his loins to renewed life.

Breaking contact, she nibbled at his neck and tugged his leather hair tie loose, letting it fall to the ground. She pressed a thick lock of his hair to her face, inhaling. "Do you know you taste like mocha? Everywhere? I want to drizzle sweet cream all over you."

"I'll be sure to raid Consuelo's kitchen." He smiled in anticipation. Pushing her back to the soft earth, he slowed to gaze at her. Passion he'd thought never to experience again made him want for more than today. He cupped her cheek. "You're an amazing woman, Dakota."

"Glad you finally see the real me." Her serious expression belied her playful words. She kissed the palm of his hand with a tenderness that gave him pause.

The Ardor *overwhelms her, too. Neither of us wants a mate.* Ignoring an insidious stab of regret, he focused on enjoying his first coupling in over seventy-five years.

He pressed his lips to hers, covering her with his body, and his loose dreadlocks curtained them from the world. He slid a hand to her breast and strummed a taut nipple through the thin pink fabric.

She sucked in a breath.

Trailing kisses along her jaw, he worked toward her ear. "You know a man's body, Dakota. Now, let me learn yours."

"The accelerated course—please." She murmured hoarse words against his ear, and bursting lavender sent gooseflesh across his torso. The *Ardor* didn't lie. She burned for release.

Already aching for her, he'd bring her to crazed madness before a full taking. Sliding a hand under her waistband, he sought the apex of her thighs. A flimsy triangle of smooth fabric covered her mons, like the shredded panties he'd retrieved from the jungle floor. A thong, according to the Internet.

Following the laced edge down, he moved the patch of fabric aside, delving one finger into her slick channel. As he circled the stiff button of flesh with a finger pad, her delightful whimpers made him press his length against her thigh.

With a groan, she interrupted the action, shoving down her stretchy pink shorts. Matteo helpfully obliged and removed them altogether. Wadded lavender lace, and a scrap of matching silk, flashed inside the knit bottoms. Instantly, he regretted his haste, wishing for the sight of her laid out in the seductive lingerie.

Sitting up, she pulled the matching form-fitting top over her head, leaving him no time to mourn the lost view. His gaze riveted to her weighty breasts and peaked nipples. Heaven's gates had swung wide open.

He pressed her back to the ferns with a feline growl. Another time, he would ask her to parade in nothing but her small clothes. Only days ago, he would have thought a queen under him an impossibility. And already he planned for more of her.

Magnetically drawn, he cupped both creamy mounds, thumbing their fleshy nubs. She gasped, and wrapping dreadlocks in each hand, pulled him down to her. With her pleading whimpers urging him on, he tasted each nipple in turn, suckling them to pebble-hard points. He rose up to take her lips again. *It has been so long...*

****

Only Dakota and Matteo existed in her new reality. Within the intimate space, his molten copper gaze gathered light from nowhere, and reflected such intensity, she wanted to drown in his hidden depths.

Mocha fragrance saturated the ropes of golden hair caressing her face, spearing arousal to her core. Lust drove reason from Dakota's mind. Amid the maelstrom of heat, he kissed her with surprising tenderness.

She rubbed her cheek against his, and he buried his face into her neck. "Your lavender *Ardor* makes me insane. I wanted you even before first sight."

"Really? Lavender?"

"Oh, yes." He inhaled against her skin. "Another reason your lilac-colored hair surprised me."

"Hm. In my favorite color spectrum." She smiled into his dreadlocks. An instant later, his comment caused a belated sting. *He's only attracted to my smell.* In grudging realization, Dakota admitted that with Matteo, she *might* need more than a pheromone connection. She dismissed the nonsense.

She couldn't sort through emotion and lust. Without a touch, his scent, so close and invading, teased her most intimate flesh. Too lost to be frightened, she ignored the warnings drifting through her mind.

"How do you do this to me?" Almost driven, she caressed the shell of his ear with her cheek.

He lifted and met her gaze. His skin held a subtle sheen. Not a play of light. "I would ask the same, but it's an old question without an answer."

Answering heat traveled her skin, sending the rational thought to stop through her mind. She ignored it. "I think my cat wants to romp with us."

Matteo dropped his head on his forearm and rolled to his side. He lifted her hand to his lips for a short kiss. "As does mine. If I *do* shift, *run like hell.*"

What? With a fiery taking of her mouth, he stole her question, and his *Ardor* mocha teased her deep inside. He trailed kisses down her abdomen then pushed her legs apart. Gaze landing on her smooth mons, his chest rumbled and vibrated against her thigh.

"Your grooming style has a certain appeal." The rolling growl didn't pause, merging with his voice. He trailed a fingertip over her naked mound, and she sucked in a breath, lifting her hips to meet him. Probing her folds with his silky tongue, he settled on the center of her universe.

In one last lucid instant, she met his gaze, before his suckling attentions stole her reason. Another assault of mocha amplified the sensations, and left her reeling. While playing her clit with his tongue, he reached up to tease a nipple, adding another instrument to the symphony of pleasure.

Hips straining against his face, she cried out, unsure if she'd said actual words. She wanted him inside her right damned now. Moving up over her, Matteo had gotten the message.

Her lips parted at the sight of him in the twilight jungle. Driving need carved the planes of his face, and a dark shimmer traveled his torso giving him an otherworldly glow.

She sucked in a breath. With one hand, he lifted her hips from the ground, and his masculine flesh sought her entrance. He froze in place and locked his hooded gaze to hers.

She nodded at his silent question.

Sheathing himself to the hilt, he filled her to bursting. Her gasp joined his groan. He seemed to savor the moment, holding her hips tight against his, and she reached up to caress his face, treasuring the desperate need she found there.

His arms trembled, and he uttered a male roar, pulling back and thrusting into her. Another wave of arousal pulsed through her core, and her hips moved of their own accord. She met him stroke for stroke in the oldest dance.

Realizing his strength, she doubted she could free herself—not that she wanted to try. She grabbed his wrist and urged him on. "Don't hold back. You won't hurt me."

A rolling snarl came from his chest. He pulled out

and thrust into her, setting their rhythm. Each stroke perfectly timed, perfectly placed. Not one to climax easily, her budding orgasm surprised her. "Oh, God."

"In my arms," Matteo growled. Lifting her against his chest, and still on his knees, somehow, he kept their rhythm. She had no time to ponder how he held her off the ground so easily. He buried his face into her neck, pressing the front of his canines into her skin, just short of pain. He snarled low and long. *The man is lost.*

Mocha *Ardor* spread desire to places on her body he hadn't touched, and suddenly, she understood. "Yes, bite me, please."

With his groan vibrating against her skin, he closed his fangs around the flesh at the base of her neck, and desire thrummed through her core. The act seemed so natural, like something she'd been missing for years.

His next thrust chased away the hint of pain, leaving only pleasure. He plunged into her again, and his pounding rhythm triggered a gush of fluid.

"More. Please." Always a dominant bed partner, she pleaded.

Wrapped in his steely embrace, and restrained by his teeth, Dakota let go of everything but this moment. Matteo's thrusts sent waves of pleasure through her center, while his luscious hardness grew inside her, like nothing she'd ever experienced. He released his hold on her neck, nipping the sensitive skin with his lips.

"Wait for me—please." Barely understandable, his tone sounded almost desolate.

Too late. Dakota's climax started deep inside and crashed over her with tsunami force. Crying out, she had a faint worry that Pantoja could hear them. An instant later, she didn't care.

Matteo's increasing size seemed to slow his

movements, though he kept trying. Waves of pleasure traveled from her core leaving a trail of gooseflesh in their wake. Clamping her thighs around his hips, she couldn't seem to get close enough. He synchronized with her body and moved inside her with each aftershock.

Hoping to give him more, she ground her hips against him. No man had filled her this way. Matteo roared his release and his essence jetted inside her. Finally spent, Dakota collapsed onto him, her sensitized nipples grazing his chest.

She rested against his shoulder, unable to move. "Ohmigod, *what was that?*"

****

"So sophisticated and, yet, so naive." Matteo stroked her hair, cherishing the muted lavender that telegraphed her sated bliss. *"Espinhos de Prazer.* We're cats, after all."

"Pleasure spines?" Dakota's eyes widened, and she looked down at the joining of their bodies. She giggled. "Can't argue with that."

"Not true spines. But like our natural brethren, the ridges bring forth a queen's fertility." Matteo kissed her ear and gently laid her onto the ferns. Cradling himself in her hips, he stayed sheathed in her feminine embrace.

The shimmer along his arms vanished, and he sighed in relief. Several times during their lovemaking, he'd nearly succumbed to the beating urge to shift. He'd been every kind of fool to take her—with only one regret. *Wait for me.*

Overwhelming need must have forced the plea, or more likely, he'd denied the depth of his attraction. The reason didn't matter. Males at the wedding would line up for her choosing. Any one of them could offer her a real jaguar queen's life, a place in both the feline and human worlds.

His lust-fog lifted, and the narrowly averted catastrophe became clear. Cristiano's overzealous save-the-species thinking hadn't considered all the risks. In making love to Dakota, Matteo had risked devastating consequences.

An involuntary shift, followed by an accidental mating, would have left Dakota the widow of a living mate. Unless she joined him in the jungle, she'd be alone and celibate for life. No queen had ever endured such a fate.

He pushed away his dismal thoughts and rolled to his side with her still in his arms. Soothing lavender surrounded him, and he wanted to stay here forever. For this moment, with her curled against his chest, he pretended she belonged to him. Her breath puffed against his skin, and she snuggled into him. Long minutes later, Matteo noted the waning light, dreading their return to the real world.

"*Senhor* Matteo?" A flashlight beam danced in the distance. Alejandro called from the cave's entrance at the dark perimeter. "The *patron* send me to check on *Senhorita* Dakota. She is well?"

Dakota lifted her gaze to Matteo's, and a slow smile lit her eyes. "She's *very* well, thank you."

The murmured comment wasn't meant for Alejandro's ears. Flush with male satisfaction, Matteo propped up on an elbow and nuzzled her nose. "The *senhorita* wished to see the cave. We'll return before full dark."

"Okay, *senhor*." Alejandro's voice held a hint of a smile, and then his footfalls disappeared into the tunnel.

"Your room or mine?" she whispered.

Matteo had tasted a possible future with Dakota and now mourned his loss. Time to shatter their illusion.

Misery put a knot in his throat. "It's best if we sleep alone tonight—"

She lifted to an elbow and raised one brow. "Sure. No strings. We sleep solo."

Matteo had offended her again. "You're beautiful, smart—sexy as hell. But the risks are too high."

Huffing air through her nose, she sat up and snatched the wad of clothing next to them. She pulled on her string panties and shorts in one move.

In bitter irony, his body already roused for her. The physical torture was nothing compared to the pain of hurting her feelings. He had to make her understand the risks. "I nearly shifted. Next time—"

Her cool gaze over a tight smile stopped him. "Next time? Find someone else." Tugging her stretchy pink top over her head, she covered her luscious breasts. The action somehow brought a slammed door to mind.

There is no one else. Not that it mattered. Were he in a room full of queens, he would see only Dakota.

His breach of lovers' etiquette had earned her righteous fury. Desperate to soothe her, Matteo grabbed her forearm. "An accidental mating would be disastrous—for both of us."

"*Mate!* Where do you get this crap?" She skillfully twisted from his grasp. "You're not that hot, *Casanova. My* cat was just fine."

He couldn't tell if she was insulted, sexually frustrated, or truly didn't know her own mind. Like him, maybe all three.

So much for no strings.

Without another word, she rose and strode toward the tunnel.

Chapter Seventeen

Morning light peeked through the vertical blinds hiding the veranda. Bleary-eyed, Dakota threw the silky cotton sheets back and rose to start her day.

By the time she'd gone to bed the night before, she'd put Matteo out of her mind. *No strings, no commitment.* All fine. He wasn't the first great sex she'd had. Okay, he was the best great sex she'd had. *Ever.*

Tough luck for him. He'd let his jerk shine through—again. She was over him. Worrying about Pantoja all night long, she hadn't lost a wink of sleep over Matteo.

Pulling on yellow crop pants and a sleeveless white blouse, Dakota mentally prepared herself to pick up the Fox at the airport. Dakota loved her mother and was proud of her, but Mom was just so much the Steel Fox. Worse, she expected the same from her daughters.

Using the mirror more out of habit than need, Dakota braided a few locks into a headband and puffed blah-brown wisps from her face. Memory of being a powerful jaguar gave her some consolation over her lost *Thunderstorm* and *Spring Lilac* mane.

According to Kelsi, Dakota's light brown hair was responsible for her jaguar's cafe-au-lait rosettes. Her cat pattern looked awesome. Human hair? Not so much.

Nine AM, according to her phone. She had plenty of time to grab coffee and a quick bite at Consuelo's buffet. Dakota stepped out to the veranda with an eye for the coffee pot.

While she poured her fix, she pointedly ignored Matteo huddled with Cristiano and Jaime at a nearby table. Paying no attention to the jerk's sculpted torso, she focused on the food spread, her mouth watering at the sight of a snowcapped peak of French toast. She plucked a wedge heavily coated with powdered sugar for her plate. Matteo's biceps hadn't even dampened her appetite.

The men smiled at her, and Matteo gestured to an empty seat next to him. Returning a grin to Cristiano and Jaime, she waved off Matteo's invite. "I've got to run this morning, but thanks."

The Fox would've been proud. Ladylike, firm—and she hadn't lied. Dakota claimed the most distant table from the men and pulled out her phone, scanning an imaginary to-do list.

Alejandro said they'd leave for the airport around eleven, so she planned to check on Pantoja. The three men at the far table likely discussed his fate. However, she doubted feeding him had crossed their minds.

Avoiding eye contact with Matteo, she still fumed over their abbreviated … hook up. No strings *was* her motto. She hadn't expected a happily ever after, just one damn night—or maybe a hundred. The contradictions in her head just pissed her off.

Shoving further thoughts of the dread-headed jerk from her mind, she finished her meal and returned to the buffet to pack for Pantoja. A minute later, with a juice-filled travel mug and a plate of Consuelo's best, she strode off to make her delivery.

Seemingly from nowhere, Matteo appeared, blocking her path to the kitchen door. He glanced at her feet and snorted. "You're not dressed for the jungle, and Pantoja is already well fed. You think we'd starve him?"

"How did you—never mind." Dakota glanced down. True enough, her slip-on sandals would get her killed—or at least they would be trashed. She lifted her chin. "Starvation did cross my mind."

"Aside from being unnecessarily cruel, I wouldn't

alienate your recruit. He's a valuable asset, at least for the time being."

As his low-voltage coffee scent worked magic on her foul mood, she sighed in resignation. Mother Nature was a merciless bitch.

"I should've known." She lifted the plate to him. "Hungry?"

"For your company, nothing more." He took the platter and led her to a poolside table next to Jaime and Cristiano. At Matteo's glance, the Salazar males grinned at each other before leaving with coffee mugs in hand.

Like a gallant knight of old, he seated her. Matteo pulled his chair next to hers. He took her hand, his thumb stroking her inner wrist. "I apologize for last night's debacle. You must know I wanted you. I still do."

Distracting tingles traveled up her arm. She rotated from his touch to allow brain function and let him to take her hand, if only to avoid more drama. His wants or needs made no difference to her—really. Still, she grudgingly acknowledged that his admission soothed her ego. And she *was* curious. "What's the deal then?"

"It's complicated." Matteo studied their clasped hands. "After my decades in the jungle, I must fight to stay human. I can't risk a shift."

"Or you'll be stuck as a cat. Got it." Dakota stiffened, but didn't pull from his touch. "We decided not to shift, and all was fine. So what gives?"

"All was wonderful, but not fine." He smiled without looking at her. "I thought I had enough control, but I was wrong. Making love with you … I nearly lost the battle." His desolate gaze found hers. "Not until after did I realize the risk to you. You're so new to your cat. If an accidental mating chained you to a feral, I'd never forgive myself. You'd never forgive me."

"Feral?" Dakota planned to corner Kelsi at the

next opportunity. Clearly, she'd omitted a few key points. Dakota squeezed his hand, encouraging him to continue.

A dark history haunted his eyes, the copper seeming to swirl. "A shifter who loses his humanity can't be salvaged."

Dread made it hard to find her voice. "What happens to them?"

Matteo cleared his throat, the way men do when choked up. "Untold centuries ago, a feral shifter and natural jaguar produced a litter of hybrids. The cubs were—wrong."

Dakota pulled her hand from his to cover her gasp. "You mean a male sired cubs with a *cat*?"

"Yes, you begin to see." Matteo straightened in his seat, seeming more controlled. "It is said the Jaguar Princess herself destroyed the feral and his entire family. Now, to prevent the shifter race from becoming an animal species, the *Enforcer* terminates ferals. It has always been so."

"Oh, God. You're the *Enforcer*. Have you—" She couldn't imagine looking a friend in the eye then executing them.

Lines bracketed his frown, and he stared at the jungle for a long moment. "Many years ago. I destroyed two—males I had known well."

"I'm sorry." Her words were so inadequate. Long before Matteo lost his mate, guilt had likely swallowed him whole. Maybe grief had only tipped him over the edge. Dakota wished for a rewind, so she could un-ask the question.

His curt nod signaled the subject closed.

We can never be together. An unexpected sense of loss stung her eyes, and welling tears blurred her vision. "You risked your *life* to make love to me?"

"*My* life? Not so much to wager." When he found her gaze, his smile didn't reach his eyes. "But I rolled the dice against a hidden peril. Now, I *crave* life—with you."

Dakota's lips parted in stunned silence. Hope for *something* she couldn't define insinuated itself into her heart. Unbidden, the image of Kelsi leaping into Jaime's arms came to mind. No guy had spoken to Dakota's soul, ever. Men *wanted* her—plenty of that action. None had ever *needed* her. Tears burned her eyes.

Retaking his hand, all of her improbable thoughts ended with *make him mine.* "But you didn't go cat. Neither did I. You might be stronger…"

He frowned. "Were the risk only to me, no consequence could keep me from your bed. But nothing is worth enslaving you to a feral mate—chaste and eternally bound."

Marking a mate had more daunting ramifications than the forced monogamy Kelsi had mentioned. If Matteo hadn't even thought of the lifelong celibacy scenario, likely Kelsi didn't know about it either.

Catastrophe narrowly averted. Matteo feared for Dakota's lifelong happiness, and all she could think about was how to fix it so they could be together again. Neediness was a foreign emotion, and she didn't like it. "I'm sorry. I was being selfish."

"Never. I want the same." The affection she saw in his gaze stopped her heart. He cupped her face and leaned in. "After decades alone, to hold you even once … I'll keep that memory with me forever."

So will I. Dakota swallowed the golf ball suddenly lodged in her throat. "What now?"

Snorting through a sad smile, he released her hand. "Enjoy the wedding. Every jag male will compete for your attentions. With luck, I won't have to break up challenge duels."

Dakota widened her eyes. After baiting her with a glimpse of a love she'd never thought possible, he planned to walk away without looking back? "So, the big bad *Enforcer* will just hand me off to any male who comes along?"

"Bitter word games, Dakota? *Hand you off?* Never." His narrowed gaze turned troubled. "Because I am the *Enforcer*, the thought of watching males court you terrifies me."

Foreboding put a physical weight in her chest. Dakota had to know. "Why?"

At first, it didn't appear Matteo had heard her whispered question. Seeming lost, he glanced at Cristiano and Jaime's empty table. "If I go cat—and lose my humanity—who must put me down?"

Sucking in an anxious breath, Dakota shook her head.

"*No one.* And my family will *die* trying."

Chapter Eighteen

Matteo's fear he'd kill Cristiano and Jaime was palpable. And after seeing him overpower Jaime in the underground cell, Dakota didn't doubt he could. "I'm a bridesmaid in my sister's wedding. But you could skip it."

Frowning, Matteo shook his head. "Jaguars are solitary, territorial, and possessive. Now, after decades without females, our deprived males gather in mixed company. The *Enforcer* must be there."

"Okay then, be my *big bad* date. I'm *not* looking for a husband, and an escort will dampen unwanted interest." Someone else surely said that. Dakota couldn't believe she'd just tied herself to a hot guy she couldn't touch.

His eyes widened, and he straightened in his chair. "You'd do that?"

"Uh—yeah, stop mayhem on Kelsi's big day? Sure, why not?"

Only one reason why not came to mind. However, the grateful smile that lit his eyes made the self-torture worth it. Besides, killings truly ruined a wedding.

Matteo sank back against his bistro chair in obvious relief. "You *are* an amazing woman."

"Yep, just don't forget it." Dakota lifted one corner of her mouth in a sardonic smile. She hoped she didn't regret being so damn helpful.

Dressed in jeans, white cotton shirt, and an Uzi, Alejandro stepped onto the veranda from the kitchen entrance. "*Senhorita* Dakota? You go to airport, now? Yes?"

"I was just leaving for the chopper." She eyed a

utility vest with bulging pockets draped over his arm and the Uzi in his hand. "What's with the Rambo outfit?"

Both men turned confused looks on her.

"The guns?" She waved at Alejandro's arsenal in disgust. "I need to stop at the university library before Mom's plane gets here. They'll never let us in."

Matteo folded his arms across his distracting torso. "You'll be guarded at all times off the plantation. The library will accommodate an American celebrity who needs a bodyguard. Have no worry."

Alejandro raised a hand, interrupting them. "This is true, *senhorita*."

"The guns will freak out my mom." Her protest lost some steam. In truth, she understood their concern. Accepting the inevitable, she nodded with pursed lips. "Haven't you ever heard of concealed carry?"

"A show of force wards off trouble." While knitted brows telegraphed his worry, Matteo's narrowed eyes relaxed, and he lifted her chin with a finger. "I'd guard you myself, but this morning, we plan how to use your Jose. Promise me you'll follow Alejandro's instructions."

"Sure." Puffing a resolved sigh, Dakota turned to follow Alejandro to the chopper.

****

Later in Cristiano's office, Matteo outlined his strategy to find this Colonel Brad Shelton, while Cristiano and Jaime fired question after question. Together, they ran through several scenarios. Few ended with success. Too much hinged on Pantoja's reliability.

"Matteo, my familiar killed his lover. You saw Pantoja. You really think he'll be loyal to us?" According to Jaime, during Kelsi's rescue, his geriatric pet jaguar had come to his aid, dispatching the isolated commando called Nuno. Reading the floor, the younger shifter scrubbed a hand over the back of his neck. "Erico held a knife at her throat and…"

"You had no choice. And Kelsi is safe." Cristiano shook his head, eyeing each man. "Pantoja's all we have."

Jaime didn't respond. Abruptly rising, he stalked from the room. No matter how necessary, killings haunted a male. Matteo knew more than most. He gazed after him, but there was nothing to say. Only time would fade the wounds.

"He'll have to heal in his own way," said Cristiano.

After an awkward pause, they returned to their mission and reviewed their sketched-out plan one last time.

****

Matteo unloaded the AR 15 Alejandro had provided and stowed the weapon in its assigned locker. Jaime was right. Pantoja's grief appeared soul-deep. Money never overrode the demand for vengeance. Matteo needed a better read on their mole. On his way to the cave, he pulled out his phone and dialed Alejandro for an overdue update. Worry for Dakota had plagued him all morning.

Voicemail. Another new invention. The recorded greeting caught him off guard. Rather than stammer a message, he sighed, tapping the red "end" button that wasn't a button.

Alejandro may not be near a *cell tower*. Everyone told him how unreliable the phone connections were, yet all carried them as though they were needed for life. Shaking off a sense of doom, Matteo broke into a jog, making quick work of the trek to the cell.

As he neared the barred-off alcove, Jaime's voice slowed his pace. The big male stood close to the bars, holding them in a loose grip with his arms spread wide. "Matteo tells me you're willing to help us find Shelton."

Tension in Jaime's tone told Matteo not to break the moment. He had no doubt Jaime intended the conversation to be private. Normally, Matteo wouldn't eavesdrop, but the merc would show his true colors to his lover's killer. Jaime would gain the read that the shifters sorely needed.

Sitting cross-legged on the mattress, Pantoja returned a hateful glower. "I'd say '*willing*' is a stretch."

Jaime dropped his gaze to the damp earth before clearing his throat. He raised a surprisingly kind gaze to Pantoja. "Your Nuno didn't suffer."

Pantoja lay down and turned, giving Jaime his back.

Jaime rested his head against the bars. "I didn't kill him, but I *am* responsible. His death was unavoidable."

The merc's taut shoulders convulsed. It struck Matteo that this man's grief for his male mate seemed no different than his own for Anna.

"I still wanted—wanted to say, I'm sorry for the pain I've caused you." Jaime waited a few seconds before turning to leave. At sight of Matteo, he paused and blinked the shine of tears from his eyes.

Matteo greeted him with a hand on his shoulder. Neither male spoke before Jaime strode toward the tunnel leading to the surface.

After waiting a few minutes to give Pantoja time to recover himself, Matteo turned the key in the rusty lock and stepped inside. Pantoja looked up from his pallet.

Matteo omitted pleasantries. "Are you still willing to help us? Help Brazil?"

Swinging his legs to the side, Pantoja sat up, his

shadowed expression dour. "You still have three million *real*?"

"We do, for good information—and loyalty. Five hundred thousand now, the same amount with every goal met."

"And these goals are?"

"First, locate Shelton. Tap his phone—yours, too."

"Sure, done. But you'll get nothing. We're disciplined, unlike you." Pantoja scanned the open cave beyond Matteo. "Where's the *senhorita*?"

No doubt he preferred to speak to a compassionate, attractive woman instead of a male shifter. Maybe he even sensed that Matteo would rather kill him where he sat than trust him. The swamp scum had threatened Dakota and his people.

"She's none of your concern." Brewing fear for Dakota, and her name on this filth's lips, made him want to attack. He throttled back a snarl. "What exactly do they intend to do with our DNA?"

Pantoja's calculating gaze studied him. "You're the deserter from the forties—and a changer."

Surprise nearly toppled Matteo's composure, but he managed to keep his features neutral. *Satan had spawned the Internet.* Apparently, Pantoja took Matteo's silence as a yes.

"Did command ever tell you the whys? The whole plan?"

No, they hadn't. Again, Matteo allowed silence to lead the interview.

"Ask your smart girl about DNA splicing. A soldier who survives in the jungle is worth something. One who thrives there—that's unheard of." If Pantoja lied, he did so with skill. "But military life didn't suit you, did it?"

"Nor you."

The prisoner's widened eyes told Matteo he'd hit his mark. The evil internet worked for him, too.

He studied his captive, perhaps ally. "Money for facts, not conjecture. Now, we need to return you to Shelton."

"He'll never believe I just went AWOL."

"He might." Matteo lifted one corner of his mouth. "I understand you like tequila."

****

Sitting at the small breakfast bar of his Manaus barrack's apartment, Colonel Shelton pushed his plate of half-eaten eggs aside, squeezing the phone to his ear with his shoulder. He pulled a scratch pad from his fatigues shirt pocket along with a stubby pencil.

After Shelton submitted his compelling evidence of werejaguars, Butler hadn't wasted any time contacting him. Video intel was always effective.

The general had already talked to the research nerd, Valentine. "Can you make it happen?"

"Yes, sir. As long as you're flexible."

Several seconds of tense silence charged the line, before Butler sighed. "How so?"

"I'd like to use our CIGS boys and some local talent for the delivery. They trained in a real jungle—not like our Pacific wanna-bes." Shelton spared no manners on General Deacon Butler, the motherfucker who'd pushed for his court martial.

Butler's pet project, the Hawaiian jungle training program, used a rainforest without poisonous anything. *Try the Amazon, asshole.*

"*Mercenaries?*" Butler practically hissed.

"A local security team that poaches a couple of our guys for jobs—during their leave. They haven't gotten anyone killed, yet, and the men have brought home a few skills." Shelton had taken a huge risk with the merc admission, and he held his breath for the payoff.

More silence reigned. "Okay, your mission—your call."

Cha-ching. Nearly breaking his pencil lead, Shelton carved a five-pointed star into the scrap of ruled paper. Butler wanted the shifters, bad.

"Just remember, a black-op fail leaves your dick hanging out. Discretion is paramount. Keep the goddamn media—and local authorities—out of it—or you're on your own."

"Understood." Shelton had no doubt Butler would leave him to drown.

"Our lab will be set up in forty-eight hours." Butler gave a rundown of the lab's location and mission objectives.

Shelton jotted the given coordinates under the star. *Panama Hell.* No wonder Butler had agreed to mercenaries. "Yes, sir."

Their mutual loathing throbbed on the line. It had to kill Butler to ask Shelton for anything. "Colonel, have the package there—on time."

Shelton used every bit of his military discipline to stay civil. It was his turn to be on top, and the timing would never be better. Only he could deliver what the brass wanted.

He sweetened his tone. "Yes, sir. However, let's plan for success—an invincible jungle soldier. I've been thinking. In a few months I hit the age limit for promotion."

Only the U.S. military got away with age discrimination. After his next service anniversary, brigadier general was off the table.

"It's a long process, you know that. I can't promise such a thing." Butler spoke like Shelton was an idiot and hadn't done any research.

"We both know there's an open position—and the promotion board meets next month. My name needs to be on the agenda, *sir*."

Butler's quivering jowls were likely red. "You trying to twist my arm?"

"I'm making a persuasive argument." Shelton kept his voice neutral, giving the man a minute to realize his situation.

Butler snorted. "I doubt there's time to file the paperwork."

"I'll prepare a high-priority retrieval operation in four hours. You can manage the same for a key asset. Werejaguars—with bows on their collars." Shelton held his breath.

More silence filled the line followed by Butler's heavy sigh. "I'll try—POTUS has to sign off."

"We'll be as on time as you are. I'll await your report, *sir*." Shelton added the last with disdain and ended the secure call. *Motherfucker.*

No doubt, Butler regretted shoving Shelton into this swamp-ridden Brazilian hotbox. In a sweet twist of fate, his career's death sentence had turned into a financial windfall. Now, he might even add a golden parachute stamped "Brigadier General".

Shelton didn't believe in coincidence. Fate—or God—had placed him here to do his patriotic duty. Before he retired, he'd give the U.S.A. an unprecedented jungle asset. America could secure the remote rainforest borders of their allies, and none would dare breach them. No more Vietnam disasters.

Using a burn phone from his briefcase—he didn't trust his apartment's hard line for team communications—he typed a text.

Shelton: **Meeting @1100, office.**

One confirmation. Maybe Pantoja was out of range.

****

Shelton's U.S. Army nine-man team stood at attention, crammed into his small office at the Manaus Brazilian jungle warfare-training center. Each sounded off with rank and code names by way of introductions. Lieutenant Liu—now Tiger—studied the solitary standout merc.

"At ease." At Shelton's command, they shifted stances. All eight men wore jungle green and brown fatigues, the regular Army and retail patterns easily distinguishable to any with a military background. "What's said here stays here. Understood?"

Looking each man in the eye, Shelton paused for a *yes, sir.* "Our mission is a live asset extraction and transport through the most dangerous jungle in the world—the Darien Gap. You've all trained for this."

A couple of U.S. soldiers shared a smile. However, Liu sent a pointed look at the extra man before raising a brow at Shelton.

"As you can see, we've brought in some well-trusted Panamanian help." He nodded at his hired man, Zorro. Not from Panama, but he spoke Spanish, so close enough. "Another joins us later. He was unavoidably detained. We're all one team."

Shelton sent another assessing look around the room. Satisfied the rangers would accept the new men, he rested against the edge of his desk in an effort to appear relaxed. "Now for the good news. This op will expedite your next promotion. Our objective—intercept a key Army Research Lab scientist who's defecting to Venezuela—and taking her research along with her."

Nothing motivated a U.S. soldier like treason. Shelton scanned the disgusted American expressions.

"Intel says our PhD plans to rendezvous with Venezuelan operatives in Manaus— this afternoon. ARL wants their AWOL doctor back to complete a high-priority project in the Gap— *before* they take her to detention. This is a black op. Any who want out, now's the time."

After a dramatic pause, Shelton rose and squared his stance. "Tiger, pull that table to the middle here. Gather 'round, men. We don't have much time."

The Amerasian complied, and Shelton spread out a map covered with notations. Pausing, he retrieved his buzzing phone from his pocket.

Butler: **POTUS on board. Committee agenda confirmed.**

He smiled. *Golden parachute.*

****

Later, in his empty Manaus CIGS office, Shelton slammed down the hard line's receiver, and the phone objected with a belched chime. AWOL and in the drunk tank. Just like old times. Pantoja's jump off the wagon could fuck up everything. Shelton cursed, jerking open a narrow closet.

At least he had some civvies handy. A U.S. colonel couldn't be seen bailing out a local, so he changed into streets—jeans and a collared shirt. Shelton checked his wallet for payoff money.

Depending on how long since Costello's last drink, he might be sober in time for their mission. If he weren't the best damn eggbeater pilot in the western hemisphere, Shelton would leave his drunken ass behind.

He folded the finalized map and placed it in his attaché. He had smart men, and they'd made good recommendations. No one else could pull this off with four hours' notice. *No one.* He glanced at his cell phone.

Just enough time to bail out Pantoja and make the mission rendezvous outside of Eduardo Gomes.

****

Alejandro sat across from Dakota in one of the helicopter's five cream-colored leather seats. His utility vest stuffed with ammo and a holstered Uzi contrasted with the plush interior. He should be wearing a suit and tie. She cringed again at the thought of explaining this to the Fox.

The cabin blocked most of the engine's roar, and Alejandro advised on security procedures without shouting. Pausing his tutorial, he took a swig from his water bottle and placed it in the mahogany console's cup holder. "When we land, stay in the cabin. I secure the site."

"What site?" With all Alejandro's precautions, possibly he planned an alternate route to pick up her mother. "We're going to the airport, right?"

"*Sim*. A private helipad. Still, I search area and building entrance."

"My mother's going to freak when she gets a load of you and Paulo." She pushed her chin toward the cockpit. Their stocky pilot, a mocha-skinned, black-haired man sported a similar vest holding two handguns.

"*Desculpa*. It must be this way."

At the sight of Dakota's bodyguards, the Fox might wait two seconds before she interrogated everyone about the need for weapons.

To reach her purse, Dakota released the harness clip at her midsection, half-wondering if the logo-clad buckles were gold plate. She slumped into the butter-soft cushioned seat with her phone in hand. No access.

Shutting down the disconcerting anticipation of dealing with the Fox, Dakota scrolled through a stash of downloaded periodicals. *Genome Research* looked like a good choice, given the circumstances.

Most of the abstracts focused on DNA

transformations related to cancer. Dakota theorized a shifter-specific stimulus—like Matteo's scent—could trigger a mutation allowing a latent to manifest their jaguar. *If the catalyst could be isolated...*

Well-immersed in her second paper detailing induced mutagenesis, the jolt of their landing wrenched Dakota from her scientific rabbit hole. Both men had unbuckled and now looked out the starboard windows, their frames taut with palpable tension. Dakota straightened in her seat with renewed apprehension.

Alejandro scrutinized an approaching ground controller, placing his hand on his Uzi. The uniformed man signaled to Paulo to shut down the chopper. Paulo snapped staccato Portuguese over his shoulder at Alejandro, too fast for Dakota's comprehension. Heart pounding, she tossed her phone into her purse.

"Keep engine running," Alejandro ordered their pilot in English, his voice low and full of menace. Maybe he hoped to hide his command from the crewman.

The helipad controller neared the chopper, stopping about twenty feet away. Paulo pulled a handgun and held it low at his side. For the second time, the groundsman drew his lit baton across his throat in a clear command to cut the engine.

Nothing about his orange vest and short-sleeved navy uniform set off Dakota's radar, but their pilot kept the rotor turning.

"What's wrong?" she asked.

"Trouble, I fear." Alejandro looked poised to take off in an instant. "We've never seen him before."

With a shake of his head, the controller bent at the waist and strode into the wind under the whirling blades. Before the crewman reached the chopper, Paulo unlatched his door, cracking it open. "Get back! Where is Bento?"

Dakota understood the shouted Portuguese.

"...wife's sick. Turn off your engine, or I'll call the—" Like lightning, the crewman pulled a semi-auto from under his vest and fired two precision rounds.

Paulo's head jerked back, as glass pebbles and bone fragments burst into the cockpit. Safety glass peppered Dakota's arms and face. In slow motion, Paulo's body listed sideways toward the copilot's seat.

Before his limp torso hit the leather, Alejandro pushed her into the opposite door of the cabin, cutting off her scream. Blocking her body with his, he blasted his Uzi, shattering the remaining windows. Stubborn sections of crackle glass clung to the frame.

"Get us out of here!" Dakota yelled. She lunged, reaching over the pilot's backrest and tried to pull Paulo to the side. The dead man's weapon lay on the cockpit floor, well out of reach. His body trapped the other handgun, the grip just visible underneath his midsection. *Damn!*

She looked out the empty window frame and scanned the helipad for new threats. A glistening crimson pool ate up the concrete around the crumpled body outside. The gentle whop-whop of the blades sounded almost reverent. Her frantic attempts to move Paulo's corpse seemed at odds with her eerily slowed surroundings.

In her time-lapse world, Alejandro sluggishly pulled a full magazine from his vest, guarding her while she tried to make room for him at the controls. He shoved the cartridge into place, and his empty clunked on the floor. The thud jolted her back into real time.

As though waiting for that sound, men in fatigues swarmed the chopper, shooting whenever Alejandro showed himself. Dakota dove for cover, dropping to the cabin floor behind the copilot seat. Alejandro returned fire from his knees.

Dakota rose enough to reach across the console, squeezed her arm between the pilots' seats, and struggled to reach the holstered gun wedged under Paulo's flaccid body.

Behind her, the sliding door opened, and vise-like hands clamped onto her ankles and yanked. Alejandro wheeled around in a crouch. Dakota clawed for the gun and screamed in fury as her fingertips grazed the Glock logo. Alejandro's expression contorted while he raised and lowered his Uzi. Likely, he feared hitting her.

More hands grasped at her legs, sliding her over the blood and safety glass smattering the leather. She kicked against their iron grips, but they held her firm.

When waiting arms locked around her torso and pulled her vertical, they released her ankles. Dakota elbowed into a flak jacket, a wasted move. Without hesitation, she planted a spike heel into the thigh behind her. Satisfaction over the resulting bellow was short-lived.

"Crazy lady, knock it off." A soldier growled in her ear.

American! Suddenly cinched into a familiar sleeper hold, she realized her attacker held back, allowing her small puffs of sandalwood-scented air. A hint of sour milk tainted the fragrance.

As shadows seeped into her vision, Alejandro lunged after her. "Cat ... run, *senhorita!*"

Run? I'll shred these assholes. From behind, her captor held her tight against his body and sniffed her neck, of all things. Sandalwood cologne closed in around her. Planning to rake his face, Dakota visualized white fur and claws. Nothing happened, no heat, no spark.

"Don't do it, *senhorita.*" *Pantoja!* He pressed cool steel against her temple. "We won't harm you."

She'd kill the rat bastard.

"Don't hurt her!" Skidding to a stop at the chopper's threshold with a stricken expression, Alejandro dropped his Uzi to the cabin floor with a thud, and he raised his hands. Recognition lit his eyes. "You son of a dog!"

The edges of Dakota's vision faded to black. *Mom.*

"Give her the damned HCG shot…" The distant voice funneled into silence.

Her last thought: *Ovulation stimulant.*

Chapter Nineteen

Waiting all afternoon for Alejandro's report had turned Matteo into a short-fused stick of dynamite, lit to explode. His leg bounced against the sofa he sat on, while Kelsi paced the Salazar parlor. He'd let Pantoja loose, and only eight hours later, Dakota and her guards were missing. Not a coincidence.

"You didn't text Dakota you were arriving today?" Kelsi halted, her knuckles white on the phone at her ear.

The guarded feminine voice on the other end denied changing travel plans. Behind the the adjacent loveseat, Cristiano stood, gripping the back of the smaller off-white couch.

Kelsi's devastated expression sucked the last sliver of hope from Matteo's chest. She dropped the phone to her side, leaving her mother's concerned questions posed to the living room at large.

Jaime circled the sofa and enfolded her in his arms and gently extracted the forgotten phone from her hand. He pressed the device to Kelsi's ear, mouthing the planned response at her.

Gathering himself for action, and nowhere to go, Matteo's body went rigid where he sat. All day, dread had beaten at him and, now, the enemy had stolen Dakota. He'd thought himself dead inside. The pain said otherwise.

Kelsi took a couple deep breaths before taking control of the phone pressed to her head. "Sorry, I dropped my cell. No—no, Mom. I must've misunderstood her. She's in Manaus shopping, and we had a bad connection." Tears filled her eyes. "Oh, hey, Jaime wants to say hello." Taken unaware, the big male accepted the cell phone his mate thrust in his face. And for an interminable few minutes, he exchanged pleasantries with his future mother-in-law.

Kelsi grabbed a tissue from an endtable's decorative dispenser, never pulling her lethal gaze from her mate.

Jaime signed off with Mrs. Gorman and turned without a minute's reprieve before facing Kelsi's fury. "You have your answer. The evil bad people—you failed to mention—did send Dakota a text." Her pained expression broke Matteo's heart. "How could you hide a *kidnapping* from me?"

Taking her in his arms, Jaime stammered another apology, obviously consumed by her distress. Like any good male, he'd only protected his mate. Matteo felt for both of them.

Kelsi turned, and her furious, tear-filled glare landed on him. "No more lies." The tears tipped over, and desperation replaced her rage. "Get her back— *please.*"

Jaime's pleading expression begged him for the same.

Cristiano squeezed Matteo's shoulder from behind. "I'm sorry, my friend. We know this is hard for you, too."

They all looked to him, the *Enforcer*, for direction. Burying his own fears for Dakota, Matteo cleared his throat against emotion. He had to focus on strategy. "We will. The hardest part comes first. We wait."

"For *what*?" Kelsi shoved from Jaime's embrace, glaring at Matteo. "You're kidding, right?"

Matteo paused. Since his shaky faith in Pantoja dwindled by the minute, he carefully considered his words. "If we leave by boat or car, we lose access to intel. No one can call us, nor can we access the surveillance—that's if Pantoja keeps his bargain."

Kelsi planted her fists on her hips. "You *still* trust him?"

The shriek in her voice hurt Matteo's ears, her aggressive stance painfully reminding him of Dakota. "No lies, so *no*, I don't. Nevertheless, whoever took her wants—needs—her alive. We can afford to follow our original plan a few more hours."

A chime sounded from Matteo's phone, which rested on an end table. The three stared at Alejandro's caller ID photo for a transfixed beat. Matteo snatched it, hitting the speaker button. "Report."

"I'm in the air. Our guests are missing. Pilot's gone." The foreman's voice cracked. "Full report when I get there. ETA one hour."

The line went dead. So did Matteo's heart.

Kelsi asked about one new terrifying scenario after another. Jaime fought a losing battle trying to reassure her. Matteo ignored the couple's strained conversation. He understood the need for the cryptic communication, but damn Alejandro's brevity.

"He said, missing—*not gone*." Matteo raised his voice above Kelsi's near hysteria.

When she looked up at him, reason, and maybe hope, returned to her gaze.

"Dakota lives. I'm positive. However, the pilot's dead."

Kelsi dropped her head against Jaime's chest.

"Paulo." Jaime clenched his jaw. "He was a good man."

Matteo had stayed behind to plan their defense. The enemy had moved faster. Dakota had paid for his incompetence. And Paulo, too, the poor bastard. Guilt racked Matteo. He hesitated, gaining control of his voice.

"I'm sorry. We'll bring her home, I swear."

"Jaime, take care of your mate." Cristiano spoke quietly to the couple and then gestured for Matteo to join him. "We'll be in my study."

The two men strode down the hall, brisk with intent. Tad sat at Cristiano's expansive, hand-carved desk with a cell phone and two tablet-shaped screens laid out before him. After Dakota hadn't returned on time, Alejandro had recruited him to monitor the programs she'd set up.

"Anything?" Matteo asked with more urgency than he'd intended to show.

The young man looked up, brows knitted over his dark eyes. "Nothing yet—no locations, texts or voice conversations. Papai?"

Kicking himself for forgetting Tad's worry, Matteo placed a hand on the teen's shoulder. "Your father's okay."

Tad's eyes misted, and he blinked the shine away. "Good, that's good." He raised his brows at Cristiano. "The others?"

Cristiano shook his head. "We don't have details, yet. They were attacked. Dakota's missing. Paulo's been killed."

The news chased the youth from Tad's features, his mien hardening to twenty years his senior. "Paulo was a nice guy. I'm friends with his two sons."

"I'm sorry." Matteo offered inadequate words for a lost life. The close-knit ties of the human familiars struck him anew. Nothing happened to one without impact on the others.

Tad rose, seeming lost somewhere between man and child. With a nod, the boy disappeared, and he narrowed a warrior's gaze at Matteo. "I'll do anything to save the *senhorita*. Only tell me what is needed."

"For now, take a break, get dinner. It's going to be a long night." Matteo gave him a shoulder hug with one arm, though he longed to console the lost child with a full embrace. "We'll need your help to find her. Rest up."

An hour later, Cristiano set a new, previously unused phone on his office desk and looked to Matteo. "Nicolas and Raoul are two of our strongest. Amadeo is out of the country, but will make haste to join us."

Matteo's oldest friends would be great assets in the operation. Nicolas could hide anywhere. "Add the three of us, and even without Amadeo, that's enough for a snatch and grab retrieval."

"Agreed." Cristiano glanced at the beeping phone's screen. "They'll locate Raoul and arrive by dawn. Nicolas has a military helicopter. Just like always, he trains and keeps up on the latest warfare technology. And he brings two skilled humans along."

Raoul had always been reclusive. However, when Nicolas found him, Raoul would answer their call. Matteo wondered if he'd taken another human wife. "He still with his tribe?"

Cristiano smiled. "Yes."

The copper tang of blood filled the air, announcing Alejandro's arrival. Dark brown stains spattered his white shirt and jeans.

Not bothering to hide his intent, Matteo turned in his seat and sniffed the air, sorting through the traces, searching for any hint of Dakota. All the blood was human. He collapsed back in relief.

Cristiano leaped to his feet and pulled a rolling leather chair next to Matteo. "Alejandro, sit."

Waiting for the foreman's return had frayed Matteo's patience. "Tell us what happened."

Every few words, Alejandro rubbed his face as he

related Dakota's abduction. "Pantoja held a gun to her head." At Matteo's snarl, Alejandro raised a hand. "He hinted he was still with us."

Matteo leaned in, ready for battle, but with no one to fight. "How?"

"He said, 'We won't harm you,' but he looked at me when he said it. It could be a message or a trick. I couldn't tell, but he frightened her with that gun so she wouldn't shift."

"I don't buy it. She would fight." Matteo turned to Cristiano. "What else would keep her from shifting?"

"If a latent needs to be around a full shifter..." Cristiano let the thought hang in the air.

Dakota had only shifted once, with Matteo. Twice, counting the partial for the talon. Only a total inability to go cat would've stopped her from fighting her attackers. A hidden weight pressed him further into his seat. "She can't shift to protect herself."

"We'll find her." Cristiano's eyes hardened. "Alejandro, what happened next?"

"They'd tied up Bento and locked him in a supply closet. He was unharmed, but good and pissed off."

Matteo hung on every word. Bento could be a useful ally. "We need to speak with him."

"Yes. He wants us to pay his respects to the attackers. He even waited to call the police until after I took off." Alejandro raised a brow at Cristiano. "Mrs. Gorman wasn't on the plane. Has she called?"

Cristiano frowned. "She never arrived. It was a ruse to get Dakota."

"So the demon Pantoja betrayed us after all." Alejandro snorted, sagging back against his chair.

Matteo reviewed the timeline in his head. "We can't be certain. Three hours before the false message arrived, Jaime and I confirmed him asleep in his apartment. And at five AM, he was still out cold in the same bed."

"So there's a small hope he's with us." Shaking his head, Alejandro looked down at his bloodied clothing. "I'll get a crew on the chopper. It flies, but it's a mess, too. I need to change and notify Paulo's family."

"Please tell them I'll come at the earliest possible hour." Cristiano rubbed a hand down his face.

He'd always taken a death of a human familiar hard. Shifters lost many over the years due to age, but the grief was different if they died in your service. Matteo understood. He had spared Cristiano this one. Paulo had died at Matteo's order.

Shoving his regret aside, he refocused on Dakota's rescue. "Before you go, Alejandro, I need your advice."

"Of course, *Enforcer*." Alejandro had looked into Pantoja's eyes, seen him with the gun to Dakota's head.

"What does your gut tell you about our mole?"

The man appeared surprised by the question and was slow to respond, rubbing his chin. "I think he's with us. But my instincts could be wrong."

Matteo exchanged a look with Cristiano, who returned a slight nod. Matteo included both men in his gaze. "Then we're agreed. We wait for Pantoja's phone taps. But at dawn, we move. Questions?"

****

Well after midnight, Matteo paced down the hallway to Dakota's suite. Driven to keep a piece of his queen with him during this long night, he'd stooped to theft. He scanned for witnesses before turning the knob.

Feminine sniffles sounded behind the door opposite Dakota's suite. Kelsi's grief tugged at his heart, adding fuel to his own sorrow.

Faint lavender greeted him inside. Dim light from

the veranda leaked into the chamber, and the near darkness suited him. He didn't bother with the light switch. Pulling back the midnight-blue bed cover, Dakota's scent blossomed from the macaw-print bedding, as he'd hoped.

For the hundredth time today, his throat tightened against an onslaught of fear for her—and for himself. Losing Dakota would likely drive him into the jungle forever. He pressed a parrot-covered feather pillow to his face, and instead of soothing his ache for her, her scent only deepened his sense of loss. Worry would make this night true hell on earth.

The door snicked open behind him, and he started. Light from the hall spilled into the room. Kelsi's red, swollen eyes widened, and she stopped short at the entrance. "What're you doing here?"

"I..." Gravel tumbled in Matteo's voice. Embarrassed and irritated over the invasion to his privacy, he couldn't very well tell her he planned to wallow in Dakota's scent like a cub separated from *mamãe*. "Nothing."

Kelsi's gaze dropped to the pillow still in his hands, and her tense features softened. "Yu do love her, don't you?"

Matteo's lips parted, but he trapped the words threatening to escape. Yes, he loved her. He reeled with the revelation. "I'll get her back. And kill any who harmed her."

"Do that." Kelsi closed the distance between them, leaned down and sniffed the pillow. She placed a hand on his forearm. "Guess it's a cat thing. I wanted her scent with me, too."

"Take it." As though he intended to cut off an arm, he reluctantly offered her the lavender-perfumed pillow. "She's your sister."

Kelsi stepped past him and reached across the bed, grabbing the pillow's mate. "She always hugs one while she sleeps. When we were kids, she piled them in her bed."

With a nod, he snugged his treasure under one arm. Without more to say, and so much said, Matteo let himself out the patio door.

Only meters away, the night hummed with lonely insect song, and he longed to roar his need for his mate into the jungle. He ignored the urge to shift. Dakota needed her *man* to come for her.

Returning to his makeshift bed on his suite's hardwood floor, Matteo curled around her scent. Even though her partial shift had impressed him, she'd only fully shifted with him the one time. Maybe latents needed practice before they could solo. Had she gone cat when they snatched her, she could have saved herself. Matteo should have taken her on a run in the jungle instead of selfishly making love in the cave.

Worry stole his ability to sleep before battle. Through the open patio curtain, a full moon inched across the sky, still hanging well above the trees. Unable to delay another minute, Matteo rose to launch Dakota's rescue.

The t-shirt he'd worn to bed carried her scent from the pillow, so he decided not to change. The other shifters would need the trace to track—and her fragrance on his body would warn them Matteo kept her close. In a weak moment, he wished he and Dakota *had* marked one another.

He strode down the hall to the main house. The kitchen was dark and empty, save the coffeepot's digital readout, glowing a red three AM. Steam puffed from the brewing appliance.

Cristiano's fresh scent lingered, so he was up,

too. Mugs sat in the same location they'd been seventy years ago. Some things just had a place in the world. And Matteo had found his—at Dakota's side.

Toting steaming coffee, he strode through the parlors to Cristiano's closed office. Light snuck out under the door along with snippets of conversation. "He'll have to show us. Send your coordinates—and that video."

Nicolas must have reported in. With a perfunctory knock, Matteo entered.

From his executive leather chair, Cristiano lifted his *burner* phone, as he'd called it, turning the folding phone from side-to-side. "I'm so anxious, I slept with this under my pillow—or didn't sleep. Good thing, too."

Matteo dragged an armchair to sit opposite him. "What video?"

"Nicolas is in the Gap to get Raoul. They sent a runner for him, and he had news. His tribesmen reported a military-type group hiking a captive north—a white female."

The office walls closed in around Matteo.

Chapter Twenty

A burning need for action sped Matteo's heart, and he jumped from his chair, leaning over the desk to search the screen. "Is it her?"

"We'll know in a few minutes. Until Raoul learned about Dakota, he'd assumed it was slave traffic."

Barring Matteo, Raoul was the most reclusive of all the shifters and likely knew little to nothing about today's technology. "How did *he* get a video?"

"A tribesman's son was home from the city and had a cell phone. Raoul had sent him out with a patrol, intending to collect evidence for the authorities."

Blood rushed in Matteo's ears. "It's her. I know it."

Raoul's territory within the Darien Gap rivaled the Amazon's lethal danger. The thought of Dakota hiking the Gap in human form weakened Matteo's legs, and he dropped back into his leather chair.

"They're moving fast. The U.S military is likely involved, as Pantoja claimed." Cristiano opened his book-style computer and tapped the keys. "We need that video."

"If the Yanks are in this, why not just fly her to the States?" The question consumed Matteo, and he drummed his fingers on the shiny mahogany. "Instead, they stop in Panama and march her through a demanding mountainous jungle known for swallowing people whole."

They must want to hide Dakota. However, with the United States' immense resources, they could hold her at a convenient and vastly more secure installation.

Shaking his head, Cristiano frowned. "Maybe her captors' try to conceal her from their own?"

"Rogues on a for-profit mission?" Matteo groaned. "If so, we have more variables, more players. And no government oversight."

A ping drew Cristiano back to his screen. "Got it."

He positioned the display between them and started the recording. The angle suggested the cameraman was high in a tree. Obviously tired, with hands cuffed behind her back, a soaked Dakota marched in the middle of a single file line of equally drenched soldiers. Drizzle obscured the picture.

He didn't need to see her face. The cadence of her gait, the shape of her body, and damp locks escaping from the hairclip was all he required. He'd know Dakota anywhere.

"It's her." Terror shook Matteo's usual systematic approach to battle, urging him to charge in with guns blazing and no plan.

"Raoul's given us a leg up. We know where they are, and we can catch them." The clip ended, and Cristiano folded the screen over the flat keyboard.

Matteo agreed. "Let's prep to move out. We have what we need. No reason to wait on that faithless Pantoja."

Thirty minutes later, Alejandro, Cristiano and Matteo strode toward the war-torn helicopter. Even from several meters away, chemical disinfectant assaulted Matteo's nose.

In the pre-dawn night, cabin lights shone through the helicopter's empty starboard window frames. The pilot's shattered window held tenaciously together around two fist-sized holes. Heavy, clear tape reinforced the crackled glass.

An unfamiliar man in coveralls emerged from the cockpit and handed Cristiano a clipboard. "She's ugly, but flight-worthy."

Cristiano fired numerous questions at the man, and they circled the bird together in deep discussion.

Invading insects swarmed the interior fuselage lights. Grimacing, Jaime pulled the bullet hole-ridden cabin door open. "*Meu Deus.*"

Alejandro's frame tensed. Matteo put a hand on his shoulder, scanning the puckered leather inside the craft. Duffles of weapons and supplies occupied the floor in place of the rear-facing seats and console.

Imagining the deluge of bullets streaming at Dakota, Matteo shuddered. And the foreman had stayed with her. Admiration for him grew. "You're a fortunate man, Alejandro."

"I could've been luckier, *senhor.*" Alejandro seemed to brace himself before climbing into the helicopter.

Matteo saw nothing but courage in the quiet man.

Jaime and Alejandro clicked their harnesses in place, and Matteo climbed into the copilot's seat. Blades spun overhead, and despite the sound-blocking headphones, the engine roared in his sensitive ears. With Cristiano at the controls, Matteo gripped the door handle to close them in for takeoff.

Tad sprinted across the lawn toward them, holding an open laptop in one hand and flagging them down with the other. *News!* Matteo pointed out the racing youth to Cristiano, and he nodded, flipping a switch that slowed the engine.

As Matteo dropped onto the helipad surface, Tad rushed up to meet him. Breathless, he skidded to a stop and took in the chopper with widened eyes. At sight of his father dozing inside, Tad's brows knitted, and he seemed to count his father's breaths.

"I'll take care of your *papai.*" Matteo yelled over

the throbbing engine, guessing the boy's worry.

"Please do." Tad pulled his gaze back to Matteo, angling the screen toward him. He pointed to a blinking light on a map display. "Colonel Shelton's phone lit up in southern Panama. I've sent this to *Senhor* Cristiano's phone."

"How do you know it's Shelton?" Matteo hollered.

Tad shrugged. "Guess I don't. It's the account Dakota noted would be for him."

"Good work. Send regular updates. We'll have to catch your communications when we can."

Tad sent another furtive glance toward his father, who slept soundly in his seat, having gone most of the night without sleep. With pleading eyes, the boy's lips parted. "*Enforcer*, I—"

"You're too valuable here, monitoring transmissions. We won't receive communications in the air or the jungle." Still shouting, Matteo braced for another round with Tad to keep him out of the ground-level rescue mission. "Plus, I'd never override Alejandro's orders to his son."

With a heavy sigh, Tad's body deflated.

Matteo clapped a hand on his shoulder. "Our communications expert must be at the radio."

"Radio?" Seeming distracted from his disappointment, Tad's brow furrowed. "We don't—"

"Old-timers' wi-fi." Matteo managed a smile.

Smirking, Tad seemed to accept his surveillance role. "Bring her back."

"We will." Matteo climbed into the leather seat next to Cristiano.

He waved at the boy who'd retreated to the edge of the concrete, still holding his open laptop. Flipping switches, Cristiano cranked the engine to a new noise level. He studied his panel of gauges with lines carved into his forehead.

The bullet-pocked machine lifted them vertically in a smooth motion. Air whistled inside the cabin, bowing the taped window inward, but the roadmap-patterned glass held together. After a few minutes, they angled into the inky sky.

"Cruising altitude. We should reach Nicolas's coordinates late this afternoon." Cristiano's voice sounded inside Matteo's headphones. "Tad tried again?"

Matteo nodded. "Alejandro watched his man die yesterday. He's not going to risk his son today."

"You made a good choice."

"One, anyway." He'd permitted Dakota to go to the airport. He'd ordered Paulo to his death. Matteo's poor judgment had allowed enemies to abduct Dakota. He couldn't bear to think about what scientists would do to her. Matteo studied the instrument panel's wood grain. All so easily avoided. "I should've escorted her to Manaus."

Cristiano snorted. "My friend, when they put that gun to her head, you'd have leaped into their cage. They'd have you both."

Struck by the truth of it, Matteo stared out his window into the night sky. Everything had changed. Human existence meant nothing without Dakota. Lavender seemed to blossom from his shirt, and he could still sense her hips cradling him long after their lovemaking. Were she here now, in his self-centered weakness, he'd damn them both and mark her.

Below the chopper, dawn's first light painted an ocean of mist-laden treetops that stretched between the horizons. The quiet beauty veiled a deadly peril beneath. Dakota, unable to shift, traveled in an equally lethal jungle.

Lost in his jaguar for so many years, Matteo hadn't concerned himself with the human aspects of life. At some point, he had bought into saving the species, most likely when he'd met Dakota. Now he *cared*— about everything.

His graying friend should appear no older than early thirties. Cristiano's territory held no trace of his scent. *He hasn't shifted in years.* Matteo prayed another latent waited for him. "Why didn't you court Dakota yourself?"

Cristiano chuckled. "Kelsi described her as brilliant and *wild*. Sounded more suited to you."

"Thank you for dragging me out into the world." Words Matteo thought he'd never say. The admission came hard.

"Really? Finally?"

The two men laughed, the way family did when they accepted and forgave each other's shortcomings.

Matteo rose and sidled between the seats, sitting on the cabin floor across from Jaime. Out cold, Alejandro slumped against a duffle tipped on its end, using the bag as a makeshift pillow. He snored with each inhale. Wind from the open window lifted his hair, giving him a comical appearance.

Matteo hadn't thought he'd use Alejandro's munitions instructions so soon. Opening one of the canvas bags, Matteo retrieved an AR 15—semi-automatic rifle. The weapon struck him as ugly in comparison to the walnut-stocked Springfield he had used against Hitler.

Jaime caught Matteo's gaze and touched an unseen control on his headphone. "You know how to use that?"

"Alejandro gave me a demonstration. Impressive."

Even without the forty-round magazine in the catch, Matteo checked for an empty chamber. He mentally reviewed loading, firing, and unloading.

Jaime studied him. "Just try not to shoot one of us."

Matteo lifted the rifle from his lap. "That's why Alejandro packed this for me."

The devastating fully automatic rifle had been impressive, but if he needed to shoot anyone during the raid, Matteo wanted controlled single-shot accuracy. Surprisingly, after all these years, his aim had stayed true.

Though they had planned for a violent confrontation, Matteo hoped to bring Dakota out in stealth.

I will bring her home.

****

Dakota had awoken on a plane's bare metal cargo floor, chained to a heavy steel ring built into the fuselage wall. After countless hours handcuffed in the spartan military transport, her captors had transferred her to a huge gray helicopter marked U.S. Army. About an hour later, they landed in a cleared patch of ground deep in a mountainous rainforest. Freshly cut branches edging the perimeter still wept clear sap.

Without a sense of time, she endured hours of a jungle-downpour hike, darkness falling before they reached their destination. She had no idea how long she'd been on the plane. The foliage and mountains here bore no similarity to the Salazar wilderness. She could be anywhere.

The only good news was that they'd apparently left her mother at the airport.

Now, she and her guard—Tiger they'd called him—stood before a camo-domed tent. Bone-deep fatigue muted her terror, and sleep deprivation made her cranky. "Look, asshole—Tiger—whatever, I'm from Omaha, Nebraska—the USA. I've got rights."

Dakota jerked against the soldier's ironclad grip on her bicep, but he overpowered her, shoving her through the tent flap.

He narrowed almond-shaped eyes, and they seemed to glint in the dark. "You gave those up, don't you think?"

Ignoring his odd comment, Dakota blinked against her surprise at his brawn. Always strong for a woman, she'd held her own against male sparring partners back home. This guy looked fit enough, but strength-wise he smoked her earlier guard. In addition to more muscle, Tiger had a few inches on her, putting him at a little over six foot.

Inside the tent, he flipped on a lantern. A lashed-together cane cage gave her a preview of her immediate future. Eerie crisscrossed shadows adorned the mottled canvas walls. *Bamboo cell or nighttime jungle?* Unless her cat materialized, the mini jail was definitely safer.

"Why are you doing this?" She asked again, trying to gauge her enemy's knowledge of the blackmail threat. With his dark hair and inky lashes, she'd have thought him decent looking—except for the hateful glare.

With his free hand, Tiger pulled open the cage door. "You know why, so shut it."

"Actually, I don't." She wasted her breath on him. Questions about her mother's whereabouts burned in her mind, but she didn't dare ask. If they were unaware of the Fox's arrival, Dakota didn't want to enlighten them.

Recognizing the sandalwood she'd noted just before the sleeper hold had overtaken her, the cologne struck her as odd. The rainforest swelter made the other soldiers stink. She narrowed her eyes at him. This was the asshole who had put her out.

"Your English is too good, *Tigre*." Every time she mentioned her U.S. roots, he seemed to cringe, so she worked that angle, stressing the Portuguese pronunciation used by the other soldiers. "You're American, aren't you, *Tiger*? You know the Bill of Rights? That pesky document?"

"You and your rights are a pain in my ass. Get in, traitor." Keeping his iron grip on her arm, he glared at her with sable-ringed, red-amber eyes. The dim light gave the unique gem tone an eerie luster. No mystery why they called him Tiger.

He pointed at the open-poled door. "Now, or I'll plant you the hard way."

"Me, a traitor? You're the one kidnapping American citizens."

Another glance at the cage—with four conveniently placed knotted loops—jumped her heart into overdrive. She tried again to shift. *Dammit all!* Her jaguar had deserted her. Maybe, latent really meant *intermittent.*

From behind her, Tiger gripped her shoulders, and she braced against his anticipated shove. Pressing his nose under her ear, he sniffed and groaned like a hungry man fixated on fresh cinnamon rolls. "You smell like some flower dipped in vanilla."

A new kind of fury overtook her. "The last man who touched me without permission wears a cast."

Tiger put one hand on the top of her head, and with the other, put more juice in his grip on her upper arm. "Get in, *sweetheart.*"

Another glance at the looped restraints sent dread pulsing through her. Exploding a head butt to his nose, warm fluid spattered the back of her neck. His angry yell urged her on. Whirling, she landed two rapid-fire sidekicks to his groin and kneecap. Howling and hugging his nether parts, the bastard refused to drop.

Dakota turned to rocket out of the tent but stopped short. Pantoja stood at the entrance, the tent flap in his hand. A nearly imperceptible shake of his head told her nothing, except he didn't want her to blow his cover. She couldn't trust him.

"*Tigre*! Cage her, now. Use the restraints." Pantoja barked in Portuguese.

Almost casually, he shook his head, drawing his sidearm. "Stop the bullshit, lady. Get in and lay down. We both know you understand me."

Implausible escape scenarios flew through her mind, each quickly discarded. Her lost momentum forced her to back down, not her best thing. She had to be patient. Maybe with some time, she could shift and turn the lethal jungle into her salvation.

Pantoja gestured to the cage floor. "Your feet in the loops, like a good girl."

Disheartened by her failure, she complied, but not without a seething look at Tiger. "This guy's too friendly. Keep him away from me."

Appearing semi-recovered and upright, Tiger pressed the bridge of his bleeding nose and pulled down, eliciting a quiet crunch. "Damn, *Asas*. I wasn't—" He glared at Dakota. "You just…"

"Right," said Pantoja, or *Wings* as Tiger had called him.

Pantoja stepped to a clear line of sight, still covering Dakota with his weapon. Tiger reached through the canes and snugged the hemp-like loops around her ankles. "Turn to the side."

He cut the zip-ties holding her arms at her back. She'd never been so sore in her life. Rolling her shoulders, she rubbed her wrists.

"You must hurt after being tied for so long." Pantoja's sarcastic barb tempted her to out him to Tiger as a mole.

However, she couldn't afford to doubt him this soon, so she tucked her revenge away for later. Maybe, she'd gone too far when she'd scratched his ear. Complying with Pantoja's gestured command, she slid her hands into the fibrous straps, putting all her murderous thoughts into her glare.

Obviously reading her, Pantoja's eyes widened before he glanced at the younger man. "*Tigre*'s your guard tonight. If he touches you improperly, I'll kill him myself."

Tiger sputtered another denial. She ignored the two men.

With little play in the restraints, Dakota dropped her head to the tarp in disgust. Apparently, caging her didn't qualify as improper. *Where is a goddamned rat when you need one?*

Dakota still hadn't determined who had abducted her. While the equipment had U.S. markings, the soldiers appeared to be of mixed nationalities. They spoke Spanish or Portuguese as often as they spoke English. Pantoja even wore different patterned fatigues from the others. All were very well armed, including her new guard.

After Pantoja left, Tiger rifled through a duffle on the floor near the camp-style lantern, pulling out a bottle of water and a t-shirt. Dakota eyed him through the sapling bars as he dropped to sit on the canvas-covered ground next to her. Soaking the shirt, he gingerly dabbed the cotton to his face, grimacing with each touch.

His eyes watered, and he snorted through his swollen nose. He glared down at her. "Sweet dreams. I'll be *right here.*"

Chapter Twenty-One

Several hours and two fuel stops later, the helicopter dropped in altitude. Matteo's ears filled to bursting, and he shook his head against the sensation.

"Jaime, up front, please. Time to land," Cristiano commanded.

The big male got up and slid between the seats in a nimble move belying his size, and claimed the copilot's station. Curious about flying a helicopter, Matteo rose to stand behind them. The tree-covered hills below grew near, and the chopper leveled out above the rolling canopy. Raoul had always enjoyed the mountainous Darien jungle, saying he could easily escape the rainy season's swamps.

Cristiano scanned the treetops. "We're closing in on the coordinates. Watch for—"

Jaime pointed. "There."

Belatedly, Matteo noted a red flag protruding from the treetops. Cristiano positioned their bird over a nearby clearing and skillfully dropped into the sea of green. Sixty meters of chopped back foliage gave the sensation of dropping down a hole.

After settling on a small level patch of ground, Cristiano slowed the engine and cut it off. Matteo stepped out of the helicopter, the insect noise sounding strangely hollow.

Nicolas and Raoul rushed to him, and the group exchanged arm clasps that turned into back-slapping hugs. Jaime, Cristiano, and Alejandro joined them, doing the same.

A geometric pattern suggesting a jaguar covered Raoul's chest, flagging his affiliation with the indigenous Emberá. He sniffed and raised a brow at Matteo. "You wear a queen's scent to taunt starving males?"

Slugging Matteo's upper arm in jest, the fairer skinned Nicolas smirked. "You have a death wish, *Enforcer?*"

Not anymore. Matteo laughed. He had missed these shifters. "You wish to try?"

Cristiano observed their exchange, and Matteo detected more joy than mirth in his expression. He owed his friend a great debt.

"Help, please." Alejandro hauled a duffle from the cabin, gesturing to more inside the chopper's hold. The men turned to the damaged chopper and all sobered.

Nicolas grimaced. "I'm sorry about your man, Cristiano."

"Thank you." Cristiano grabbed a canvas bag and strode off, likely following scent to Nicolas's campsite. He'd never handled the loss of one of his people well.

Matteo ached for him, suffering for his own part in ordering Paulo to his death. He grabbed a bag and followed Cristiano.

Raoul fell in beside him with a rucksack on his back. During the short hike, he gave a full report of Dakota's trail and sightings. "They plan something medical. Their camp has a lab and hospital equipment."

His announcement struck fear into Matteo's heart. *Dissection?* Maybe they didn't care if Dakota lived.

While the others ate a waiting meal, Matteo grabbed his AR 15 and commandeered Raoul for a scouting mission. Visions of Dakota on an autopsy slab assailed him. He couldn't wait twenty minutes for everyone to eat. They'd return with intel and plan their nighttime raid.

Raoul shifted to his black on charcoal jaguar for their journey. Although he kept his pace slow through the steep pathless jungle, Matteo still trailed him by several meters. Biped travel frustrated the hell out of him. Even with his naturally enhanced stamina, his legs only churned so fast.

Two hours from their campsite, Raoul halted at a black palm tree and shifted to human, waiting for Matteo to catch up. Dakota's terror-laced blood scent came from the tree's three-inch-long thorns. Matteo hissed air through his teeth.

"Your girl did that with intent. According to my scouts, she brushed trees along their route, obviously leaving a trail. After the rains started, she ran into this one."

Matteo had mentioned his fear that water might've washed away Pantoja's scent, and she'd remembered. No one could've missed the dangerous thorns. However, the barbs caused infection, and their bite could be deadly. "We move."

Raoul melted back to jaguar and took off. Shouldering his rifle, Matteo redoubled his efforts to keep pace with the huge cat through the rugged terrain. A faint mechanical chugging sound pulsed from the forest ahead, growing louder with each step. A few minutes later, at the crest of a jagged rise, Raoul froze with his front paw suspended, lifting his head to a sniffing position.

They'd reached the enemy camp. Dreading what he'd find, Matteo dropped to all fours and crawled commando-style, staying at Raoul's rear. Fortunately, the diesel engine would cover any sound of their approach.

Raoul peered over the edge and pulled his tail forward in a *come ahead* signal. With his heart pounding in his ears, Matteo complied. If the mercs had harmed Dakota, he feared he'd lose his last scrap of military savvy and mount a one-man charge.

On a terrace below, two small square tents

flanked a larger canvas Quonset with a rumbling gas generator at its rear. A man in green scrubs exited the main tent's square entrance, pausing to speak with a sentry. A few smaller domed camo tents formed a loose-knit perimeter among the trees.

Raoul dropped back below the rise before shifting to human. "The big barrel-shaped tent holds a surgeon's room, I think. I've never really seen one."

Not surprising, since Raoul never ventured near civilization, nor did adult shifters ever need surgery. Occasionally, an injured child might see the inside of an operating room. Matteo himself had only seen 1930s pictures.

"Circle right. Move in and find Dakota. I'll cover you." While his friend shimmered black, returning to jaguar, Matteo found a tree suitable for rifle cover.

He should be scouting for Dakota. Smothering his fury over his weak biped assignment, he slung his weapon over his shoulder and found a vine-covered tree. He scaled about thirty meters up the ceiba's horned trunk to a decent sniper perch. The easy climb surprised him. He'd retained jaguar strength, too.

Blending in with the darkening jungle, Raoul circled the camp's perimeter, hissing every few minutes to give Matteo his position. Human ears would never detect the sound over the insects and generator. Minutes seemed as forever, and Matteo despaired of getting a precious glimpse of his mate-to-be.

Rustling fabric came from just inside the jungle. On the far side of the main tent, parrots in the canopy squawked their distinctive warning, followed by the feline cough he had been desperate to hear. *Raoul's found her!*

Heart in his throat, Matteo scanned the camp's perimeter with new intensity. They must be holding her deeper in the forest. All the better for the jaguars.

Dakota and a two-guard escort emerged from the trees. Each gripped one of her arms, pulling her along. Matteo leaned in, and the sour note of fear in her scent curdled his blood.

"You goddammed motherfucker, let go of me." Matteo's gentle queen had arrived.

"Keep it up, sweetheart. Your ankle bracelets go back on in two minutes." Walking on her far side, an Asian soldier with blackened eyes and a swollen purple nose glowered down at her, favoring his right leg.

Matteo grinned. *That's my girl.*

The soldier led her toward the central tent. They weren't wasting time with their plans. Matteo had hoped they would stand down for the night, but lights glowed inside the hospital tent.

Matteo peered down the rifle's scope. Confirming Dakota was injury free flooded him with relief. As an afterthought, he flashed the red targeting laser on the injured man's camo hat. The beam shone bright in the dark.

At the guard's side, Dakota did a double take at the dancing red dot and immediately fell silent. She slanted a furtive glance toward Matteo's position.

The Quonset sentry stepped aside, and Dakota's guards pulled her inside the main tent. The canvas door unrolled behind them in a heavy swish, closing the entrance.

Matteo growled low in his chest. Unbidden, heat traveled his skin. Recalling her normal, unimpeded gait, and the guard's damaged face, he shut down the involuntary shift.

"What do you mean, I have to wait?" An angry male voice wrenched Matteo back to his surveillance. A fireplug of a man dressed in scrubs planted fists at his hips. He glared up at the sentry. "Do you know who I am, Lieutenant?"

"Yes, sir, Major, sir. My orders are to hold you until they're ready, sir."

"Even in the middle of the goddamned night, that's my goddamned operating room, soldier. Nothing happens without my say-so."

A surgeon! Autopsy images scrolled through Matteo's mind. Avoiding the liuetenant's line of sight, Matteo targeted the red beam on the backside of the doctor's green skullcap. *He'll never touch Dakota.*

"Where's Shelton? He can brief me on this damn need-to-know operation." Dr. Fireplug prowled in front of the sentry, appearing ready to attack.

Of the countless Matteo had killed in war, he'd never killed an innocent man. Like this surgeon, others in the camp probably had no idea why they were here. Angling his rifle off target, Matteo dropped his head on his forearm.

A black glow at the base of his tree drew his attention. The light faded, and Raoul materialized, dark-skinned and naked, waving him down. Descending a few feet, Matteo released his hold and dropped the final twenty meters, landing next to his friend.

Raoul scanned him up and down. "No broken ankle. You *did* stay in the jungle too long."

Matteo had no patience for Raoul's laidback approach to everything. "You heard them?"

"Yeah, and her scent's soured. We going in?"

Dakota had been terrorized. Pulse-pounding rage rushed through Matteo. For an instant, he wished he'd taken the shot. He wanted to kill them all, but he forced himself to think strategically. "We all come out alive. You bring Cristiano and the others. I'll work some kind of distraction."

Raoul regarded the ground with unusual interest. "All right. Just don't turn into an idiot while I'm gone."

He wheeled in a black glow, and a six-hundred-pound charcoal cat launched into the jungle. Matteo needed to buy the shifters at least two hours' travel time. *Dakota's time.*

Chapter Twenty-Two

The shifters had come for Dakota. Nothing else explained the dancing red laser target on Tiger's head. Since the sniper had passed on such a clear shot, they must not be ready to move in. Whoever operated the rifle had been invisible in the trees.

Matteo was nearby. It had to be him. She hugged the thought to her heart. Staying alert and ready to act was the only help she could offer. In her excitement, even Tiger's threat to tie her feet had lost its edge, until he pushed her through the square doorway.

At sight of an exam table—equipped with stirrups—in the center of the canvas room, she froze in place. Behind her, the rolled flap dropped, dimming the light.

"Sit," Tiger commanded. Scanning the room with a frown, his gaze settled on the table. The unreadable look he exchanged with the other soldier confused her. A chink in their armor?

As directed, she claimed a metal chair next to a stainless-steel side table. As much as she wanted to resist, she feared pushing the shifters to act until they were ready. *Stay focused.*

Rolling metal storage units, with see-through doors above and drawers below, lined the wall. Supplies and clear, peel-open packages holding gyn speculums and a box of exam gloves filled the inner shelves, reminding her of any other gynecologist's office.

Makeshift weapons were woefully absent.

Two men in scrubs emerged from an interior space. Before the flap dropped, the opening framed an operating room table with a toolchest-style cart at the head. Dakota recognized an anesthesia machine next to the red supply cart. In a tent?

One of the orderlies nodded at Tiger. "Thanks, guys, we'll take it from here."

"Think so? Dude, look at my face." Tiger scowled at them.

The unknown male snickered. "If she got the whole dose, we're good."

"Med sticky's on her back, just like you said." Tiger's voice sounded distant.

Willing her body to lunge from the chair did nothing. Dakota parted her lips to yell, and instead, her jaw dropped open. After several ineffective attempts to close her mouth, saliva trickled down her chin, startling her.

Dakota tried to shrug her shoulders to detect a transdermal patch. Her body didn't respond to that command, either. Tiger must have slipped on a medicated adhesive while she'd slept coma-like after her grueling hike.

Her sudden helplessness terrified her, but the mystery drug overpowered any physical response. Her heart didn't pound, and her breathing slowed.

"She looks wasted, not cooperative. Thought you needed her for an experiment?"

"Yep, that's right." The man gave Tiger a stern look with his cryptic answer. Both their voices sounded hollow. "You're not needed here."

Visions of dissection—or God forbid—vivisection ignited her terror. Horror sucked the air from Dakota's chest, or maybe their sedative had depressed her respirations. She had the careless thought that respiratory arrest waited in the next minute.

I need to run. Her eyelids fell to half-mast, and she snapped them open. Unfortunately, nothing else would move. Dakota had never been so vulnerable.

Matteo's here.

"Oh yeah, up we go."

Hands, too many for her foggy brain to count, lifted her onto a hard mattress. Her head listed to the side. Moving reflections in the cupboard glass created an illusion of motion, making her queasy. Something snugged around her arm above her elbow.

"A little pressure." Not Tiger. The new male voice sounded muffled. Something dull pushed against her skin. The band released, and a cool path snaked up her arm. "And done."

The bumpy sway of what must be a gurney seemed determined to rock her to sleep.

****

Matteo checked on his captive sentry one last time. The unconscious soldier lay gagged with a sock. Matteo had hogtied his wrists and bare feet with vine fiber strips. Shifter scent covering his prisoner's fatigues would keep dangerous wildlife at bay for a few hours. And the man breathed. Matteo needed him quiet, not dead. No reason to kill until necessary.

About twenty minutes after they took Dakota into the tent, the blustering surgeon had arrived under guard. "Shelton better have a good explanation for this shit."

They planned to cut her open—or worse. And, like her antianxiety medication, their anesthetic might not work. Without another choice, he had left his sniper perch in search of a *distraction*. Instead, he'd found a guard.

Dakota's out of time. From the camp's perimeter, he peered through leafy cover. Getting to the surgery tent would be simple. However, once there, he had to create a diversion that wouldn't put Dakota at risk.

Hugging the adjacent tent for cover, he sprinted to the rear of the Quonset, certain the noisy generator would hide any sound of his approach. Bright lights within silhouetted a cupboard positioned just inside the canvas wall.

Using the cabinet to hide his presence, he unsheathed Pantoja's knife and slit an eye-level peephole into the tent. Iodine almost overpowered Dakota's scent.

A body-shaped blue mound lay on an operating room table. At the head, clamps held a paper drape aloft. Wisps of chestnut hair trailed over the table's edge. *Dakota's under there.* Something hidden supported her drape-covered legs, separating them into a V. The sight sucked the breath from Matteo's chest.

"What the fuck is this, Shelton?" Dr. Fireplug bellowed and gestured to Dakota on the pedestal table in the center of the tent. "ARL sent me to harvest ova from a new primate species. This girl's no damn monkey."

They'd put Dakota to sleep and planned to steal her *eggs*—her unborn children. The sons and daughters Matteo longed to father. After all the scientific advances he'd read about, it wouldn't surprise him if they could grow a baby without a mother.

Horror threatened Matteo's reason, and his skin shimmered with rage, reflecting off the canvas. Reining in his fury, he reassured himself these demon-spawn needed her alive.

"That's the point, Major. She isn't human. Maybe not even a primate. And that's all you need to know." Standing off in the corner, the tall, middle-aged Shelton wore a white paper jumpsuit and spoke with authority. "Get on with it."

Matteo memorized his face—for later.

The doctor's spiked brows rose over his surgical mask, nearly brushing his skullcap. "Good God. Like an *area fifty-one* thing?"

"You could say that. Not a damn word of what

happens here leaves this tent." Shelton eyed the staff in the surgery suite, including the entire team in his warning.

Since they didn't plan an autopsy or worse, a live dissection, Matteo paused outside the tent, weighing his next move. Even if the doctor took Dakota's eggs, after Raoul brought the shifters, they could retrieve her unborn when they extracted her. However, Shelton could plan to send the ova out by helicopter. Still, if Matteo charged in, the risk to her was too high.

A man at Dakota's head checked gauges on a machine next to her, seeming to watch her vital signs. "We're golden here."

"Twenty minutes and done." The surgeon patted Dakota's drape covered thigh. "Let's see what you really are, little miss."

Interpreting the anesthetist's comment to mean Dakota was healthy and insensible, Matteo settled in for an anxiety-ridden wait. He scanned the perimeter of the camp at his rear for any sign of a patrol.

"Goddammit, keep her down. I can't work on a moving target." The surgeon's thundered demand whipped Matteo's attention back to the portable surgery suite.

Still draped, Dakota, bucked on the table. Matteo gasped and splayed his hands on the canvas. He prayed she was strapped in place under the blue sheet. The gowned doctor sat on a stool between Dakota's legs, both hands holding her thighs in place.

"Jesus H." Obviously stressed, the man at her head checked glowing numbers on the machine angled next to him and grabbed a syringe of milky fluid. "She's got enough on board to drop an elephant. Any more, she might not wake up."

Shelton strode to the anesthetist and grabbed his

wrist. The unknown drug fell from the startled man's grasp. "We need her alive." Shelton waved at two corpsmen already rushing to the table. "Hold her down."

She's feeling this! Matteo's hands shook with restrained rage, and images of Shelton's mauled throat filled his mind.

Corpsmen converged on the table to restrain Dakota. The anesthetist jerked his hand free, snapping orders for meds, openly disobeying Shelton's order.

In the melee, draping and a hospital gown fell to the floor, leaving Dakota's upper body exposed to all while the men restrained her. The indignity rankled Matteo on a new level.

Grumbling, the surgeon returned to his despicable task of stealing Dakota's unborn babies. Enraged, Matteo ripped open the tent wall and leaped several feet inside, leveling his rifle at the surgeon.

"Touch her, maggot, and you die." A chest-deep growl filled his voice, betraying his jaguar heritage.

A masked woman in greens shrieked and backpedaled into a supply cupboard. The sound of cracking glass rang through the space. Jerking a wide-eyed look at Matteo, the startled surgeon extended gloved hands out to his sides. A curved probe-like tool fell from his grasp, thudding on the tarp. "W-whatever you say."

The distinctive metal scrape and click of a semi-automatic's racked slide resounded from the head of the table. "I don't think so."

Dread stealing his breath, Matteo jerked to see the new threat. Without a flicker of concern, Shelton pressed the gun's muzzle to Dakota's temple. The bastard's steely-gray eyes didn't waver.

He stroked the trigger's edge with an index finger. "Stand down, *catman.*"

"Jesus Christ!" Wide-eyed gaze riveted on the gun, the anesthetist scrambled back, rocking the supply cart behind him.

Matteo had forgotten the most dangerous man in the tent. Full of self-loathing, he should have known Shelton hid a weapon under his white coverall.

A plastic breathing tube protruded from Dakota's mouth. In the tense silence, her involuntary movements tapped the clear plastic against the semi-auto's barrel. Their medicine had finally slowed her struggle.

Stock still, Shelton glowered at Matteo. "Your call, *catman*. We can settle for only DNA."

A whoosh of air cut into the silent standoff. Next to the terrified anesthetist, a canister-style piston pushed a breath into Dakota's lungs. Her body arched in a silent gag.

The sight of his strong Dakota so vulnerable broke Matteo. Swallowing his impotent fury, he looked to the side and dropped his rifle. "Help her, *please*."

Pantoja and the Asian with the damaged face rushed in from the front of the tent. Raccoon Eyes scanned the OR, and stopping short, gaped at Shelton holding Dakota at gunpoint. Pantoja, his mouth a firm line, cast an eye around the suite, likely noting possible weapons.

"Don't just stand there, secure the prisoner," Shelton barked.

The pair raced around the surgical team and the small table of instruments. Pantoja shoved his gun in Matteo's face, and Matteo tried to read him with little more than a glance. Their mole straddled both sides too well. Raccoon Eyes yanked Matteo's hands behind him and clamped his wrists together with steel cuffs.

Dakota's fight had abated, and the surgical team seemed more relaxed. Not Shelton. He kept his weapon at Dakota's head and eyes on Matteo. "Behave."

Even if Matteo shifted, he couldn't save her. Shelton would kill her before he completed his change. Matteo had failed her. *Just like Anna.*

"Search him," commanded Pantoja, gaze locked with Matteo's.

Raccoon Eyes confiscated Matteo's gun and knife. Pantoja glanced at the blade and shifted to the side, blocking Shelton's line of sight. Not daring to look to him for help, Matteo put all the threat he could into his return glare. When the time was right, both men would die.

****

"Take him to the front and wait." Furious with their failure and delay, Shelton lifted his weapon toward the ceiling, clicking the safety into place. He glared at the shaken anesthetist. "Wake her up. We're done here until the area's secure."

Pantoja shoved their prisoner past the surgery team who pulled the blue covers from the jaguar woman. "Eyes forward."

At Shelton's back, her seal-bark coughs reassured him that she lived. If nothing else came out of this cluster fuck, they had another subject. A male. That should please the PhD nerd.

As Liu and Pantoja marched the catman from the hospital Quonset to the adjacent command tent, Shelton brought up the rear. A few soldiers loitering near a camp lantern eyed their detail, likely drawn by the security breach commotion. In their midst, a plaid-shirted civvy raised a hand as though Shelton might stop and chat.

Valentine. Brilliant—as a fence post. And he carried that fucking dog. The man didn't have two brain cells to rub together.

Shelton ignored him, staying focused on securing

the mysterious werejaguar. No human had ever moved so fast. D'Cruz had blurred into the operating room suite. If he did indeed turn into a giant jaguar, and if he had enhanced strength to go with his speed, Shelton doubted shackles would hold the hell-spawned monster.

Fortunately, they didn't need chains. A gun at the female's head had easily contained the violent mutant.

Pantoja led them into the austere command office. Shelton needed to know if D'Cruz acted alone or if he'd brought company, right damn now. He grabbed two straight-backed gray metal chairs from the matching aluminum desk and set them in the middle of the small room.

"Chain his legs to the rungs. That'll slow him down, man or cat." Shelton was sorely tempted to berate his men over their failed security. Instead, he jutted his chin at Pantoja. "*Asas*, double the guard on command and get a patrol—you lead—and secure our perimeter, goddammit."

"Yes, sir." Pantoja pushed the prisoner into the chair and handed another set of shackles to Liu. "You okay, Tiger?"

Liu nodded.

Shelton kept his gun on his captive, while Liu clamped the prisoner's ankles into heavy steel bands. Liu snorted and shook his head as though the catman's odor offended him. The sweaty male didn't smell that bad. Liu staked out a guard position just inside the closed entry.

Gripping a fistful of ratty dreads, Shelton pressed the semi-auto's muzzle to the wildman's head. "*D'Cruz* is it?"

Fiery copper eyes glared back. The abomination curled his upper lip, exposing a disturbingly large, curved canine. Shelton swallowed against his mouth's sudden dryness. He tamped down the hard-wired instinct to flee a predator. Hoping to mask the involuntary response, he sneered.

However, D'Cruz sniffed the air and lifted one corner of his mouth, as though he'd actually smelled Shelton's fear.

Cat or not, Shelton recognized a hardened man when he saw one. Only this freak atrocity had a weakness. "No reason for you—or her—to die. We want you alive. It's a real shame you didn't cooperate. None of this would've happened."

Pulling keys from his pocket, Shelton unlocked his desk's hutch and extracted a small gray lock box. He entered the combination into the dial and, at the click, extracted a nine-inch lead-filled leather blackjack.

Liu's eyes turned to saucers.

With a smirk, Shelton moved his chair a couple feet in front of D'Cruz and took a seat. He planted his elbows on his thighs and held the cudgel up for the catman's viewing pleasure. Or maybe his own. Absently caressing the worn leather, Shelton recalled the Iraqi scum who'd last tasted its pleasures. The stronger they were, the more satisfying. Though he was strictly heterosexual, the anticipation dropped heat to his groin.

He studied the unnatural copper gaze, craving a glimpse of alarm, an undercurrent of terror. A nostalgic smile curved his lips. "Let's cut to the chase, *catman*. Who's with—"

A familiar yap came from outside the tent. "Taco, come back here!"

At the base of the door flap, the ratty Chihuahua with over-sized ears burrowed into the room, his tail wagging his body side to side. Whimpering a placating note, he belly-crawled to D'Cruz's feet and rolled onto his back.

"For the love of Christ." Shelton lurched to his

feet.

"Taco, you naughty boy, come to Daddy." The weighty canvas flap pulled away from the entry's support strut, and Valentine squeezed inside. Liu wheeled to intercept the intruder with a shooter's stance, and leveled his sidearm at Valentine's midsection.

Shelton fisted his hands at his belt. "Valentine, get the hell out."

Stopping short, the doctor's bugged eyes fixed on the gun, and he belatedly raised his arms. "I say, Lieutenant Liu, that's hardly necessary."

"Shit." Liu dropped his weapon and heaved a breath. "Dr. V, you can't be here."

Shelton caressed the trigger of his nine-mil, unsure whether to shoot the ratty dog or the too-stupid-to-live geneticist. The crosshatched candy-apple-red shirt made an irresistible target. "Valentine, turn around and walk."

At sight of his Chihuahua begging a tummy rub from D'Cruz, Valentine glanced up to him with raised brows. "Huh. He likes you."

With narrowed eyes, D'Cruz didn't appear any more impressed by Valentine than Shelton. He uttered a big-cat snarl, surprising Shelton and knocking the bemused expression from Valentine's face.

Valentine's stunned look transformed to a hesitant grin. "Mr. D'Cruz, sir, I suspect you have *very* interesting genetics."

"Get him the fuck out of here." Shelton added his own growl at Valentine.

Liu forced the research nerd against the canvas flap and hollered for back up. Two fatigue-clad soldiers appeared at Valentine's sides and gripped his arms. The idiot looked surprised.

"Let me take Taco. Here, boy." Behind his wire

rims, Valentine's eyes shone with tears. *Yellow bastard.* Struggling against his captors, the needy wimp grasped at the air for his dog. The guards finally dragged him off.

The mutt bit Shelton's pant leg, growling as though he were a Doberman pinscher. Furious, Shelton shook his booted foot until the fabric ripped, launching the yelping Chihuahua toward the door. "Keep that mangy cur out of my sight, or he'll be jaguar kibble."

Taco scurried to follow his master and halting at the safety of the threshold, wheeled around with hackles ridging his back. The mutt growled a bark and darted off in Valentine's wake.

The man was a menace. Shelton returned to his seated prisoner.

Chapter Twenty-Three

"I'm alone." Matteo slurred the words again through swollen flesh, his lips throbbing with a pulse of their own.

As the *Enforcer*, he'd used a blackjack, too. However, the receiving end was a new experience. He wouldn't allow Shelton to wear him down and force him to shift. Even as human, he might be able to break his steel restraints. Dakota needed him, but he had to be patient. Only a stealthy escape in human form gave him a chance to bring her out with him.

Further, if Shelton was distracted by Matteo, and focused on gaining intel on incoming shifters, he might leave Dakota unharmed. No matter what Shelton did to him, Matteo couldn't reveal the other shifters. He tried to come up with a small tease of information to leak.

Shelton cleaned the smooth black leather with an almost loving caress. Crimson streaked the white cloth. "Still? You're here all by your lonesome?"

"I'm the only one."

Shelton came to attention. "The only one, what?"

With fury at a slow burn, Matteo spat red mucous and a tooth on the tarp floor. More DNA for the picking, though they'd already swabbed saliva and drawn blood. "You figure it out."

Bracing for the anticipated blow, his self-preservation instinct to shift rose yet again. The blackjack couldn't hurt him, not permanently. However, a shift would mean the end for him and likely Dakota.

Instead of another tap, Shelton laid his cudgel gently on the desk. Standing with hands on hips, perspiration dotted his brow, and sweat plastered his white tank to his frame. He'd removed his camo shirt about twenty minutes ago. The soft colonel probably spent most of his time in the frigid air conditioning.

"Tiger, get Mouse in here." Shelton sat at the desk and made the screen come alive. "I want you both to know what we're really dealing with."

A few minutes later, a smiling scrap of a boy entered the tent. His gaze landed on Matteo, and his mouth froze in an O. He looked from Liu to Shelton. "What's goin' on, ya'll?"

"Where am I?" From well beyond the tent walls, Dakota's slurred speech sounded weak. *She's awake.* The distant sound of her voice buoyed Matteo, giving him hope.

None of the three riveted to Dakota's transformation video seemed to hear her. Matteo tensed against the urge to charge to her rescue. Impotent fury consumed him, crystalizing his resolve to wait. Cristiano would arrive soon. He only needed to hold out a little longer.

Shelton turned off his computer and dismissed Mouse, saying something about guard duty. Straining to hear more from Dakota, Matteo had missed the exchange.

Liu stayed riveted to the screen until it went dark. He glanced over his shoulder at Matteo with a surprising flicker of sympathy. The lieutenant turned a shuttered expression to Shelton. "Sir, a few hours of swamp heat and no water might loosen his tongue."

"Do that."

"Yes, sir." Liu approached and lowered to unshackle Matteo's legs. Earlier, his foul stench nearly made Matteo's eyes water, but now his swollen nose blocked the man's odor.

No Geneva Convention rules here. And given the mixed nationalities of the troops, and their lack of knowledge of even the main goal, Shelton's operation had to be a rogue action.

"Bring him back at oh-three-hundred hours—the girl, too. She ought to be awake enough by then." Shelton met Matteo's gaze for a beat. "We'll see if Mr. Catman gets cooperative."

Bile rose to Matteo's throat. He hadn't spared Dakota a thing. He glared at Shelton's back as the whoreson paced to the entrance.

Shelton stuck his head outside. "Sergeant, get four men. Prisoner detail. On the double."

A solid *Yes, sir* came from beyond the canvas wall. Within minutes, the space filled with armed soldiers. Once again, Shelton pressed his gun to Matteo's head. "Your girl pays tenfold if anything happens to my men. Got it?"

As his torn, swollen, lips were stretched too tight to move, Matteo nodded. While Liu reshackled his ankles, Matteo prayed they relocated him near Dakota. Waking helpless during the aborted surgery and choking on the plastic tube had to have terrified her. Like air to breathe, he needed to hold her in his arms, needed to know she was unharmed.

Liu arrayed the four soldiers around Matteo, and they marched him into the jungle. Steel chain between his ankles jerked Matteo's strides short. Frustrated by his nonfunctioning sense of smell, he snuck glances into the treetops outside the main camp's perimeter. *Where the hell are they?* Worse, he couldn't detect Dakota. Fifteen minutes later, there was still no sign of the others.

"Charlie-echo-bravo." Pantoja's familiar voice came from the depths of the darkened understory.

"Jag one," Liu responded.

Pantoja emerged from cover, leading six soldiers with grease-painted faces. A few had greenery attached to their helmets. With a glance at Matteo, he gestured for Liu to join him several yards away, likely unaware of Matteo's sensitive hearing.

Pantoja snorted. "He looks a little rough."

"Yeah, the old man wore himself out. No answers though. See anything out there?" Liu's Portuguese was as good as Dakota's.

"Shit ton of snakes."

"No jaguars?" Liu's tone held a hint of suspicion.

Pantoja smirked, however, his focus lasered in on the lieutenant. "No. You see any cats?"

His tacit denial of the shifters' existence gave Matteo a sliver of hope that the faithless merc might still be of use. According to the height of the moon overhead, if Pantoja planned to help, he needed to do it now. Three AM had to be less than a couple hours away.

Liu lifted his camo cap to wipe his glistening brow. He leaned in and whispered. "Shelton showed you that video?"

Pantoja cocked his head without answer.

"The *cat show*?" Liu asked.

"I've seen it. So the werejag flick finally hit the theaters." Pantoja raised his brows. He was smart to let Liu lead the exchange.

Liu snorted. "I think it's faked. You know, to freak us out into doing this shit." He paused and studied Pantoja. "Or do you believe this jaguar crap?"

"Don't know. Don't care. Money's money."

"They don't pay me that much." Liu thumbed over his shoulder at Matteo. "Dude's way different, but a *werejaguar*? Anyone could've faked that video."

"I could've, easy. Doesn't matter to me." Pantoja kept a straight face. "After I report off to Shelton, I'll relieve you for a few hours. We swap guard duty. No one else."

Liu shook his head. "He wants the girl back at oh-three-hundred for questioning."

Pantoja shrugged. "No problem. The girl's at your camp. I'll stop in. You get a little shuteye first and then deliver her."

Pantoja had blatantly lied about everything. He wasn't that stupid. He'd intentionally leaked that the holding camps were close together. Matteo tucked the info away.

After another twenty-minute march, they entered a ring of a few domed tents. Liu led them straight to a strip and pole cage at the far edge. Trees formed the corner posts of the enclosure, their trunks circled by steel chains attached to heavy shackles. Even standing right next to the cell, he detected nothing of Dakota's scent. She'd never been here.

They'd built this kennel just for him.

****

Insects hummed, and precious air moved over Dakota's face. Even the heavy humidity didn't bother her. She sucked in a reassuring gulp of oxygen and released it, savoring the easy breath.

Goo stuck to her lashes and clouded her surroundings. A familiar wrist restraint stopped her hand short of her face, so she blinked hard to clear the ointment.

They'd returned her to the same cage. Regaining her senses, she moved each extremity, testing the straps. Furious tears leaked from the corners of her eyes. Never in her life had she so wanted to sob in uncontrollable rage.

They'd proven they could do anything to her. Visions of waking on a stainless-steel table, with a Y-shaped incision exposing her empty body cavities, transformed her rage to out-of-control hysteria.

Screaming, without rational thought, she yanked frantically at her cuffs. The canes rattled with her useless efforts.

Terrified of losing herself to a panic-driven insanity, she willed her dysfunctional response into oblivion and pressed her wild arms and legs to the tarp. Body rigid, she lay panting. Her rapid breathing had nothing to do with her physical efforts. She concentrated on the mottled green and brown canvas above her and forced slow breaths into a natural rhythm.

The surgical assault had changed something fundamental inside her. And her pathetic reaction to the four-point restraints was a part of it. Acting the victim would only get her dead. Dakota had to focus on escape. For the hundredth time, she imagined white fur and massive claws. Nothing. If her jaguar would cooperate, she could be out of here in seconds. She discarded the useless thought.

I control my destiny. She might need some help, but she would get out of this mess.

As before, the tent hid her from the rest of the camp. Uttering a sound of disgust, her dry tongue stuck to the roof of her mouth.

Dark had fully fallen, blurring the tent's camo pattern in shadow. *He hadn't actually come.* Only her wishful thinking had conjured Matteo. Tears stung her eyes anew.

"Ma'am, can you hear me? You okay in there?" According to the hesitant, twangy voice, she had a newb guard from the American Deep South.

He'd called before, she was certain, but she'd been too engrossed in her meltdown to answer. He'd heard her losing it. Terror, rage, and now humiliation. She almost welcomed his interruption. His voice brought her back to the present, and she concentrated on the here and now. "I'm seriously pissed off, is all."

"Um, okay." Shuffling footsteps came nearer the tent wall. "Can I come in?" His voice nearly squeaked. What kind of guard was this guy?

"I need the *ladies' room.*" Her brittle lips cracked in a new spot with every word. "And water."

"Glad you're awake. I heard you know the drill." A short, wiry soldier probably only in his late teens, and dressed in fatigues, released the chains connected to her tight woven-fiber bracelets.

After rubbing her chafed wrists under the cuffs, she scooted toward her feet. New slack in her leg shackles allowed additional movement.

He raised his rifle at her. "Sorry, ma'am. I gotta stay."

Dakota sat up and glared at him. Not only did he intend to watch her squat, he had called her *ma'am*, as though she was fifty or something. With every muscle screaming, she felt seventy. She shrugged aching shoulders and rubbed her thighs.

"I'm rightly sorry, ma'am." Puppy-brown eyes met hers over his rifle site. The poor kid looked more distressed than she felt.

Groaning at his sincerity, she grabbed a coffee can of cat litter near her shackled foot. In a small attempt at privacy, she gave him her back and lowered unfamiliar green cotton pants. They'd changed her clothes while she was unconscious. With business completed, she pulled up the lightweight scrubs and tied the drawstring snug.

Bayou Boy offered a bottle of blessed water in exchange for her used can. She gulped with abandon. Insect song and the crackling plastic bottle filled the warm night air. If they drugged her again, so be it. The tepid water was ambrosia.

"Charlie-echo-bravo." From the voice, her regular

guard, Tiger, had returned.

"Jag-one." The southern kid responded with what must be a code.

Tiger's blackened eyes and swollen nose had turned purple-green already, and he walked straight enough, entering the crowded space. "Hey, Mouse, it's your lucky day. Major's pissed. I've got to cover the rest of your shift."

"You? The *GI Joe golden boy* messed up?"

Tiger dropped an overstuffed camo duffle next to the canvas wall and tossed a backpack on top of it. "It's bullshit."

"Yeah, sure, but hey, sucks to be you." The smaller man taunted with good-natured license. "She's done needin' her hands. I was fixin' to—"

"I got it." Tiger grabbed a backpack from the ground and handed it to him. "Tell Ace to be on time. I got another shift after this."

Dakota tensed, riveted to their exchange. Tiger rushed the kid out for a reason. Maybe he wanted to get her alone. For revenge or—wait! *Another guard-duty shift?*

His assignment could be anything, but if there was another prisoner, like her mother. She shuddered. Or maybe she hadn't imagined Matteo. Dakota fought to keep her expression neutral and her worries in check.

All smiles, the southern boy left, zipping the dome's flap behind him. Maybe, if she distracted Tiger enough, he would let something slip. Feigning cooperation, she played nice and lay down, reaching her hands toward the rails.

"That's okay." Her gaoler kept his voice low. "Stretch for a few."

Surprised by his offer of this small freedom, Dakota lifted to one elbow. She put real appreciation on her face. "Um, thanks. I never got to tell you I'm sorry about—"

"Forget it. It's a prisoner's job to fight back. But I want you to know, your perfume, whatever, surprised me, that's all. I wouldn't..." Apparently, Tiger wanted to make nice, too.

She nodded, not buying his line. "So why'd you get double duty?"

"Sorry, can't chat about me. But I'm curious about you." Tiger put his finger to his lips in a shush signal. "I saw a video of you changing into a great white cat. Did you fake it?"

She didn't need his unspoken instruction to lie. "Yes."

"Who's the man in the video?" Again, Tiger shook his head.

"Go away."

He pointed to the ground and mouthed, *He's here.*

"Where?" she whispered. Dakota's heartbeat pounded inside her head, driven by hope and worry. In the same instant, logic smothered her optimism. Tiger had no reason to help her, and every motivation to get information.

Not far. His cryptic, lip-synced answer could mean anything. She'd been a fool.

Disgusted with her own weakness, she dropped to her back and glared at him through the wooden rails. "Get the hell out."

Tiger circled to the head of the cage, and Dakota resigned herself to the four-point restraints for the night. Rattling the post chains, he angled his head toward an air vent. "When you get thirsty, remember you asked for it."

Dakota studied him, and he mimed the shush signal again, totally confusing her.

Someone scratched at the tent flap. Tiger jumped to his feet, leveling his rifle at the flap. "Code!"

"Um, oh bother. Echo. Bravo…"

Gusting a sigh, Tiger lowered his weapon and pinched the bridge of his nose as though gathering self-control. He unzipped the canvas. "You're early."

A slightly built man ducked into the tent, wearing oversized, sagging fatigues. A too-pointed cartoonish nose dominated his features, and an army cap pushed his ears out to the sides through wisps of gray hair, adding to his comedic appearance. He plucked wire-rimmed glasses from his chest pocket and perched them on his nose. The nerd package was complete.

Placing a small canvas bag on the tarp floor, the odd man lowered to sit crosslegged a couple feet outside the sapling bars. "I was afraid I'd get lost and be late."

"Okay, just keep your voice down. And make it quick." Tiger whispered. He stepped outside and circled the tent before returning. "All clear for now."

Dakota sat up, studying the new arrival. Camo failed to disguise him as anything close to military. However, for some reason, Tiger tolerated this clownish soldier's eccentricity. Suspicions put her on full alert. If this shoestring of a man had orchestrated her involuntary surgery, maybe she could learn what they'd done to her.

"This is Dr. Valentine, a geneticist. He's told me some freaky shit, and after that operating room cluster, I believe him. Listen to him." Tiger kept his voice low. He turned his full attention on the doctor. "If I scratch the canvas, we got company, so shut down the convo."

Nodding, Valentine unzipped his duffle. A black button golden nose poked out of the bag.

Tiger aborted his exit, wheeling around with widened eyes. "Are you nuts? I told you not to bring that dog."

"I couldn't leave him. Taco cries without me, so everyone knows when I'm gone." Valentine whispered back. He tucked the tiny pup under one arm. "I give you my word, he'll stay quiet."

"Nice you bet our lives on it." Tiger pursed his lips and stooped over to exit the tent. In the next instant, the zipper traveled the track, closing Dakota in with the unknown doctor.

Valentine scanned her body with a clear lack of sensual heat. His eyes widened, and a slow smile curved his lips. Then, he seemed to recall his purpose. He parted his lips a couple of times, as though he didn't know what to say.

Dakota could hardly follow the events, nor did she dare trust either man. All the same, hope kept her voice low. "Why're you here?"

"You, my dear, have *very* interesting genetics." He glanced at the canvas flap separating them from Tiger, knitting his brows. "And I've been a fool."

Dakota had no trouble believing that. "And?"

"You're my life's work, you see." He offered a smile that didn't reach his gray eyes. "Colleagues ridiculed my research. Journals refused to publish my papers. One rejection even advised me to submit to a tabloid. As though—"

"You think I'm a shapeshifter, too?" Dakota hedged, adding accusation to her tone. She couldn't afford to substantiate this man's research.

He cocked his head, and lines formed in his brow, as though she'd somehow hurt his feelings. "You disappoint me, Miss Dakota. I've studied the mirrored double-helix complex that made you—and your friends. No one will convince me your metamorphosis was a special effects video."

Two double helixes? Even with her survival at

stake, the scientist in her wanted to dive into the lab and see this DNA marvel for herself. She shook off the temptation to ask a million genome questions. "What did you do to me? In the operating room?"

"Thanks to your friend Mr. D'Cruz, nothing. They put you to sleep and woke you up. Thank God." Valentine looked at the ground, the tent wall, at any place but her.

She glared at the top of his head. "Not buying it. You did something."

He looked up with a frown. "Oh, it's true. The procedure was aborted before…" He searched the ground for a moment. "They—*we* needed your ova for more in-depth study. Against my protests, they'll try again, tomorrow."

"You *motherfuckers*," Dakota whispered. Heart racing, she scanned the tent. Somehow, she would get out—tonight. *Matteo had been in the trees.* The other shifters had to be with him.

"Agreed." He spoke in a matter-of-fact tone. "The pursuit of knowledge isn't always justified."

Ironic that the enemy held the key to her species, possibly even the shifters' survival. In that instant, she both hated and admired Valentine. "Why. Are. You. Here?"

He slapped his thighs and blew out a breath, startling the little Chihuahua curled in his lap. "Shelton is a bad man."

Dakota snorted at the obvious.

Valentine gave her a half smile. "More importantly, he's acting on an inaccurate assumption. You are human. And, as such, have human rights. I tried to tell him, but…"

A *mirrored* double-helix meant *four* DNA strands. One helix pair for jaguar and one for human?

Welling tears veiled her view of the doctor. So much had happened, so fast, she hadn't realized how she'd feared losing her humanity. "I'm still human?"

"Of course you are. There, there. No crying, now. You're God's creation—and He doesn't make mistakes."

Taco rose and wiggled through the bars, padding into Dakota's lap. Standing with paws on her chest, he covered her cheek with doggy kisses, making her grin through her tears.

"Taco will do back flips to make you happy." With a fatherly smile, Valentine dug in his duffle and handed her a plaid handkerchief. Somehow, the ludicrous accessory didn't surprise her.

"You're not afraid I'll eat him?" She'd meant the question to be funny, but surprised herself, waiting on edge for his answer.

He smiled and shook his head in silence, glancing at the door again. "No more than Lieutenant Liu would."

"You mean Tiger?"

"They do call him that in camp. He's like you, you see, but with a variant."

It took a couple beats for Valentine's meaning to sink in. *Tiger's a latent, too.* Maybe he really had smelled her shifter scent, and his sandalwood fragrance hadn't been cologne. She gave a long look after him. "A variant? Just how different?"

Scraping sounded in the domed enclosure. She startled, and Valentine darted a glance at the door. "Miss Dakota, we're out of time."

He reached into his duffle and pulled out a portrait keychain, showcasing his baby, Taco. With a closer look, she realized a data storage device backed the picture. She met his gaze with raised brows.

"My research—in exchange for Lieutenant Liu's protection. You must take him with you. They'll do anything to make him shift. And he's at risk because of me." He whispered, dangling the proverbial carrot near the wooden poles separating them.

Dakota's jaw dropped open. She couldn't take her eyes from the tiny hard drive. The shifters could beat extinction with that data. She reached for the keychain and snatched her hand back. Nothing this good could be this easy. Liu might be no more shifter than Valentine. This escape could be Shelton's elaborate ruse to plant a spy. "Anything could be on that drive—or nothing."

His distressed gaze misted over. "*Please.* Take it. Take him. You must leave. They plan to interrogate you in a couple hours." He wiped a hand down his face. "Followed by another ova retrieval."

The metal zipper's whir yanked their attention. Liu slipped in. "We're okay. Just a guy taking a leak."

Dakota sighed in relief.

Liu pulled supplies out of his oversized duffle as if it was Mary Poppins' carpetbag. Sliding a machete into a belt at his waist, he fixed his attention on Dakota. He tossed rubber boots at her. "We leave now, or never. What is it?"

Chapter Twenty-Four

With the dark night surrounding him, Matteo lay on the damp earth, spread-eagle within the sapling cell. Lacerations inside his mouth throbbed and filled his palate with the salty tang of open flesh.

At least, Shelton's ministrations hadn't damaged his enhanced vision. Night had fallen an hour ago, and Matteo scanned the twilight-shrouded trees again for signs of Cristiano.

Though it was not yet midnight, Matteo strained to hear any change in the insect chorus. He expected Cristiano to free Dakota first, as he should. They would come for Matteo, soon.

After about forty-five minutes or so, his hopes dimmed and he suspected Shelton's men had intercepted the shifters. A patrol passed through the jungle about fifty meters out. Their routine, clipped communications gave no hint they'd spotted Cristiano's team. Further, none within the camp seemed to detect the passing force.

The steel shackles weighed heavy on Matteo's wrists and ankles, much more substantial than the brittle handcuffs. Even so, escape would be easy as a jaguar. His increased mass would snap the metal.

However, if he failed to regain human form, and his opposable thumbs, he couldn't rescue Dakota. And trapped as a jaguar, he would lose her forever.

Worthless Pantoja paced outside of the cage while Matteo, glaring at his back, decided how long the merc would live. Even if Pantoja kept faith in the end, he'd let them take Dakota into that butcher shop.

With each minute of darkness that passed, Matteo became more certain something had forced Cristiano to abort any rescue attempt.

One by one, lights within the camo domes winked out around the campfire's glow, and still, no jaguar's hiss to send Matteo into action. Facing the jungle, Pantoja halted behind the tree nearest Matteo's head.

"Are the changers here?" Pantoja whispered so quietly, Matteo thought he'd imagined it. The merc resumed his path around the cage.

Doubting the man's intent, Matteo leveled a glare at him. Pantoja kept an unrushed pace and paused again in the same spot. "You hear me. Don't be an ass-wipe. After Shelton's done with her, they take her back to surgery."

With blood pounding in his ears, Matteo growled deep in his chest. Anxious to move and furious, he barely stifled an impatient snarl when Pantoja started another lap.

One decision made. The merc would live another day. Matteo would lie down with Satan himself to free Dakota. Once in the jungle, he'd find Cristiano and the others and leave Pantoja to face his fate.

"That patrol will be back in forty minutes. There's no radio contact here." Pantoja lifted his chin. "And just so you know, *I* did that. You ready?"

Matteo resented the smug bastard and wanted to knock the arrogant look from his face. However, if Pantoja told the truth, it might take humans a half an hour moving fast on foot to reinforce this position.

"At your signal." Matteo gritted through clenched teeth.

Since the surgeon had expected a monkey, Shelton likely tried to hide Matteo and Dakota from most of the troops. He'd only shown the video to a few on his squad. However, Shelton's secrecy had given the jags a distinct advantage. With the exception of the few guards, his troops wouldn't expect jaguars.

Accepting help from Pantoja grated on Matteo's last nerve. However, without sure knowledge Dakota was safe, he couldn't wait on Cristiano any longer.

Pantoja completed another circuit and scanned the area. Dropping to his knees, he unlocked one shackle. "Hold still until I say. Then we move."

Matteo tipped his head a degree. He'd still prefer Pantoja dead.

On the far side of the campsite, the sentry Matteo had left tied up in the jungle exited a one-man tent. He hoped he didn't regret leaving the soldier alive.

"*Asas*, want a few minutes before lights out?" the sentry asked.

Pantoja gave the man a casual glance and dropped the key next to the shackle. Rising from his squat, he stretched as though nursing sore muscles. "I'm good. Tiger's due around midnight."

"Too bad, I'd like a couple minutes alone with that guy."

Pantoja laughed. "I'll pass along your love."

He resumed his route around the cage. Across the campsite, Matteo's freed prisoner sat on a flipped bucket, glancing at him with narrowed eyes and cleaning his rifle. Finally, the sentry crawled into his canvas den.

All the while, Matteo imagined Dakota, restrained and vulnerable. *Waiting for help. Waiting for me.* Raccoon Eyes might even take revenge for his damaged face. With a mix of dread and fury, Matteo's heart pounded.

Pantoja's footfalls mimed a metronome inside Matteo's head. After forever, the sentry's tent went dark. Pantoja's gait didn't change.

Knowing the enemy needed Dakota healthy did little to quell Matteo's fears. He'd only known this kind of terror the night Anna died. He shoved the crippling memory back into the depths of his mind. Rash action born of panic wouldn't help Dakota.

She would fight until her last breath, so Matteo would do the same. Schooling himself to patience, the pounding in his ears lessened, and his breathing slowed. After several minutes of listening to Pantoja's pacing, his footfalls stopped.

"I think he's down for the night." Whispering, Pantoja unlocked the remaining shackles and opened the cage door. Matteo crawled from the cell and rose up next to him, stretching sore muscles. He missed the instant jaguar healing. Pantoja slung a backpack over his shoulder.

Matteo clenched his jaw until had they traveled several meters into the jungle. "I work alone."

"Fuck that. You changers owe me a shit-ton of cash, and I can't stay here, not now." Pantoja tossed him a bottle of water. "Drink up, catman. I don't want to carry your furry ass."

"Keep up, merc, because I won't carry yours." Matteo fought a grin. Maybe the mole would live a couple more days.

****

Dakota fingered the hard drive, looking into Valentine's eyes, willing him to agree. "You should come with us."

From behind him, Lieutenant David Liu, Tiger's real name, stiffened and narrowed red-amber eyes at her. He mouthed, *We need to go.*

Valentine lifted his dog for a kiss and got love in return. Dakota couldn't tell if he hadn't heard her or simply ignored her.

"Miss Dakota, you tempt me. However, Taco and I would be a terrible burden. We'd slow you down, and you'd be apprehended."

"Eventually, they'll know you downloaded this."
She lifted the key chain. "You'll go to prison for
treason."

"Perhaps." He seemed too easily resigned to a
fate in Leavenworth.

"You think you deserve it, don't you?"

"Perhaps."

Guilt must consume the geneticist. Worried for
this strange doctor, Dakota ignored the heavy sigh from
Liu. She couldn't leave Valentine behind. "Who'll take
care of Taco if…"

He nuzzled his dog and turned to her, his eyes
shining up behind his wire rims. Clearly, Taco was his
world. "He doesn't tolerate anyone but me. Oddly,
though, he likes you. And the other one, Matteo is it?"

"I'm kind of a dog person." She responded
absently, consumed with visions of this frail-looking man
surrounded by hardened criminals. However, she
couldn't argue with his reasoning. He'd get them caught,
for sure. Reaching through the bars, she stroked Taco's
velvety ears. "Later, if … we'll find a way to take care of
him."

Valentine placed the dog into his duffle and
stood, tucking the bag under one arm. "Goodbye, Miss
Dakota. It's been a pleasure."

"Dr. Valentine, could you help with one more
thing?"

At his nod, Dakota pushed down her misgivings.
"Do you know what happened to my mother? Did they
grab her, too?"

His eyes were gentle. "You and Liu—and now
D'Cruz—are our only subjects."

They hadn't captured her mother. Dakota
slumped back and sighed in relief. *Matteo's a subject!*
She glared at Liu. "You didn't say he'd been captured."

"What the hell did you think I meant?" he whispered and then blasted a sigh.

They had Matteo. Escape just became a secondary goal. What if he shifted to get loose or to protect himself? She had to free him. "We go, now."

Valentine looked from one to the other with raised brows. "I'd best let you two get started."

Liu met the shorter man's gaze. "Dr. V—" He cleared his throat and blinked. "Thanks."

He gave Valentine a man hug, and the doctor responded with awkward half pats on Liu's back. If not for Dakota's sudden need for speed, she might have found the exchange amusing.

"Come with me." With a glance at Dakota, Liu led Valentine out of the tent in an emotion-charged silence. After a few fretful minutes, he returned. Wiping his nose, he sniffed and focused on his never-ending duffle. Sloshing from inside his backpack broke the silence. "He'll stay in my tent here. Didn't want him hiking in the dark."

Despite Liu's reluctance to bring the geneticist along, he undoubtedly shared her worry for Valentine.

"That's good," her voice cracked. No one had ever given up so much for her. "I doubt I'd be that brave."

Behind Liu, the zipper traveled the tracks signaling an intruder. At the whirring noise, Liu whipped around just as Pantoja stooped through the opening. Liu raised his rifle to Pantoja's face. Just as fast, Pantoja leveled a handgun back at him.

"Damn, *Asas*. Use codes much?" whispered Liu.

Their shocked expressions turned icy as they glared at each other.

Nothing about Pantoja reassured her. He'd let them take her to the operating room. *Pantoja has betrayed us.* Now, she'd never get out of here. Desperate, she glanced at the open flap behind him. He blocked her path.

He angled his head at Dakota without breaking the fierce standoff. "Why's she loose, Tiger?"

"Why didn't you use the code, *Asas*?" Liu's whisper was as strident as Pantoja's.

They would wake the whole camp. But Pantoja *was* whispering. Dakota tried to read him. He evidently didn't want anyone to know he was here. When he glanced at her, his intense gaze seemed to hold a message. Maybe the Fox's intuition was hereditary. Dakota had no choice. She would out Pantoja and hope for the best.

Dakota stepped between the two men, grabbing both weapons by the barrel, shoving their aims to the ground. "Put your guns away, now. Both of you."

Neither man complied, but they didn't fight her grip on their weapons, either.

"Jose, I'm glad to see you," whispered Dakota. She would flush out his intent, one way or the other.

Liu's brows rose. "*Jose*, my rifle's ready to fire. Don't think your handgun will be faster."

"Stop it." Dakota snapped at Liu. "Jose's here to rescue me," she turned to their *mole*, "aren't you?"

With all the whispering, they sounded like a nest of pit vipers. She glared at their double agent, betting her life on him.

He ignored her question and lifted his chin at Liu. "Explain."

Dakota lost what little patience she had. "Later. I trust him, so you will, too. Let's go."

Leaving them to kill each other, she slipped on the pilfered boots, courtesy of Liu, and slung his backpack of water bottles over her shoulder. Before she could slide out of the tent flap, each man grabbed her by the arm.

Jerking free, she wheeled to face them. "Now what?"

Pantoja pulled zip-ties from his pocket, holding them up between them. "Prisoner formation."

The offending plastic strips transfixed Dakota, spurring her heart into a gallop. With a sudden urge to flee, she shifted her weight to the balls of her feet. "Not happening."

He twirled the ties in front of her. "Matteo's waiting to meet us."

She wrenched her gaze to Pantoja's dark eyes, studying him. "He's free?"

Pantoja nodded. "Thanks to me."

With a shaky sigh and heart pounding, she turned, placing her hands at her back.

"The thanks I get for risking my life," he grumbled near her ear.

Next to her, Liu smirked, seeming amused by her sudden distrust. Distress over the restraints must have shown in her eyes, and wiped the mirth from his expression. He angled to the side, watching closely while Pantoja looped the ties around her wrists, linking them together.

Dakota squeezed her eyes shut and forced a slow, shaky breath. Living with panic her whole life should have made this easier. However, submitting to the cuffs—even as a ruse—conjured a new kind of terror. A drip of perspiration trickled between her breasts.

Swallowing her fear, she dared to look at Liu. His dark amber gaze reflected only concern. To hide her embarrassment, she gritted her teeth and glared resolutely at the canvas behind him.

Liu glowered at Pantoja over her shoulder. "The

cuffs come off when she says. Double-cross us, I'll kill you."

"Back at you." Pantoja scowled. "Anyone asks— we're marching her to the main camp. Shelton's orders."

****

Matteo rested his rifle on a forked tree limb in front of him. Surveilling his planned rendezvous site thirty meters below, he adjusted to a more comfortable position on his branch while he waited for Pantoja. He checked his rifle site. Pantoja had stashed his AR 15 along their path to Dakota's camp, surprising Matteo.

Sending Pantoja in after her had nearly killed him, but their mole could walk in and escort her out. Pantoja's reasoning—and the cached rifle—had earned Matteo's trust. However, worry over their delay was wearing his confidence thin.

"We thought you were in chains." Cristiano's conversational voice came from ground level, interrupting the insect drone.

"So you were around somewhere." Matteo's broken nose couldn't even sense the male jag directly beneath him. No more than a shadow between the tree trunks below, Cristiano had snuck in undetected.

He chuckled. "Raoul said you planned a diversion. Nice job."

"Didn't want to be an inconvenience." The *legendary Enforcer* would never live down capture by humans—or worse—sending in a human to rescue his mate-to-be. Annoyed, but refusing the bait, Matteo dropped to the ground next to his naked friend. A growl rumbled in his chest. "You're late."

"We brought Alejandro. It took more time."

"Any sign of Amadeo?"

"Not yet. It was a slim hope he could get here fast enough. We waited for Dakota's camp to fall asleep and your boy Pantoja brought her out in handcuffs. Nice we don't need to rescue you, too." Cristiano's good-natured smile didn't relieve the sting of sarcasm.

He looked out into the dark, watching for something. A few seconds later, whispers of foliage told Matteo someone approached.

Three male shifters in jaguar form emerged from the rainforest, each hissing a quiet greeting. Raoul's charcoal pelt faded into the dark, and Nicolas's classic orange and black coloring made him extremely useful. Jaime looked almost identical to Cristiano's jaguar appearance. Matteo couldn't detect a scent from any of them.

Their arrival soothed his need for action. With luck, they would do no more than race to Nicolas's hidden helicopter. "Nice to see you, my friends. While I give Cristiano report, establish a close perimeter around us."

Jaime and Nicolas launched onto tree trunks, racing up into the canopy. Alejandro trailed in with a grease-painted face, wearing matching camo fatigues, and toting a backpack of supplies. Though louder than the others, he traveled quietly for a human. Raoul padded a few meters away and circled the small group.

Greeting Alejandro with the fist bump that seemed to have replaced casual handshakes, Matteo thanked him for his help.

The foreman snorted. "I'm just a mule, packing supplies—and clothes."

"Clothes? Ever-sensitive Cristiano." Matteo shared a smile with his naked friend. In truth, after recalling how Dakota's *Ardor* had assaulted him, he preferred the other males wore pants.

Alejandro chuckled. "He thinks of everything, that one."

After nearly losing his life at the airport, the foreman had insisted on joining in Dakota's rescue. "I lost her," he'd said.

"And you're never *just* anything, my friend. You've risked your life for Dakota, twice now. I'll never forget."

"It's nothing. The Salazars are family," Alejandro mumbled. If given the chance, Matteo would honor this self-effacing man as well as his future generations.

Family. Isolation no longer held any appeal. The realization bored into him. He had Dakota and her sister, and the Salazars' clan. A full life waited for him—if they got Dakota out in one piece. He cleared his throat against a sudden bout of emotion.

"Yes. We are family. Cristiano chose well." He squeezed Alejandro's shoulder and then turned to Cristiano. "Pantoja's inside to bring her out."

The embarrassing announcement barely scraped past Matteo's throat. Cristiano's eyes widened. "Interesting. A million well spent?"

"For now." Matteo gave a noncommittal shrug. He still worried he'd risked Dakota's life on a faithless mercenary.

Cristiano's brows knit together. "Dakota had a visitor. After a few minutes, he and Pantoja marched her out of the camp in handcuffs. Could he have recruited another?"

"Who? What direction?" Unease quickened in Matteo's gut.

"Toward the main camp. The soldier wore U.S. camo—looked mixed race."

"Asian? With blackened eyes?"

Cristiano nodded.

"He's her guard." Growling, Matteo could barely force the words out. "She fought him and—"

"We were ready to take her, but caught your scent and wanted to even the odds." Cristiano grimaced. "Your Pantoja has turned on us."

"Shelton plans to interrogate her at three AM." Matteo wanted to rail at him for delaying even a minute to free her. "That maggot Pantoja has taken her early. He only released me to prevent Shelton from discovering his treason. We need to extract her now."

Cristiano frowned with narrowed eyes. "Agreed."

"The merc's mine. Let's move." A feline snarl filled Matteo's voice. Terror for Dakota sent adrenaline through him, and his rage over betrayal added more fuel.

"Follow us. Better yet, ride." Cristiano's unprecedented offer humbled Matteo. Shifters bore only their children on their backs, ever.

Raoul barked a roar into the night, signaling the other males to return. Following Cristiano's lead, he bumped Alejandro and swung his dark head towards his back with a coughed snarl.

The foreman's mouth dropped open, and he turned widened eyes to Matteo. "Does he mean…"

"Yes, he does. One day, you'll tell your grandchildren the story." Matteo tried to reassure Alejandro, as well as himself. "God willing, I will, too."

With a black glow limning his form, Cristiano dropped to all fours, melting into an amber-eyed, black-on-black patterned jaguar. His jag form had gained mass over the years, maybe even more than Matteo's.

"So you do shift. Good to know." With profound gratitude, Matteo leaped astride the muscular back. He threaded fingers into Cristiano's pelt and grabbed a fistful of fur. With his other hand, he patted Cristiano's shoulder. "Thank you, my friend."

Cristiano gave an almost human-sounding snort and loped off. After Alejandro seemed steady aboard

JUNGLE SALVATION

Raoul, Cristiano increased their speed to just short of full throttle.

Chapter Twenty-Five

Matteo waited impatiently as Raoul emerged from his shift, rising from all fours. The ancient accepted a pair of dark green and brown pants from Alejandro. "I didn't close in to see her, but caught her scent. They're about thirty minutes outside the main camp."

No one asked why Raoul didn't get near to investigate. Dakota's queen fragrance could easily turn the jaguar-shifter males against each other. An unnatural silence charged the space between the men. They pulled on camo gear, while Alejandro smeared grease paint under Jaime's eyes.

With enemies so near, deep in the jungle, none would've chosen human form. Matteo understood their sacrifice. At least while human, they respected his relationship with her. After sharing a meaningful glance with Cristiano, he included Jaime and Nicolas in his gaze. "Thank you, all."

Raoul nodded with a half-smile. "Mark her soon, my friend."

If only he could.

****

Dakota followed Pantoja's shadowy form through the darkened jungle, supposedly to rendezvous with Matteo. Liu brought up the rear with eerily quiet footfalls. She'd checked more than once to make sure he followed.

Tugging again at the loose plastic strips, their give reassured her of an easy escape. She took small comfort that with only a few strides she could lose herself in this blackness.

From above, a harsh squawk cut into the monotonous drone of insects, startling her. Neither of the men seemed fazed. Near blindness in the stagnant jungle night made the unfamiliar sounds more ominous. Willing herself to calm, she sniffed the mold-tainted air for any trace of mocha. "How much further?"

"Soon." Pantoja whispered as she had in case a patrol followed. "We're circling back to him now."

Without sight or scent of Matteo, every step grew heavier, casting doubt on her decision to trust Pantoja. She fingered the data-filled key chain in her back pocket. It hadn't landed in the jungle-floor compost layer, yet. One of the backpacks Pantoja or Liu carried would've been more secure. However, if she needed to bolt, Dr. Valentine's work had to come with her.

"Halt!" Not quite shouting, Liu shoved past her and grabbed Pantoja's arm. He flashed a low-level beam at the ground a mere yard in front of Pantoja, spotlighting a coiled diamond-backed snake. "Fer-de-lance gets a wide berth."

The pit viper raised its triangular head, tasting the air with its tongue, and the tubular body curled in on itself. Dakota sucked in a breath and stepped back, and Pantoja joined her.

"Damn, Tiger, you're freaky. How'd you see him?" Pantoja's tone held awe.

The next second, two shadows dropped from above, landing on either side of the men. The black shapes fought in the dark, and Liu's lantern hit the ground, backlighting their struggle. Two more assailants exploded from the blackness on either side of Dakota. One with a shock of thick, wavy hair grabbed her upper arm, his vise-grip hold digging painfully into her flesh.

Terror of renewed captivity ignited a powder keg of pent-up fury. Dakota exploded in a torrent of motion. Yanking free of the loose plastic ties, she elbowed her assailant and wheeled with a throat strike.

Mid-move, the powerful man clapped an iron hand around her wrist, and in the same smooth motion, he locked her free arm against his bare torso. Dakota roared in impotent rage, fighting for escape. Pulling her in close, his chuckle rumbled against her breasts, and citrus-tinged cinnamon blossomed from his skin. *Shifters!*

Expecting the unknown male to release her, Dakota ceased her struggle and sighed in relief. Instead, her captor tucked her hand against his chest. Almost nose-to-nose with her, his mercurial eyes mirrored the dim light.

"We're here to save you, *niñita.*" His murmured Spanish hummed against her ear, sending gooseflesh down her arms. Cinnamon blossomed around her, and her arousal spiked unbidden.

The male smiled, lifting his nose to a sniffing position.

If she'd had a free hand, she'd have slapped him.

Given she ran for her life, her unexpected reaction put her on full alert. A shift's heat wave traveled her torso, and she stifled the change. *Now? Kitty needed to work on timing.*

A hooded mercury gaze and parted lips banished his amused expression. "*Dios mio, senhorita*, you *do* have fire." He nuzzled her neck and inhaled. "And lavender."

Rescue or not, no one would restrain her again. Ever. Certainly, no weak-minded male so easily distracted by her scent. She kneed him square in the balls.

He doubled over and groaned, releasing her. She leaped back and glared at him. "You're late. I rescued myself. Get your head in the game."

Leaving her amorous ally to recover, she swung

around to save the rest of her team. Cristiano and Jaime restrained Pantoja, who hissed whispered explanations.

"What are you?" Matteo straddled Liu on the ground, and his taut broad shoulders loomed over his victim. He spat words in Liu's face, while holding a knife at his throat.

He was going to kill him. Dakota raced to Matteo's side.

****

The Asian kid pushed at Matteo's forearm with surprising strength for a human. "I'm one of you!"

"No. You're *other*." Matteo spoke through an involuntary hiss.

Since the man's rancid stench made Matteo want to slit his throat, maybe his nose had healed. Heat traveled Matteo's skin, and his pending shift's glow reflected off his prisoner's odd reddish-gold irises. Barely a man, the U.S. soldier appeared only a little older than Tad.

"Holy shit!" The kid gulped with wild eyes. "You're gonna change, aren't you?"

His Adam's apple bobbed, grazing Matteo's blade. A bead of crimson trickled down his neck. The soldier's pupils dilated to black, enveloping his golden gaze. Sour adrenaline tainted his blood's already foul scent. His fright had escalated to terror.

Matteo needed intel. He'd get nothing from an incoherent prisoner. With an iron will, he shut down his change to jaguar. "Nothing but plain human. Sorry to disappoint."

Too late. His captive thrashed his head side to side, fighting an unseen battle. While Liu bucked under Matteo, a tawny glow shimmered across his skin, and he roared, animal-like.

"Don't hurt him!" Dakota's panicked voice cut

through the melee. "No, David! Don't shift now!"

Leaping off the flailing man, Matteo stared, rapt, at a blossoming igloo of howling amber light. "*Mio Dios.*"

The nimbus resolved, leaving an oversized tiger crouching amid shreds of camo fabric. Liu panted in clear distress. White canines gleamed, and his jewel-toned eyes blazed in the darkness. He swung his massive feline head side to side, and snarled at the entire group. When his gaze found Dakota, he locked on her.

Without an apparent thought in her brilliant mind, Dakota sprinted toward the nine hundred pounds of cat. "You're okay. Stay with us."

Matteo grabbed her just before she could hug the snarling beast. "Don't touch him. He's out of his mind."

"Let me go! David doesn't know what's happening." Screaming, Dakota jerked in his arms. "I promised to help him."

Matteo eyed the newly shifted tiger, easily the size of any jaguar shifter. Liu's tail whipped side to side, and Matteo dragged Dakota a couple meters away, snugging her backside against him. He lowered his lips to her ear. "We'll take care of him, I swear it. But you're not going near an out-of-control cat."

The massive tiger wheeled and lunged into the darkness, leaving Matteo and the others exchanging perplexed looks.

"Holy shit," whispered Pantoja.

Beside him, Jaime loosened his grip on Pantoja and turned widened eyes to Cristiano. "Do we have shirttail relatives, *Papai*?"

Cristiano shook his head, gaping after Liu's trail. "Not that I know of."

Matteo stared after the tiger in wonder, gentling his hold on Dakota to an embrace. He didn't want to let her go.

Still gazing after Liu, she leaned back into Matteo, laying her arm over his.

Her touch soothed the unbearable dread that had eaten at his soul. *What if I'd lost her?* Curling Dakota tighter in his arms, he snuck a kiss to her ear. He glanced at Raoul, the eldest. "Have you ever heard of tiger shifters?"

Raoul pulled his gaze from the big cat's trail. "Never. Stinks, though."

Dakota knitted her brows. "You don't like sandalwood?"

Snickers from the other shifters made Matteo's chest rumble. There was only one reason the tiger smelled good to Dakota. To make matters worse, Raoul's scent covered her body. Matteo stifled the growl and glared at the male.

Raoul smiled wide, his teeth stark in the night. Clearly, he enjoyed taunting death. "Mark her soon, my friend."

"You're repeating yourself, Old One," Matteo deadpanned.

Dakota glanced from Matteo to Raoul. "You smell good, too, *Old One*." She gave his crotch a pointed look. "How's the package?"

Raoul's mocking smile faded to a droll stare, before he strode—not too freely—to pick up the flashlight. "Let's move."

The male's lingering scent on Dakota created a vivid mental picture for Matteo. Fury might have taken over, if not for Raoul's impaired gait. Matteo laughed outright, striking out after him.

"We can't leave David behind!" Dakota pulled at Matteo's arm and turned her misty aqua gaze on him.

"Dawn's too near. There's not time to chase

down the tiger. And nothing's safer than a cat in the jungle."

Dakota looked longingly after the tiger's trail, lines marring her brow. "You can't know that. He's all alone, and he's never shifted." Her voice broke. "He risked his life to help me escape—and I promised him sanctuary."

The others drew near. It seemed no male could ignore a jag queen's tears. Pantoja put a hand on her shoulder. "Matteo's right. According to Shelton, Liu's the best jungle soldier in the U.S. Army. Add the cat—he's made for the rainforest."

Cristiano nodded. "This is Raoul's territory. When it's safe, he'll find Liu and bring him to us." He raised a brow at the older male. "Won't you?"

"Sure." Raoul snorted, lifting his chin. "But he sleeps outside the hut."

"He owns my life for bringing you out. I swear we'll honor your vow." Matteo tried to soothe Dakota's worry.

"I just hope he doesn't run into Amadeo." Raoul smiled, taunting her with the veiled threat.

"Who?" she asked with widened eyes.

"A shifter from Ecuador." After a quelling look at Raoul, Matteo scanned the perimeter. "I'd hoped he'd be with us by now."

"Oh." She gazed up at Matteo. "I knew you'd come."

Matteo drank in the sight of her. Ignoring the lingering pain of his injuries, he kissed her, long and slow, only vaguely aware of the others' retreat. He wanted to inspect every inch of her. "Nothing could keep me away. Tell me you're unharmed."

"I'm okay." She frowned and trailed a gentle finger over his brow. "But you're kind of banged up."

"Not anymore." He looked into her sea-green eyes, and knew he was home. "Now, I'm whole again."

Jaime paced to them. "Sorry to interrupt. Running for our lives and all." He shoved a thumb over his shoulder toward Pantoja. "He says we might have a thirty-minute lead on a full force patrol, but they'll send out their swiftest scouts."

Matteo growled deep in his chest. "Raoul, take point. We're moving out, *now.*"

Raoul's smile widened, showing his back teeth. "*Sim, Enforcer.* Immediately, as you say."

Ignoring his insolence, Matteo turned to Nicolas. "Check our back trail and report. Recon only. Do *not* engage."

Nicolas nodded and disappeared into the dark understory. After a minute, the rustling of fabric sounded as he disrobed several meters away. He'd cache his clothing in the jungle. With Nicolas's natural jaguar coloring and his renowned stealth skills, Shelton's patrol would never detect him in the dark.

Raoul took the flashlight and waved the group to fall in behind him. He led them off at a jog. In front of Matteo, Pantoja and Alejandro's easy breaths told him both were fit for the downhill retreat. The shifters would hold their speed to human tolerance. Behind Matteo and Dakota, the Salazars kept a relaxed pace.

"Where're we going?" She jogged at Matteo's side, just where he wanted her.

"Nicolas's chopper is at the base of the mountain. If we maintain pace, it's about an hour and a half away."

As though summoned by their conversation, helicopter blades whopped high above, sending birds squawking down from the canopy. The rainforest's cathedral ceiling and the night would conceal them from the sky's prying eyes. Still, Matteo couldn't dispel a sense of foreboding.

"Move off the trail." Raoul slowed and led them into thicker cover, his flashlight casting his shadow among the trees. He halted between thick trunks growing close together.

Dakota stopped and grimaced into the dark above them. "Damn."

Cristiano pulled up beside their small gathering with Jaime at his side. "They might have spotted us."

More twenty-first century technology had to be at play. Matteo didn't doubt his friend, but needed education—fast. "How?"

Alejandro joined, frowning. "Thermal imaging—only if they found a thin spot in the trees." He looked up into the black awning of branches. "They need line of sight to detect our heat signatures. If they get lucky, we'll show up as green shapes through their goggles—or in a live camera feed."

Matteo nodded. "Like the German tanks used, but mounted on a chopper."

"Way more accurate, now," added Cristiano.

Dakota focused on Pantoja, Shelton's spy tech. "Could they have trailed us with an infrared camera drone? Like your dragonfly that recorded me?"

Pantoja missed—or ignored—her hinted sarcasm. "Unlikely. Shelton bought the best, and our thermal drone was much bigger than my little bug. We would have likely spotted anything they sent."

"And too noisy to sneak by shifter ears." Alejandro's grim expression eased into a smile. "Shifters will hear a chopper before it reaches us, too."

Matteo was out of his element. Nicolas's helicopter was several kilometers away, and in the dark, even shifter eyes might miss a random bare spot ten stories overhead. Twenty-first century tech had outpaced him, and lives were on the line. He glanced from Dakota to the men clustered around him. "Recommendations?"

"If they *do* locate us, they still have to catch us. Can we double our pace?" Jaime rubbed his chin, glancing at Jose and Alejandro. Likely, he worried that Matteo would slow them down, too.

"We'll try. No other choice."

They had left so much unsaid. For any hope of getting home, they had to get their escape flight off the ground and stay out of firing range. Nearly impossible with commandos on their heels. But, somehow, they had to get to the helicopter undetected.

Matteo's gaze landed on Dakota, and his profound love for her stopped his heart. No matter what happened to him, she would return to the safety of Brazil. "Dakota, can you shift?"

"I think so. Something about being around shifters." She smiled, and in the next moment, her skin shimmered a dark glow. Relief washed through him.

"If we get in trouble, follow Cristiano and Jaime into the trees. No soldier will catch you."

Eyes flashing, she fisted her hands on her hips. "Oh, no, you don't. We stay together."

Unaccustomed to dissent, he narrowed his *Enforcer* gaze on her. "You're not—"

Dakota's lips parted, no doubt in rebellion; however, Nicolas erupted from the blackness behind them, cutting short their battle of wills. He sprinted to a stop in front of Matteo. Bent over, bare-chested and winded, he motioned to Alejandro to douse his low-beam lantern.

Darkness engulfed them, and Matteo sensed a palpable wave of anxiety travel through their party. Suddenly, the insect chorus seemed even louder.

"Report," he demanded, instinct keeping his

voice to a whisper.

"Nine men—five minutes—behind me. Fell into the trees from the sky! Rappelled from—the canopy," Nicolas wheezed out between breaths.

Dakota's eyes widened. "They sent in *tree-jumpers*?"

Matteo's ignorance frustrated him, but worse, his lack of knowledge might get them killed. "Explain."

"Elite airborne stuff—like my jumpmaster. Paratroopers land in trees and climb or rappel down."

Matteo raised his brows. Dakota jumped out of planes? Why was he surprised?

Nicolas still sucked wind. "Yes. Crazy men."

Traveling in human form would get them caught, but Matteo had no choice. Even if he could shift, he wouldn't leave Alejandro and Jose behind. For all his doubts over Pantoja, the man had proved true in the end.

"Nicolas and Raoul, drop back and trail us. If Shelton's men get close, let us know."

Both nodded and, not bothering to find privacy, they stripped and shifted.

Already striding past Dakota, Matteo locked eyes with her. "Salazars, if we need to split, go cat and take Dakota on ahead."

The pair stepped toward her, and she puffed a sigh that Matteo hoped signaled resignation. He glanced at Raoul and Alejandro, and his worry for the foreman grew. None could carry him now. "If needed, we'll cover their retreat."

Alejandro collected Raoul and Nicolas's discarded clothing. "*Sim, Enforcer*."

Matteo lifted his rifle. "Let's move."

****

Dakota followed Matteo's shadowy form through the rainforest in the pitch-black night. They'd been running almost flat out for several minutes. The jungle floor and sparse undergrowth teemed with lethal critters, so she didn't dare leave his wake. Jaime and Cristiano trailed right behind her, apparently taking Matteo's protection order to heart.

A bite from anything, and Dakota would need to shift to clear the poison. The thought brought reassuring heat to her skin. A smart girl would just shift to cat for this run, but she wanted to be near Matteo. And he ran as human.

She looked over her shoulder. "Alejandro, Jose, stay single file behind Matteo. His scent will clear out poisonous snakes and bugs."

They nodded, breathing harder than the last time she'd glanced at them.

Since reuniting with the shifters, the urge to shift—her misdiagnosed panic disorder—had returned in full force. Now, she feared going furry by accident.

Alejandro and Pantoja chased behind the Salazars in single file, their breathing more labored with each stride. Even downhill, the breakneck pace had used them up.

Prior to manifesting her cat, Dakota couldn't have sprinted in the jungle sweatbox, either. Matteo hissed them to a halt in a level clearing devoid of ground cover save decomposing leaves. Bark-covered columns stretched upward, supporting a murky black ceiling devoid of moon or stars.

Sucking wind, Alejandro lifted the tail of his camo shirt and wiped his brow. He turned on his hand-held lantern, using the damp cloth to cover the lens, lowering the beam to candlelight.

Dakota tugged on his backpack's shoulder strap. "I got this."

Alejandro hesitated before handing over the

canvas bag. Matteo caught her gaze and gave a discreet nod before turning to the Salazars a few paces away. "Cristiano and Jaime, it's time to take Dakota—you'll travel faster as cats. We'll be right behind you and meet at the chopper."

The two men nodded, disrobing with lightning speed. Alejandro, still breathing hard, collected their clothing and then filled the backpack Dakota held out. The Salazars, with identical, muscular V-shaped torsos, raced silently into the darkened jungle, and Dakota lost them. She had expected Jaime's sculpted physique, but Cristiano's taut build surprised her.

Matteo lifted one corner of his mouth. He'd busted her checking out the Salazar goods. She shrugged a shoulder. They had more important things to worry about.

White light filtered down from the thick canopy high above. Nicolas dropped naked from cover to a lower branch. "*Enforcer*, we've gained on them. They're about twenty minutes behind."

Matteo nodded. "Cover our rear."

Nicolas's whispered update sent a short-lived wave of relief through Dakota. Their small lead wouldn't get them safely off the ground.

Matteo's gaze settled on the two humans. "Nice work. We can do this."

Pantoja nodded, but Alejandro looked too fatigued to respond. Neither appeared optimistic. She sent a weak smile to Matteo. She didn't buy his optimism either. They were in deep shit.

His special treatment of her would get the others—and maybe him—killed. Unfortunately, their need for stealth didn't allow a pushback discussion.

At the thought of separating from Matteo, a knot formed in her throat. She blinked back tears. Crying wouldn't help. Avoiding his gaze, she tugged off her V-neck scrub top and wadded it.

When Alejandro reached for her bundle, she slid Valentine's precious hard drive into his hand. Hidden under the balled-up shirt, she closed his fingers around the keychain and pulled him close.

His eyes widened, but he didn't say anything. She leaned in cheek to cheek, her lips grazing his ear. "This data can save the shifter species. If you have to, hide it in the jungle."

"We put a small pack around your neck. Take it with you, to safety," Alejandro barely whispered in broken English. He sent Pantoja a furtive glance.

Anticipating a battle and possible recapture, she didn't dare carry the data. "By now, Shelton knows I've got it. He won't suspect a human."

A quiet jingle at Alejandro's hip told her he'd pocketed the drive. "*Sim, senohrita.* As you say."

She finished stripping and put the rest of her clothing into the backpack. Matteo reached for the bag before Alejandro could take it. "Leave her to shift."

Surrounded by men, Dakota suspected he tried to give her a semblance of privacy. His concern for her modesty was sweet.

She smiled at him. "Since we run for our lives, I can go without a dressing room."

No hint of amusement tempered his stern countenance. "Any man who drools over you might die."

"Oh boy. I think they're a little busy for that, don't you?"

He didn't respond.

Nearby amid the stark tree trunks, ultraviolet light shaped two bodies, melting Jamie and Cristiano into giant, shadowy beasts. Their eerie glow played over the stark planes of Matteo's face, making him appear even more lethal.

The Salazar shifts triggered the familiar panic in her chest, reassuring her that her cat lay in wait. She could fight. "I don't need to be coddled. We're stronger together, I know it."

Matteo ignored her protest, cupping her face with his hands. "You're brave—I know this. However, I sent Jaime to safety, too. He's our only mated male. You're both too important."

She parted her lips to object and, as though he tried to force her to reason, he firmed his caress to a hold.

"I can't live without you." His serious tone dropped to pleading. "We're out of time. No argument— please."

"But…" *I can't live without you, either.* He had one thing right. They *were* out of time. Dakota nodded, emotion stinging her eyes. No matter what the future held, she would not let him die for her.

Matteo enfolded her in his arms for a half-minute—not nearly long enough. Another time, with his bare chest pressing against her breasts, he'd have set her body on fire. Now, only desperate longing to share the future with this man consumed her.

Dakota slid a hand behind his neck and, wadding dreads in her fist, planted a demanding kiss on his lips. "Meet me at the chopper, dammit," she ordered. "You might be my first love, so don't screw it up."

From above, Nicolas's dark glow lit Matteo's copper eyes over his broadening smile. He pressed his forehead to hers. "You *are* my last love, so save me a seat."

Heart swelling with his confession, she caressed his cheek in farewell. A burnished reflection highlighted his copper gaze. In the pitch-black night, she couldn't fathom what light created the gleam. *So not human.*

A strange, sour note tainted his comforting mocha. No one needed to tell her that she smelled his fear. Her heart stuttered under her breastbone. *I can't lose him.* Terror had likely turned her own scent rancid, too.

A man had finally filled her heart to bursting, and now she had to leave him. She bowed her head with an entreaty for strength and safety for all of them. Praying had become a habit. "Amen," she whispered.

The mere thought of cream-colored fur propelled a fiery wave over her skin. A split second later, static energy consumed her. Dark purple light obscured the world, and a falling sensation dropped in her stomach before she fell to all fours. The effortless metamorphosis confirmed her theory that she needed a shifter present to change.

Liu had been latent when she'd tried to go cat in his presence. Or maybe a tiger wouldn't help her shift at all. Regardless, she'd probably need a full jaguar shifter nearby to shed her fur, too. She'd worry about that later.

New feline sight revealed a twilight jungle previously hidden from her human senses. She rose to her full cat height and sought Matteo. He grinned, coming next to her and ruffled her sensitive ears. She pressed back into his hand and his reassuring coffee scent.

"Now, go with Cristiano. He'll protect you with his life."

A few feet away sat a large black jaguar. Obsidian rosettes set in black fur had hidden his presence from her human eyes. Cristiano's amber gaze shone back at her from the broad jaguar face, reflecting an indiscernible light. Her private moment with Matteo hadn't been so private.

Towering over her in jaguar form, Cristiano

lowered his massive head and bumped her shoulder. The body language needed no translation. *Get moving.*

Sitting a few feet away, another black jaguar sent her an icy glare. Jaime's clear blue eyes and facial scar had followed him into his feline form. He rose to four paws and swung his tail side to side in obvious impatience.

A final glance at Matteo made her want to rise up and plant her throbbing cheeks against his, one after the other.

Matteo's eyes misted over, and he pushed her away. "They're on our heels. Go!"

Dakota snarled, wheeling to lope off with her escorts.

Chapter Twenty-Six

Matteo ordered Raoul to the trees to scout ahead and then he circled back to lead the party of humans on the ground. Matteo kept their pace to a human sprint.

Though he'd been tempted to ask the shifters to carry Pantoja and Alejandro, their added weight would slow the cats down. Worse, using their combat force as beasts of burden would leave them all vulnerable. Quelling his reservations, he had ordered the shifters to the trees to guard their flanks.

Tough battle choices that put the humans at higher risk grated on his conscience. Matteo vowed not to leave them.

Lagging far behind, Alejandro's heavy breathing turned to strident wheezes. Each inhale sounded like air blown through a blade of grass.

Matteo glanced over his shoulder. Pantoja flagged, too, but not as though his heart might stop. Nicolas dropped to the trail behind the two men and coughed a snarl, urging the humans to keep up.

"Halt," whispered Matteo.

Alejandro stumbled to a stop, and Matteo turned in time to catch him. He kept a hand on the wobbly man's shoulder. If the enemy hadn't already spotted their heat signatures, they need only listen for the discordant harmonics dominating the cricket song.

Pantoja, breathing hard but recovering quickly, glanced at Alejandro with a furrowed brow. "I've got our six."

As he strode past Nicolas to their back trail, the cinnamon cat launched onto a tree trunk before rocketing into the dark above.

Pantoja jumped. He scowled after the shifter.

"Goddammit, don't do that shit."

Breaking to a jog, the merc took up a position a few meters behind them, selecting a clump of broad-leafed plants at the base of a giant ceiba tree. A good choice for cover against human eyes and the heat-seeking goggles Alejandro had warned about. No wonder Shelton had hired Pantoja.

Alejandro seemed steadier. The stooped man's breathing had quieted, and he wiped his watering eyes. "*Senhor*, you and the others catch your Dakota. I'll stay here and slow them down."

Humbled by the offer, and relieved by his ability to speak, Matteo gripped Alejandro's shoulder. "No, my friend. We stand together, here."

Rocky terrain up the mountain on one side of their position offered good advantage. "Join Pantoja. I'll cover you from above and we'll put them in a crossfire."

"Yes, *senhor*." Alejandro straightened, finally taking an easy deep breath. "If we're overrun…" He fingered his pocket and looked to the side, as though searching for words. With a sigh, he met Matteo's gaze. "Tell Consuelo I love her—and Tad. I'm so proud of him."

"Of course, my friend, but you'll tell them yourself." Matteo gave the standard encouragement that all men needed when death hovered close by. Warriors facing battle often exacted such promises—and their comrades honored them.

Grim-faced, Alejandro nodded.

Matteo needn't ask him for a similar commitment. He'd already told Dakota he loved her—and he'd failed his only family, the Salazars. But Cristiano, more brother than friend, deserved to know he loved him.

As Alejandro turned to leave, Matteo halted him

with a touch. "Tell Cristiano…"

The foreman's weak smile didn't light his eyes. "I will, but he knows. He never gave up on you, you know. He'd say, 'When Matteo returns to us.'"

Matteo had no words. He'd thought himself so alone. And he'd been so wrong.

****

Dakota kept pace with Cristiano, dodging downed trees and tortuous vines covering the jungle floor. Then he accelerated down into the darkened crease of a steep ravine, taking their speed even higher. Her newfound stamina surprised her. Foliage and tree trunks blurred past, and a frond slapped her muzzle. Since Jaime followed at her rear, nearly on top of her, her tail tapped his snout.

Staccato gunfire echoed through the understory. Dakota skidded with her haunches under her and hooked left into the trees, circling to their back trail. Cristiano and Jaime's scents, so clear to her jaguar nose, laid out a path akin to runway lights.

She put everything she had into her flight, easily scaling the ravine's edge, gaining flat ground. A torrent of gunfire drove her to a full-on sprint.

Within seconds, the two males caught up, and Jaime launched himself on top of her. Again, someone tried to restrain her. Whipping to her back, she ripped three-inch-long claws down his muzzle, plowing bloody furrows through his scar. He snarled a protest, though the gashes mended while she watched.

Next to Jaime, Cristiano blew out a gusty sigh and growled. He shouldered Jaime aside. Dakota got the impression he'd given in. They could hold her down, but they couldn't carry her.

Dakota sprang back into her race to Matteo. Gunfire came in isolated bursts and grew louder with each stride. Closing in on the steep mountainside battle, and panicked for Matteo, she searched for his scent. Sulfur residue invaded her nose.

Jaime and Cristiano surged ahead of her, and both issued challenging roars into the air. Responding snarls came from either side of the skirmish. The acrid smoke crippled her sense of smell, leaving her nose blind. She'd already learned to rely on scent, and its absence disturbed her.

Cristiano coughed a low-pitched snarl, and his clear message, *Follow*, surprised Dakota. He dropped them to stalking speed and led them to high ground. She mimicked his uphill belly-to-the-ground crawl and they wove through velvety elephant-leaved foliage.

An ominous whistle of air broke through the gunfire, followed by a blast that quaked through the jungle floor. Dakota pinned back her battered ears, barely stifling a snarl.

Cristiano halted at the top of the rise, swinging his tail forward on one side, signaling Jaime and Dakota to join him. Sliding up between the two black jags, she peered through spiked, grassy cover.

About ten yards in front of them, Alejandro and Jose huddled behind a huge tree trunk. In the near-pitch dark, two pairs of enemy soldiers had flanked them. Nicolas stalked the human forces on the high side of the battle, and Raoul circled them in the trees below. Dakota's jaguar vision allowed her to see the action.

Instead of night-vision goggles, the commandos had cameras mounted on their helmets. Possibly, they transmitted imaging as well as provided thermal sight. The enemy teams focused on Alejandro's tree. Fortunately, they showed no awareness of the spying jaguar trio or the pair of cats stalking them.

Cristiano turned a hardened amber gaze her way.

The human intelligence within disturbed her, yet, at the same time, reassured.

He snorted an order to *stay* and Dakota imagined he poked a threatening finger at her. With a last warning look, he and Jaime stole onto the battlefield.

The two males stalked from tree to tree, in a clear attempt to avoid the enemy's infrared line of sight. Dakota kept a keen eye on the nearest commando team, ready to provide a distraction—what, she didn't know. As she'd feared, the pair of soldiers drew up even with Alejandro's tree. One took aim.

"Damn and hellfire," Matteo cursed in quiet Portuguese high above her on the perimeter. A single report split the air, dropping the would-be shooter to the ground.

"Holy Jesus, ya'll, I'm hit." The puppy-eyed guard squealed. *Mouse.*

Dakota gasped, staring at the sweet wiry kid who'd been her reluctant guard. He was no tree-jumper. Reinforcements must have swelled the enemy ranks.

Mouse was a baby. He should be clubbing in Baton Rouge, hoping to get laid—not bleeding out in the jungle. Dakota let out an almost human-sounding wail. Her mournful cry joined the battle din.

Mouse's partner dove to lie next to him, and he tied something around the kid's thigh. After searching the trees above, he rose to one knee, raising his rifle. In the same instant, another blast sounded, and a puff of mud and leaves erupted at his side. He plunged back down to cover.

"Gods, Polo. I'm bleedin' somethin' fierce." A sob broke Mouse's childlike voice, ripping a cry from Dakota.

Another shot came from the trees, and Polo jolted with the report. He grabbed his shoulder. "Goddamnit."

She couldn't hide in the shadows and watch the little Mouse bleed to death. Medics hovered on the sidelines, while the kid cried. Bolting from cover without a logical thought, she only knew she had to protect them. At sight of her, Polo scrambled to cover Mouse. She closed the gap and crouched over the two soldiers, pulling them under her body.

****

Matteo recalled the baby-faced Mouse from Shelton's office. Though his precision shots had ensured the soldiers below would live, Dakota's high-pitched howl had shuddered through Matteo and amplified his guilt. Remorse always followed a battle's first blood.

Refocusing on the firefight, he searched for the biggest threat—that damn rocket launcher. If needed, he would leave the trees to neutralize it. *It.* Rather the live person manning the weapon.

From the lower ridge, a blur of white shot to mid-battlefield and dropped atop the soldier called Polo and the wounded kid. *Dakota!* Blood left Matteo's head so fast he thought he might tumble from his canopy sniper nest.

Extending a paw to trap the escaping Polo, she pulled him under her body. Neither man had gotten a shot off before she had covered them. However, round after enemy round peppered dark splotches across her creamy body. After jumping with the first hits, she settled in, apparently determined to shield the two men.

Shelton's troops had no worry of hitting their own with the big white target protecting their soldiers. An invisible band cinched Matteo's chest tight, and he forced a breath. He crawled along his branch to a position above her, and prepared to drop into the fray.

"Jaime! Cristiano!" Matteo's desperate shouts announced his already exposed position.

303

Even though she clearly disagreed, nothing mattered except Dakota. The Salazars already stalked toward her, leaving Nicolas and Raoul to cover Pantoja's position. The sight of them gave Matteo hope.

From a cluster of trees in the rock face, a missile screamed down into the field, detonating grenade-like in front of the Salazars. Both jaguars soared several meters, with legs flailing, and thudded to the ground, unmoving.

With their bodies intact, Matteo was certain they lived, but losing them put the battle in jeopardy. And worse, now the males were vulnerable. Matteo sucked in a tense breath, willing Cristiano and Jaime to rise. Neither moved.

If Shelton had ordered the heavy artillery, he didn't care how many shifters died—as long as he captured Dakota. Fury welled up, and Matteo's heart kicked hard against his sternum. Any compassion he had held for the humans evaporated. As he had years before, Matteo shoved his reaction deep within and refocused on the objective.

An outcropping of winding strangler figs flagged the rocket launcher's location, and Matteo shredded the jungle patch with gunfire. A satisfying cry traveled the forest, before a stovepipe gun fell in seeming slow motion, end over end, into the undergrowth below. Jaime and Cristiano still hadn't moved.

The hollering man under Dakota continued his struggle, but he would escape only at her pleasure. While bullets flew, she licked the back of his neck.

"Quit fightin', Major—I mean Polo." Mouse's twang cracked, sounding boyish, as he lay motionless under Dakota's crouched body. "Miss Dakota … ma'am, it's you, right? You won't hurt us, will ya?"

She nudged him with her muzzle.

Major? Dakota likely held their commanding

field officer. Too bad. Strategically, an officer should be the first one in Matteo's crosshairs. He wouldn't take a shot at her pets. Instead, he searched the battlefield for the one man who would die today. *Shelton.*

A pair in camo closed in on Dakota's six. Matteo laid down fire in front of them, and they dropped to the ground.

****

Polo had ceased rebelling against Dakota's shelter, relieving her. He and Mouse seemed to understand she only protected them. Across the field, Cristiano and Jaime breathed. She sent up a prayer of thanks. They would live. Hope rose that they could stop this mess before anyone else got hurt. She cuddled the two soldiers into the safeguard of her body.

"Die, you animal freaks!" Hatred in the voice was palpable. Two clapped reports rang out behind her, and she braced for the spray of bullets that would surely follow.

Instead, a male cry came from Pantoja's position, yanking Dakota's attention. Alejandro clutched his chest, and blood trickled from his mouth.

"Oh, God, no!" Dakota's head swam with shock.

He reached out at nothing, before he toppled against the tree's broad trunk. Two commandos had eased in behind her and found a shooting position. She'd been so busy protecting Mouse and Polo that she'd missed the bad guys. The enemy ... like the two under her.

Pantoja lunged to pull the foreman's flaccid body to deeper cover. Rising to a four-point stance, with every muscle taut, Dakota willed Alejandro to move, to breathe, to show any kind of autonomic response, a sign of life. Her heart lodged in her throat. Nothing. *He's gone.* The realization sucked the air from her chest.

As though in that instant, they realized she'd transformed into a threat, Polo and Mouse scrambled from her as fast as their injuries would allow. Gunfire from Matteo's sniper spot chased behind them, while Polo half-dragged, half-carried Mouse toward the treed perimeter. In the wild battle, Matteo aimed to encourage their flight. Didn't he know that compassion only killed your own?

Numbing guilt combined with grief. Dakota had shown mercy and protected the enemy, and their adversaries had taken full advantage. They'd shot Alejandro right in front of her. She might as well have pulled the trigger. Dakota let loose another pain-filled howl. Loaded with righteous anger, her red-hazed, tunnel vision honed in on Alejandro's killer.

The murdering slime huddled under his leafy cover with the other soldier, as though he thought the murky night hid him. "They wanna be the next dominant species?" His quiet chuckle sounded forced. "I'm gonna have one o' them furry bastards mounted over my fireplace."

With flattened ears and a rage-filled roar, Dakota lunged, reaching them in three strides. Both commandos leapt to a shooting stance, and before her target could level his rifle, she collapsed the redneck motherfucker.

Howling underneath her, he twisted onto his belly, and, in a frantic attempt to escape, he lifted to his hands and knees, and crawled, clawing the earth. She sank talons deep into his back. With a blood-curdling scream, the murdering scum gouged furrows in the ground scrabbling for freedom—all in vain.

His forgotten teammate fired two point-blank rounds into Dakota's chest. The sledgehammer impacts sent fire through her torso, and she swung her glare at the shooter.

"Damn." Redneck's wingman backpedaled fast.

Her prey's panicked squeals connected to something visceral, a gut-drive she couldn't ignore, and she forgot the fleeing soldier. Overpowering cat instinct drove her to go for the back of his neck. With a yawning strike, she cut off his shrieks, and the abrupt silence shocked her. His body slackened to dead weight in her clenched jaws.

Savory blood filled her mouth, and the salty flavor coated her tongue, like a perfectly seared... Disgusted by her vulgar reaction, and equally enthralled, nausea churned her stomach. Repulsed by her primal response, she tossed the limp corpse to the ground. An urge to take flight stormed through her, and she retreated backwards a couple yards, staring at the mangled body. The redneck lay unmoving just a yard in front of her.

A human body.

A man.

The enemy had turned her into a killer.

A patrol emerged from the dark perimeter and closed in. Facing the three commandos, she crouched low to the ground, roaring her pain and fury.

Or, maybe she was just a born killer. *Bring it, assholes.*

Chapter Twenty-Seven

"Hold your fire!" Shelton yelled from his cover position within the trees. Shooting from all directions stopped, and an eerie silence followed. After her savage kill, he'd doubted his men would follow his stand-down order. Releasing a controlled breath of relief, he was proud of them.

The huge white cat was Dakota Gorman from the video, he was certain. He wished he could see her in daylight. Even in the green and yellow thermal rendering, she was a magnificent specimen. Mission success hinged on delivery of a live werejaguar. Shelton stayed glued to the thermal imaging command feed, wondering how many cloaked shifter signatures lay hidden within the rainforest cover. Failure wasn't an option. He had no choice. "Doolittle, you're up!"

Mechanical reports sounded from his tranq-sniper's location, and the Gorman jaguar flinched with each hit. Barely visible fan-tailed darts lodged in both of her flanks and another hung from her shoulder. Doolittle's veterinary team had scored big. Still, they'd have to track her while the drug took effect.

Shelton had no idea what she was doing out in the middle of the battle, or why she had hovered over his men like a mother hen protecting her young. At least, she had forgotten them, and his boys were safe. Two big cats charged from the trees toward her position.

In the same instant, three soldiers trained for animal capture rushed to intercept the sabretooth-tiger-sized jaguars. Shelton couldn't be prouder of his brave boys. One stopped yards away and aimed a shuttlecock-shaped net launcher. Shelton leaned in, willing success.

"Damn you, Dakota! *Run!*" The catman yelled

from his position in the trees above her, firing at the capture team. Shelton tapped his mic.

"Polo, reinforce Doolittle's squad." To make sure he captured the female, Shelton would have to cut his losses and give up the catman. "And neutralize the sniper at three o'clock."

****

As Matteo had suspected, his warrior princess cringed at spilling blood. Now, she had made her first kill. Anguish shone in her eyes. He longed to soothe her, and take her to safety.

Unable to do either, Matteo took aim and sprayed warning fire in front of the trio closing in on her. The capture team retreated with their useless net gun. A four-man squad materialized and took up strategic flanking positions, allowing the zoo team to retreat. This group was armed for war.

Bullets whizzed through the leaves around Matteo, and then a cannon ball hit his chest, knocking him back. Grappling at anything to keep his perch, the AR 15 tumbled from his grasp. Matteo's breaths came hard and painful, hampered by the blood filling his mouth. He coughed, sputtering crimson.

Certain he'd taken a hit from a rocket-grenade, the small hole below his collarbone was a surprising relief. He could live through a small-arms caliber round. Light-headed, he teetered deeper into cover, but kept line of sight. The battle raged on.

The lead soldier charged, targeting Dakota with his rifle. A bullet couldn't do her permanent damage. Still, Matteo had never felt so helpless in his life, watching the enemy close in on her. He tensed, readying to shift during his freefall.

However, she'd proven herself battle ready. He needed to have faith in her. Raoul and Nicolas streaked to her position, and Nicolas leaped in front of her.

Matteo willed the shimmer from his skin in relief, but the edges of his vision closed in. Blood still pumped from his chest wound, plastering his shirt to his body. He'd underestimated his injury.

Nicolas, in his cinnamon cat form, roared at their attacker, forcing the commando into a hasty, stumbling retreat.

"Oh-shit-oh-shit." Backpedaling hard, the stumbling soldier dropped his rifle and pulled a machete from his belt. In the same instant, Nicolas launched at the falling man, who made a wild swing with his blade. Gunfire erupted from the trees.

Meters below Matteo, Nicolas's jaguar head thudded to the ground, while his massive feline body sailed over his attacker, landing in a crumpled heap. His claws raked the air before he melted to decapitated, naked human. *Oh, God, no!* Balance deserting him, Matteo grabbed a branch. The wood cracked in his grip.

The lightless shift confirmed Nicolas was truly gone. Raoul lunged to their fallen comrade with a mournful howl. Matteo shared his pain.

Uncontrollable rage shook his frame, and grief pummeled him. He couldn't hide in his humanity any longer. If all shifters present were lost, the jags would never recover. Dakota, his friends—and his species— were out of time.

Now, the enemy, armed with machetes, bore down on the helpless Salazars. This battle could be the demise of them all.

Simple math—one or four deaths—laid out his irreversible course. Resigned to his fate—he met Dakota's hardened gaze. She snarled with her ears pinned back.

A different kind of grief stole the air from his

lungs. "I'm sorry."

****

Matteo was sorry. Not nearly as sorry as Dakota. He'd tried to provide cover for Alejandro and Pantoja, and her grave lapse in judgment had killed them all. Above her, Matteo disappeared into the jungle canopy. The shifters needed his sniper cover. Maybe some could escape with their lives.

She'd been a fool. In sadistic self-torture, she forced herself to look at Nicolas's beautiful, athletic—headless body. Dakota raised a blistering glare at the camo-clad soldiers bearing down on the fallen Salazars. *No more.*

They stalked hesitantly toward the motionless black jags with raised machetes. Another tranq-rifle team armed with a net gun followed them in. Raoul roared a charge, and Dakota answered with her own. They launched as one toward the enemy troops surrounding the two helpless cats.

Shelton's men would imprison, or kill, all of the shifters. If only she had followed orders and stayed hidden. No do-overs in war. Her people needed her to toughen up. Shoving her guilt to a place packed to bursting, she raced alongside Raoul.

From the foliage along the low-lying ridge, an unfamiliar tawny jaguar sprinted toward them. He roared, announcing his presence to the enemy. Gunfire chased his trail, lifting wet leaves from the jungle floor. Amadeo had joined them after all. Rounds put bloody patches on his coat, and he ignored them. The sight of the massive cat, moving with a confidence she didn't feel, buoyed her hopes.

Raoul dropped away, circling to flank the human squad.

Dakota checked for the new cat's scent, but all

she got was a snoot full of sulfur. The powerful jaguar veered toward her, and together, they raced to the defenseless Salazars. No wonder, they'd hoped Amadeo would get here in time to help. He lunged ahead of her and plowed the field. With incessant gunfire dappling his pelt, he took down one soldier, delivering a skull-crushing bite. The crack of the helmet split the air.

Behind him, a commando wheeled with his machete drawn, and angled for a lethal strike against Amadeo. *Not again.* She'd nurse her conscience later. Dakota leapt, landing between the soldier and the big male shifter. The man halted; she didn't. She raked hooked claws across his body, ripping a swath through his biceps. The machete tumbled from his useless hand, and he screamed, cradling his ragdoll arm against his stomach.

Amadeo nudged her shoulder, and they broke through the enemy line to a protective position in front of the downed Salazars. Dakota followed his lead. At their retreat, medics rushed in to retrieve the fallen. Amadeo stuck to her side like glue, always a little ahead of her. Matteo had probably given him a protection order, too.

The impotent syringe darts still hung from her sides; she'd forgotten them. Several yards away, Pantoja crouched near Alejandro with a rifle in one hand and smearing mud on his clothes with the other. Relieved that he was in one piece, she coughed a snarl at him. He raised his head but gave no response.

When he advanced from tree to tree toward them, she understood. He must have heard her. With her twilight vision, it was easy to forget that without thermal imaging, the humans endured the pitch-black night. Dakota glanced up, hoping Matteo knew to provide cover for Pantoja. Staying focused on the jaguars, the enemy seemed to have forgotten the shifter's mole-turned-ally.

When he finally huddled next to the Salazars, she released a shuddering sigh.

The medics cleared out in a rush with their two stretchers, and a barrage of volleys ensued. The minute of impromptu truce was over. Raoul stalked nearer with a barked snarl, ignoring the round of bullets that parted his fur. Rage in his mercurial eyes gave him a demonic air. Amadeo shouldered in front of her and issued a similar challenge. They would make a stand here, all of them.

"Hold your fire!" One last shot sounded, and then a soldier with a thermal camera on his helmet, Major Polo she realized, strode to the center of the fray. He planted himself in front of the jaguar trio, raising one arm. The other hand rested on a side arm holstered in a vest.

Amadeo crouched in front of Dakota and snarled at him.

Polo glanced at the big male and swallowed, before he met Dakota's gaze. "Doolittle, pull back!"

The capture team halted, shifting glances at Amadeo. They had to be relieved. He was ginormous, a full six inches taller than Raoul.

"We'll retreat. Give us some space."

He didn't need shifter permission to retreat. All they had to do was back off. Not wanting to take her eyes from Polo, Dakota sniffed to detect anyone at her rear. Nothing but sulfur. After allowing Alejandro's killer to sneak in behind her, she dared a glance.

Both Salazar males showed signs of rousing, taking deep breaths. She dropped back, worried for their safety. In their hazy state, they could walk right into the enemy lines.

Cristiano raised his head and blinked. A short two yards away, Jaime stood and shook as though shedding water from his fur. The motion made him stagger. Firm evidence that they lived relieved Dakota, and her protective instincts surged stronger than ever.

Planting herself in front of them, she returned a glare at the major, snarling low in her throat.

Pantoja casually leveled his rifle at Polo, seemingly unaffected by the rifles instantly locked on him. "Major Airborne, drop your weapons. Back up."

A red dot appeared on Polo's chest. The major nodded at Pantoja's heavily accented English, but didn't move. "Shelton tells me you're a turncoat merc. Working for bigger money?"

"I protect Brazilian treasures. Now, shut up and drop your guns."

Polo shook his head. "How about we just back up? Let you take your wounded and leave?"

Raoul snarled low and long, giving the impression he'd prefer to tear the humans apart. All eyes landed on him. Jaime padded to angle in front of Pantoja, so close, he brushed against him. His intent to shield him couldn't be clearer.

Unaware of Jaime's approach, Pantoja started at the contact and then shrugged, looking side to side at the cats. "Major Polo, sir. Your guns only kill me. Don't you wonder how you're alive?"

Polo held Dakota's gaze. "I think I know."

Polo lifted the camera up, leaving him blind. He must want her to see his eyes. His brows drew together. "Take your wounded and go. Please."

She glanced at Nicolas's body still where he'd fallen a few yards away. They had to bring him and Alejandro home. She gave Pantoja a pointed look and hoped her plea showed in her eyes.

He gave a slight nod. "Major, we need stretchers."

Polo glanced at him and raised a hand high and

circled an index finger. "Medic, two stretchers. Drop 'em at our left flank. Now."

"Polo, I didn't authorize a retreat." Shelton's strained voice, the one that had threatened Matteo in the operating room, came from inside the major's helmet. "And we need that body!"

The transmission was crystal clear to Dakota's hypersensitive hearing. Flicking her ears, she snapped her attention to Polo.

He widened his eyes, seeming to realize she'd heard the message. Evidently, she hadn't hidden her eavesdropping skill. He held her gaze, pressing a button near his ear. "Communication garbled. Four casualties, enemy down two." He cupped hand over his mouth. "We'll regroup and trail them."

She couldn't tell if he'd wanted her to hear his last or not.

"A life for a life." The major had looked right at her, and his lips had barely moved.

****

Even a couple hours after leaving the battlefield, the stink of sulfur still clung to Matteo's fur. He snorted to clear his muzzle. Traveling through the canopy, he safeguarded the shifters' rear during their retreat down the jungle mountainside, intentionally avoiding Dakota.

He was so proud of her. Even her disastrous soft-hearted move to protect Mouse and Polo had been borne of courage. After her shaky start, she'd been a fierce opponent, saving Matteo's head from the machete-wielding enemy.

Ahead with Cristiano and Jaime, she trekked through the lower treetops, the three of them guarding Pantoja and Raoul hiking below. The grieving Raoul was more vulnerable in human form. Pantoja trailed him, less sure-footed in the dark than the shifter male. Dawn would break soon.

Each man dragged a U.S. Army stretcher, travois-style, with the bodies of their lost brethren strapped in place. Raoul had reverently placed Nicolas's head in Alejandro's backpack. Hardly a hero's processional.

Another of many downed trees blocked their path. The two teamed up on one stretcher, and then the other, lifting their blood brothers over the deadfall. *Too slow.* To make matters worse, they left a rutted trail in the mud that a blind man could follow. The abhorrent idea of leaving their fallen to the jungle never came up—and it wouldn't.

Matteo thought to steal a minute of mourning with his family, and a sudden need to regain human form accosted him. Consumed with their escape, he had yet to try. Pausing on a sturdy branch, his heart pounded in fear. The time had come to determine his fate. He willed heat over his skin.

Nothing. Not even a flush of warmth.

As though to torture him, the scents of the people he valued most drifted in on a slow-moving air current, including Dakota's. The beloved he would lose. He stifled a forlorn cry clawing at his throat. *Dakota.* Her essence found his nose and drove home the true value of his sacrifice. She would be safe.

He'd made a solid choice, and, even if he could, he wouldn't change it. Hope's keen edge cut deeper than he'd imagined. Matteo had known his cat would take over, but his heart had had faith in a reprieve—the love conquers all fallacy. Instead, hope's razor flayed him with reality.

Survival instinct was strong. Could he *take a fall* when Cristiano came for him? Fear of killing his friend and brother weighed him down, and Matteo dropped to his belly on the branch beneath him. Trying again, he imagined skin and dreadlocks.

More nothing.

Matteo had executed two ferals, secure in the knowledge they were all animal and a danger to the species. Forever lost to heaven's grace. Now, trapped in his cat with his sentient thoughts, he doubted this heretofore truth. Rather than replacing a shifter's identity with a jaguar's mind, maybe cat instinct only grew stronger.

That belated revelation offered no help now. He shook off the useless reverie. Safety for Dakota and his family came first.

Hissing a signal to Cristiano, Matteo reversed to scout for Shelton's men. Within minutes, he located a twelve-man patrol, several with thermal imaging cameras on their helmets. Moving fast, they were closing in on the slow-moving shifter party.

High above, Matteo slid through the trees, circling their forward perimeter. Satisfied another team didn't march nearby, he tracked their human pace from roughly three stories above.

The soldiers moved efficiently through the unholy Darien Gap terrain, using machetes with skill. They would catch the shifters in less than thirty minutes. Their lead pointed out hazards to the men behind him. Halting at unpredictable intervals, he flipped his heat-sensing camera down from his helmet, scanning the trees and jungle cover.

"Anyone see anything? I got nothing." Major Polo's familiar voice grabbed Matteo's attention. "Radar, report."

Dakota's high-ranking prisoner had held on to his command. Surprising, since his battle retreat had lit Shelton's fuse. The colonel probably didn't have another choice, since Polo led a team of highly specialized jungle troops.

Morning brought natural twilight to the understory, so Matteo kept under cover. Thermal imaging could still spot him in the foliage. He stretched out along a wide branch directly over the major's head, the wood's mass blocking his heat signature.

Radar trudged through the mud to the front. "Still no jaguar sign, Polo. Only two men transporting casualties. They might've split up."

"I don't think so." Polo glanced to the canopy, pointing. "The cats're likely up there."

"We checked the trees. They're pretty smart for animals. I think they hide from the IF." Radar looked side to side and dropped his low voice to just above a whisper. "The old man says these catpeople could take us over. I'm not gonna lie, I'm kinda freaked. You see them take those rounds? Like goddamned Superman."

Polo kept searching the canopy. "I saw. Bring up the rear and keep an eye on the old man. He was sucking air on the last rise."

Polo's subdued tone sounded discouraged. Coming out of hiding had been a long-standing shifter dinner-party topic. Men like Polo saw a shifter's humanity first. Others didn't. Suspicion and hate had taken hold. Worse, the crazy digital-age technology had already forced the shifters' decision. The species' war for existence weighed on Matteo's heart. Maybe Polo understood.

Radar ambled toward his spot at the rear, nodding at a lone soldier striding to the front. The tall man with the familiar gait joined Polo on point. *Shelton.* "Whatchya got?"

"Not a damn thing."

Polo aimed his night vision toward Matteo's camouflaged location. Out of time, Matteo gambled on his gut instincts. He stayed within deep leaf cover to avoid being obvious and leaped to a narrow branch, leaving his body heat in clear line of sight.

"Colonel, we've got company," Polo said in a low tone, jutting his chin at Matteo's position.

When Dakota had eavesdropped on Shelton's battlefield transmission, Polo had recognized Dakota's sharp hearing. He had to know Matteo could hear him, too. Matteo prayed his instincts about the major held true.

Dropping his camera to his forehead, Shelton scanned in Matteo's direction. Matteo shot off through the treetops to lead the patrol away from Dakota and the other shifters, adding a limp to sweeten the lure. The well-disciplined soldiers gave chase without shouting orders. Only fabric rustled behind Matteo.

"Colonel, I think he's wounded." Polo had embraced Matteo's ruse.

"Roger that."

Behind Matteo, the silent commandos moved fast. They were good.

An hour later, Matteo had drawn Shelton's men to a craggy mountainside, the rougher terrain and thicker ground cover slowing them. He'd made brief appearances, limping like a protective mother killdeer, leading predators from her nest.

With his life forfeit anyway, dying in battle was preferable to making Cristiano execute him. Matteo could save his friend that heartache. No matter what, Shelton wouldn't live to make a second attempt to steal Dakota's unborn.

The soft colonel flagged at the end of the patrol of hardened troops. Radar stuck to his side. Matteo's prey wouldn't get more isolated than this minute. He stepped off his two-story perch, and with legs spread wide, he sailed to the jungle floor at their rear.

Both men whirled to face him. Shelton fired his side arm and Radar engaged with his rifle. Matteo lunged and raked Shelton from face to torso, shredding flesh and clothing. A gargled scream erupted, before he staggered back and dropped insensible, the jagged wound at his neck streaming blood into the mud beneath him. Radar blasted a steady stream of gunfire and blocked Matteo's final death blow, the fully automatic rifle cutting a cavernous seam the length of Matteo's body. Matteo staggered sideways. Scorching pain consumed him along with a sudden fear that Radar's next volley could take his head as easily as a machete. He couldn't die before Shelton.

Recalling Dakota's torture at his orders gave Matteo the courage to face his own end. He crouched to leap onto Shelton for a final—lethal—hold.

Polo jumped in front of Matteo, a machete in one hand and the other outstretched with an open palm. "Stop! Goddammit, stop!"

Behind him, soldiers rushed in to tend Shelton, who coughed when they applied pressure to his gushing neck wound. Another knelt with a sleek stovepipe gun, the lethal grenade launcher, aiming the missile-tipped barrel at Matteo.

Glaring at Polo, Matteo snarled long and loud, thrashing his tail. A gaping wound ran the length of his side, and hellfire speared deep into his chest. Blood filled his mouth.

He longed to share his pain with all of Shelton's men—save Polo. Defying Shelton, Polo had given the shifters—and most importantly Dakota—a way out.

The major glanced at the rocket launcher. "Hold your fire!" He turned a pleading expression to Matteo. "I can't let you kill him. You know that."

Matteo could slay Shelton before either soldier reacted. However, if the idiot with the launcher fired, the grenade would take them all out, Polo included.

A few tense seconds of stalemate ticked by. If Matteo's final act was to kill an innocent, he'd die a truly feral death.

Polo held his gaze, seeming to read Matteo's indecision. "Let Shelton go." He spoke quietly and lifted his chin in Dakota's direction. "Find the others, your people."

I have no people. But he could be true to himself.

Obviously, Polo had known where the shifters were the whole time. He would never know the real reason Matteo retreated. He couldn't kill an innocent.

Crouching, Matteo walled off his pain and exploded to a tree trunk a few meters to the side. Gunfire and the grenade launcher's whistle sounded behind him. Matteo scrambled up into the canopy as the grenade exploded a safe distance from the shouting men below.

Chapter Twenty-Eight

Several yards from Nicolas's tree-limb covered helicopter, Dakota sat on her haunches in the jungle. They'd left the copter hidden from the enemy to allow Matteo more time to catch up. Staying in jaguar form, pacing and sniffing the stagnant air, she'd hoped to catch the first possible scent of his arrival.

She hadn't seen Matteo since he'd bolted from the battle to find a sniper perch. Cristiano had assured her that he'd dropped back to guard their retreat. Worry for Matteo consumed her. And fretting never solved anything. She thrashed her tail, needing to do more.

Dressed in borrowed fatigues, Cristiano joined her and threaded fingers into her ruff. He looked toward their back trail with a furrowed brow. "Matteo is a skilled soldier. He'll come."

With the sunrise and still no Matteo, a subtle tension had grown within their party. Cristiano plainly tried to reassure himself as much as Dakota.

Her eyes stung in a very human way, and a desolate mewl erupted from her throat. She wanted to hold Matteo, lose herself in his scent and tell him she loved him. This time, without the snark.

"Our friends need us." Without waiting for her, Cristiano glanced at the heartbroken gathering and then walked away. He was right. She needed to join the mourners and offer what solace she could. She rose to her paws to search for the fatigues she'd refused earlier.

They were still neatly stacked behind the tree, where she'd left them. After shifting, she slid on the oversized shirt and pants, followed by military issue jungle boots. Dread slowed her steps more than the oversized footwear.

The men lingered near two tarp-covered bodies resting on the ground outside of the helicopter. With tears tracking his cheeks, Jaime knelt, and laid a hand on what she suspected was Alejandro's chest.

Pantoja stood at his side, giving Jaime's shoulder a supportive squeeze, and the big male allowed it. *The lion and the lamb.* Somehow, they'd come to terms. She wondered if she'd ever be worthy of such grace.

Near the other corpse, Nicolas's guards, Sebastian and Manuel, held each other. Both sets of shoulders convulsed. With inactivity, the loss of Alejandro and Nicolas had taken hold of their team.

Cristiano emerged from the chopper fuselage carrying a couple bottles of water. He approached Raoul and Pantoja at the edge of the group. Both men appeared spent, and each accepted the water.

Raoul twisted off the lid and drained the plastic container. "He never returned from his scouting mission. Since Shelton didn't bother to follow us, I suspect they have him. We need to go back."

Dakota stopped short, her gasp drawing everyone's attention. No one offered a soothing alternative theory. Rather, they turned away and joined Nicolas's men standing over his body. *Alejandro and Nicolas—my fault.*

Though Paulo's death seemed eons ago, inside her mind, his murder replayed in brilliant color. If only she had fought harder—or died trying. Now Matteo, her love, was missing. Staring at the mourners' backs, her chest constricted, and she fought to keep her balance.

Dakota bit the inside of her cheek—hard— wrestling her inner pain into submission. Blood's metallic taste filled her palate. She needed to grow a pair and offer her sympathies.

Instead, she charged Raoul and got in his face.

"You left Matteo behind?"

His mercurial eyes flared, and he tossed his empty bottle to the vines at their feet. "No. I carried my slain friend home to rest."

Raoul had left Matteo to Shelton, and now he stabbed a red-hot poker of guilt into her gut. As rage coiled inside her, heat pulsed over her skin.

Cristiano wedged between them, and an innate power flashed in his eyes. He gripped her shoulders with a subtle shake. "Dakota. Think. If Shelton knew our location, we'd have incoming. Matteo did that." His voice cracked. "I'd never leave my brother behind."

His words sank in. She blew out a breath through pursed lips, and the dark shimmer circling her vision bled away. "Okay ... okay."

Cristiano jutted his chin at Nicolas's grieving men. "I need to be with them."

Ashamed, she nodded. Cristiano paced to the mourners. Seeming to have forgotten her, Raoul appeared lost and frozen to his spot, staring at the motionless tarp-covered mound a few yards away.

An empathetic tear tracking her cheek surprised her. Dakota scrubbed it away. She'd only known Alejandro and Nicolas for a short time, but Raoul had lost someone as dear to him as family.

Unsure it was safe, she stepped to his side and touched his arm. Like him, she kept her gaze on the body-shaped tarp. "I'm sorry. For everything."

Without looking at her, he nodded, more in dismissal than acceptance. He trudged with weighted steps to join Nicolas's few mourners.

Dakota's freedom had cost too much. They'd lost Paulo. Now, two more men had died—because she'd gone soft. Her idiocy had killed them. A special kind of grief isolated her. Unfit to join the bereaved, she sat on a fallen tree.

A box of tissue materialized in front of her, and she snatched it. While she dabbed at her eyes, Pantoja claimed a spot on the log next to her. "Give Raoul some time. Grief always partners with anger. I wanted to slaughter those who killed my Nuno. Now, I'm fighting with you."

"But you saw. Alejandro's killer got behind me while-while I protected the enemy." Her voice cracked. "It's my fault."

"Any who've seen battle think they've committed evil sins—that their judgment cost lives. Don't cheapen Alejandro's sacrifice. He died with honor, protecting his people—as all fallen soldiers do."

Maybe in time, she would understand. Not today. Sniffing, she wiped her nose.

Pantoja hugged her with one arm. "Nicolas's freaky end could've happened anywhere on that field. Forgive yourself."

A few yards away, Cristiano held Raoul in his arms. Dakota didn't doubt he'd overheard her conversation with Jose. He met her gaze over Raoul's shoulder and then turned to the mourners. "My friends, the Maker calls for Nicolas."

****

Matteo teetered near the top of the canopy. Though the pain had lessened, even two hours later Matteo's wounds hadn't yet healed. His only consolation was that he would heal faster than Shelton.

Matteo had left the colonel and his men on the mountainside. At last sight, they limped toward their hospital camp. Their surgery tent may come in handy—if Shelton lived that long.

The shifters should have left Panama by now, however, below Matteo, they circled Nicolas's funeral pyre. He spied on his friends, wishing he could honor Nicolas as the brave male deserved. Instead, Matteo lurked in the shadows, wounded and weak-minded, not ready to face the others or his future. He'd kept his distance. So far, the sulfur stench coating his fur had hidden his scent from Cristiano, and most importantly, from Dakota.

With her so near, courage to face his fate waned. Dropping down to a sturdier branch, he wondered if Raoul would tolerate a feral poacher in his territory. Not likely.

Even if he found sanctuary, he'd lead a solitary existence in the jungle. Dakota would mate another, and his life would be hell on earth. The thought made Matteo's decision simple, and he resolved, yet again, to meet his execution with dignity.

"Nicolas has no Honduran shifter family to return him to our Maker." Cristiano's voice broke. Matteo understood the unspoken question. They traveled Raoul's territory.

"I'm proud to call him brother," Raoul announced. "He'll rest in my jungle, and I'll join him at the Maker's timing."

With their decreasing numbers, few had blood relatives to see to their final needs. Matteo was grateful Nicolas would rest in a lifelong friend's home, just as Matteo would rest in Cristiano's territory.

"Nicolas led an honorable life…" Cristiano started the ceremony. Each would say a few words before fire returned Nicolas's body to Mother Earth.

After descending from the treetops, Matteo tried twice more to regain his human form, and each attempt bore the same dismal results. Giving up, overwhelming sadness almost drove him back into the jungle. Once again, hiding from humanity called to him. He shook his head and snarled. Nicolas deserved better. Matteo padded to the perimeter of the service.

Shifter flesh burned fast and hot. The smoke would give away their location. Cristiano must plan to evacuate immediately following the service.

Dressed in oversized fatigues, Dakota stood with the males circling the bright flames. Cristiano draped an arm over her trembling shoulders, occupying Matteo's place at her side. Maybe he would pursue her, after all.

Matteo gazed at Dakota, drinking in the sight of her. Tears stained her cheeks, and he longed to console her. He wanted to brush the chestnut locks from her exquisite features and kiss her pain away.

No doubt, fighting and death had injured her heart, but her fiery spirit would prevail. War made courageous people stronger. And Dakota was the bravest female he'd ever known. Love for her welled up, threatening to burst him into pieces.

He wanted to hold on to this feeling, the part of her that consumed him, and take it with him into the hereafter, but he doubted the veil allowed for such nonsense.

Only Raoul or Cristiano would be strong enough for her. At least he wouldn't live to see her mated to another. Matteo was grateful for the small blessing. He just hoped Cristiano delayed his execution until after Dakota was safely aboard the chopper.

****

Dakota wiped her eyes again as the last embers died away. One more time, she searched for Matteo. Worry escalated to fear. They had to leave, with or without him. Her heart pounded, and she readied herself to battle with Cristiano to wait for a few more minutes.

Cristiano turned from the bed of glowing ash and grimaced. He scanned the jungle. "He's here."

Sulfur lay heavy over Matteo's faint mocha fragrance, but she detected it, too. She wheeled around in anticipation. Amadeo, the huge tawny jaguar from the battle stepped from elephant-leaf cover. The gunpowder stink clung to him. In her over-wrought worry for Matteo, she had assumed the big jag was guarding their flank—he had disappeared when they set out. Knowing it was rude and not caring, she searched behind him for Matteo.

Amadeo drew near, and gazed at her with molten copper eyes. A sinking sensation rocked her, and she stepped back to catch her balance. How had she not seen his eyes in battle? With slow realization, she recalled that he'd never really looked at her on the field. They'd been busy, but in hindsight, she suspected intent.

Buried under the sulphur smell, she found Matteo's espresso—and recognized his rust-colored rosettes. *Matteo had shifted!* Dakota reeled and grabbed Cristiano's arm. People talked in garbled voices around her, but she understood nothing. The battle's gunpowder miasma had masked Matteo's trace. There was no Amadeo.

I'm sorry. Matteo hadn't left the battle to look for a sniper perch. Instead, he'd shifted and left Dakota for good.

"How could you?" Sorrow spiked her strident wail.

Fresh tears stung her eyes, and she rushed to him. He was so tall he nearly met her nose to nose. She ruffled his ears in a mix of fury and tenderness.

Matteo's copper eyes looked so natural against his lion-toned fur. And so sad. The shifter party formed a half-circle around them.

"That you, D'Cruz?" Pantoja grinned. "Good to see you. Nice back up. You one big, bad-ass motherfucker."

The grim-faced shifter males didn't join in his Portuguese banter. Instead, an ominous tension charged Raoul and Jaime's shared glance.

Pantoja looked side to side. "I miss something?"

Dakota ignored him, as did the others. Gripping the fur under Matteo's ears, she pulled his gaze to hers. "Don't you dare leave me. Not like this."

Matteo dropped to his belly, and she followed to her knees. True panic shook her frame. Recall of Matteo's previous near-execution slammed into her. Dakota turned and scooted back into Matteo, facing Cristiano and the others.

Cristiano stepped toward them, and tears glistened in his amber eyes.

Dakota spread her arms out, blocking his path to Matteo. "No! Stay back. He's fine. He'll be *fine*."

Cristiano shook his head. A single tear tracked his cheek. Raoul and Jaime closed in at his flanks, leaving Pantoja looking from one to the other with widened eyes. "What the hell did he do?"

"Nothing! Except save us all," Dakota screamed, turning an accusatory glare on Cristiano. "You knew! You lied to me. You planned to go back for him? Yeah, right."

"He's feral, *pequeno*. Even if you don't know the danger, he understands." Cristiano turned his tortured expression to Matteo. "My friend—my brother, shift, now. For all our sakes."

They feared he'd sire a litter with a natural jaguar and devolve the species into God knew what. Fighting sobs, Dakota pressed her forehead to Matteo's soft muzzle. His raspy tongue laved the damp streaks from her face.

Jaime tugged at her arm. "*Papai*'s right."

She jerked from his gentle grasp, her gaze locked with Matteo's. "Please."

"Dakota, you only torture him. Let me take you to the helicopter." Jaime's tone was gentle, pleading even.

Kelsi had said Jaime had marked her while she was in *human form*. With new inspiration, she shook Matteo. "Mark me! Now. If you're mated, there's no reason to—to hurt you." She couldn't say *execute*. She looked over her shoulder at Cristiano. "Right? *Swear it*."

Cristiano's lips parted, and he jerked a nod with sudden hope in his eyes "Please, my friend. Do as she says."

Matteo shook from her grasp and backed up on his belly.

"Damn you. Shift your dead ass," Dakota shouted.

A dim, translucent halo rose from his fur and winked out. Still, he made no move toward her.

"You'd rather *die* than mark me?" An anguished sob punctuated her heartache.

Jaime gripped her forearm with more force and pulled her up, glancing at Cristiano. "It's not so simple. If Matteo marks you, and later you mate another, instinct will drive your mate to challenge him—and Matteo *will* kill him." He glared at Matteo. "Try again."

Dakota jerked from Jaime's iron hold. No way would she sentence Matteo to eternal loneliness in the jungle while she married someone else. She stepped out of the oversized boots and whipped off her scrubs. Heat shot over her torso, and electricity crackled through her body.

"He'll shift—I know it." Her last words sounded like yowls. In full jaguar mode, and wholly committed, she advanced on her prey. Matteo belly-crawled in reverse and then rose up to meet her.

He batted at her with sheathed claws. She snarled and struck right back, before launching a cat-style tackle, putting all her shifter strength into the takedown.

Jaime stepped toward the fray, as though he planned to cut in on Dakota's assaultive mating dance. Tail thrashing, she held Matteo down and growled at Jaime, daring him to even think about interfering.

Cristiano blocked his son with an outstretched arm. "If Matteo truly resists, she can't best him. We'll leave them to make their own choices."

The men filed out, and Dakota was grateful for the privacy.

From her hold on Matteo's back, she rubbed a painful cheek across his ear. *Not enough.* Instinct demanded she mark his muzzle. At some level, she knew this should be slow and easy—romantic, but there wasn't time to linger. They would indulge later, in safety—and as human—she hoped.

****

The crescendo of lavender beat at Matteo, demanding he accept her claim. His gut told him Dakota would lead the shifter species to recovery. She needed a mate at her side in the human world, not just in the jungle. Matteo let loose a desolate yowl.

If he accepted her mark without returning his own, Matteo's execution would free her to mate again. However, the grief of losing a mate lasted decades. The thought of her suffering needlessly tore him up inside. Better to resist now.

Dakota's enticing growl threatened his logic. Her scent on his fur tortured him, and his cheek glands throbbed in thoughtless rebellion. Frantic to control his jaguar instincts, he struck at her again. This time he added claws and a warning snarl.

To his knowledge, no female had ever mated a

feral. Dakota risked an eternity of the unknown to save him. His heart swelled for his courageous queen. Love for her combined with her seductive *Ardor* and, together, they banished his last shreds of logic.

Weak humanity succumbed to wild nature. Rolling to his back in submission, he exposed his throat for Dakota's pleasure. He had just enough sense to know crushing guilt would consume him—later. He was all animal now.

Chapter Twenty-Nine

Pinning Matteo on his back, Dakota pressed her muzzle hard against his, grinding against one jawline then the other. He was hers. Nothing had ever felt so right. She followed up with an affectionate bath, holding his tawny face between her white paws.

Matteo returned her feline kisses with a good laving of his own—but no scent markings. If he left her hanging, she'd kill him herself. She snarled her frustration.

His chest rumbled against hers. The meter of his throaty warning connected deep inside, like the cautionary tremor of an impending earthquake. He flipped them so fast she didn't perceive the move. Behind his rounded ears, slivers of sun filtered through the morning canopy.

Massive canines circled her throat, and for an intense few seconds, Matteo held her motionless on her back. Dakota's heart pounded in excitement rather than fear, the urge to fight him glaringly absent. This must be a dominance thing—and only Matteo could ever restrain her.

As though she savored the first sip of an extraordinary espresso, coffee filled her senses. Unexpected arousal slammed into her feline body. Matteo growled low against her skin. No doubt, her scent had announced her reaction.

Matteo released her, and she rose unsteadily to all fours. Seeming to smile at her near swoon, he flicked his whiskers and stretched his tawny muzzle down to hers. His chest rumbled while he pressed his essence deep into her fur. *Ardor* consuming her, she wobbled on her four legs and let out a helpless whimper.

He rubbed his body along hers, and his scent enveloped her with a sense of security, along with a certainty she was loved above all others.

More than anything in this moment, she needed to tell him she loved him. Words he might never whisper in her ear. She stifled the ugly thought. *He'll tell me ... one day.* Dakota had made her choice and resigned herself to live with it.

As much as she wanted to go for a jungle run with him, they needed to get out of this hellhole and back to Brazil. She headbutted him and rose to all fours. With a thought, she willed away her fur, and wished it could be so easy for Matteo.

She wrapped her bare arms around his neck and buried her face in his ruff, enjoying his scent. "I love you, Matteo. We'll figure this out, somehow."

****

Dakota's shift to human, or maybe her touch, launched scalding heat over every inch of Matteo's body, lifting his fur to hackles. Fast approaching incoherence, he screamed in pain, sending Dakota scuttling backwards crab style.

Anna's shifts had always made Matteo want to change with her, but nothing like this involuntary plunge into a fiery inferno.

"Ohmigod, you've got this." Dakota dropped onto her bottom, and tears welled in her widening eyes. "For us, Matteo. Sweet cream forever."

My gatinha.

Bright light stole Matteo's vision. Far worse than his last shift, this change was stuck in the hellfire phase. After an eternity of searing agony, high voltage shocks traveled through his convulsing muscles. He cried out in anguish an instant before his consciousness stole blissfully away.

****

Panting against the recalled torture, and anticipating more, Matteo's head lay in the cradle of his cramping arms. He clenched his fists, savoring the feel of the human action, and he thanked the Maker. He was truly human again. And his gunshot wounds had healed. Involuntary quivers in his torso and extremities turned to disabling spasms. He was afraid to move.

Lavender quieted his riotous muscles. Dakota must lie stretched out next to him, her cool flesh chilling his over-heated skin. Afraid to find himself in a dream, he slivered his eyes open. She had stayed with him. His heart swelled in his chest. His courageous girl had kept vigil over him. "Are you an angel?"

Only inches away, her shining teal gaze met his. "I love you. I knew you'd come back to me."

Tears dotted her lashes over a joyful smile. Her love welcomed him to humanity and would bring him home forever.

"I'll always come back to you, my last love." Smiling, Matteo reached for her, stretching his tortured flesh. Vexed, he growled and aborted the caress. Pain had stolen the moment and quelled his doubts. He lived.

"You're really awake—and *really* sunburned." Sniffling, she pressed a finger to his tender shoulder. "Or something. And you've got more rockin' spots."

"Shifters don't sunburn." His new bass voice rumbled with a hint of gravel.

"Oooh, and you got some old-time Barry White goin' on, too." She rubbed her nose to his. "I like."

Lying together naked and newly mated, she spoke of another man? The woman tested him. He lifted to an elbow and grimaced. "What?"

She giggled, eyes dancing, and pressed her lips to his. "Never mind."

"You're still amazing." He returned her tender kiss with his own.

Smiling, she trailed a finger along his jaw. "You remembered."

"I'll never forget." He rubbed his nose to hers and pulled back. Even the tip of his nose was tender. Looking around, he realized the others were gone. "Did they leave without us?"

"I've heard a couple choppers, but nothing close enough to be ours taking off. But we need to move." Dakota rose and grabbed her discarded fatigues, tossing the pants and boots to Matteo. "This top's like a dress."

"Keep the boots. Don't want your pretty feet cut up." Handing them back, he cringed at the thought of the fabric against his skin. With ginger care, he pulled on the heavy cotton pants. "How long was I out?"

"Fifteen minutes, maybe?" She dropped the shirt over her head and lifted her light chestnut waves through the collar, her signature hair clip long gone.

A panel attached to the shirt's hem dropped to cover the tops of her shapely thighs. The tail must tuck into a waistband to protect human soldiers from insects—smart. She finished off her attire with the military-issued jungle boots. Nothing dimmed her allure. Only his tortured skin kept him from ravaging her right there.

"Shall we?" She extended a hand, as though they were lovers planning a walk on the beach.

Matteo threaded his fingers in hers, and they broke to a jog. Long before they closed in on the chopper, Matteo detected Cristiano's anxiety-laden scent. The sour notes announced his fear. He must have rushed out to greet them in the trees.

Cristiano's gaze landed on Matteo, and he stopped short, scanning Matteo up and down. "Thank

God."

He cleared his throat twice, before striding to Matteo with outstretched arms. The embrace hurt like hell, but Matteo didn't pull away, instead, savoring the human touch. They broke apart to share a warriors' grasp with both arms. Matteo smiled wide. "Dakota's biped shift dragged me along—through hell—but I'm here."

"I dared to hope a mate's lure would bring you back to us." Cristiano darted a glance and a not-so-subtle sniff at Dakota. "Apparently, best wishes are in order."

"Yes, indeed." She beamed at him, radiant, and winked. "I told you so."

Matteo gave her a half grin, and Cristiano belly laughed. "Matteo, my brother, now, I really fear for you. A lifetime of I-told-you-so's are in your future."

Filled with joy, Matteo nodded and tucked her against his body. "And I'll cherish every one."

Cristiano looked skyward, to where the canopy blocked the heavens. "A U.S. Army chopper has flown nearby twice, now."

"Shelton's not with them. I almost killed him, dammit." Matteo gave a brief replay of their showdown, grudgingly admitting his weakness for Polo. "The fly-by could be a routine search flight. I'd have ordered one."

Dakota exchanged a glance with Matteo, and he wondered if she felt as guilty as he did. His shift—and their mating—had delayed everyone else's escape. "Thank you for waiting. What can we do?"

"Take off after the next pass?" asked Cristiano.

With a nod, Matteo straightened. "Let's move."

The trio broke into a jog, eating up the several meters to the chopper site. As soon as they cleared the trees, Nicolas's man waved them to the helicopter. In black jaguar form, Jaime dropped from overhead and, upon landing, shifted to naked human. Cristiano tossed a wad of camo at him.

"Their bird just passed by again." Jaime tugged on pants while he spoke. "Same one as before. I don't think they've spotted us, but it won't be long."

****

Dakota joined the others removing branches and vines hiding Nicolas's helicopter. Even to her untrained eye, the machine had a workhorse look to it—nothing like Cristiano's airborne Mercedes. "What *is* this?"

"A *Black Hawk*." With awe on his face, Pantoja eyed the chopper and turned to Matteo. "Can I drive?"

"You have hours on this model?" interrupted Cristiano. "Nicolas was our pilot."

Pantoja snatched a branch from the tail section. "I—"

"Fine time to mention that." From her perch atop the helicopter's tail, Dakota widened her eyes at Cristiano. She tugged at a woody vine wedged on the rear rotor, perspiration beading her forehead. "Jose is certified on Sikorsky models UH-60 and HH-60. That close enough?"

He laughed. "UH-60 *is* a Black Hawk."

"Oh. Okay," said Dakota, too busy to feel embarrassed.

"How do you know this, *senhorita*?" Pantoja looked up at her from under dark furrowed brows.

Dakota tossed the offending vine to the ground and sent him an amused glance. "Military records and a good memory."

Pantoja shook his head. "Smart girl."

She dropped to the spongy earth. Per Cristiano's orders, she and the others piled the camouflage branches a good football field away from the chopper.

Pantoja surveyed the cargo section. "Nice. Auxiliary fuel tanks."

Cristiano sighed and cast a last look toward the funeral site. "That's Nicolas."

Next to him, Raoul tracked his gaze. "I'll come by soon, my friend."

Mention of Nicolas put a knot in Dakota's throat. "So even after death, he saves us."

Pantoja leaped into the pilot seat. Having a few hours on the Black Hawk, Sebastian joined him as copilot. Dakota followed Matteo into the spartan, hard-surfaced interior. Inside, an odor of death joined the fuel and plastics.

Alejandro's tarp-shrouded body rested on a plastic pullout shelf extending into the chopper's tail. No one mentioned the smell. They would take him home with dignity.

So much loss. All to save her ass.

Across from her and Matteo, Jaime strapped into a shoulder harness. Cristiano and Raoul claimed seats on either side of him. She and Matteo buckled in and held hands.

Manuel, Nicolas's other guard, sat on the floor. Matteo glanced around and unbuckled. "We can shift if injured. Strap in—"

"No, sit here. Only some of us can shift." Cristiano shrugged out of his harness and rose. "Our mated males stay belted in."

Knowing how hard it was to accept special treatment, Dakota squeezed Matteo's hand. He sighed and settled back onto his seat.

Manuel glanced at his phone before turning toward the cockpit. "We burned seven minutes uncovering the Black Hawk."

"Roger that." Pantoja pressed a series of buttons on a complicated instrument panel, and the engine whined to life. With each thrown switch, the motor's pitch grew higher, and the machine shuddered. Cringing at the sudden pain in her ears, Dakota accepted the headphones Jaime tossed into her lap with a grateful nod. Raoul and Matteo donned headphones, too.

Tapping her foot, she looked over her shoulder. Pantoja still checked gauges and pushed buttons. Finally, in a slow roll, the chopper left its covered location and taxied to the center of the clearing.

Manuel raised his phone again. "Two minutes 'til next pass."

Cristiano gave him a slow nod. "Jose…"

"Hold on to your asses and enjoy the ride." Pantoja's unrealistic confidence unnerved Dakota.

Before she could interject, the chopper rocketed almost vertical through a tunnel of green, leaving her stomach somewhere on the jungle floor. They burst into the glaring sunlight. Out the side window, another chopper angled toward them.

"Bring it on, *Yanks*." Pantoja hooted.

High above the trees, he banked the Black Hawk so hard that the window view of the horizon swirled into an ocean of canopy. Dakota's body seemed suspended against the harness. Cristiano's hold on Matteo's seat kept him from slamming into the side door.

Leveling out, the helicopter accelerated and the back end lifted. Facing the rear, Dakota's body separated from the seat, pushing against the nylon straps once more.

Cristiano rose to his knees and scanned the sky. He pressed a button on his headphones. "Jose, Chinook angling in fast at five o'clock. They've got more speed."

"Oh yeah! But we have moves—and they don't have me," Pantoja yelled back, wildly exhilarated, adding a war whoop.

Raoul seemed unflappable. "Maybe with shifters

on board, they won't shoot us down."

With a half-smile, Cristiano shook his head. His apparent lack of concern over their maniac pilot relieved Dakota. Their nonchalance must be a flyboy thing.

Another sharp bank serpentined into a nosedive. The maneuver drove the harness into her body and once again left her stomach behind. Cristiano slid across the chopper's metal floor, and Raoul grabbed his outstretched hand, catching him. Terror replaced Dakota's confidence in Pantoja.

He wove the helicopter through a gauntlet of treetops, while his copilot Sebastian shrieked like a ten-year-old girl. Foliage blurred past on both sides of the machine, and a few hacked branches clunked against the fuselage.

Matteo squeezed her hand. "Be ready to shift."

"I'll shift when you do." She put all kinds of threat in her voice.

He nodded.

Before they could adjust to the winding course, the chopper climbed nearly vertical, popping up over the canopy, the greenery meeting the horizon in all directions.

With her skydiving addiction, Dakota had flown in many small planes and, when traveling, she had taken a few helicopter tours. Nothing had prepared her for this airborne rodeo.

Cristiano bolted from one window to the other, searching the sky. "We've gained. Dive again."

When they dropped altitude, Dakota gritted her teeth against a scream. To her surprise, they flew level without the steep banking motions.

"Excellent choice, Jose," said Cristiano.

They flew above the lazy path of a small river. Below them, two dark bare-chested men in a canoe waved with big smiles. It seemed the Black Hawk flew just over their heads, and maybe it did. Dakota might even recognize their faces if she saw them again.

"I think we've lost the Chinook. The sky is clear—for now." Cristiano pulled back from the window and dropped to sit on the floor.

An hour later, over southern Panama, static hummed from the chopper's audio. "This is the Colombian border patrol. Unmarked helicopter, identify yourself."

Dakota groaned. All this way to run into a border detail.

Cristiano furrowed his brows and leaned between the seats into the cockpit, as though his proximity would intimidate the authorities.

Pantoja threw a roguish smile over his shoulder. "Roger, border patrol." His Spanish sounded as native as his Portuguese, impressing Dakota. "VIP escort. Authorization, niner-niner-tango-alpha-delta. And say hi to Maria for me."

"Asshole. Maria says get lost. Cleared to pass."

"Mwah." Pantoja sent a loud kiss into his mic. "Roger that."

Sebastian and Manuel exchanged smiles from their front-facing seats. From across the fuselage, Jaime raised a brow at Matteo. "You hire interesting help."

"I hire help who can do the job." He beamed at Dakota, squeezing her thigh. "Actually, our warrior princess spotted his potential."

"Hardly a warrior."

Jaime snorted. "You're like your sister. Beware, Matteo. The Gorman ladies are too gutsy for their own good."

"Agreed." Matteo laughed. "Her courage scares the shit out of me."

Heat warmed Dakota's cheeks, and she shoved his shoulder in retaliation. However, a glance at Alejandro's shrouded corpse slapped her sober. "If only I had a do-over."

The steady thump-thump of the bladed rotor filled the silence. Matteo clasped her hand, stroking her skin with his thumb in silent support. She squeezed back and rubbed at her eyes, willing the tears to wait for later. Time healed. She clung to the thought. Though, it might take decades.

After a few minutes of silence, Jaime looked to the cockpit and turned on his com link. "Jose, my new friend, will you accept a late invitation to my wedding?"

Pantoja laughed. "Can I get a better room?"

"I think the bamboo suite might be available." Dakota found Matteo's gaze, and his scent rose above the mechanical smells of the cabin, fluttering in her core. The silent promise in his eyes sent heat through her torso, and her skin shimmered. In a panic, she shut down the involuntary shift.

Cristiano and Jaime chuckled.

Flames heated Dakota's cheeks once more. With the *Ardor*, nothing would be private, ever. "Don't do that to me in public!"

Matteo lifted the headphone from her ear and leaned in. "They only laugh at your glowing skin. Now that we're mated, your scent is only for me."

"That's a relief." Now, if she could just get control of the jump to jaguar.

****

The sun hovered below the trees as Pantoja perched the Black Hawk on the Salazar helipad. Anxious to see Kelsi, Dakota released her harness and leaned forward to peer out the window.

Jamie sprang from his seat to do the same. He

opened the cargo door and, in one leap, landed at his mate's side. Trailing him, Dakota dropped to the concrete. She paused awkwardly, waiting in line for her hug.

After an intense embrace with Jaime, Kelsi rushed her. Dakota held her sister in a charged moment of relief and didn't want to let go. Until now, she'd taken so much in her life for granted, including her sister. Finally, she pulled back enough to meet Kelsi's misty gaze.

"I thought I'd never see you again." Even though they had talked—and sobbed—once on the phone, Kelsi appeared as overwhelmed as Dakota felt.

Dakota smiled through tears and defiantly rubbed them away. "I figured if my big sis could escape skin traders, I could give a few Army Rangers the slip."

"Not the living in your older sister's shadow thing again, please." Kelsi snorted a laugh and wiped her eyes.

The chopper's engine cut off, leaving the familiar insect melody sounding hollow and distant. Quiet weeping came from the far edge of the concrete.

Consuelo! During their Manaus stop to refuel, Cristiano had sent word of Alejandro's death. Of course, his family would be here to greet him.

With silent tears streaming his face, Tad appeared shell-shocked while he supported his mother. Cristiano took her petite frame in his arms, and she fell against him.

Raoul and Jaime bore Alejandro's tarp-covered body from the helicopter and placed him, and the composite board supporting him, onto a waiting gurney.

With soul-wrenching sobs, Consuelo dropped over the camo mound and spread her arms over her husband. Dakota's eyes teared so fast they didn't even sting. Tad, still appearing lost, kept a hand on his mother's back and one on his father's body.

That should be me, not Alejandro.

When Tad and Consuelo learned the truth, they would never speak to her again. Her incompetence had torn a family apart. Part of her, a part she didn't recognize, required an incalculable penance.

Seeming to sense her paralyzing guilt, Matteo leaned body-to-body close, threading his fingers with hers. He lifted her hand for a gentle kiss, and gave her a much-needed boost of courage.

While Consuelo composed herself, Cristiano stayed close. Kelsi and Jaime joined Raoul, and together, they formed an impromptu reception line. Matteo kept a firm hold on Dakota's arm, and she trudged the gallows' walk to offer her unworthy condolences. Inadequate words for a life debt she could never repay.

Chapter Thirty

Dakota chided herself for her cowardice and, when her turn came, she hugged the kind matron who had treated her as family. "I'm so sorry. Alejandro was—"

Is my hero. Dakota couldn't finish aloud.

"Thank you, *senhorita.*" Consuelo's response seemed robotic. *Safe.*

Cristiano stood at Tad's side with an arm around his shoulders. The young man nodded, and his lips parted, only for him to swallow several times. Certain he would hate her later, Dakota fought a sob. "I'm sorry."

Matteo extended a hand and, instead of a handshake, he gripped Tad's forearm in an old-time warrior arm-clasp and didn't let go. "Alejandro's courage humbled me. I know it's small comfort, but your father died a hero."

Tad squared his shoulders, and he nodded. "Later, I need to know…"

"When you're ready." Matteo converted his warrior's grip to a gentle, two-handed clasp. "For now, know this. Before our last battle, he told me that you were his pride and joy."

The gangly youth clenched his jaw, and he jerked a nod. His dark eyes aged in front of Dakota, and in the next moment, a man met her gaze.

"Tad, your father died saving me." She held back a full confession. They were both too brittle for that much truth. She searched Tad's expression for brewing hatred, and the anvil forged from remorse weighed heavier in her chest.

Quiet, Tad held her gaze. She couldn't look away. Words continued to tumble out. "I don't know how I'll handle that—ever. He'll always be my hero."

Tad jutted his chin as though Dakota had offended in some way. "Guarding the shifters was his honored place in life."

Dakota blinked in surprise and fingered Valentine's hard drive in her pocket. "He didn't save only me. He may have saved the shifters."

Tad knitted his brows. "How?"

She owed so many insurmountable debts. "I'll tell you the whole story later. If you or your mom ever need anything, anything at all," she shared a glance with Matteo, "we've got your back."

****

After arriving at the plantation, Dakota showered and later joined Cristiano and Matteo, reviewing the plantation's security. Urgency dictated their defense couldn't wait.

Jaime and Kelsi had stayed with Alejandro's family. Secretly, Dakota couldn't have been more grateful. The Mendes family's grief was too entangled with her guilt.

Standing in the hall outside her suite, Matteo opened the door and turned his molten copper gaze on her. "Our mating was unconventional. Allow me this one tradition."

She smiled at his romantic notion. "Okay. But if I'm asleep before my head hits the pillow…"

Beyond exhausted, she draped her arms around Matteo's neck, and he scooped her up as though she weighed nothing. He carried her across the threshold and stopped at the edge of the bed, holding her close. Maybe there was something to this tradition stuff.

The turned back blue and yellow bedding invited the couple to crawl in. A tray of chocolate-covered strawberries and a small pitcher of heavy cream graced the endtable, along with a cooling stone holding a bottle of champagne. In the midst of their return, someone had thoughtfully prepared for a romantic moment. The sight warmed Dakota's heart.

Mocha *Ardor,* and imagining his taste mixed with sweet cream, teased her into nuzzling Matteo's skin. "Will you always smell this good?"

"*Always.*" He nipped at her neck. "And so will you."

"I love you, Matteo," she whispered the words against his ear that she never thought she would say to a man.

Laying her on the silky sheets, his dreads fell around her, drowning her in espresso. He framed her face with his hands. "My courageous warrior princess. I will love, honor, and cherish you, until death parts us."

He took her lips in a gentle kiss. Caring tenderness was a new experience. Only now, with Matteo, did she know true love. In wonder, she savored the pure affection between them and kissed him back. Emotion stung her eyes, and a single tear escaped.

"You weep?" Matteo kissed it away and gazed at her with furrowed brows.

In the midst of profound loss, she'd found her soulmate. "Happy tears."

He dropped his cutoffs to the floor and joined her in the bed, pulling her backside into his body. Dakota covered his arm at her waist and snugged him in closer. His thickening manhood against her rump made her smile. "So, you're *not* tired."

He trailed light kisses from her shoulder to her ear. "Your *Ardor* overcomes any fatigue, but the morning is not so far off, either."

As he spoke, mocha pearled her nipples and speared arousal to her core. Apparently, his scent also had a superpower over exhaustion. Dakota pressed her buttocks into his groin. "Morning is lightyears away."

She added her cotton top and drawstring pants to the small denim pile on the hardwood floor. Turning to him, she slanted her mouth over his and relished their simple joining. He played his tongue against hers, the caresses slow and gentle.

Love for this man threatened to burst from her, the man who'd risked his humanity to save her. She wanted to crawl inside him, learn his innermost self, and allow their spirits to intertwine.

Emotion made her breathless. "Matteo, I love you so much, it's scary. Is it this way for all mates?"

Too late, she realized she had likely brought Anna to his mind, and she regretted her question. Grief for his deceased wife had no place in their first mated joining. She parted her lips to apologize.

He kissed her to silence and gazed at her with a smile. "Thank the Maker. I thought you'd made me insane."

"Make love to me, my mate, my love."

He did. Slowly and gently—and Dakota had never felt so treasured.

****

Lying on his side, Matteo gazed at his sleeping queen. The way her lashes rested on her cheeks and her hair swept over the pillow, she appeared angelic. She'd always his angel.

When dawn had come, he'd been afraid to open his eyes for fear he'd only dreamed of claiming her. However, the brave jaguar queen who'd wagered a life of loneliness to save him slept innocently beside him.

Her brow furrowed at some inner quandary, and she whimpered. He longed to kiss her worry away. As though she sensed his adoring gaze, her eyes fluttered open.

"Good morning, *gatinha*."

She smiled back, and for an instant, her somnolent troubles left her expression. "Back at you, *Romeo*."

He trailed a finger along her jaw. "Your dreams distressed you. War does that to all. They'll fade in time."

Lips tight, as though unwilling to bare her soul, she shook her head. She blinked, and a teardrop escaped the corner of her eye.

Cupping her face, Matteo's concern for her tugged at his soul, and he couldn't leave her to face her demons alone. "Tell me."

"I was sure I'd dream of Alejandro." She closed her eyes, appearing to gather courage. "Instead, I dreamed that Valentine walked to the gallows, and I—I pulled the lever." Her voice caught. She lifted to an elbow and scrubbed at her damp cheek with the heel of her hand. "They'll put him away for life. Treason's a big deal in the U.S. I have to keep my promise to him."

"The tiny dog?"

She nodded, staring at the ceiling. "I wish…"

With a gentle hand on her face, he pulled her gaze to his. He shook his head. "After besting a hellborne gauntlet, you fret over a Chihuahua."

"Not just the dog. But that's all I can do for Dr. V—or anyone." She lay back on her pillow and pressed a thumb and forefinger to her eyes.

Matteo was grateful to Valentine, too, however, the U.S. military would keep the geneticist's prosecution under wraps, as well as his location. He had no idea how to locate Valentine or his beloved Taco.

Matteo knew firsthand the grave need to keep a battlefield oath. Honoring those obligations healed a survivor's soul. He would ease her pain. "I understand."

****

Wedding tasks filled the days following Alejandro's funeral, and Dakota was grateful for the distraction. In the midst of her sadness over Alejandro and Nicolas, she'd found joy with Matteo.

Dakota pressed the hem of her sister's wedding gown to the dining room table, holding the inner edge flat, while Kelsi penned another distant cousin's name onto the silk.

"So putting the girls' names inside the gown does what, exactly?" asked Dakota.

"It's like catching the bouquet—good luck in love. Since the reception will be sort of speed dating for shifters, I've got a lot of names." Kelsi shook out her hand. "I'm getting writer's cramp."

Dakota arched a sardonic brow. "So the males will take a whiff and see who shifts?"

A chuckle broke Kelsi's tense expression. "Hopefully, more civilized than that. When's Matteo due back?"

His surprise trip to Manaus a couple days ago had taken forever. Apparently, mates didn't tolerate separation well. Dakota sighed in anticipation. "He's coming in today with Mom. That should be an interesting ride." She laughed. "Not sure why it takes a two-day trip to reinstate his identity. I could've done it online for him, easy."

A young, round-faced woman with near-ebony skin and dark eyes entered the dining room carrying a small tray of coffee mugs and a thermal carafe. "*Senhorita* Dakota, you asked to talk with the *patron*. He say in his office."

"Thanks, Isabel." Dakota swirled her hair more securely into her tortoiseshell clip, meeting the fill-in housekeeper's gaze. "You can skip the English. I need to use my Portuguese."

The woman's quick nod and smile held an element of relief.

Kelsi capped the pen and tossed it on top of the rumpled silky white mound. "Go on, I'll take a break and recheck the list."

The permanent marker rested on a nine-thousand-dollar designer gown. *Indelible ink.* Dakota reached to set the pen to safety.

"Come. I'll bring coffee," Isabel said, switching to Portuguese. The woman's presence drove home Consuelo's absence. Dakota straightened and forced a smile. The dress wasn't important.

A week had passed, and Consuelo's anguish still haunted Dakota. Only Matteo's stalwart support had seen her through Alejandro's funeral. Following Isabel to Cristiano's office, Dakota blinked away the sting of tears.

The door stood open, framing Cristiano behind his desk chatting with Jose. New, lustrous dark hair made him look anything but the ancient shifter *patron*. He appeared young enough to be Jaime's brother, maybe even his twin.

Glancing at her, Cristiano rose and shook Jose's hand. "So, we're agreed. Upload the video as we discussed with Matteo."

Video? Today, other matters took priority, but she made a note to investigate the comment later.

Jose turned to leave and, seeing her, he halted with a large grin. "Thanks for the referral. As of now, I have a very good job for life."

She laughed. "Awesome, just don't make me look bad."

"I'll do my best." Still beaming, Jose stood aside,

allowing the women to enter before excusing himself.

Thanking Isabel, Cristiano rose from his leather desk chair and stepped around to take Dakota's hand in both of his. "Good morning."

The housekeeper set their coffee on a small table in the corner and made a discreet exit, closing the door behind her.

He gestured for Dakota to take one of the four chairs at the round table and claimed a seat across from her. "You've worried me, holing up in your room. How can I help?"

"I can't change the past—" Emotion stole her voice. Saying their names, *Alejandro and Nicolas,* would make her puddle up. "I mean—our losses. So I *need* to pay it forward."

"I understand. More than you know." The pain of his burden showed in his sad amber gaze.

"I'm so sorry." She reached to give his hand a squeeze. Cristiano had ordered lifelong friends to their deaths. "This must be even more horrible for you."

He pursed his lips, and glanced out the window for an instant, obviously not interested in that discussion. "You asked to see me, Dakota?"

Somber, she extracted Valentine's keychain from her pocket and dropped Taco's picture on the marble tabletop. The metallic clank gave away the frame's added weight.

Cristiano picked it up, turning it over in his hand. "What's this?"

"Valentine's research."

His burning gaze shot to hers. "The one who freed you?"

Dakota nodded. "I've got limited genetics knowledge, but the data looks formidable."

His eyes widened. "Research on us?"

"Yes, and no. He found two latents. You know David Liu—the tiger. And several years ago, an unknown Central American female."

Cristiano leaned in, and his gaze seemed to bore into her. "Where?"

"Her location isn't in the files, sorry." Uninterested in the nameless latent, Dakota's mouth went dry. She had to redirect the conversation.

"She could be very important to us."

Keeping her promise to Valentine was more important than finding an unknown latent. Cristiano might be able to help if he could forget about locating female shifters for even a minute.

"Look, the U.S. will charge Valentine with high treason. Maybe they already have. All he asked in return for his life's work—and my freedom—was for me to take care of Liu and Taco. I intend to do it."

Cristiano studied her a moment before spearing fingers through his hair. "Raoul has your tiger, safe and sound. But who's Taco?"

Dakota tapped the marble tabletop next to the picture keychain. "His baby, the Chihuahua."

Cristiano obviously fought a smile. "A dog?"

She nodded, deadly serious. "He asked a small thing of me—considering."

"I see." Sobering under her intent regard, Cristiano sipped his coffee. "We have connections that might help, but I'll need to explore our options."

"There's more." Dakota hesitated to share her ambitions to revive the shifter species.

After completing one bachelor's degree and later dropping out of medical school, not to mention two other unfinished degrees, Dakota's academic career was a family joke. The Fox called her flighty.

People had died to save Dakota, but more

importantly, they'd given everything for the species. Serious research could snatch the shifters from the jaws of extinction. The lost lives and Valentine's incarceration must count for more than one person. And Dakota would honor their memory.

If Cristiano dismissed her need to validate their sacrifices, her composure might crumble. And nothing could happen without Cristiano's support. The Fox might front another round of tuition, but research costs would be in the millions.

"Go on," Cristiano nodded, appearing solemn. Maybe he understood the importance of the moment.

A glance at the ever-present mailing tube in the corner gave Dakota courage. "I plan to build on Dr. Valentine's work. Last night—online—I applied for the Federal University's genetics doctorate program."

"You're a bright girl. I'm delighted." His gaze tracked hers to the cardboard cylinder stamped *FAMILY*. "Finally, someone will show real interest in my genealogy chart."

"I'll definitely put your lineage research to use."

A knock sounded at the office door.

"*Senhora* Gorman's helicopter arrives in five minutes," Isabel said from the hall.

Research funding would have to wait. Dakota jumped from her seat, astonished at how eager she was to see her mother. Even more surprising, Dakota needed to hold Mom in her arms.

Leaving Cristiano to catch up as he could, she rushed out of the house and joined Jaime and Kelsi, already standing at the edge of the helipad. Dakota patted a rhythm on her thigh while the chartered helicopter lowered. A half-minute later, Cristiano halted at her side.

Engine noise grew louder, and the chopper wind whipped Dakota's hair into a frenzy. Her gaze riveted to the familiar smiling face peering out the side window of the descending chopper. Wisps of the Fox's trademark platinum hair framed her high cheekbones, but the rest of her long locks were likely in a loose chignon at her nape that never left its place.

The wheels touched down, and Mom waved at the reception party. Matteo appeared next to her in the window, and at sight of him, Dakota lit up inside, her stomach doing a little flip. He smiled back, placing an open hand on the window. The Fox glanced from one to the other, and her pleasant expression wilted.

Dakota had no worries her mother had been openly rude to Matteo. The woman was way too cultured to engage in a blatant snub. However, it appeared he hadn't won her over during their trip.

The helicopter door slid open, and Matteo, holding an Uzi and sporting a sidearm at his hip, stepped lightly to the ground. He turned and offered a hand to help the Fox exit the cabin, but Cristiano stepped in front of him. "Thank you for escorting Mrs. Gorman."

The obvious dismissal didn't seem to faze Matteo, and he rushed the several feet into Dakota's waiting embrace. He lifted her from her feet and buried his face into her neck. "I missed you so much."

"I hope so. Serves you right for leaving me all alone," Dakota said.

Mocha *Ardor* caressed her while she kissed him, and she nearly forgot her mother's arrival. She dragged herself from Matteo's coffee allure and looked over his shoulder to catch the scene.

Gracefully exiting the helicopter, Mom accepted Cristiano's offered arm. She lit on the ground and, as though she were fragile, he cradled her hand in both of his. He'd get over that. "Mrs. Gorman, I'm so pleased to meet you."

Dakota turned and kissed Matteo's cheek. "I love you. Mom will, too. Just be prepared."

"For what?"

Dakota laughed. "Put it this way, she's earned the *Steel Fox* tag."

She strode toward her mother and without preamble, wedged in front of Cristiano and wrapped the Fox in her arms, holding on too long and too hard. Tears stung her eyes, and she squeezed tighter.

Hugging back, her mother chuckled near Dakota's ear. "My, my. I'm glad to see you, too, sweetie."

"I missed you." Dakota couldn't come up with anything better. Responding with, *I thought you might be caged in a lab,* seemed like a bad idea.

The Fox held her at arm's length, and in intuitive mom fashion, the Fox sobered and studied Dakota. "Baby, what's wrong?"

The penetrating scrutiny left Dakota feeling exposed. Fortunately, Kelsi and Jaime rushed to join them, saving her for the time being. Matteo tugged Dakota's hand and tucked her under a supportive arm.

Kelsi made introductions, and the Fox turned her analysis on Cristiano. "You're Jaime's *father?*"

With a broad smile, he nodded. "And shamelessly proud of him, too."

The Fox didn't look impressed. In fact, she did the one-brow raise that Dakota knew so well, announcing doubt. "You look younger than I expected."

Cristiano's newly dark hair gleamed in the sunlight, and the skin around his eyes had snugged up. With the pair standing side by side, the Fox would never buy they were father and son.

"Aging well is a fortunate Salazar trait." Cristiano's beguiled expression appeared identical to

Jaime's when he gazed at Kelsi. "I see where the Gorman girls get their beauty."

The idea of the paternal Cristiano interested in her mother shook the concrete beneath Dakota. She snapped a questioning look to Matteo.

He shrugged, totally unhelpful.

Jaime and Kelsi glanced at each other and grinned, nearly devolving into laughter.

"You're too kind." The Fox returned her classic all-business smile to Cristiano.

Seeming undaunted by her cool reception, Cristiano tucked her arm in his and led her through the gardens toward the house. "Your girls are a blessing upon our family."

The Fox shot a glance at Matteo over her shoulder, her corporate façade crumbling. "Girls?"

Cristiano's shoulders tensed. "I meant only—"

"It's nothing, Mom." Dakota couldn't deal with Fox drama right now. Her controlling mother would not tolerate losing another daughter to Brazil, not yet. "I've decided to go into genetics. I applied for the PhD program at the university in Manaus."

"Yes, they have an accelerated curriculum," Cristiano added.

Accelerated? That tidbit hadn't been on their website. Maybe he'd sensed Mom's anxiety over the announcement and just plain lied. That worked for Dakota.

Cristiano tugged her mother along. "Your daughter is quite brilliant."

"Yes, very brilliant." The Fox deadpanned and narrowed her eyes at Matteo. The hint of scrutiny disappeared, and she turned raised brows to Dakota. "You've never mentioned an interest in genetics. What brought this on?"

Grateful Cristiano had minimized the five-year doctoral commitment, Dakota cringed at the suspicion in her mother's voice. She hadn't anticipated this conversation, so she dodged Mom's question. "I hope to get done in a few years."

Lying wasn't always bad. Kelsi's international marriage had rocked the Fox's foundations, and now, Dakota's defection might topple the building. Today was not the time for full disclosure.

Several inches taller than Mom, Cristiano smiled down at the Fox. "There's no telling the impact Dakota's keen mind will have on the world. You must be so proud."

"Yes, of course." When Mom glanced over her shoulder, a vertical line between her perfect eyebrows deepened, and her forehead crinkled, distressed in a way Dakota had never seen.

The Steel Fox was afraid—maybe even terrified—of losing her daughters? The thought astounded Dakota. Mom had always seemed an invincible force and all about Gorman Paper, Inc.

Dakota turned a radiant smile on Matteo. "After the wedding, would you like to see the amazing Omaha, Nebraska?"

****

Cristiano personally escorted Celeste and Dakota to the sunlit *Waterfall Room*, its rattan sitting area complete with a wall fountain. The sparkling cascade bathing the sculptured rock-face created a soothing melody. He had saved the favored-guest quarters for the mother of the bride.

After inviting Mom to an evening barbecue, Cristiano took his leave. Dakota helped her unpack, waiting for any sign of her mother's reactions—to everything. She closed the dresser's top drawer.

Facing the bed, the Fox stilled with her hands splayed on either side of her open suitcase. Her tense shoulders rose and fell with her heavy sigh, and the relaxing waterfall song rang hollow in the room.

From behind, Dakota wrapped her arms around her mother, and rubbed her cheek on the Fox's shoulder. "You've been a great mom, and I love you."

Her mother's frame straightened, seeming to reject Dakota's embrace. "Why?"

"Why do I love you?" Confused, Dakota gripped her mom's upper arms and turned her around, and her mother allowed it.

The Fox's teal eyes misted over, but her gaze didn't waver. "First Kelsi, and now you. Why are you leaving me for another country?"

Mom's intuition had struck again. Dakota parted her lips with a ready lie, however, the tremulous tears dotting her mother's lower lashes stole her words. The Steel Fox slew Wall Street dragons on a regular basis. The woman had never appeared so vulnerable. "Please, *please,* tell me that man with the machine gun and ratted-horsetail hair is not the reason."

Despite the Fox's tears, Dakota recognized the controlled tone from childhood interrogations. Defensive comebacks shot through her mind, and she discarded them, dropping her arms to her sides. "You raised us to think for ourselves—and now, we do."

"That's not an answer."

Long office hours and cancelled vacations had never represented a mother's love. Until today. Mom had worked to protect her daughters. The realization slammed into Dakota and filled her with a new empathy for her stalwart mother.

"There's so much more to Matteo. You'll see. Trust me. I know he makes a rough first impression."

The memory kicked up one corner of Dakota's mouth. *Your hair is blue.*

Mom's eyes narrowed, and a hint of the metal returned. "I did trust you. And you promised good news. I'm still waiting."

Dakota put all the love she could into her gaze. "You gave all you had for us. I don't remember you even going out on one date after Daddy died. I never understood. But I get it, now."

"You understand that I loved my daughters? That's your big epiphany?" The Fox snorted.

Seeing the woman's motivations in a new light, and more importantly, understanding them, Dakota ignored the bait to battle. She smiled wide and cupped her mother's cheek. "I never doubted you loved us. I just never understood your drive to work so hard. We had friends with single parents. You were different. What was so important about paper products? Nothing. You worked for something much more precious to you. Us. I'm way late, but I get it."

The Fox's eyes widened and she dropped to sit on the bed. "Are you pregnant?"

I'm trying. Dakota chuckled at her inside joke. "No. But like you, I've found something vital to work for. Something worth any sacrifice."

"And..."

Dakota pushed the suitcase to the center of the bed and settled next to her mother, their thighs touching. "Take a closer look at Kelsi. She used to have the beginnings of crow's feet. They're gone. Now, she has newborn-babe skin."

Mom knitted her brows. "I don't understand."

"Cristiano *is* Jaime's dad. He's got to be at least your age."

Widening her eyes, the Fox stiffened. "Father?

Brother more like it. He's no older than thirty-five, if he's a day. I'm tempted to roll my eyes."

Dakota smiled at her mother's rules of behavior, raising a hand, palm out. "Total truth—he's Jaime's *papai*. Something here, in this place, slows aging. Cristiano, nor Jaime, has ever had any kind of illness. Same with Matteo. Their health has to be genetic. Either from their DNA—or something in this place. If we could isolate that gene…"

The Fox puffed a breath. "I've never been ill, either. So that's not unusual."

Surprise wiped the smile from Dakota's face. Mom had always been healthy. Maybe she *did* hide a jaguar. Their family could stay together for centuries. Only an unmated male could say for sure. Recalling Cristiano's possessive moves when greeting her mother, Dakota planned to corner him at the earliest opportunity. "Mom, have you noticed any unique—"

The Fox looked up at her from under lowered brows. "Is that your real interest in Matteo? To stay young?"

Dakota shook her head, and hair escaped her clip, falling into her eyes. Her *Ardor* question could—and should—wait. She placed a hand over her mothers, and Mom squeezed it tight. "Mom, I really think he's the one."

The Fox bowed her head, covering her face with her free hand, muffling a groan. She lifted Dakota's fingers to her lips for a kiss. "At least tell me he has a job."

"He's in security," Dakota thought fast, "and coffee. Give him a chance—please. I did. It was the best decision I ever made."

Gripping the edge of the mattress under her, the Fox nodded. She studied the floor as though searching for words then looked up, meeting Dakota's gaze. "You really think you can find the *fountain of youth*?"

Mom would love Matteo in her own time and in her own way. Dakota embraced the change of subject. "I've already identified patterns to track." *And they leave really big paw prints.* "I plan to investigate while I'm at the university. Cristiano may even fund private research. I need to speak with him."

"The Nebraska Medical Center has state-of-the-art everything. Surely, they have a genetics program. You could enroll there." The last ended as a question. Tiny lines appeared in the Fox's brow, giving her a pleading look.

"I need to be near my subjects to study them." Dakota smiled at the obvious.

Mom sat up straighter and wiped the corner of one eye, her features melting into their familiar intrepid beauty. "I apologize. I've been selfish."

"You've been worried. I was, too." Dakota needed to reassure her mother, but more, she wanted Mom's life to be full of joy.

Mom nodded, seeming to retreat into her own thoughts.

She deserved so much more than eighty-hour weeks and boardroom drama. Love had come full circle. Dakota would work for her mother, just as her mother had sacrificed for her daughters. The shifter catalyst gene had to exist. Dakota would identify it and ensure her mother's jaguar came out of hiding.

She nudged her mother's shoulder with her own and, when Mom looked up, gave her an encouraging smile. "The program doesn't start for a few months. How about a couple summer houseguests? You could get to know Matteo."

The Fox framed Dakota's face in her hands. "All

he really needs to do is love you as much as I do."

Speechless, Dakota's lips parted and she blinked a sting from her eyes.

The Fox's smile dropped away, and her scrutiny intensified. "You *are* changed, in some way. More serious, or confident. I've always feared the day you found your passion." She gave a quick nod. "You'll be unstoppable."

"That's—thanks, Mom." A rogue tear tracked Dakota's cheek. Thirty-four-years old and, yes, her mother's opinion still mattered.

Dakota hated to withhold their shifter genetics, especially now, when she felt so close to her mother, but the Fox would need time to adjust. They'd all agreed to wait to enlighten her.

Burgeoning commitment to her role in their high stakes save-the-species campaign gave Dakota a calm sense of purpose. Her mother's life may hinge on her success. She would tell Mom the whole truth when the time was right.

****

Matteo and the other shifters stared at the life-sized image of Shelton paused on the parlor's big screen. At the closing of Dakota's forced-march video, the news station had frozen the headshot portrait-style, framed by Darien Gap flora.

Blurred faces had filled the picture except for Shelton's crisp image, and the editors had kept Dakota's identity anonymous. However, the story of U.S. military involvement in human trafficking had broken nationwide, followed by a groundswell of Brazilian fury.

As Matteo pulled Dakota against him in the overstuffed chair, his chest rumbled with impotent rage, breaking the room's silence. A dark glow shimmered from his forearms. "They'll never touch you again, I swear."

"No, they won't," she said through gritted teeth. Sitting in his lap, Dakota pulled his arm tighter around her waist. He held her with a mate's need for touch, and her nearness gave him much-needed control over his ire.

On the sofa next to them, Jaime tucked a sniffling Kelsi under his arm.

Cristiano, his mouth a grim line, sat in a matching cream-colored chair across from them. "Jose sent this to the news through untraceable servers."

Cristiano pressed a button on the remote. Voice-over identified Shelton as a top-level U.S. Army colonel stationed in Brazil.

The news anchor didn't hide his disgust. "The U.S. government promises a thorough investigation. According to their spokesman, General Deacon Butler, Colonel Shelton's present whereabouts are unknown."

Cristiano pressed the remote, darkening the monitor. "My money says they've hidden Shelton away. Only they're debriefing, not interrogating him."

"They can't let him off. The pressure will be too high." Dakota sounded so certain. "If they connect him to human trafficking, he'll never recover. The American people won't tolerate slavery of any kind—and a U.S. Army colonel? They'll fry him."

Isabel, face flushed, rushed into the parlor and straight to Cristiano, holding out a cell phone.

"*Patron*, it's *him*." She mouthed the words with dramatic, widened eyes. Nearly dancing out of the room, she paused at the hallway and fanned her cheeks. "His aide called, first, and then *he* came on the line. I could hardly speak."

Smiling at her whispered amazement, Cristiano covered the mic and glanced around their group. "Please excuse me." He rose and headed toward his study with brisk strides. "Ah, President Franco. Thank you…"

"Is that—" Dakota's mouth hung open. "As in the *Brazilian* president?"

Matteo grinned. "Likely. I haven't bothered to check who's in office. Too many important things to research."

Jaime didn't seem any more surprised than Matteo that his father chatted with the country's leader. "*Papai* will work every front to get justice for our family."

Kelsi nodded. "He's relentless."

"I should've killed the self-inflated bastard. That would've been justice." Matteo wondered how often he would regret leaving Shelton alive.

Dakota pressed her lips to his ear. "Getting him wouldn't have been worth hurting Polo. I'm good with how things are."

Matteo hugged her, grateful for her kind heart.

Jaime kissed Kelsi with unabashed desire. "Warm the bed, *meu anjo*. I need a word with Matteo."

Blushing to her roots, she gave him a playful slap. "You're so naughty."

As she jumped from the sofa, Jaime swatted her bum. "That I am."

For the first time in decades, the sight of a loving couple filled Matteo with anticipation, rather than melancholy. Clearly amused, Dakota grinned at him over her shoulder and snuggled back against his torso. New optimism flickered in his chest. Life waited, and Matteo would join with abandon.

Lavender blossomed around them, cloaking his body in sizzling heat. He hardened against Dakota's rump and readjusted her position for comfort. Even his nipples peaked with the onslaught. *My mate.* He tightened his arms around her, discreetly taking in her scent.

"That's my cue." She stood, leaving his condition exposed to the world. After a few strides of a seductive strut, she looked over her shoulder, tasting her upper lip. "Don't make me start without you."

Matteo groaned, the mental image turning his brain to mush. He tracked her ass until she disappeared into the hallway and broke the spell.

"Ha! You have trouble waiting, my friend." Jaime's snort yanked Matteo from his anticipation.

With exaggerated indulgence, he stretched an arm out along the back of the sofa and folded one leg over the other, waiting while Matteo gathered his wits.

He blew out a gusty breath. "Apparently, this needs to be quick."

"I won't keep you." Jaime's dancing blue eyes sobered, and his Adam's apple bobbed with a swallow. "Alejandro was to be my best man. Would you do me the honor?"

Chapter Thirty-One

Dakota clutched her small white orchid bouquet in the stifling heat of the two-hundred-year-old Salazar chapel. With a lot of luck, armpit rings wouldn't mar her strapless teal sheath. Silk was such an unforgiving fabric.

She and Matteo were the only attendants with Jaime and Kelsi at the front of the church. The forty or so guests filling the pews waved tasteful engagement-photo fans, *Senhora* Vargas's brainchild. However, she'd forbidden the wedding party from using them. *Flapping like chicken is undignified.*

The priest droned on. The happy couple before him seemed oblivious to the swelter, though Dakota tracked a bead of perspiration from Jaime's forehead to his jaw and then to the floor.

Across from her, broad-shouldered Matteo looked fittingly solemn in his hastily tailored gray tuxedo. Prior to the ceremony, he'd tugged at the stand-up collar of his coordinating shirt. She smiled, recalling his protest. *Good thing shifters are hard to kill. This is strangling me.*

She was quite proud of his look, with his dreads pulled back into a fishbone pattern, and gold-beaded tawny ropes draping his back. Added to his hair, his molten gaze and high cheekbones could grace the cover of *Gentlemen's Quarterly*.

During the hours it had taken for Dakota to create the chic style, he'd fidgeted and complained like a five-year-old boy. She smiled.

He caught her perusal and lifted a mocking brow.

"You're so hot," she mouthed at him. *And mine.*

Heated copper promised a payoff later, and her heart fluttered. She refocused on the priest to quell her body's smoldering response.

Behind her in the second pew, sniffles sounded. In a rare loss of composure, the Fox cried real tears. Most of the time, she kept her emotions under wraps. Dakota suspected sadness caused the puddle.

A familiar yappy bark interrupted the priest's monologue, accompanied by the clatter of canine toenails on stone. Muffled laughter sounded in the small nave. Dakota wheeled around in wild expectation.

Taco raced through rainbow patches of light born of the stained glass, scampering down the aisle between the six rows of pews. Dakota stooped, and the Chihuahua leapt into her open arms. He laved her face in a fervor, whimpering with affectionate demand.

She giggled, generating an echo of laughter through the small gathering.

In a blur of green plaid, Dr. Valentine rushed through the chapel's main doors, his pointy nose nearly twitching within his pinched features. He ducked low to scoot down the center aisle, as though he might actually hide from the wedding guests. The notion upgraded Dakota's giggle to open laughter.

Obviously chasing the doctor, David Liu stopped short at the threshold and shook his head. He caught Dakota's eye and smiled. So much better looking out of uniform. More than one girl in the back pews ogled him. Not missing their interest, he nodded to either side. "Ladies."

Laughing, Dakota rushed as fast as her sheath dress allowed to greet Valentine, ignoring the toenails snagging the silk bodice. "I can't believe you're here!"

The doctor's entry had stalled the wedding ceremony. Standing between a beaming Kelsi and Jaime, Father Souza smiled at the commotion.

"You're a naughty boy." Winded and speaking

low, Valentine extracted Taco from Dakota's arms. "My apologies. I thought he needed to potty, and as soon as his little feet touched the ground, he took off like a shot."

"You're safe!" Tears stinging her eyes, Dakota wrapped the odd geneticist in a hug, squishing the squirming Chihuahua between them. "How?"

Valentine patted her bare back and stiffened, noticeably uncomfortable with the physical contact. Matteo joined them, and Taco renewed his struggle, straining toward him.

"Oh, no you don't." Valentine tucked the pup into his arms. He glanced from one to the other, giving Matteo a double take. "My, you healed exceedingly well."

Smiling wide with dancing eyes, Matteo nodded.

Belatedly, Valentine seemed to recall Dakota's question, and his expression lit up. "Oh, yes. Would you guess? Brazil sent a nice attorney to offer me asylum— and a job! And something about testimony later."

A physical weight left Dakota's body. The man who'd given up everything to free her would live a full life—with his beloved pup.

From the first pew on the groom's side, Cristiano shared a laugh with Matteo. Beaming at her, Matteo looked way too satisfied with himself.

"You did this?" she asked.

Matteo signaled to *Senhora* Vargas to find seats for the welcome gatecrashers. "With a little help from Cristiano."

Somehow, they had managed to get Valentine out of the U.S., and Matteo had never said a word. Cristiano's call from President Franco came to mind, followed by Matteo's two-day *errand* in Manaus.

She raised a brow. "You're a sneaky cat."

All of the shifters had met, or heard stories about,

the eccentric geneticist and his baby, Taco. Kelsi didn't miss a beat over the break in ceremony. Smiling, she and Jaime descended the one step into the nave to greet the late arrivals.

Dakota reached for Matteo's hand, and he tucked her under his arm. The wedding party gathered around the doctor, and a new optimism flooded through Dakota.

****

Matteo was grateful the wedding service neared the end. Surprisingly, he had understood most of the priest's Latin. He stole another glance at Dakota. *Spring Lilac* curls trailed from her crown over a swirl of *Thunderstorm* braids. She called the style an updo. He called it ravishing. Or hypnotic.

Seeking courage, Matteo fingered the sapphire solitaire in his pocket. His apprehension made no sense. She wouldn't decline. Only death severed a mating.

Anna had loved him, but in the end, love hadn't been enough. He had risked so much, mating again. A cowardly part of him required Dakota's vow she would never leave. He sighed, returning his attention to the service.

"Allow me to present Mr. and Mrs. Jaime Salazar." The priest repeated the English announcement in Portuguese, and the small congregation rose with applause. Dakota kissed her sister's cheek, and Matteo shook Jaime's hand, adding a slap on the back. The jubilant couple joined their family filling the main aisle.

Taking the two strides to Dakota, Matteo met her teal gaze, and took her hand. While they waited at the fringe of the bride and groom's small crush, he savored the touch of their intertwined fingers. The wedding atmosphere, his fears—whatever the reason—he could wait no longer. He leaned to nuzzle at her ear.

"Dakota, I love you. Marry me? Now?" Pulse

pounding, he searched her expression for any hint of hesitance.

At her radiant smile, he released a relieved breath. Her lips parted with what he hoped was agreement. Then, with a confused expression, she scanned the guests. Her perusal settled on her mother hugging Kelsi. "As in *today*—now?"

She hadn't said yes. He'd been an ass. Of course, she wanted her own wedding. He put all his love into a tender kiss. "Just say yes. All brides want their day. You'll have yours."

Dakota gazed at him, and a slow smile curved her lips. "The yes part is easy."

Matteo's heart wanted to explode, and he fought the urge to lift her up and swing her around. Then her hesitation sobered him. "But—"

She glanced at her mother again. "*But*—I promised the Fox I wouldn't bother her with a wedding."

A smile put shards of emerald in her oceanic gaze—his inspiration for her promise ring. He'd tortured the jeweler for three hours to get the exact hue.

"Almost forgot, the *anel de compromisso*." Reaching into his pocket, he retrieved the two-carat blue-green solitaire and slid the band onto her right ring finger. She gazed at the princess-cut stone gracing her hand.

"That rock's a promise ring? It's—" Her voice caught. When she met his gaze, tears hovered on her lower lashes. "You coordinated it with my gown—sneaky cat."

"Actually, the stone matches your eyes." Laughing softly, he kissed her forehead and thumbed a teardrop from her cheek. Let others fall for her fashion-diva front. She couldn't hide her inner strength from him. "We'll select our *alianças*, our wedding rings, together."

As though they were alone, she slid an arm around his neck and planted a fierce kiss on his lips. "Are you free at sunrise?"

Matteo's heart soared. Life with his bold Dakota held a promise he had never imagined. "I can hold out a few more hours."

The End

www.majewell.com

JUNGLE SALVATION

EVERNIGHT PUBLISHING ®

<u>www.evernightpublishing.com</u>